HELLBENT

Also by Gregg Hurwitz

HELLBENT

Gregg Hurwitz

MINOTAUR BOOKS ☙ NEW YORK

HELLBENT. Copyright © 2018 by Gregg Hurwitz. All rights reserved. Printed in the United States of America. For information, address St. Martin's Press, 175 Fifth Avenue, New York, N.Y. 10010.

www.minotaurbooks.com

The Library of Congress Cataloging-in-Publication Data is available upon request.

ISBN 978-1-250-11917-9 (hardcover)
ISBN 978-1-250-11918-6 (ebook)
ISBN 978-1-250-18500-6 (international, sold outside the U.S., subject to rights availability)

Our books may be purchased in bulk for promotional, educational, or business use. Please contact your local bookseller or the Macmillan Corporate and Premium Sales Department at 1-800-221-7945, extension 5442, or by email at MacmillanSpecialMarkets@macmillan.com.

First Edition: January 2018

10 9 8 7 6 5 4 3 2 1

To Gary and Karen Messing
and
Darra and Zach Brewer.
You don't get to choose your family,
but sometimes you luck out.

"And now that you don't have to be perfect, you can be good."

—John Steinbeck, *East of Eden*

HELLBENT

Evan's scuffed knuckles, a fetching post-fight shade of eggplant, ledged the steering wheel. His nose was freshly broken, leaking a trickle of crimson. Nothing bad, more a shifting along old fault lines.

He inspected his nose in the rearview, then reached up and snapped it back into place.

The Cadillac's alignment pulled to the right, threatening to dump him into the rain-filled roadside ditch. The seat springs poked into the backs of his thighs, and the fabric, dotted with cigarette scorch marks, reeked of menthol. The dome light housed a bare, burned-out bulb, the brake disks made a noise like an asphyxiating chicken, and the left rear brake light was out.

He should have stolen a better car.

Rain dumped down. That was Portland for you. Or—if he was being precise—a country road outside Hillsboro.

Big drops turned the roof into a tin drum. Water sluiced across the windshield, rooster-tailed from the tires.

HELLBENT

He sledded around a bend, passing a billboard. A moment later smeared red and blue lights illuminated the Caddy's rear window.

A cop.

The broken brake light.

That was inconvenient.

Especially on this car, since a BOLO had likely been issued. The cop would be running the plate number now if he hadn't already.

Evan blew out a breath. Leaned harder into the gas pedal.

Here came the sirens. The headlights grew larger.

Evan could see the silhouette of the officer behind the wheel. So much like a shooting target—head and chest, all critical mass.

Hillsboro prided itself on being one of the safest cities in the Pacific Northwest. Evan hoped to keep it that way.

As he popped the brakes and jerked the wheel, the heap of a car rocked on its shocks, fanning onto an intersecting road.

Two more cop cars swept in behind him from the opposite direction.

Evan sighed.

Three patrol cars lit up like Christmas, sirens screaming, spreading out across both lanes and closing in.

That was when the thumping from the trunk grew more pronounced.

1

No Version of Being Too Careful

Evan moved swiftly through the door to his penthouse suite at the Castle Heights Residential Tower, his RoamZone pressed to his ear. The phone, encased in hardened rubber and Gorilla glass, was as durable as a hockey puck and essentially impossible to trace. Every incoming call to 1-855-2-NOWHERE traveled in digital form over the Internet through a labyrinth of encrypted virtual-private-network tunnels. After a round-the-world tour of software telephone-switch destinations, it emerged through the receiver of the RoamZone.

Evan always answered the phone the same way.

Do you need my help?

This time, for the first time, the voice on the other end was a familiar one.

Jack Johns.

Jack had plucked Evan from the obscurity of a foster home at the age of twelve and placed him in a fully deniable black program buried deep inside the Department of Defense. Jack had turned Evan into Orphan X, an expendable assassin who went where the U.S. government would not and did what the U.S. government could not. Jack had fought for Evan to stay human even while teaching him to be a killer.

The only father Evan had ever known was calling this line now, a line reserved for those in mortal danger. And he had answered Evan's question—*Do you need my help?*—with a single syllable.

Yes.

Evan and Jack had an elaborate series of protocols for establishing contact. Never like this.

For Jack to call this number meant that he was up against what others might consider world-destroying trouble.

All Evan had gotten over the phone so far was that one word. Static fuzzed the line infuriatingly, the connection going in and out.

He was gripping the phone too hard. "Jack? Jack? *Jack.*"

Eight years ago Evan had gone rogue from the Orphan Program. At the time he'd been the Program's top asset. Given the sensitive information in his head, the bodies he'd put in the ground, and the skills encoded into his muscles, he could not be allowed to exist. The most merciless of the Orphans, Charles Van Sciver, had taken over the Program and was hellbent on tracking down and eradicating Evan.

Vanishing was easier when you already didn't exist. The Orphan Program lived behind so many veils of secrecy that no one except their immediate handlers knew who the Orphans were. They were kept in separate silos and deployed through encoded comms that preserved plausible deniability at every level. Double-blind protocols ensured that even the handlers' whereabouts were often unknown by higher headquarters.

And so Evan had simply stepped off the grid, keeping only the operational alias he'd earned in the shadow service, a name spoken in hushed tones in the back rooms of intel agencies the world over.

The Nowhere Man.

He now helped the desperate, those with no place left to turn, people suffering at the hands of unrepentant and vicious abusers.

His clients called 1-855-2-NOWHERE. And their problems were solved.

Antiseptic. Effective. Impersonal.

Until this.

Evan's tense steps echoed around the seven thousand square feet of his condo. The open stretch of gunmetal-gray floor was broken by workout stations, a few sitting areas, and a spiral staircase that rose to a loft he used as a reading room. The kitchen area was equally modern, all stainless steel and poured concrete. The views up here on the twenty-first floor were dazzling, downtown Los Angeles shimmering like a mirage twelve miles to the east.

Despite all that space, Evan was having trouble breathing. He felt something wild clawing in his chest, something he couldn't identify. Fear?

"Jack."

The reception crackled some more, and then—finally—Jack's voice came through again. "Evan?"

It sounded as if Jack was in his truck, an engine humming in the background.

"I'm here," Evan said. "Are you okay?"

Through the receiver he could make out more road rolling beneath Jack's tires. When Jack spoke again, his voice sounded broken. "Do you regret it? What I did to you?"

Evan inhaled, steadied his heart rate. "What are you talking about?"

"Do you ever wish I'd never taken you out of that boys' home? That I'd just let you live an ordinary life?"

"Jack—where are you?"

"I can't tell you. Dollars to doughnuts they've got ears on me right now."

Evan stared out through the floor-to-ceiling, bullet-resistant Lexan windows. The discreet armor sunshades were down, but through the gaps in the woven titanium chain-link he could still see the city sparkling.

There was no version of being too careful.

"Then why are you calling?" Evan said.

"I wanted to hear your voice."

Over the line, tires screeched. Jack was driving fast, this much Evan could glean.

But he couldn't know that Jack was being pursued—surreptitiously, yet not so surreptitiously that Jack didn't notice—by five SUVs in rolling surveillance. Or that a Stingray cell-tower simulator was intercepting Jack's signal, capturing his every word. That within five minutes the *thwap-thwap-thwap* of rotor blades would stir the clouds and a Black Hawk attack helicopter would break through the night sky and plummet down, fanning up dust. That thermal imaging had already pegged Jack in his driver's seat, his 98.6-degree body temperature rendered in soothing reds and yellows.

All Evan knew right now was that something was terribly wrong.

The static rose like a growl, and then, abruptly, the line was as clear as could be. "This is looking to be my ninth life, son."

For a moment Evan couldn't find his voice. Then he forced out the words. "Tell me where you are, and I'll come get you."

"It's too late for me," Jack said.

"If you won't let me help you, then what are we supposed to talk about?"

"I suppose the stuff that really matters. Life. You and me." Jack, breaking his own rules.

"Because we're so good at that?"

Jack laughed that gruff laugh, a single note. "Well, sometimes we miss what's important for the fog. But maybe we should give it a go before, you know . . ." More screeching of tires. "Better make it snappy, though."

Evan sensed an inexplicable wetness in his eyes and blinked it away. "Okay. We can try."

"Do you regret it?" Jack asked again. "What I did?"

"How can I answer that?" Evan said. "This is all I know. I never had some other life where I was a plumber or a schoolteacher or a . . . or a dad."

Now the sound of a helo came through the line, barely audible.

"Jack? You still there?"

"I guess . . . I guess I want to know that I'm forgiven."

Evan forced a swallow down his dry throat. "If it wasn't for you, I would've wound up in prison, dead of an overdose, knifed in a bar. Those are the odds. I wouldn't have had a life. I wouldn't have been me." He swallowed again, with less success. "I wouldn't trade knowing you for anything."

A long silence, broken only by the thrum of tires over asphalt.

Finally Jack said, "It's nice of you to say so."

"I don't put much stock in 'nice.' I said it because it's true."

The sound of rotors intensified. In the background Evan heard other vehicles squealing. He was listening with every ounce of focus he had in him. A connection routed through fifteen countries in four continents, a last tenuous lifeline to the person he cared about more than anyone in the world.

"We didn't have time," Evan said. "We didn't have enough time."

Jack said, "I love you, son."

Evan had never heard the words spoken to him. Something slid down his cheek, clung to his jawline.

He said, "Copy that."

The line went dead.

Evan stood in his condo, the cool of the floor rising through his boots, chilling his feet, his calves, his body. The phone was still shoved against his cheek. Despite the full-body chill, he was burning up.

He finally lowered the phone. Peeled off his sweaty shirt. He walked over to the kitchen area and tugged open the freezer drawer. Inside, lined up like bullets, were bottles of the world's finest vodkas. He removed a rectangular bottle of Double Cross, a seven-times-distilled and filtered Slovak spirit. It was made with winter wheat and mountain springwater pulled from aquifers deep beneath the Tatra Mountains.

It was one of the purest liquids he knew.

He poured two fingers into a glass and sat with his back to the cold Sub-Zero. He didn't want to drink, just wanted it in his hand. He breathed the clean fumes, hoping that they would sterilize his lungs, his chest.

His heart.

"Well," he said. "Fuck."

Glass in hand, he waited there for ten minutes and then ten more.

His RoamZone rang again.

Caller ID didn't show UNIDENTIFIED CALLER or BLOCKED CALLER. It showed nothing at all.

With dread, Evan clicked the phone on, raised it to his face.

It was the voice he'd most feared.

"Why don't you go fetch your digital contact lenses," it said. "You're gonna want to see this."

2

Dark Matter

The burly man forged through fronds and the paste of the jungle humidity, his feet sinking into Amazonian mud. A camouflaged boonie hat shadowed his face. A cone of mosquito netting descended from the hat's brim, breathing in and out with him. The ghostly effect—that of an amorphously shaped head respiring—made him seem like a bipedal monster flitting among the rotting trunks. Sweat soaked his clothes. On his watch a red GPS dot blinked, urging him forward.

Behind him another man followed. Jordan Thornhill was gymnast-compact, all knotty muscle and precision, his hair shaved nearly to the skull, a side part notched in with a razor. He'd taken off his shirt and tucked it into the waistband of his pants. Perspiration oiled his dark skin.

They'd left the rented Jeep a few miles back, where dense foliage had finally smothered the trail.

They kept on now in silence, mud sucking at their boots, leaves rustling across their broad shoulders. Strangler vines wrapped massive trees, choking the life from them. Bats flitted in the canopy. Somewhere in the distance, howler monkeys earned their names.

Thornhill kept tight to the big man's back, his movement nimble, fluid. "We're a long way from Kansas, boss. You even sure this dude has it on him?"

The invisible face beneath the boonie hat swiveled to Thornhill. The netting beat in and out like a heart. Then the man lifted the netting, swept it back over the brim. Surgeries had repaired most of the damage on the right side of Charles Van Sciver's face, but there remained a few feathers of scarring at the temple. The pupil of his right eye was permanently dilated, a tiny starfish-shaped cloud floating in its depths.

Souvenirs from an explosive that had been set by Orphan X nearly a year ago.

As the director of the Orphan Program, Van Sciver had the resources to eradicate most of the physical damage, but rage endured just beneath the skin, undiminished.

Thornhill grew uneasy under Van Sciver's gaze. That shark eye, it had an unsettling effect on people.

"It was on his person," Van Sciver said. "I have it on good authority."

"Whose authority?"

"Are you actually asking me?" Van Sciver said. The scars didn't look so bad until he scowled and the skin pulled taut, stretching the wrong way.

Thornhill shook his head.

"The real question is, is it still there?" Van Sciver said. "For all we know, it could be riding in the belly of a jaguar already. Or if there was a fire—who the hell knows."

"Sometimes," Thornhill said, "all a man needs is a little luck."

Yes, luck. For months Van Sciver had lived inside a virtual bunker built of servers, applying the most powerful deep-learning data-mining software in computational history to finding some—*any*—trace of Orphan X. The recent directives from above had been clear. Van Sciver's top priority was to stamp out wayward Orphans. Anyone who'd retired. Anyone who hadn't made the cut. Anyone who had tested questionable for compliance.

And most important, the only Orphan who had ever—in the storied history of the Program—gone rogue.

The Program's large-scale data processing had at last spit out a lead, a glimmer of a fishing lure in the ocean of data that surged through cyberspace on a daily basis. Even calling it a lead, Van Sciver thought now, was too ambitious. More like a lead that could lead to a lead that could lead to Orphan X.

The story behind it had quickly become legend in the intel community. It went like this: A midlevel DoD agent had once, through a labyrinthine process of extortion and blackmail, acquired a copy of highly sensitive data pertaining to the Orphan Program. A few aliases, a few last-known addresses, a few pairings of handlers and Orphans. These key bits and pieces had been captured from various classified channels outside the Orphan Program in the seconds before they autoredacted.

The agent had hoped it would hasten his rise inside the department but quickly learned that he'd caught a hot grenade; the data was too dangerous to use. He'd kept it as an insurance policy despite standing orders to the contrary that originated from Pennsylvania Avenue that any and all data pertaining to the Orphan Program *must* be expunged. Rumors of this shadow file persisted over the past months but had remained only rumors.

Until the powerful data-mining engines at Van Sciver's disposal had caught the scent of this shadow file and verified its existence by shading in bits of surrounding intelligence—like gleaning the existence of invisible dark matter by observing gravity effects around it. The midlevel agent had sensed the crosshairs at his back and had gone to ground.

In more ways than one.

In the end it hadn't been an Orphan or a fellow agent who had brought him down but an unexpected trade wind.

Van Sciver had promised himself that when the time came, he'd leave his bunker and get his boots muddy for a lead that might bring him to Orphan X. So here he was, squelching through the boggy muck of another continent, reaching for that shiny lure.

They smelled it before they saw it. A slaughterhouse stench lacing the thick, heavy-hanging air. They crested a slope. Up ahead the snapped-off tail rotor of a Sikorsky S-70 was embedded in the trunk of a banyan, cleaving the massive tree nearly in half.

Thornhill waved a hand in front of his face. "God*damn*."

Van Sciver drew in a lungful of aviation fuel and rotting flesh, a reek so strong he could taste it. They shouldered through a tangle of underbrush, and there it was. The downed fuselage rested on its side, nudged up against an enormous boulder like a dog trying to scratch its back. A tired seventies army-transport chopper repurposed for private charters, sold and resold a dozen times over, now being slowly devoured by the jungle.

The pilot had been thrown through the windscreen. His body, held together by the flight suit, was cradled tenderly upside down in the embrace of a strangler vine twenty feet off the ground. His flesh seemed to be alive, crawling with movement.

Fire ants.

A rustling came from the fuselage, and then a desiccated voice: "Is someone there? God, please say someone's there."

Van Sciver and Thornhill drew close. Van Sciver had to crouch to see inside.

The NSA agent hung lifeless from the sideways seat, his arms dangling awkwardly, a roller-coaster rider in the twist of a corkscrew. The shoulder harness bit into a charcoal suit jacket and—given the heat—seemed to be making some headway through the underlying flesh as well.

The agent's fellow passenger had managed to pop his own seat belt. He'd landed with his legs bent all wrong. A shiv of bone jutted up through his pants at the shin. The skin around it was puffy and red.

Tears glistened on his cheeks. "I thought I was gonna die here. I've been alone with . . . in the middle of . . ." His sobs deteriorated into dry heaves.

Van Sciver looked past him at the dead agent and felt a spark of hope flare inside his chest. The body looked reasonably well preserved hanging there. Van Sciver forced his excitement back into the tiny dark place in his chest that he reserved for Orphan X. He'd been close so many times, only to have his fingertips slip off the ledge.

"The harness kept him off the ground," Van Sciver said to Thornhill. "Away from the elements. We might have a shot."

The passenger reached toward Van Sciver. "Water," he said. "I need water."

Thornhill darted inside, hopping gracefully through the wreckage until he stood beneath the agent, practically eye to eye.

"He's fairly intact," Thornhill said. "Not gonna place at the Miss America pageant, but still. We got us a good-looking corpse."

The passenger gave with a dry, hacking cough. "Water," he whispered.

"Let's get the body out," Van Sciver said.

"I'll unclip the harness," Thornhill said, "and you ease him down. The last thing we need is his festering ass disintegrating all over the fuselage."

"Please." The passenger clutched the cuff of Van Sciver's pants. "Please at least look at me."

Van Sciver removed the pistol from his underarm tension holster and shot the passenger through the head. Taking hold of the passenger's loafers, he dragged the man clear of the fuselage. Then he returned to the downed helo, and he and Thornhill gently guided the agent down. It involved some unpleasant grappling. The stench was terrible, but Van Sciver was accustomed to terrible things.

They carried the corpse gingerly out into the midday blaze and laid it on a flat stretch of ground. Thornhill's eyes were red. Choking noises escaped his throat. They took a break, walking off a few paces to find fresh air. When they got back to civilization, Van Sciver realized, their clothes would have to be burned.

By unspoken accord they reconvened over the body. They stared down at it. Then Van Sciver flicked out a folding knife and cut the clothes off.

The bloated body lay there, emitting gases.

Thornhill was ordinary-looking by design, as were most of the Orphans, chosen so they could blend in, but his smile was unreasonably handsome. He flashed it now.

"This shit right here? We are livin' the dream."

Van Sciver reached into his cargo pocket, removed two sets

of head-mounted watch-repair binoculars, and handed one to Thornhill.

"Any idea where it would be?" Thornhill asked.

"Fingernails, toenails, hair."

They tied their shirts over their mouths and noses like *bandidos*, got down on all fours, and began their gruesome exploration.

The first hour passed like a kidney stone.

The second was even worse.

By the third, winged insects clustered, clogging the air around them. Shadows stretched like living things. Soon it would be nightfall, and they could not afford to wait another day.

Thornhill was working the agent's hair, picking through strand by strand. Finally he sat back on his heels, gulped a few quick breaths, and spit a wad of cottony saliva to the side. "Are we sure it's on him?"

Van Sciver paused, holding one of the agent's jaundiced hands delicately. It was gooksenecked at the wrist, ready to receive a manicure. The skin shifted unsettlingly around the bone.

Sweat trickled down into Van Sciver's eyes, and he armed it off. He could still see through his right eye, but after so much meticulous concentration the blown pupil and bruised retina gave him trouble focusing. He could feel the muscles straining. He did his best to blink free the moisture.

Then he froze, seized by a notion.

Leaning forward, he parted the dead man's eye. Its pretty blue iris had already filmed over. He thumbed at an upper lid, splaying the lashes. Nothing. He checked the lower lid next.

And there it was.

A lash hidden among others. It was glossier and more robust, with a touch of swelling at the insertion point.

It was a hair, all right. Just not the agent's.

With a pair of tweezers, Van Sciver plucked out the transplant and examined it more closely.

The lash was synthetic.

This was not the future of data storage. It was the *original* data storage. For billions of years, DNA has existed as an information repository. Instead of the ones and zeros that computers use to render digital information, DNA utilizes its four base codes to lay down data complex enough to compose all living matter. Not only had this staggeringly efficient mechanism remained stable for millennia, it required no power supply and was temperature-resistant. Van Sciver had reviewed the research and its big claims—that one day a teaspoon of synthetic DNA could contain the entirety of the world's data. But despite all the outlandish talk of exabytes and zettabytes, the tech remained nascent and the costs staggering. In fact, the price of encoding a single megabyte with digital information was just shy of twenty grand.

But the information on this single eyelash was worth more than that.

To Van Sciver it was worth *everything*.

It contained nothing directly related to Orphan X—Evan was too adept at covering his trail—but compared to the expansive data Van Sciver had been sifting through, it held a treasure trove of specifics.

Holding the lash up against the orange globe of the descending sun, Van Sciver realized that he had forgotten to breathe.

He also realized something else.

For the first time he could recall, he was smiling.

3

Everything He Held Dear

Venice was a beautiful city. But like many beauties, she was temperamental.

Furious weather kept the tourists inside. Rain hammered the canals, wore at the ancient stone, bit the cheeks of the few brave enough to venture out. The storm washed the color from everything, turning the Floating City into a medley of dull grays.

Nearing the Ponte di Rialto, Jim Harville spotted the man tailing him. A black man in a raincoat, bent into the punishing wind a ways back. He was skilled—were it not for the weather-thinned foot traffic, Harville never would have picked him up. It had been several years since he'd operated, and his skills were rusty. But habits like these were never entirely forgotten.

Harville hiked up the broad stone steps of the bridge, the Grand Canal surging furiously below. He reached the portico at the top and cast a glance back.

Across the distance the men locked eyes.

Everything He Held Dear

A gust of wind howled through the ancient mazework of alleys, ruffling the shop canopies, making Harville stagger.

When he regained his footing and looked back up, the man was sprinting at him.

It was a strange thing so many years later to witness aggression this naked.

Instinct put a charge into Harville, and he ran. Vanishing up a tight street, he took a hairpin left between two abandoned palazzos and shot across a cobblestone square. He had no weapon. The man pursuing him was younger and fitter. Harville's only advantage was that he knew the city's complex topography as well as he knew the contours of his wife's back, the olive skin he traced lovingly each night as she drifted off to sleep.

He shouldered through a boutique door, overturned a display table of carnival masks, barged through a rear door into an alley. Already he felt a burning in his legs. Giovanna liked to joke that she kept him young for fifty, but even so, retirement had left him soft.

He careened out onto a *calle* at the water's edge. Across the canal a good distance north, his pursuer appeared, skidding out from between two buildings.

The man saw him. He flung his arms back, and his jacket slid off gracefully, as if tugged by invisible strings. Rain matted his white T-shirt to his torso, his dark skin showing through, the grooved muscles visible even at this distance.

The man's eyes dropped to the choppy water. And then he bounded across, Froggering from pier to trash barge and onward, leaving two moored gondolas rocking in his wake.

Dread struck Harville's stomach like a swallowed stone. He registered a single thought.

Orphan.

The man was on Harville's side of the canal now, but propitiously, a wide intersecting waterway provided a barrier between them. As Harville began his retreat, the man vaulted over an embankment, rolled across a boat prow, and sprang up the side of a building, finding hand-and footholds on downspouts and window shutters. Even as he went vertical, his momentum barely slowed.

That particular brand of obstacle-course discipline—parkouring—had come into popularity after Harville's training, and he couldn't help but watch with a touch of awe now.

The man hauled himself through a third-story window, scaring a chinless woman smoking a cigarette back onto her heels. An instant later the man flew out of a neighboring window on Harville's side of the waterway.

Harville had lost precious seconds.

He reversed, splashing through a puddle, and bolted. The narrow passages and alleys unfolded endlessly, a match for the thoughts racing in his head—Giovanna's openmouthed laugh, their freestanding bathtub on the cracked marble floor, bedside candles mapping yellow light onto the walls of their humble apartment. Without a conscious thought, he was running away from home, leading his pursuer farther from everything he held dear.

He sensed footfalls quickening behind him. Columns flickered past, lending the rain a strobe effect as he raced along the arcade bordering Piazza San Marco. The piazza was flooded, the angry Adriatic surging up the drains, blanketing the stones with two feet of water.

Quite a sight to see the great square empty.

Harville was winded.

He stumbled out into the piazza, sloshing through floodwater. St. Mark's Basilica tilted back and forth with each jarring step. The mighty clock tower rose to the north, the two bronze figures, one old, one young, standing their sentinels' watch on either side of the massive bell, waiting to memorialize the passing of another hour.

Harville wouldn't make it across the square into the warren of alleys across. He was bracing himself to turn and face when the round punched through his shoulder blade and spit specks of lung through the exit wound as it cleared his chest.

He went down onto his knees, his hands vanishing to the elbows in water. He stared dumbly at his fingers below, rippling like fish.

Everything He Held Dear

The voice from behind him was as easygoing as a voice could be. "Orphan J. A pleasure."

Harville coughed blood, crimson flecks riding the froth.

"Jack Johns," the man said. "He was your handler. Way back when."

"I don't know that name." Harville was surprised that he could still form words.

"Oh. You mistook me. That wasn't a question. We haven't gotten to the questions yet." The man's tone was conversational. Good-natured even.

Harville's arms trembled. He stared down at the eddies, the stone, his hands. He wasn't sure how much longer he could keep his face out of the water.

At some point it had stopped raining. The air had a stunned stillness, holding its breath in case the storm decided to come back.

The man asked, "What are your current protocols when you contact Jack Johns?"

Harville wheezed with each breath. "I don't know that name."

The man crouched beside him. In his hand was a creased photograph. It showed Adelina nestled in Giovanna's arms, feeding. She was still wearing her pink knit cap from the hospital.

Harville felt air leaking through the hole in his chest.

He told the man what he wanted to know.

The man rose and stood behind him.

The water stirred around Harville. He closed his eyes.

He said, "I had a dream that I was normal."

The man said, "And it cost you everything."

The pistol's report lifted a flight of pigeons off the giant domes of the basilica.

As the man pocketed his pistol and forged his way through the floodwater, the hour sounded. High on the clock tower, the two bronze forms, one old, one young, struck the bell they'd been ringing across these worn stones for five centuries and counting.

4

Are You Ready?

Evan was still sitting in the kitchen, the Sub-Zero numbing his bare back, the glass of vodka resting on his knee. The phone remained at his face. He felt not so much paralyzed as unwilling to move. Movement would prove that time was passing, and right now time passing meant that bad things would happen.

He reminded himself to breathe. Two-second inhale, four-second exhale.

He reached for the Fourth Commandment: *Never make it personal.*

Jack had taught him the Commandments and would want—no, *demand*—that Evan honor them now.

The Fourth wasn't working, so he dug for the Fifth: *If you don't know what to do, do nothing.*

There was no situation that could not be made worse.

The vodka glass perspired in Evan's hand.

The phone connection was as silent as the grave.

Van Sciver said, "Did you hear me?"

Evan said, "No."

Are You Ready?

He wanted more time, though for what, he wasn't sure.

"I said, 'Go fetch your digital contact lenses. I have something you want to see.'"

Two-second inhale, four-second exhale.

"Let me be perfectly clear," Evan said. "If you do this, nothing will ever stop me from getting to you."

"But, X," Van Sciver said pleasantly, "you don't even know what I have planned."

The line cut out.

Two-second inhale, four-second exhale.

Evan rose.

He set the glass down on the poured-concrete island. He walked out of the kitchen and past the living wall, a vertical garden of herbs and vegetables. The rise of greenery gave the penthouse its sole splash of color and life, the air fragranced with chamomile and mint.

He headed across the open plain of the condo, past the heavy bag and the pull-up bar, past the freestanding central fireplace, past a cluster of couches he couldn't remember ever having sat on. He walked down a brief hall with two empty brackets where a katana sword had once hung. He entered his bedroom with its floating Maglev bed, propelled two feet off the floor by ridiculously powerful rare-earth magnets. Only cable tethers kept it from flying up and smashing into the ceiling. Like Evan, it was designed for maximum functionality—slab, mattress, no legs, no headboard, no footboard.

He entered his bathroom, nudged the frosted-glass shower door aside on its tracks. It rolled soundlessly. Stepping into the shower, he curled his hand around the hot-water lever. Hidden sensors in the metal read his palm imprint. He turned it the wrong way, pushing through a slight resistance, and a hidden door broke free from the tile pattern of the stall and swung inward.

Evan stepped into the Vault, the nerve center of his operations as the Nowhere Man.

Four hundred square feet of exposed beams and rough concrete walls, crowded from above by the underbelly of the public stairs leading to the roof. An armory and a workbench occupied one side.

A central sheet-metal desk shaped like an L held an impeccably ordered array of computer towers, servers, and antennae. Monitors filled an entire wall, showing various hacked security feeds of Castle Heights. From here Evan could also access the majority of law-enforcement databases without leaving a footprint.

The door to the massive gun safe hung ajar. Beneath a row of untraceable, aluminum-forged, custom-machined ARES 1911 pistols, a slender silver case the size of a checkbook rested on a shelf.

Evan opened it.

Ten radio-frequency identification-tagged fingernails and a high-def contact lens waited inside.

The device, which Evan had taken from the dead body of one of Van Sciver's Orphans, served as a double-blind means of communication between Evan and his nemesis.

Evan applied the nails to his fingertips and inserted the lens. A virtual cursor floated several feet from his head.

He moved his fingers in the space before him, typing in thin air: HERE.

A moment later Van Sciver's reply appeared: EXCELLENT. ARE YOU READY?

Evan took a deep breath, wanting to hold on to these last precious seconds before his world flew apart.

He typed: YES.

Jack finally decided enough was enough and pulled his truck over onto a broad dirt fire road that split an endless field of cotton. Dust from the tires ghosted its way down the deserted strip of road. He couldn't see the chopper in the darkness, but he heard it circling high overhead. He threw the truck into park, kept his eyes pegged on the rearview, and waited, his breath fogging in the winter chill.

Sure enough, SUV headlights appeared. Then another set. The vehicles parked ten yards off his rear bumper. Three more black SUVs came at him from the front. He watched them grow larger in the windshield until they slant-parked, hemming him in.

He traced his fingers absently on the driver's window, drawing patterns. Shot a breath at the dashboard. Then, groaning, he climbed out.

The men piled out of the vehicles in full battle rattle, M4 carbines raised. A few of the men held AK-47s instead. "Both hands! Let's see 'em."

"Okay, okay." Jack wearily patted the air in their direction, showing his palms.

He was still pretty goddamned fit for a man in his seventies, but he'd noticed that his baseball-catcher build had started to soften over the past few months no matter how many push-ups and sit-ups he did each morning. The years caught up to everyone.

He breathed in fresh soil and night air. The cotton stretched out forever, dots of white patterned against brown stems, like snow melting on a rocky hillside. It was Thanksgiving Day; the harvest looked to be running late.

He watched the men approach, how they held their weapons, where their eyes darted. They moved well enough, but two of them had their left thumbs pointing up on the magazine well grips rather than aligned with the AK barrels. If they were forced to switch shooting sides, the charging handles would smash their thumbs when they cycled.

Freelancers. Not Orphans. Definitely not Orphans.

But there were fifteen of them.

A few grabbed Jack, patted him down roughly, and zip-tied his hands behind his back.

One man stepped forward. His shaved head gleamed in the headlights' glow. The plates of his skull ridged his shiny scalp. It was not a pretty head. It could have used a bit of cover.

He raised a radio to his lips. "Target secured."

The others shifted in place, boots creaking.

"Relax, boys," Jack said. "You did good."

The guy lowered the radio. "You're finished, old man."

Jack pursed his lips, took this in with a vague nod. "He'll come for you." He cast his eyes across the freelancers. "With all the fury in the world."

The men blinked uncomfortably.

The door of the closest SUV opened, and another man stepped

into view. Compact and muscular. He threw his sculpted arms wide, as if greeting a long-lost relative.

"You're a hard man to track down, Jack Johns," he said.

Jack took his measure. "Jordan Thornhill. Orphan R."

Surprise flickered across Thornhill's face. "You know me?"

"*Of* you anyway," Jack observed. "When you live as long as I have, son, you have eyes and ears in a lot of places."

"You're fortunate," Thornhill said, "to have lived so long."

"Yeah," Jack said. "I was."

The whoomping grew louder. A Black Hawk banked into view over the hillside and set down before them. Dirt and twigs beat at them. Jack closed his eyes against the rotor wash.

As the rotors spun down, a pair of geared-up men emerged. They wore flight suits and parachutes and looked generally overprepared. Three more men and the pilot waited inside the chopper.

Jack shouted, "A bit of overkill, don't you think?"

Thornhill shouted, "We owe a debt of gratitude to helicopters this week!"

Jack didn't know what to make of that.

"Well," he said, "let's get on with it, then."

The two men in flight suits took Jack by either arm and conveyed him over to the helo. The others hauled him in. As they lifted off, Jack caught a bird's-eye view of Thornhill vanishing back into the SUV as smoothly as he'd appeared. Two freelancers headed to search Jack's truck, and the others peeled off to their respective vehicles and drove away.

The helo rose steeply and kept rising. Black Hawks have an aggressive rate of climb, and the pilot seemed intent on showing it off. This wasn't gonna be a joyride. No, this trip had another purpose entirely.

Jack had done more jumps than he could count, so he knew how to roughly gauge altitude by the lights receding below.

They passed ten thousand feet.

Fifteen.

Somewhere north of that, they stopped and hovered.

One of the men donned a bulky headset and readied a handheld digital video camera.

Are You Ready?

Another slid open the doors on either side.

Wind ripped through the cabin, making Jack stagger. Given his cuffed wrists, he couldn't use his arms for balance, so he took a wide stance.

The cameraman shouted, "Look into the camera!"

Jack did as told.

The cameraman listened to someone over his headset and then said, "What are your current protocols for contacting Orphan X?"

Jack shuffled closer, the wind blasting his hair, and squinted into the lens. "Van Sciver, you can't honestly believe this will work on me."

The cameraman listened again and then repeated his question.

Jack's shoulders ached from his hands being cinched behind his back, but he knew he wouldn't have to bear the pain much longer.

"There is nothing you could ever do to make me give up that boy," Jack said. "He's the best part of me."

The cameraman winced, clearly catching an earful from Van Sciver over the headset, then squared to Jack with renewed focus. "I'd suggest you reconsider. We're at sixteen thousand feet, and you're the only one up here without a parachute on."

Jack smiled. "And you're dumb enough to think that puts you at an advantage."

He bulled forward, grabbed the cameraman's rip-cord handle between his teeth, and flung his head back.

There was a moment of perfect stunned silence as the parachute hit the cabin floor.

The wind lifted the nylon gently at first, like a caress.

And then the canopy exploded open, knocking over the men in the cabin. The cameraman was sucked sideways out the open door. The Black Hawk lurched violently as first the chute and then the cameraman gummed into the tail rotor.

The Black Hawk wheeled into a violent 360. Jack gave a parting nod to the sprawled men and stepped off into the open air. On his way out, he saw the powerful ripstop nylon wrapping around the bent metal blades.

By instinct Jack snapped into an approximation of the sky-diver's stable position, flattening out, hips low, legs spread and slightly bent. His hands were cuffed, but he pulled his shoulders back, broadening his chest, keeping his hanging point above his center of gravity. The wind riffled his hair. He watched the sparse house lights wobble below, like trembling candles holding strong in a wind. He figured he'd have hit 125 miles per hour by now, terminal velocity for a human in free fall.

He'd always loved flying.

Jack thought of the malnourished twelve-year-old kid who'd climbed into his car all those years ago, blood crusted on the side of his neck. He thought about their silent hikes through the dappled light of an oak forest outside a Virginia farmhouse, how the boy would lag a few paces so he could walk in the footprints Jack left shoved into the earth. He thought about the way his stomach had roiled when he'd driven that boy, then nineteen years old, to the airport for his first mission. Jack had been more scared than Evan was. *I will always be there,* Jack had told him. *The voice on the other end of the phone.*

The ground was coming up fast.

I will always be there.

Jack shifted his legs and flipped over, now staring up at the night sky, letting gravity take his tired bones. The stars were robust tonight, impossibly sharp, the moon crisp enough that the craters stood out like smudges from a little boy's hand. Against that glorious canopy, the Black Hawk spun and spun.

He saw it disintegrate, a final satisfaction before he hit the ground.

Evan stood in the darkness of the Vault, breathing the dank air, watching the live feed with horror.

The dizzying POV of the camera flying haphazardly around the cabin, banging off tether straps, jump seats, screaming men. And then airborne, free of the cabin, spinning off into the black void. The only sound now was the violence of the wind.

Evan's brain was still stuck thirty seconds back when Jack had walked out the cabin door as calmly as if he were stepping off a diving board.

Are You Ready?

The virtual ground came up and hit Evan in the face.

Static.

Evan's last panicked text to Van Sciver remained below: NO WIAIT STOP I'LL TELL YOU WHEREWW I AM

His next exhalation carried with it a noise he didn't recognize.

The cursor blinked.

Van Sciver's response finally arrived: TOO LATE.

Evan removed his contact lens and fingernails and put them back in the case.

He walked out of the Vault, through his bedroom, down the hall, and across the condo to the kitchen area.

The glass of vodka waited on the island.

He picked it up with a trembling hand.

He drank it.

5

Common Interests Are Important

For the first time in memory, Evan slept in. "Slept" wasn't quite right, as he was awake at five. But he lay in bed until nine, staring at the ceiling, his mind re-forming around what he had witnessed, like a starfish digesting prey.

At one point he sat up and tried to meditate, but every breath was punctuated not with mindfulness but a red flare of rage.

Finally he went and took a shower. He soaped his right hand and ran it up and down the tile, leaning his weight into the arm to stretch his shoulder. It had been recently injured, and he didn't want the tendons and ligaments to freeze up.

Afterward he got dressed. Each bureau drawer held stacks of identical items of clothing: dark jeans, gray V-necked T-shirts, black sweatshirts. This morning in particular, it was a relief to move on autopilot, to not make any decisions. Clipping a Victorinox watch fob to his belt loop, he padded down the hall into the kitchen.

The refrigerator held a jar of cocktail olives, a stick of butter, and two vials of Epogen, an anemia med that stimulated the production of red blood cells in the event of a bad bleed. Three contingency saline bags stared back at him from the meat drawer.

His stomach reminded him that he hadn't eaten in almost a day. His brain reminded him to make a sweep of his various safe houses scattered across L.A. County to take in the mail, change the automated lighting, alter the curtain and blind positions.

He had never wanted to leave his condo less.

There is nothing you could ever do to make me give up that boy.

Behind his front door, he took a deep breath, preparing himself to transition modes. Here at Castle Heights, he was Evan Smoak, importer of industrial cleaning products. Boring by design. He was fit but not noticeably muscular. Neither tall nor short. Just an average guy, not too handsome.

The only person who knew that he was not who he seemed was Mia Hall, the single mother in 12B. She had a light scattering of freckles across her nose and a birthmark on her temple that looked like it had been applied by a Renaissance painter. Because all that wasn't complicated enough, she was also a district attorney. When it came to Evan's work, they had settled on an unspoken and uncomfortable policy of don't ask, don't tell.

He pressed his forehead to the door, summoning greater resolve. *He's the best part of me.*

He stepped out into the hall, got on the elevator.

On the way down, the car stopped and Lorilee Smithson, 3F, swept in. "Evan. It's been a while."

"Yes, ma'am."

"Always so formal."

The third wife to an affluent older gentleman who had recently left her, Lorilee was a vigorous practitioner of cosmetic surgery and body sculpting. She'd been beautiful once, that much was clear, but it was increasingly unnerving how her forehead remained frozen in an approximation of surprise no matter what the rest of her features were doing. She was fifty years old. Or seventy.

She wove her arm through Evan's and gave it a girlfriendy shake. "There's a craft class right now—scrapbooking. You should really come. Preserve those childhood memories."

He looked at her. She had three new lines radiating out from her eyes, faint wrinkles in the shiny skin. They looked pretty. They made her face look lived in. Next week they'd be gone, her face ratcheted even tighter, a tomato about to burst.

He contemplated the least number of syllables he could make that would get her to stop talking.

He said, "I'm not really a big scrapbooker."

She squeezed his arm in hers. "C'mon. You have to try new things. At least that's what I'm doing. I'm going through a transition right now, as you might have heard."

Evan had heard but had absolutely no idea how to reply to her. Was this one of those times that people said, "I'm sorry"? Wasn't that a stupid thing to tell someone whose asshole husband had left her? "It'll get easier" sounded equally platitudinous.

Fortunately, Lorilee wasn't much for silences. "I'm getting out there again, you know? Been seeing a new guy—a wedding photographer. But it's hard to tell if he really likes me for me or if he just likes my money."

She pursed her inflated lips and gave his arm another little shake.

He patted her wrist, using the gesture as subterfuge to disentangle himself from her. But when he did, his hand came away powdery with tan dust. He looked down at her arm and saw the bruise marks she'd tried to conceal. Three finger-size marks from where someone had grabbed her.

She covered her arm with her purse, looked away self-consciously. "He's okay," she said. "You know how those artist types are. Temperamental."

Evan had no reply for that.

It was none of his business. He thought of Jack walking into space as if stepping off a diving board. Evan needed to get food, and then he had people to kill.

Her smile returned, though it labored to reach her cheeks. "That's why I'm scrapbooking. They say common interests are important."

A sudden dread pooled in Evan's gut. "Where did you say the scrapbooking class was?"

The elevator doors parted on the lobby to reveal a bustling crowd of Castle Heights residents massed around various craft tables that had been erected for the event.

Every head turned to take in Lorilee and Evan.

Evan made a snapshot count. Seventeen residents, including HOA president Hugh Walters. They all looked eager for small talk.

Evan finally made it into the subterranean parking garage, closed the door behind him, and was about to exhale with relief when he noticed Mia and her nine-year-old son sitting at the bottom of the stairs.

Mia shot him a tentative glance. He couldn't blame her for looking hesitant. He'd gone to her last night, ready to leave behind his aliases and untraceable help line to see what it might be like to attempt a normal relationship. In the wake of Jack's call, he had left her—and the conversation—hanging.

Peter craned his neck, his charcoal eyes staring up. "Hi, Evan Smoak."

Evan said, "What's new?"

Peter said, "Braces suck."

"Language," Mia said wearily.

"What're you doing down here?" Evan asked.

"Mom's hiding out from the scrapbooking lady."

"That's not true," Mia said.

"Is too. You called her 'pathologically chipper.'"

"Well, she is." Mia's hands fluttered, then landed in her chestnut curls, a show of exasperation. "And I just needed a moment away from . . . chipperness."

Peter's raspy voice took on a mournful note. "I wanted to see, is all. Plus, she had a bowl of Hershey's Kisses."

"Okay, okay," Mia said. "Go ahead. I'll be up in a sec."

Peter scampered up the stairs, paused before Evan, gave a chimpanzee smile to show off the new hardware. "Do I have anything stuck in my braces?"

"Yeah," Evan said. "Your teeth."

Peter smirked. Then he fist-bumped Evan and shot through the door into the lobby.

Mia stood. She did a slow half turn, stretching her arms, letting them slap to her sides. "That was an odd conversation," she said. "Last night."

He came down the stairs. It was hard to be this close to her and not want to move even closer. She was the first person he'd ever met who'd made the notion of another life appealing. He'd had to overcome a lifetime of instinct and training to summon the courage to go to her door last night.

It felt like a decade ago.

He said, "I'm sorry."

"I'm not looking for an apology," she said. "Just an explanation."

Evan thought of a digital video camera hurtling around the cabin of a plummeting helicopter.

He cleared his throat, a rare nonverbal tell. "I'm afraid I can't give one."

She tilted her head. "You look terrible. Are you okay?"

That image flashed through his mind again: Jack stepping out of the Black Hawk, vanishing into the void. It seemed like a dream remnant, resonant and unreal.

"Yes," he said.

"Are we gonna talk about what happened?"

"I can't."

"Because of whatever . . . things you're into."

"Yes."

She looked at him more closely. In his childhood Evan had endured countless hours of training at the hands of psyops experts, training that involved brutal interrogation that lasted hours, sometimes days. To ensure he gave nothing away with his body language or facial expressions, they'd monitored everything down to his blink rate. And yet today emotion had left him loose and vulnerable. He felt as if Mia were looking right through his façade. He stood there, exposed.

"Whatever happened this time," she said, "it hurt you."

Evan locked down his face, held a steady gaze.

She gave a concerned nod. "Be careful."

As he walked past, she caught him around the waist. She hauled him in and hugged him, and he felt himself tense. Her cheek was against his chest, her arms wrapped tight around the small of his back. He breathed her scent—lemongrass lotion, shampoo, a hint of perfume redolent of rain. He wanted to relax into her, but when he closed his eyes, all he could see was a Black Hawk spiraling out of control against a backdrop of stars.

He tore himself away and headed to his truck.

6

The Brink of Visibility

His tasks for the day completed, Evan sat at his kitchen island before a plate of steaming mahimahi, seasoned with thyme from his living wall. The plate was centered precisely between knife and fork. Offset symmetrically beyond the plate were two bowls, one filled with fresh pomegranate seeds, the other with cherry tomatoes, also plucked from the vertical rise of vegetation. His vodka tonight, shaken until bruised and served up, was 666 Pure Tasmanian, fermented in barley, single-batch-distilled in copper pots, and filtered through highest-grade activated charcoal. Ice crystals glassed the top.

He'd prepared the meal with focus.

And he didn't want any of it.

He wondered what Mia and Peter were eating in their condo nine floors below. Their colorful home with action figures on the floor, dishes in the sink, messy crayon drawings magneted to the refrigerator. When he'd first visited them, the disorder had made him uncomfortable. But he'd learned to understand it differently, as an affirmation of lives being fully lived.

He forced a bite. The flavor was good and told his body it was hungry. He reminded himself that no matter what emotions were cycling through him, he was a machine bent to a single purpose and machines required fuel.

He ate.

When he was done, he scrubbed the plate, dried it, put it away atop a stack of others. It struck him that only the top plate ever got used.

He took the vodka over to the big windows stretching along the north wall and stared out at the Los Angeles night. He could see clearly into the building across from his, like peering into a doll-house. A man emerged from an elevator, scrubbing furiously at his collar with a handkerchief. The fabric came away lipstick red. He folded the handkerchief into his pocket, walked down the hall. Evan watched his wife react happily to the door's opening. They embraced. Three floors up, a family quartet lay on their stomachs on the living-room carpet, playing a board game. Next door to them, a woman sobbed alone in a dark bedroom. An older couple on the top floor practiced ballroom dancing. The woman had a flower in her steel-gray hair. They both smiled the entire time.

All that humanity in motion. Like observing the inside of an intricate clock, gears and cogs and hidden machinations. Evan could tell the time, but he would never fully grasp the inner workings.

His gaze returned to the woman crying in the dark. As he watched her, he felt something inside him twist free, a fresh shoot of grief rising up to match hers. He'd never lacked sympathy—no, that he'd always had in spades. But he'd protected himself from empathy, had withdrawn here to his Fortress of Solitude and taken up the drawbridge.

He watched the woman sob and envied her ability to release so powerfully and so well.

His release would be paid for in blood.

He took a sip of his drink, let it slide across his tongue, cleanse his throat. Hint of dark chocolate, touch of black-pepper heat.

He dumped out the remaining vodka, then crossed to the Turkish rug near the fireplace, sat crossed-legged, and rested his hands gently on his knees. He straightened his vertebrae and veiled his eyes so they were neither open nor closed.

He dropped beneath the surface of his skin and focused on his breath, how it moved through him, how it left his body and what it took with it.

He felt the grief and fury inside him, a red-hot mass pulsing in his gut. He observed it, how it crept up his throat, seeking egress. He breathed through it, even as it raged and fought. He breathed until it dissipated, until he dissipated, until he was no longer Orphan X, no longer the Nowhere Man, no longer Evan Smoak.

When he opened his eyes sometime later, he felt purified.

He set aside his grief. He set aside his fury.

It was time to get operational.

The high-def contact lenses had their own data storage and as such could be rewound and replayed. Evan watched the footage dispassionately, a bomb investigator searching a blast site for clues.

The POV blinked on, a shuddering view of the Black Hawk's interior. Evan ignored the handcuffed man it was pointed at. Instead he watched one of the captors slide open the cabin doors to reveal paired slices of night air.

It was too dark to pick up any surface bearings. Evan could not determine how high the helo was, though one of the captors had mentioned sixteen thousand feet. As the wind whipped through and ruffled the hostage's hair, the moon jogged into sight in the corner of the open door. If Evan had a team of NASA astronomers at his disposal, perhaps he could determine the chopper's location based on star position.

But all he had in the Vault was himself and an aloe vera plant bedded down in a dish filled with cobalt-blue glass pebbles. She was named Vera II, and while she made for excellent company, she lacked the computing power of a team of NASA physicists.

He'd already done an extensive news search online and had not been surprised to find that there was no report of a Black

Hawk's crashing anywhere in the world last night. Van Sciver's non-fingerprints were all over it. If Evan wanted to pick up the trail, he'd have to shine a light in the shadows.

He focused on the footage as the freelancers in flight suits positioned themselves around the Black Hawk's cabin.

Someone off-screen shouted, "Look into the camera!"

The hostage obeyed.

Evan searched the captors for identifying tattoos, insignias, but they were geared up from their boots to their necks, only their faces showing. These freelancers loved their apparel. Evan studied their comportment, their builds, their postures. The men not in motion stood like they had two spines. Their boots were straight-laced, the preferred style of hipsters and ex-military.

Evan presumed they were not hipsters.

Van Sciver liked to use spec-ops washouts as his guns-for-hire, dishonorably discharged men who had all the training but were too brutal or unruly to stay in the service.

A voice came from off camera: "What are your current protocols for contacting Orphan X?"

The hostage kept his feet wide for balance and talked to the lens.

As the back-and-forth continued, Evan's eyes picked across the scene for any telling details—a Sharpied nickname on a rucksack, a serial number on a gun, a map with a cartoon red X on it. No such luck. They'd done a superb job of sterilizing the visual field.

The hostage squared to the lens, gave his line: "And you're dumb enough to think that puts you at an advantage."

The ensuing commotion, if viewed with detachment, bordered on comedic. The calmness of the hostage, such a contrast to the terror of his captors.

As the digital camera flew around the cabin, Evan worked his RFID-covered fingernails, bringing up virtual settings that shifted the footage to slow-motion. In the chaos perhaps something would be revealed.

He watched the scene through five, six times to no avail.

Then he changed his focus to a later segment of the footage, when the camera sailed free of the failing helo. He put on a night-vision filter, hoping to identify something on the ground, but it was whipping by too fast. Even when he moved to frame-by-frame, all the flying lens caught were blurs of occasional lights, tracts of what looked like farmland.

He was about to give up when he caught a glimpse of a bigger earthbound splotch, less illuminated than the other lights. He reversed and freeze-framed. It was darker because it wasn't in fact a light. The night-vision wash had picked it up, lightening it to the brink of visibility.

He rotated forward one frame. Back one frame. That was about all the space he had. He returned to the middle frame, squinted, instinctively leaned forward. Of course, the virtual image moved with his head, holding the same projected distance.

Fortunately, Vera II didn't judge.

Evan grabbed the splotch, enlarged it, squinted some more.

A water tower.

With a hatchet cut into it? It looked like an apple.

No—a peach.

A peach water tower.

There was one of those, all right. He'd seen it on a postcard once.

He was already scrambling to free himself of the contact lenses. Off with the new tech and in with the old.

A Google search brought up the Peachoid, a one-million-gallon water tower in Gaffney, South Carolina. It was located just off Interstate 85 between exits 90 and 92 on the ingeniously named Peachoid Road.

It wasn't a big red X on a map.

But it was pretty damn close.

7

Two Graves

Evan's Woolrich shirt sported fake buttons hiding magnets that held the front together. The magnets gave way easily in case he needed to go for the holster clipped to the waistband of his tactical-discreet cargo pants. Right now the holster was empty. He wore lightweight Original S.W.A.T. boots that with his pant legs down looked like boring walking shoes. The boots would be a pain to unlace at airport security.

In his back pocket, he had one of many passports gorgeously manufactured by a gorgeous counterfeiter, Melinda Truong.

The matter was too urgent to wait for a cross-country drive.

It was oh-dark-hundred, and the elevator was empty this early—thank heaven for small mercies. As the doors zippered shut behind Evan, he smelled a trace of lemongrass. On the floor was a pea of balled-up tinfoil, the Ghost of a Hershey's Kiss Past.

Or maybe *he* was the ghost, drifting invisibly among the living, following in their wake.

The ride down was quiet. He enjoyed it.

Evan carved through the whipping desert wind and ducked into the armorer's workshop. Lit like a dungeon, it was off the Vegas Strip and off the beaten path. Evan checked the surveillance camera at the door, verified that it had been unplugged before his arrival, as was the standing arrangement.

He smelled gun grease and coffee, cigarette smoke and spent powder. He peered through the stacks of weapon crates, across the machines and workbenches that were arrayed according to some logic he'd never been able to decipher.

"Tommy?"

The sound of rolling wheels on concrete presaged the nine-fingered armorer's appearance. And then there he was, sliding in from stage left in a cocked-back Aeron chair, welder's goggles turning him into some kind of steampunk nightmare. Beneath the biker's mustache, a Camel Wide crackled, sucked down to within a millimeter of the filter. Tommy Stojack plucked out the cigarette and dropped it into a water-filled red Solo cup, where it sizzled out among countless dead compatriots. Given the ordnance in evidence, a misplaced butt would turn the shop into a Fourth of July display.

Tommy slid the goggles up and regarded Evan. "Fifteen minutes prior to fifteen minutes prior. I could set my watch by you."

"You have it?"

"Of course I have it. What's with the ASAP?"

"I'm on something. It's highly personal."

"Personal." Tommy plucked out his lower lip and dropped in a wedge of Skoal Wintergreen. "Didn't know that word was in your lexicon. You threw in an adverb and everything."

Evan could count the people he trusted on the fingers of Tommy's mutilated hand, with digits to spare. Since the Black Hawk's disintegration, Tommy was one of the few remaining. Even so, Evan and Tommy knew nothing of each other's personal lives. In fact, they knew little of their respective professional lives either. From the occasional dropped tidbit, Evan had put together that Tommy was a world-class sniper and that he did contract training and weapons R&D for government-sanctioned black-ops groups that were not as dark a shade of black as the Orphan Program.

Tommy supplied Evan with his firepower, too, and made each of Evan's pistols from scratch, machining out a solid-aluminum forging of a pistol frame that had never been stamped with a serial number—a ghost gun. Then he simply fitted a fire-control group and loaded up the pistol with high-profile Straight Eight sights, an extended barrel threaded to receive a suppressor, and an ambidextrous thumb safety, since Evan preferred to shoot southpaw. He ordered all his pistols in matte black so they could vanish into shadows as readily as he did.

As Evan entered the heart of the lair, Tommy used a boot to shove himself away from a crate of rocket-propelled grenades, conveying himself over to a workbench where he at last creakily found his feet.

Laid out on a grease-stained silicone cloth were a laptop and a narrow pistol that looked like one of Evan's 1911s that had gone on a diet.

"I skinny-minnied this little lady up for you," Tommy said. "What do you think?"

Evan picked it up. It fit oddly in his grip. His usual pistol, sliced in half. It was barely wider than the 230-grain Speer Gold Dot hollow points it fired. He turned it over in his hand and then back. "The weight'll take some adjusting to."

"That's your way of saying, 'Thank you, brother. You're PFM. Pure Fucking Magic.'"

Evan eyed the sights. "That, too."

Tommy slung an altered holster across the workbench. "And here's a special-sauce high-guard Kydex to fit it."

Evan hefted the weapon a few more times. "To be honest, I wasn't sure how you'd pull it off."

"Pull it off?" Tommy's head drew back haughtily. "Boy, I've been calibrating a laser gun for the navy that can knock drones out of the sky. I've been field-testing self-guided fifty-cal sniper rounds for DARPA that change direction in midair. Fine-tuned a smart scope that *doesn't let you* shoot a friendly target." He crossed his arms. "I think I can handle smuggling a handgun past a few mouth-breathing TSA agents." He snapped his fingers, pointed to a sticky coffeepot gurgling behind Evan. "Fetch."

Evan poured a mug for Tommy, had to wipe his hands on the gun-cleaning cloth. Tommy slurped the coffee across his packed lower lip. Then he lit up another Camel. Evan figured the only reason Tommy didn't smoke them two at a time was that it hadn't occurred to him yet.

Tommy pulled three Wilson eight-rounders from his bulging shirt pocket and offered them up. "Test-drive it."

Evan slotted in the first mag, put on eye and ear pro, and walked to the test-firing tube. He ran through all twenty-four rounds without a hitch. Then gave a faint nod.

He came back over to the workbench. "How's the A-fib coming?"

Tommy waved him off. "I'm getting extra beats in between my extra beats. I figure I speed shit up enough, I'll go full-tilt Iron Man." He jabbed the stub of his missing finger at the arrayed items. "Let me break it down Barney style. Same everything you're used to but skinnier. 'Why skinnier, Chief Stojack?' you may ask." The finger stub circled. "Witness."

Tommy took the skinny gun and slid it into the laptop's hard-drive slot where some hidden mechanism received it. "All they'll see on the X-ray is the solid block of the hard drive. I had to go thirteen-inch screen on the laptop to make the specs fit, so they might make you take it out, power it up, all that security Kabuki-theater bullshit, but you'll be GTG. Obviously you gotta clean the piece so there's no residues that'll ring the cherries in a puff test. As for the laptop, I filled it with bullshit spreadsheets, generic documents, a few stock photos." He picked up the laptop, showed off its slender profile. "High speed, low drag." He made a production of handing it off to Evan, a waiter displaying the Bordeaux. "Go forth and conquer." He gave his gap-toothed smile. "Fair winds and following seas."

Evan took the laptop and started for the door.

"Hey."

Evan turned back.

"You're not exactly a barrel of belly laughs generally, but you seem decidedly more somber. This 'highly personal'? It's *actually* highly personal?"

"Yes."

Tommy studied him, tugging at one end of his horseshoe mustache. The crinkles around his eyes deepened with concern. "You get in a jam, send up a smoke signal. I'm not too old to cover your six, you know."

"I know. But it's something I have to handle alone."

Tommy nodded slowly, his gaze not leaving Evan's face. "Remember what Confucius say: 'Before you embark on a journey of revenge, dig two graves.'"

"Oh," Evan said, "I'm gonna dig a lot more than that."

8

Serve with Gladness

It had all been for shit.

Evan stood in front of his rented Impala on the side of Peachoid Road, staring at the street's namesake, which he had grown to despise. He held the giant fruit monstrosity personally responsible for the stagnation of his pursuit.

He didn't know precisely what he was looking for, but some indication that Jack and a ten-ton Black Hawk helicopter had struck the earth in this vicinity would have been a start.

Van Sciver's Orphans were a conspiracy theorist's wet dream. Not just at killing—they were good at killing, very good, but humans had been killing one another for a very long time. No, *this* is what they did best—erased any trace of their actions from the official world everyone else lived in. Nothing for the media, local PD, FBI, even CIA to grab hold of. They moved with the fury of a hurricane and didn't leave a dewdrop in their wake.

Evan had driven the frontage and access roads, carved through the checkerboard plots of farmland, housing, and forest surrounding the novelty landmark, searching for that dewdrop to no avail. There was no wreckage, no scorched earth, no Jack's truck abandoned at the side of a road.

The flight from Las Vegas, with a layover in Houston, had taken seven hours and seven minutes. Driving fifty-three miles from Charlotte Douglas International had tacked on another hour and twenty. A long way to come for a whole lot of nothing.

They say that revenge is a dish best served cold, but Evan preferred to serve it piping hot.

He took in a deep breath and a lungful of car exhaust.

The Fourth Commandment: *Never make it personal.*

He repeated it over and over in his head until he almost believed it.

Then he got into his Impala and drove off. He took a final loop upslope, winding through thickening forest that coaxed a distant memory of the trees surrounding Jack's farmhouse.

He checked his RoamZone. Even after a long day, the high-power lithium-ion battery kept the phone's charge nearly full. He wondered briefly what he would do if the next Nowhere Man case rang through—a *real* Nowhere Man case as opposed to the personal mission he was on now. After he helped his clients, he asked them to find one—and only one—person who needed his help and to pass on his untraceable number.

He had a rule, encoded in the Seventh Commandment: *One mission at a time.*

For Jack he was willing to make an exception.

He pulled over to get a bottled water at a convenience store. As he headed back to the car, chugging down the water, he caught a chorus of singing voices on the breeze.

Only when he turned and saw the open front door of the Baptist church across the parking lot did he realize that it was an actual choir. Drawn by the music, he walked over, climbed the stone steps, and entered. The pews sat empty, but the singers were in place in the choir stand, decked out in royal-blue gospel gowns. They were working on an a cappella hymn, practicing beneath a stark wooden cross flooded with light from behind. The choir conductor, an older man, directed from a podium. The voices rose pure and true.

Evan's form in the doorway cut the light, and the director half turned, his hands still keeping time for the singers. He gave a welcoming nod in the direction of the pews.

Evan felt the habitual pull to withdraw, but there was a power in the joined voices that hit him in the spine, made it thrum like a guitar string. He took a seat in the last row and let the hymn wash over him.

With the harmony came memories. Waking up in the dormer bedroom in Jack's farmhouse that first sun-drenched morning. Walking behind Jack in the forest, filling those boot prints with his own small shoes. The cadence of Jack's voice, how it never rose above a measured pitch during their nightly study sessions. Jack had taught him everything from Alexander the Great's battle tactics to basic phrases in the Indo-Iranian languages to toasting etiquette for Scandinavian countries—nothing was too trivial. The smallest detail could save Evan's life in the field.

Or kill him.

He thought about an Arab financier peering through raccoon eyes, wearing a half-moon laceration from Evan's garrote like a necklace. A fat man, bald as a baby and clad only in a towel, staring back at him lifelessly through the steam of a bathhouse, blood drooling from a bullet hole over his left eye. A man slumped over a table in a drab Eastern European kitchen, his face in his soup, the back of his head missing.

He thought about what he was going to do to Van Sciver and every one of his men he came across along the way.

The choir finished. Before they could disperse, the director cleared his throat to good dramatic effect and said, "Now, when you get back out there with your car pools and your grocery shopping and your punching the clock, you take a little time to think about the works you do and the life you lead. When you're back in this here church one day boxed up in a coffin, that's gonna be all that's left to speak for you." With a crinkled hand, he waved them away. "Go on, now."

The singers filed out, joking and gossiping. A few glanced Evan's way, and he nodded pleasantly. People forget anything that's not a threat, and Evan had no intention of being remembered.

He lifted his eyes to the glow behind the altar and wondered at the beliefs men held and what those beliefs drove them to do. In his brief time on the planet, he'd seen so many dead stares, so many visages touched with the gray pallor of death. But he'd never blinded himself to the humanity shining through the cracks of those broken guises. Jack had made sure of that. He'd lodged that paradox in Evan's mind and in his heart. It had saved him, in a manner of speaking. But it came with a price.

Evan started to rise when the director turned and caught his eye. The old man limped up the aisle toward him. "Our altos are flat and our tenors are sharp. You'd think it'd even us out some."

"It sounded perfect to me," Evan said. "But I've got an untrained ear."

"You must." The man sat heavily in the pew next to him, let out a sigh like air groaning through a bellows.

"I'll let you get on with your day, sir," Evan said.

"Minister."

"Minister. Thank you for letting me listen."

"A man doesn't stumble into a church for no reason."

Out of deference Evan didn't take issue with him.

The minister sat back, crossed his arms, and gazed at the vaulted ceiling. Evan felt a familiar tug to leave but realized that for the moment he had nowhere to be. The minister scratched at his elbow, clearly in no rush.

Evan considered the man's words again. Decided to rise to the challenge.

"Which matters more?" he asked.

"Which *what* matters more?"

"At the end. Which matters more? The works we've done or the life we lead?"

"Say 'I,' son. First person. You'd be surprised at how powerful the change is."

Evan took a pause. "Which matters more? The works I've done or the life I lead?"

The minister was right. The words felt different in Evan's body and behind his face.

"You assume they're different," the minister said. "One's works and one's life."

"In some cases."

"Like yours?"

"That remains to be seen."

The minister gave a frown and nodded profoundly. It took a good measure of dignity to manage a profound nod, but he managed it just fine. "Do you follow the Commandments, son?"

Evan nearly smiled. "Yes, Minister. Every last one."

"Then there's your start."

Evan held a beat before switching tracks. "I'd imagine that few people are woven into this community as well as you are."

"I'd say you imagine right."

"Has there been any word about government folks coming through town, a helicopter, a fire?"

The minister arched an eyebrow. "There has not."

"Suspicious flurry of activity down by the"—he hesitated slightly before naming his nemesis—"Peachoid?"

"No."

"How about alien spaceships cutting crop circles?" Evan countenanced the man's watery glare. "Kidding."

"What's all this hokum about?"

"I was supposed to meet a friend at the peach water tower."

"Why don't you call him?"

"Long-lost friend. We'd arranged a meet online."

"Hmm." The minister mused a moment. "You sure you got the right one?"

A jolt of anticipation straightened Evan up slightly in the pew. "The right friend?"

"The right Peachoid. Same folks built a smaller one down in Clanton, Alabama."

Evan had not in fact been following all the Commandments. He'd overlooked the first one: *Assume nothing.*

He rose. "Thank you, Minister. I can't tell you how useful your guidance has been."

"I serve with gladness."

Evan shook the proffered sandpaper hand. "As do I."

9

From Beyond the Grave

Five hours and thirty-eight minutes later, Evan was standing on the side of I-65 between Birmingham and Wetumpka, gazing up at a five-hundred-gallon version of the same eyesore.

Twenty-seven minutes after that, his headlights picked up Jack's truck parked at the edge of a fire road running between two swaths of cotton that stretched into the darkness, maybe forever.

He climbed out of the Impala, unholstered his slender ARES pistol for the first time, and approached the truck tentatively. It was cold enough out to be uncomfortable, but he didn't have any interest in being uncomfortable. He shone a key-chain Maglite through the windows and took in the damage. Slashed seat cushions, scattered papers from the glove box, holes punched through the headliner. They'd searched as well as he'd expected they would. They'd have been looking for anything that might point them to Evan.

His breath fogging the pane, Evan stared at the defaced interior and considered how many years Jack had polished this dashboard, vacuumed the seams, touched up the paint. Anger and sorrow threatened to escape the locked-down corner of his heart, and he took a moment to tamp it back into place.

He walked around the truck, searched for booby traps. None were visible.

The truck was unlocked. It was two decades old, but the hinges didn't so much as creak when the door swung open. Jack's hinges wouldn't dare.

Evan sat where Jack used to sit.

Do you regret it? What I did to you?

He put his hands on the steering wheel. The pebbled vinyl was worn smooth at the ten and two. The spots where Jack's hands used to rest.

I wanted to hear your voice.

Out of the corner of his eye, Evan caught a gleam from the molded map pocket on the lower half of the door. He reached down and lifted Jack's keys into the ambient light.

Odd.

Jack never left his keys in the truck.

He was a creature of habit. The Second Commandment had always been his favorite: *How you do anything is how you do everything.* He had drilled it into Evan's cells.

There was a likelihood, of course, that Van Sciver's men had taken Jack's keys when they'd grabbed him so they could search his truck. But if that were the case, once they were done, wouldn't they just have tossed the keys back on the seat or dropped them into the cup holder? Placing them in a map pocket low on the door took consideration and a bit of effort.

It's too late for me.

Jack had known he was about to get grabbed.

This is looking to be my ninth life, son. Dollars to doughnuts they've got ears on me right now.

And Jack would've controlled the terms. Evan guessed he would've gotten out of the truck under his own power. Left it unlocked for the search. Placed the keys carefully for Evan to find.

But why?

Sometimes we miss what's important for the fog. But maybe we should give it a go before, you know . . .

Jack had known he was about to die.

I guess . . . I guess I want to know that I'm forgiven.

Evan looked through the dirty windshield. The night swallowed up the land all around. Sitting in the cab of Jack's truck, Evan could just as well have been floating through the black infinity of outer space.

"We didn't have time," he told the dashboard. "We didn't have enough time."

I love you, son.

"Copy that," Evan said.

He pondered the darkness, his breath wisping in the November chill.

Before he died, Jack had wanted to set things right with Evan—he'd made that much clear. But maybe his words held a double meaning. What if there was something else he was looking to set right? He'd known that Van Sciver was listening. He would've spoken in code.

Evan replayed the conversation in his head, snagged on something Jack had said: *Sometimes we miss what's important for the fog.*

The turn of phrase was decidedly un-Jack. Jack had a down-to-earth, articulate speaking style, the patter of a former station chief. He was not flowery, rarely poetic, and tended to make use of metaphors only when undercutting them.

Evan looked down at the keys in his hand.

miss what's important for the fog

The realization dropped into his belly, rippling out to his fingertips.

He zippered the key into the ignition.

The well-maintained engine turned over and purred.

Evan sat.

He leaned forward so that his mouth would be that much closer to the cooling windshield. And he breathed.

A full minute passed. And then another.

Fog started creeping in from the edges of the windows. He shifted in the seat, watched the driver's window.

As fog crept to the center of the pane, a few streaks remained stubbornly clear. They forged together as the condensation filled in around them, finally starting to resolve in the negative space as letters.

In his final minutes, Jack had written a low-tech hidden message for Evan with the tip of his finger.

Evan stared at the window, not daring to blink.

At last the effect was complete, Evan's orders standing out in stark relief on the clouded glass.

GET PACKAGE
3728 OAK TERRACE #202
HILLSBORO, OR
Jack had given him a final mission.

10

A Goodly Amount of Damage

The apartment complex was so sturdy that it bordered on municipal. Ten-foot security gate, metal shutters, callbox with buzzer. Evan had approached the target slowly, winding in on the address block by block like a boa constricting its prey. Then he'd parked behind the building in the shade of a tree—Hillsboro was lousy with trees—and surveilled.

The rented Toyota Corolla reeked eye-wateringly of faux new-car smell, courtesy of an overly exuberant car washer. Evan had been watching for three hours now, which was a lot of new-car smell for a man to take.

Traffic ran past steadily. A Tesla Model S flashed by, and more Priuses than he could count. Buses creaked to a stop across the road at intervals approximating ten minutes and disgorged various domestic workers and floridly bearded young men. Evan used the reflection off the bus's windows to observe the wide parking lot enfolded in the horseshoe of the three-story complex. People came and went, and they looked ordinary enough.

Then again, so did Evan.

The same HILLSBORO HOME THEATER INSTALLATION! van drove by two times, a half hour apart. A half hour was an eyebrow-raising interval, though it was plausible that the driver had bid a job or had completed a small repair and was returning to the shop.

Evan didn't like vans.

He gave it another hour, but the van didn't reappear. Besides, what idiot would put an exclamation mark on an undercover vehicle?

He reapplied a thin layer of superglue to his fingertips. Superglue was less conspicuous than gloves and left him with full tactility. He pressed the fingers of his left hand to the window. They left five printless dots.

A rickety old Cadillac coasted to the curb across the street from Evan at the rear of the complex. An elderly man emerged, the strains of a Beethoven piano concerto still drifting through the open windows. He began to unload from the trunk various canvases, which he propped against the wall of the building. They featured cubist takes on musical instruments—a deconstructed trumpet, a piano turned inside out. There was a flair to his artwork, an inner life. The canvases kept coming. They lined the base of the building, filled a blanket he spread on the sidewalk, peered from the jaw of the open trunk. The man sat creakily, adjusted his herringbone flat cap, and nodded to the music.

Evan listened along with him. It was Concerto No. 3, one of Jack's favorites. He remembered Jack's saying that it owed something to Mozart, how all things should honor what preceded them and inspire what is to come.

He wondered how he could best honor Jack.

The question of inspiration was even thornier.

He remembered Jack's message scrawled on the foggy window. He wondered what the hell the package was and why Jack had hidden it all the way across the continent. Something essential. A long-buried secret from Jack's past that would lead to Van Sciver? Maybe even a torpedo that would sink him.

Evan checked his gun. Along with the skinny 1911, he'd smug-

gled one extra go-to-war magazine in the laptop. He'd validated the mag at a range, making sure it dropped clear. That gave him seventeen rounds, which was less than he was comfortable with. Then again, he could do a goodly amount of damage with seventeen rounds.

He heard an echo of Jack's voice: *Just don't put all the holes in the same place.*

He got out of the car. Scanning the traffic, he walked around the east wing of the building, tucking quickly into the horseshoe. At the edge of the parking lot, the callbox sprouted from the metal mesh of the security gate. It was a serious gate with a serious double-keyed lock. Another metal gate guarded the stairwell, which was itself caged.

Fire hazards to be sure, but this was a bad section of Hillsboro—whatever that meant—and the folks who lived here cared more about day-to-day safety than about the sliver percentage of a fire-induced stampede.

Jack had chosen a good place to hide the package.

On the directory, number 202 was blank. Evan scanned the other names. Given the security concerns of the residents, a button-pushing deliveryman ruse wouldn't likely get him far.

He'd bought a rake pick and a tension wrench at a hardware store and was about to get busy when a guy yammering into a Bluetooth headset clanged out of the stairwell gate. As the man strode up the corridor toward the front, Evan pretended to punch a code into the callbox's keypad.

"I heard this new ramen place is *sick*," the guy told his interlocutor and anyone else in the vicinity who might have been interested. "They have, like, a hundred flavors of shōchū."

He shoved his way out the front gate, ignoring Evan and the rest of the world, and Evan slipped through. In case he had to beat a hasty retreat, he wedged a quarter between the latch and the frame so the gate wouldn't autolock.

At the stairwell he finally got to use his pick set. He engaged a second quarter to keep that gate from locking also.

A fine fifty-cent investment.

He crept up to the second floor and down the corridor. Apartment 202 had a peephole. He ducked beneath it, put his ear to the door. Heard nothing inside.

Though the building was late-afternoon quiet, he couldn't risk creeping around the corridor for long.

The apartment lock was also double-keyed. With the rake and wrench, he jogged the pins into proper alignment and eased the door silently open.

The place was dimly lit and smelled of carpet dust and greasy food. A brief foyer led to a single big studio room. No furniture.

He made out a faint scraping sound.

Pistol drawn, Evan eased through the foyer, heel to toe, minding the floorboards. More of the studio came into view. A bare mattress. A mound of fast-food wrappers. A geometric screen saver casting a striated glow from an open laptop. Then an overstuffed rucksack.

The scraping grew louder.

He eased out a breath, peered around the corner.

A girl crouched, facing away, her forehead nearly touching the far wall. She had a mane of dark wavy hair, torn jeans, a form-fitting tank top. It was hard to gauge from behind, but he guessed she was a teenager. She was bent over something, and her shoulders shook slightly. Crying?

The closet and bathroom doors were laid open, and there was no furniture for anyone to hide behind. Just her.

He thought about the double-keyed locks and wondered—was she being held captive?

He aimed the ARES at the floor but didn't holster it. Stepping clear of the foyer, he lowered his voice so as not to startle her. "Are you okay?"

She jumped at the sound, then glanced tentatively over her shoulder. Her back curled with fear, her expression vulnerable. She looked Hispanic, but he couldn't be sure in the dim light.

"Who are you?" she said.

"I'm not gonna hurt you."

"Why are you here?"

A Goodly Amount of Damage

He drew closer slowly, not wanting to scare her. "It's a long story."

"Can . . . can you help me?"

He holstered the pistol but stayed alert. "Who put you here?"

"I don't know. I can't remember. I . . . I . . ."

Her posture suddenly snapped into shape, a bundle of coiled muscle. She pivoted into a vicious leg sweep, leading with the hard edge of her heel, sweeping both of his boots out from under him.

As he accelerated into weightlessness, he saw the glint in her eye matched by the glint of the fixed-blade combat knife in her right hand. A sharpening stone lay on the carpet, the stone she'd been crouching over, scraping away when he'd walked in. Already she'd rotated, spinning up onto her feet, readying to drive the blade through his sternum.

He struck the floor, the wind knocking from his lungs in a single clump, and it occurred to him just how badly he had misjudged the situation.

11

Enemy of My Enemy

Evan's first focus was the knife.

Darting down at him like a shiv stab, all blade, nothing to grab.

Laid out on the carpet as if he were a corpse, he swept the bar of his forearm protectively across his chest, hammering the girl's slender wrist and knocking the knife off course just before it broke skin. The tip skimmed his shirt above the ribs, slicing fabric.

His second focus was her fist.

Which she'd cocked and deployed even while her knife hand had still been in motion. He had a split-second to admire the technique—knuckles following blade with double-tap timing—before she broke his nose.

He rolled his head with the punch, tumbled gracelessly up onto his feet. She grabbed the back of his shirt, but the magnetic buttons gave way—*click-click-click*—and he spun right out of it. His eyes watered from the blow to the nose, but the escape bought him a much-needed second to blink his way back to some version of clarity. She flung the shirt aside and launched a barrage of kicks.

He parried, parried, parried, bruising his forearms and knuckles, holding his attention mostly on the knife.

She came at him again, a jailhouse lunge, but now he was ready for it. His hands moved in blurry unison, a *bong sau/lop sau* trap that simultaneously blocked and grabbed her arm. He clenched hard, slid his fist up the length of her forearm, and hit the bump of her wrist with enough force that her fingers released and the knife shot free.

They were nose-to-nose, her mouth forming an O of perfect shock. He had a wide-open lane to her windpipe—one elbow strike and she'd be over—but Jack's Eighth Commandment sailed in and tapped the back of his brain: *Never kill a kid.*

He barreled her over and pinned her with a cross-face cradle, a grappling move that left her locked up, her knee smashed to her cheek, arms flailing uselessly to the sides.

"Get off me!" she shouted. "I will kill you! I will fucking—"

He pressed his forehead to her temple, immobilizing her head and shielding his eyes. "Breathe," he said.

She inhaled sharply.

"Again."

She obeyed.

"Where is the package?" he asked.

"What?"

"What'd you do with the package?"

"The hell are you talking about?"

"You saw the message. You beat me here."

"Can you get your knee out of my ribs?"

Evan eased off the pressure. "What'd you do with it?"

She gave no answer. Each breath rasped through her contorted throat.

Blood was trickling from Evan's nose, tickling his cheek. "I'm gonna let you go, and we're gonna try this again, okay?"

Her answer came strained. "Okay."

"I'd prefer not to have to kill you."

"I'd like to say the same, but I haven't decided yet."

He released her, and they stood. They kept their palms raised, halfway to an open-hand guard. She drew in deep lungfuls, her cheeks flushed. She was expertly trained but still green.

He got his first clear look at her. Her hair fell to her shoulders, thick and dark and lush. The right side had been shaved short, but it was mostly hidden by the tumbling length of her locks, a surprisingly subtle effect. She was lean and fit, her deltoids pronounced enough to show notches in the muscle.

"I'm gonna put my shirt back on," he said. "If you come at me, it won't go well for you."

Keeping his gaze on her, he backed up and put on his shirt. Next to the rucksack, a ragged flannel rested on the carpet. He tossed it to her.

She tugged it on.

Keeping a bit of distance, they stared at each other. A wisp of agitated piano reached them from outside, the concerto hitting the third movement.

"Let's cut to it," Evan said. "I see how you move. I know you're an Orphan. I know who sent you."

"You don't know anything."

"What's the package?"

She answered him with a glare.

He risked a fleeting look at her rucksack. "Is it in there?"

"No."

He crouched over the rucksack.

"Don't touch my stuff."

He rooted around in it, sneaking quick glances down. Clothes, a few toiletries, a shoe box filled with what looked like personal letters.

"Put those *down*."

"Is there some kind of code in these papers?"

"No."

He armed blood off his upper lip. "Is the package something on the laptop?"

"No."

"If you're lying, I can hack into it."

Her mouth firmed into something more aggressive than a smirk. "Good luck."

As he started to reach for the laptop, it suddenly alerted with a ping, the screen saver vanishing.

Enemy of My Enemy

Four surveillance feeds came up, tiling the screen. It took a moment for Evan to register that they were streaming different angles of the outside of the apartment complex.

The bottom-left feed showed two SUVs blocking the horseshoe of the parking lot. Teams of geared-up operators charged for the front gate.

"Your backup's here," the girl said. "What—you couldn't handle me yourself?" Her voice stayed tough, but her chest heaved with the words. She was scared, and this time he knew she wasn't faking it.

Evan stared at the screen. The operators displayed a similar military precision to that of the men in the Black Hawk. Evan counted six of them.

Seventeen rounds. Six men.

Just don't put all the holes in the same place.

On-screen the lead operator kicked the front gate, and it clanged open. Evan heard it in stereo, registered the vibration in the floor.

He and the girl watched as the men poured into the ground-floor corridor.

He said, "They're not with me."

His eyes met the girl's, and he saw that she believed him.

Her voice was hammered flat with dread. "You left the gates unlocked behind you."

Clang. The stairwell gate flew open, courtesy of Evan's ill-spent twenty-five cents.

The men throttled up the stairwell. The girl's eyes darted from the screen back to Evan.

"Enemy of my enemy," he said.

She gave a nod.

He drew his ARES. "Get behind me. Pick up your knife."

The girl moved, but not for the knife. She shot over to the mattress and lifted it, revealing a hatch cut through the floor. She looked at him, eyes wild, hair swinging. "My stuff," she said. "Get my stuff."

The clamor of the men reached the second floor, spilled onto the corridor.

Evan snapped the laptop shut, rammed it into the rucksack,

tossed the combat knife in after. She slipped through the hatch and disappeared. The mattress fell back into place, covering the hole. He didn't hear her land. He sprinted across the room.

As he yanked up the edge of the mattress, he heard the front door smash in. Snatching the rucksack behind him, he shoulder-rolled beneath the mattress, free-falling. A thump announced the sealing of the hatch above.

He rotated to break his fall, but a soft landing caught him off guard. His boots struck another mattress, positioned on the ground floor directly beneath the one above. He tumbled off the side onto the carpet.

He looked up.

The girl was waiting.

She wrenched the rucksack from his grip, pistoned her leg in a heel stomp directed at his throat. He caught her foot in both hands and twisted hard, flinging her aside. She bounced up off the floor like a cat, shot across the room, flung open the window.

As she leapt through, he grabbed a strap of the rucksack, halting her momentum. She jerked back and banged against the outside wall, one arm bent over the sill. She wouldn't let go of the rucksack. They were both off balance, caught in a ridiculous tug-of-war across a windowsill.

Boots drummed the floor above. It was only a matter of time before one of the men looked under the mattress.

Evan dove through the window, collecting both the rucksack and the girl in a bear-hug embrace. They sailed past the elderly artist, their fall cushioned by the blanket covered with his paintings. The Cadillac's radio blared away, the C-major coda galloping along in presto.

Evan hopped to his feet, broken frames falling away, the cubist pieces now cubist in three dimensions. Through the window Evan saw a beam of light appear, a golden shaft piercing the gloom of the ground-floor apartment.

The upstairs mattress, pulled back.

He looked helplessly across the street at his rental car.

Thirty yards of high visibility through traffic.

He'd never make it.

The artist rose from the sidewalk, his flat cap askew. "What kind of damn-fool nonsense is this?"

The girl thrashed free of Evan, landing on all fours. She scampered across the blanket to get away, but it bunched beneath her knees, impeding her progress.

Evan grabbed her arm, spun her up and around, and dumped her into the Cadillac's open trunk, shattering her straight through a painting of a dissected bassoon. He slammed the trunk an instant before she started battering at it.

He snatched up the rucksack, slung it through the open rear window. "If they hear you, they'll kill you."

Her muffled shout came through the trunk. "How do I know *you're* not gonna kill me?"

"Because I would've done it already."

He hopped into the car. The keys waited in the ignition, enabling the radio and a pleasing whiff of air-conditioning.

As the concerto tinkled to a close, Evan looked out the open passenger window at the old artist. Through the window over the man's shoulder, he saw the first shadow tumble from the ceiling.

"Sorry about your art," Evan said, and peeled out.

He wheeled around the edge of the complex, blending into traffic, coasting past the open mouth of the horseshoe. He looked back at the building.

In the center of the parking lot, a man stood facing away, his head tilted up to take in the second floor. Waiting. He would have looked like an ordinary guy were it not for his posture; he stood with the perfect stillness of the perfectly trained.

Orphan.

One of the operators stepped out through the splintered door of 202 and gestured to the man with two fingers—*He's on the run, went down and out.*

The traffic light turned red, and Evan hit the brakes, peering back transfixed as the man in the parking lot sprang into motion. He hit the front gate with his foot, vaulted up, ran four pounding steps along the high fence top, then leapt onto the outside of the stairwell cage. With a series of massive lunging leaps, he scaled the cage and then swung around onto the third-floor corridor.

He jumped up, grabbed the hanging roof ledge, and spun himself onto the roof, where he stood with the command of a mountaineer claiming an apex.

He'd parkoured his way up the entire route in under six seconds. Evan allowed himself to be impressed.

The man peered down, evidently picking up the commotion on the sidewalk outside apartment #102. He began a slow rotation, pivoting like a weather vane, his eyes scanning the streets below.

Evan turned back around in the driver's seat, cranked the side-view mirror to a severe tilt, and watched the man's reflection. The man finished his rotation, staring down at the mass of cars at the traffic light. It seemed like he was looking directly at Evan in the Cadillac, but of course there was no way it was possible from that distance.

The light turned green, and Evan drove off.

12

Increasingly Rural Tangle

Keeping the needle pegged at the speed limit, Evan drove a circuitous route to the nearest freeway and ran past four exits before hopping off and shooting west through an increasingly rural tangle of desolate back roads. Gray clouds pervaded the sky, heavy with the promise of rain. Sure enough, a few drops tapped the roof, quickening to a rat-a-tat, ushering dusk into full night. Decreased visibility was good; it went both ways. Local law enforcement had undoubtedly already issued a Be On the Lookout for the Cadillac.

He had to change vehicles, but first he needed to get a good distance between himself and the men who'd raided the apartment compound. Then he would regroup, determine what the package was, and deal with the problem in the trunk and the myriad questions that came with it.

He closed his eyes, inhaled deeply, settled his shoulders. He blew out a breath, opened his eyes, and reset himself, assessing everything as if he were confronting it for the first time.

Jack's dying message.

A package.

An address.

A girl who was an Orphan—or at the very least Orphan-trained. Who was hostile.

But not allied with the crew of men, led by another seeming Orphan, who had raided the apartment complex in pursuit of her, the package, or Evan himself.

A crew that had Van Sciver's fingerprints all over it.

Which left a whole lot of questions and very few answers.

The rain thrummed and thrummed. The girl in the trunk banged a few times, shouted something unintelligible. The windshield wipers groaned and thumped.

First order of business was to do a quick equipment appraisal.

Evan's scuffed knuckles, a fetching post-fight shade of eggplant, ledged the steering wheel. His nose was freshly broken, leaking a trickle of crimson. Nothing bad, more a shifting along old fault lines.

He inspected his nose in the rearview, then reached up and snapped it back into place.

The Cadillac's alignment pulled to the right, threatening to dump him into the rain-filled roadside ditch. The seat springs poked into the backs of his thighs, and the fabric, dotted with cigarette scorch marks, reeked of menthol. The dome light housed a bare, burned-out bulb, the brake disks made a noise like an asphyxiating chicken, and the left rear brake light was out.

He should have stolen a better car.

Rain dumped down. That was Portland for you. Or—if he was being precise—a country road outside Hillsboro.

Big drops turned the roof into a tin drum. Water sluiced across the windshield, rooster-tailed from the tires.

He sledded around a bend, passing a billboard. A moment later smeared red-and-blue lights illuminated the Caddy's rear window.

A cop.

The broken brake light.

That was inconvenient.

Especially on this car, since a BOLO had likely been issued. The cop would be running the plate number now if he hadn't already.

Increasingly Rural Tangle

Evan blew out a breath. Leaned harder into the gas pedal.

Here came the sirens. The headlights grew larger.

Evan could see the silhouette of the officer behind the wheel. So much like a shooting target—head and chest, all critical mass.

Hillsboro prided itself on being one of the safest cities in the Pacific Northwest. Evan hoped to keep it that way.

As he popped the brakes and jerked the wheel, the heap of a car rocked on its shocks, fanning onto an intersecting road.

Two more cop cars swept in behind him from the opposite direction.

Evan sighed.

Three patrol cars lit up like Christmas, sirens screaming, spreading out across both lanes and closing in.

That was when the thumping from the trunk grew more pronounced.

He checked the wheel, loose enough to jog two inches in either direction with no effect on the steering. He was going to have to attempt tactical driving maneuvers in a car that should not be highway-approved.

Evan had spent a portion of the summer of his fifteenth year on a specialized course in the sticks of Virginia with Jack in the passenger seat keeping one hand on the wheel, steering him through everything from evasive driving to acceleration techniques in challenging traction environments.

Just another kid out with his old man, learning to drive.

In their final conversation, he'd told Jack, *I wouldn't trade knowing you for anything.* He felt it now not as a sentiment but as a warmth in his chest. He was glad he'd gotten the words out.

The Cadillac backfired. The motor sounded like it had a marble loose in it. Evan grimaced.

All right, Jack. Let's do this together.

He started to alternate brake and gas, playing with the pursuing cruisers, forcing them to alter their lineup. At last one separated from the pack, moving bullishly to the fore.

Evan held the wheel steady, luring the lead car closer.

A crackly loudspeaker pierced the rain. *"Pull over immediately! Repeat: Pull to the side of the road!"*

Evan called back to the girl in the trunk, "You might want to brace yourself."

The girl shouted, "Great!"

He unholstered his ARES.

Seventeen bullets.

The lead car crept up alongside him, nosing parallel to the Caddy's rear tires.

The PIT maneuver, or precision immobilization technique, was adapted from an illegal bump-and-run strategy used in stock-car racing. The pursuing car taps the target vehicle just behind the back wheel, then veers hard into the car and accelerates. The target vehicle loses traction and spins out.

The lead cop car was preparing for it now.

Unfortunately for him, so was Evan.

He waited, letting the cruiser ease a few more inches into position at the rear of the Caddy.

Then he hit the brakes.

He flew backward, catching a streak of the driver's *Oh, shit* face as he rocketed by.

The cars had perfectly reversed positions, the do-si-do taking all of half a second.

Evan crumpled the sturdy prow of the Caddy into the rear of the cruiser, steered into the crash, and stomped on the gas pedal.

The cruiser acquiesced to the laws of physics, sheering sideways. It wrapped around the grille of the Cadillac in a series of elegant mini-collisions before fishtailing off. As Evan motored ahead onto open road, he watched in the rearview as the cruiser wiped out one of its confederates, wadding them both into the roadside ditch, where they steamed in a tangle of bent chassis and collapsed tires.

One set of headlights held steady, navigating through, sticking to the Caddy's rear.

A quarter mile flew by, then another, as Evan and the last cop standing gauged each other.

The cop finally feinted forward, trying to steer into position, but Evan held him off by veering squarely in front of him. They kept on that way, swerving unevenly across the sodden road, the cruiser coming on, Evan answering with avoidance maneuvers.

The Caddy was growing weary, the reaction time a little worse by the second. Evan was pushing it to the limit, but it was a low limit.

He eyed the mirror. The cruiser gathered itself on its haunches, readying to dart forward again to deal a decisive blow.

All right, Jack. What next?

First of all, get off your heels, son. The Ninth Commandment: Always play offense.

"Right," Evan said to the empty passenger seat.

He raised his 1911, turned away, and shot out the windshield. It spiderwebbed, but the laminate held it in place. With the heel of his hand, Evan knocked out the ruined glass, and rain crashed in over him, a wave of spiky cold. Evan stomped the brake hard and whipped the wheel around. The boat tilted severely as the back swung forward, sloughing through mud. For a moment Evan thought it might flip.

But it righted itself into a sloppy 180, Evan jerking the transmission into reverse and letting the wheel spool back through his loose fists. Gears screamed.

So did the girl in the trunk.

Already he'd seated the gas pedal against the floor, capturing what forward momentum he'd had, except now he was driving in reverse.

Nose to nose with the cruiser, their bumpers nearly kissing.

The young cop at the wheel blinked at him.

They hurtled along the road, two kids in a standoff on a seesaw.

Except the seesaw was traveling fifty miles per hour.

Wind howled around the maw of the windshield. Driving backward protected Evan from the rain. He had a clear view over the top of his pistol and no bullet-deflecting glass between him and the target.

Before the cop could react, Evan jogged the wheel slightly, offsetting the vehicles, opening up an angle to the side of the cruiser.

He shot out the front tire.

Fifteen rounds left.

As the cruiser wobbled and lost acceleration, Evan braked in time with it, holding it in his pistol sights the entire way.

Both cars slowed, slowed, gently nodding to their respective halts. They faced each other about ten yards apart.

Pistol locked on the cop, Evan got out of the Caddy. His boots shoved mounds in the soggy ground. The rain had stopped, but the air still felt pregnant, raising beads of condensation on his skin. His shirt felt like a wet rag.

The cop was still buckled in, fingers locked on the steering wheel, collecting himself.

"Out," Evan said. "Hands."

The cop unbuckled and climbed out. Sweat trickled down his face, clung to the strands of his starter mustache. He stood in the V of his open door. Evan indicated for him to step clear of the car, which he did. He looked earnest and stalwart standing there before the block lettering of his cruiser: HILLSBORO PD. A holstered Glock rode his right hip. His hands were shaking, but only slightly. He wore a wedding ring.

A muffled voice yelled from the Caddy's trunk, *"Don't do it! Don't you hurt him!"*

The cop stiffened, licked his lips. "Who's that?"

Evan said, "I'm not sure yet."

The cop inched his hands down a bit.

"You have a family," Evan told him.

The cop said, "And you've got a girl in the trunk of your stolen vehicle."

"I'll admit there are rare occasions on which there's a reasonable explanation for that," Evan said. "This is one of them."

The cop did not look impressed with that.

"I'm not going to hurt her," Evan said.

"Forgive me for not taking you at your word."

The breeze swept a bitter-fresh scent of churned soil and roadside weeds. The cop's right hand twitched ever so slightly, raised there over the holster. He was the kind of guy who worked hard, helped his neighbors, stayed up late watching westerns on TV.

"Kids?" Evan asked.

The cop nodded. "Daughter. She's five." His Adam's apple lurched with a strained swallow. "I have to look her in the eye every morning and every night and know I did the right thing."

Increasingly Rural Tangle

"Think this through," Evan said. "Do I seem like a guy who doesn't know what he's doing?"

The cop's hand dove for his pistol.

It got only halfway there before Evan fired.

13

Dying Only Meant One Thing

Evan's shot clipped the rear sights of the cop's holstered Glock. The force of the round flipped the entire holster back off the cop's waistband. It made a single lazy rotation and landed in a drainage ditch with a plop, vanishing into the murky brown water.

Evan hadn't wanted to waste another bullet, but there it was. Down to fourteen.

When the cop blew out his next breath, he made a noise like a moan. He leaned over, hands on his knees.

"Couple deep breaths," Evan said.

"Okay."

"You're gonna radio in that you got me and you're taking me in."

"Okay."

"Right now."

The cops Evan had left in the wreckage several miles behind them on the road would have called in a rough location for backup already, which meant that Van Sciver would hear, because Van Sciver heard everything.

As the cop leaned in for his radio, Evan stayed tight on him in case he went for the mounted shotgun. But the cop's nerve had deserted him.

"Unit Seventeen to Dispatch. I have apprehended the suspect and am heading home to HQ, over."

"Copy that, Seventeen. We will call off the cavalry."

Evan reached around the cop, yanked the transmission into neutral, and snatched the keys from the ignition. Both men jerked clear as the cruiser forged through the mud, bounced across the ditch, and plowed off the road. Bushes rustled around it, and then it was gone.

Evan said, "March."

At the point of Evan's ARES, the cop walked off the road, through a stand of ash trees, and onto the marshy land beyond.

"Kneel," Evan said.

The cop stopped on a patch of bluegrass. His knees made a sucking sound in the wet earth.

Evan stood behind him. "Close your eyes."

"Wait." The word cracked, came out in two syllables. "My daughter? The five-year-old? Her name is Ashley. She waits up, watches for my headlights every night. Plays with her American Girl doll in the bay window by the kitchen. Won't go to sleep until I'm there." He choked in a few gulps of air. "I promised her I'd always come home. Don't make a liar out of me. Please. Don't make a liar out of me."

Silence.

"Do you have kids? A wife? Parents, then. Think about them, how they'd feel if you . . . you . . . Or if something happened to them. Think about how you'd feel if it was something someone did. Something that wasn't even necessary. If they were taken from you."

He fell forward onto his hands. His eyes were still closed, but he felt his fingers push into the yielding earth. He thought about his body landing here, taken in by the spongy ground.

He waited for the bullet. Any second now. Any second.

Would he feel it, a pinpoint pressure at the base of his skull before the lights went out?

He thought about the chewed corner of his daughter's blankie, the smell of her head, how when she was a newborn her feet used to curl when she cried.

He thought about his wife's face beneath her white veil, how he couldn't quite see her, just a sliver of cheek, of eye, until the minister had said the magic five words and he'd lifted the soft tulle fabric and uncovered her beaming back at him.

He thought about how dying only meant one thing, and that was not seeing them again. How lucky he was to have been given that purpose. And how wretched it must be for all the lost souls out there who floated through their years, adrift and alone.

Twenty minutes passed, maybe more, before it dawned on him that he wasn't dead.

He opened his eyes, peered down at his hands, lost to the bluegrass.

He pulled back onto his haunches, moving as slowly as he'd ever moved, and turned around.

There was nothing there but wind shivering the leaves of the trees.

14

A Pang of Something Unfamiliar

Evan stood at the trunk of the Cadillac. Golden light filtered through the high windows of the ancient barn, lending a fairy-tale tint to the hay-streaked ground and empty stables. He braced himself and opened the trunk.

The girl erupted from inside.

This time Evan was ready. He ducked, and the tire iron strobed by, fractions from his skull. She landed, spun, and came at him again, but it was halfhearted. She knew she'd lost her one good shot.

He stripped the tire iron from her hands and deflected her onto the ground. She lay there panting, a strand of glossy brown-black hair caught in the corner of her mouth.

"Well," she said, and spit out the strand. "Can't blame me for trying."

"No," Evan said.

She sat, laced her hands across her knees, rolled back slightly onto her behind, and looked up at him. Broad cheekbones, long lashes, vibrant emerald eyes. The pose was youthful, disarming. She might have been watching a movie at a slumber party. But there was something haunted beneath her strong features. As if in her brief life she'd seen more than she'd wanted to.

"You killed him, didn't you?" she said.

"The cop?"

"No," she said. "Not the cop."

"Who?"

"I only had him for a few months," she said. "I finally had someone who . . ." Then she went blank, a screen powering down.

"Who?" he said.

Silence.

He tried a different tack. "What's your name?"

"Joey." Same empty expression.

"What's it short for?"

Her eyes whirred back to life, clicked over to him. "None of your business." She looked up at the high rafters. "Where the hell are we?"

"Off the beaten path."

"What's the plan?"

"Leave the Caddy here. There's a working truck outside a storage shed a klick and a half north. I take that and leave you here. After."

"After what?"

"You give me the package. We can go through your things, piece by piece. Or you can tell me. But there's no way this isn't happening."

She just stared at him.

"Look, Joey, you know how this works. You are a classified government weapon—"

"No. Let's be clear." She stood up, half crossed her arms, one hand gripping the opposite elbow. Her shoulders tensed, rolled forward. Defensive. "I'm a defective model of a classified government weapon. I got pulled off the assembly line."

"Meaning?"

"I washed out, okay? I didn't make it."

"Who was your handler?"

"Orphan Y," she said. "Charles Van Sciver."

A Pang of Something Unfamiliar

Hearing the full name spoken aloud in the muffled damp of the barn—it was a profanity. For a moment Evan was unsure if she'd actually said it or if he'd conjured it, spun it into life from the primordial soup of his own obsession.

He breathed the sweet rot of old wood. His throat felt dry. "He trained you?"

"Yeah," she said. "Until he didn't."

He fought to grasp the contours of this. "Van Sciver was neutralizing the remaining Orphans. Everyone that wasn't his inner cadre."

"Yeah, well, he decided to rev up recruitment again. More assets, more power."

A stab of eagerness punctured Evan's confusion. "So that's the package? Information on Van Sciver."

"No," she said. "I don't have any of that."

"Then what were you doing in that apartment?"

"I lived there," she said. "What were *you* doing in that apartment?"

"Jack Johns sent me."

Her stance shifted at once, forward ready. "Who the hell are you? How do you know Jack Johns?"

"He was my handler."

"Bullshit," she said. "Bullshit. Where is he?"

"He's dead."

Her eyes welled with an abruptness that caught him off guard, emotion rushing to the surface. "I knew it. You killed him."

"Jack was a father to me."

"No. *No.*" Her hands were balled up tightly. "If that was true, if he was your handler, you wouldn't have killed those cops."

"I didn't."

"Never let an innocent die."

"The cops are all—" He cut off in midsentence. "What did you just say?"

It seemed all the oxygen had gone out of the barn.

"Nothing."

"The Tenth Commandment," Evan said.

She glowered at him. And then her face shifted, just slightly.

No one would have gotten the Commandments out of Jack. Evan knew that. Which meant she knew it, too.

"The First," she said. "What's the First Commandment?"

" 'Assume nothing.' " He drew in a breath. "The Eighth?"

" 'Never kill a kid.' " She brushed her hair out of her face, her lips slightly parted, her expression heavy with something like awe. When she spoke again, it was a whisper. "You're Orphan X."

The wood creaked around them. Dust motes swirled, fuzzing the air. Evan gave the faintest nod.

"Evan," she said. There was something intimate in her saying his first name. "He told me about you."

"He didn't tell me about you."

"Jack saved me when I broke with the Program."

"Saved you?"

"You know how it is with Van Sciver. Either you're with him. Or." She didn't have to complete the thought. "Look, I told you. I'm not a government weapon. I'm not an Orphan. I'm just a girl."

It dawned on him, a full-body shiver like a wash of cold water. He sat down against the Caddy's bumper. Tilted his forehead into the tent of his fingers.

"What?" she said.

"Jack wants me to look after you."

"Look after me?"

Evan gazed up at her, felt the blood drain from his face. "You're the package."

They moved beneath the bright moon, high-stepping through a field of summer squash, vectoring for the truck Evan had scouted earlier. Joey's bulging rucksack bounced on her shoulders, made her lean frame look schoolgirl small.

What the hell had Jack been thinking? Evan felt a pang of something unfamiliar. Guilt? He pictured Jack free-falling through the Alabama night and let in some rage to wash the guilt away.

"Let's be clear," Evan said. "I'm not Jack. It's not what I do. I'll get you to safety, square you away, and that'll be that."

Her face had closed off again. Unreadable. Their boots squelched.

A Pang of Something Unfamiliar

An owl was at it in one of the dark trees, asking the age-old question: *Who? Who?*

"How'd Van Sciver's men find my apartment?" she asked.

"They were closing in on Jack. They must've gotten the address somewhere, staked it out."

"You sure *you* weren't followed?"

"Yes."

"If they knew I was there, why wouldn't they just have killed me?"

"Because I'm more valuable to them."

"Oh. So they only let me live to lure you in."

"Yes."

A burning in his cheek announced itself. He raised his fingertips, felt a distinct edge. He picked out the safety-glass pebble and flicked it to the ground.

The girl was talking again. "Van Sciver had Jack killed."

He kept on, letting her process it. It was a lot to process.

She dimpled her lower lip between her teeth. "I can help you go after Van Sciver."

Evan halted, faced her in the moonlight. "How old are you?"

"Twenty."

"No."

"Eighteen."

"No."

She squirmed a bit more. "Sixteen."

He started up again, and she hurried to stay at his side. The only colors were shades of gray and sepia. The moonlight ripened the green squash to a pale yellow.

"How did you know?" she asked.

"When you lie, your blink rate picks up. You've also got a one-shouldered shrug that's a tell. And your hands—just keep your hands at your sides. Your body language talks more than you do, and that's saying something."

"God," she said. "You sound just like Jack."

He took a moment with that one.

They cleared the squash and came onto a stretch where something—pumpkins?—had been recently harvested. Hacked vines populated the barren patch, pushing up from the earth like gnarled limbs. An aftermath scent lingered, fecund and autumnal, the smell of life and death.

"It doesn't matter how old I am," she said. "I can help."

"How? Do you have locations, addresses for Van Sciver?"

"Of course not. You know how he is. Everything's end-stopped six different ways. I didn't even know where I was most of the time."

"Do you have any actionable intel on him?"

"Not really."

"Do you know why Jack was in Alabama?"

She colored slightly. "Is that where he died?"

"Joey, listen. You're raw, totally unbroken—"

"I'm not a horse."

"No. You're a mustang. You fight well. You have extraordinary coordination. But you're not finished, let alone operational."

"Jack sent you to me."

"To protect you. Not get you killed."

"I have training." She was angry now, punching every word. "I knocked you on *your* ass, didn't I?"

"You can't imagine the kind of violence that's coming."

"Did Jack advise you to just ship me off somewhere to hide for the rest of my life?"

The shed loomed ahead, a dark mass rising from the earth, the outline of the beater truck beside it. Evan quickened his pace.

"Jack died before he knew how this would all unfold. I have only one concern now, and that is finding Van Sciver and every person who had a hand in Jack's death and killing them." Evan pulled open the creaky truck door and flipped down the visor. The keys landed in his palm. He looked back at Joey. "What am I supposed to do with you?"

"I'm not useless."

"I never said that."

She came around the passenger side, got in, slammed the door. "Yeah," she said. "You did."

15

Just Geometry

The neon sign announcing the motel in Cornelius had lost its M and L, blaring a woeful orange OTE into the night. The place was rickety despite being single-story, tucked beneath a freeway ramp, the pitted check-in desk manned by a woman who smacked watermelon gum vigorously to cover the scent of schnapps.

It was perfect.

Evan checked in solo, prepaid in cash, and didn't have to produce any details of the alias he had at the ready. Not the kind of establishment that made inquiries of its patrons. The woman never looked him in the face, her attention captured by a hangnail she was working to limited success with her front teeth. The security camera was a fake, a dusty plastic decoy drilled into the wall for show.

He signed the book "Pierre Picaud," took the key that was inexplicably attached to a duct-taped water bottle, and trudged like a road-weary salesman to Room 6.

As he opened the door, Joey materialized from the shadows and slipped inside with him.

She dumped her rucksack on the ratty carpet, regarded a crooked watercolor of hummingbirds at play. "Look," she said. "Art."

"Really spruces up the place."

She gestured to a corner. "I can sleep there."

"I'll take the floor."

"I'm younger. The bed looks shitty anyways."

"I want to be right by the door," Evan said.

She shrugged. "Fine." She fell back stiffly onto the mattress, a trust fall with no one there to catch her. There was a great creaking of coils. "I think you got the better deal."

"That bad?"

"It feels like lying on a bag of wrenches. No—not *quite* that bad. Maybe, like, rubber-handled wrenches."

"Well, then."

"And I'm used to some shitty places," she said.

"That's the biggest thing the Program has on foster-home kids," he said. "We think wherever we're going isn't as bad as where we've been."

She lifted her head, putting chin to chest, the diffuse neon glow of the sign turning her eyes feral. "Yeah, well, foster homes are different for girls."

"Like how?"

"Like none of your fucking business."

"Okay."

"I never talk about it. *Never.*"

"Okay."

She let her head fall back again. Evan followed her gaze. The water-stained ceiling looked like a topographical map. He wondered if anyone ever knew what went on inside the mind of a teenage girl.

"Do you have a legend?" Evan asked her.

"Jack was getting me a passport, driver's license. It was still in process when . . ."

"Airport's out in that case. That's okay. They're expecting it anyway."

"What's the plan, then?"

"First train departs Portland at eight A.M."

"Okay. So a train. To where?" She waved a hand dismissively. "Doesn't matter."

"We'll make arrangements, make sure you're taken care of."

"Yeah."

"Anything I need to know about Van Sciver, now's the time to tell me."

She sat up, crossed her legs. "I didn't interact with him privately much, if that's what you mean."

"Anything."

"He took me when I was fourteen."

"He's the one who found you?"

"No. It was a guy. Old as death. Gold watch, always smoking, wears Ray-Bans all the time, even at night."

Something crept back to life inside Evan's chest. Something he'd thought long dead.

Boys mass in a bedroom doorway at Pride House Group Home, Evan at the bottom, always the smallest. They peer down the hall at a man but can see only a partial profile. He is extending a solid black business card to Papa Z between two slender fingers. A gold wristwatch glints, dangling from a thin wrist.

"Mystery Man," Evan said.

She cocked her head.

Most of all he remembered the helplessness. Twelve years old, his fate in the control of forces so large and unseen they might as well have been ancient gods. Being asked to jump and jump again, never knowing if there'd be earth underfoot, if he'd ever land.

Until there was Jack, the bedrock to his life.

When Joey had landed, it was with Van Sciver.

Her upturned face waited for him to say something. He wondered how she had scraped her way through her sixteen years. That pang knifed through him again, but he ignored it, turned his thoughts to business.

"How did he choose you?" Evan asked. "The Mystery Man?"

"He watched us all at first, playing in the yard. Just . . . *observing*. For some reason he picked me out one day, drove me a good ways to a marine base. I don't remember which one, but I was in Phoenix, so I'd guess now it was Yuma? He walked me into a giant training facility. The whole inside of the building had been converted to an indoor obstacle course. It had everything—barbedwire crawl, mud pits, rope climbs, tire pulls, traverse walls. The most stuff I'd ever seen, the place just crammed with it. At the end of the course, there was a bell, and when you finish, you know, you ring it. The old guy had a stopwatch. He said, 'The sole aim is to get from Point A to Point B in the fastest time possible.' I was wearing a dress and sandals. I said, 'The sole aim?' and he said, 'That's right.' "

She paused and again bit her plush lower lip. Her front teeth were slightly too big, spaced with a hair-thin gap. The imperfection was endearing. Without it her features would've been too smooth, too perfect.

"What'd you do?" Evan asked.

"I turned around and walked out," she said. "Then I circled the building from the outside, went through a service door by the end of the course, and rang the bell. I looked across at him, and he was still standing there, hadn't even started the stopwatch yet."

"Smart."

She shrugged. "It's just geometry."

"And then?"

"Two seconds later the old guy's cell phone rings. There must've been cameras there. By the time I'd walked back around, he had a syringe in his hand. I don't remember him sticking me or anything else." She paused. "I never saw anyone again."

"Where'd you wake up?"

"Maryland. But I didn't find *that* out until eleven months later when I escaped."

"Van Sciver kept you in a house for an entire year?"

"A house?" She coughed out a laugh. "I lived on an abandoned air-force installation. My bed was a mattress in a hangar. I ate, slept, trained. That's it. Usually with other instructors. Van Sciver only dropped by now and then to gauge my progress."

"Was he pleased with it?"

"Yeah. Until." She pulled in a deep breath. "One night I woke up.

Heard noises. A man crying. I don't why it's worse than when a woman does, but it was. I crept over to the raised office area, you know, up a short set of stairs. It had the only window. I looked out and saw Van Sciver stuffing an unconscious guy into a duffel bag. Then they carried the duffel toward the hangar. I ran back, pretended to be asleep. Van Sciver came in, woke me. He handed me a Glock 21, you know—the Gen4?"

Evan was suddenly aware of how cool the room was.

She said, "I asked what we were doing and he said—"

" 'It is what it is, and that's all that it is,' " Evan said.

She stared at him.

"Cognitive closure," Evan said. "Van Sciver's mode of thinking. A strong preference for order which, okay, a lot of us have. But it's paired with a distaste for ambiguity. That's why Jack cultivated it in us. Ambiguity. That's the part that keeps you human."

"Question orders," she said, her voice a hoarse whisper. "The Sixth Commandment."

He nodded.

She swallowed, was silent a moment, then continued. "So I took the gun. I didn't feel like I had a choice. Van Sciver walked me over to the duffel, told me to shoot it. I asked why. He said it was an order and orders don't come with whys. I could see the guy's outline there inside the duffel."

In the neon glow, Evan caught a sheen on her forehead. Sweat.

She shook her head, breaking off the story. "We've all done shit we regret. I regret every day of my life what I did."

Sliding off the bed, she dug in her rucksack. She pulled out a few toiletries, which she shelved to her chest with an arm, and disappeared into the bathroom. A moment later the shower turned on.

Evan looked at the open mouth of her rucksack. A piece of paper had fallen out. He picked it up to put it away for her when he saw that it was a birthday card. Tattered envelope, no address.

The front of the card featured a colorful YOU'RE 16!, though much of the glitter had been worn off from handling. A well-loved card.

Evan opened it.

A pressed iris had been preserved inside, already brittle.

Know that I am proud of you, sweet girl. That I see the beautiful woman you have grown into.
   Xoxo, M.

Evan stared at the scrawled feminine hand for a time, felt a stirring inside him. Was "M" the mom who had lost Joey into the foster system?

It certainly wasn't Orphan M; Evan had left his pieces scattered on a roadway in Zagreb.

But how would "M" have been in touch with Joey? Joey would have been taken off the grid when she was tapped for the Orphan Program. Jack must have arranged some way to reestablish contact between daughter and mother—mailbox forwarding or a dead drop. It would've been a lot of trouble to get done correctly, and Jack only did things correctly. Which meant that whoever "M" was, she meant a lot to Joey.

Evan put the card away, careful not to fragment the dried flower further, and found a plug to charge his RoamZone.

Crouched over the faint green glow, he pondered what he would do if a Nowhere Man call rang through right now. The missions formed an endless chain, each client passing on his untraceable number to the next. That was the only fee he charged for his services. He'd found that this simple act was also part of the healing process for clients, a first step on the road to putting their lives back together. What was more empowering than helping to rescue another person?

For the first time since he'd become the Nowhere Man, he felt unready to answer if the black phone rang. Holed up in a motel in Cornelius, Jack's death still unavenged, stuck with a sixteen-year-old who was at her best difficult to manage—he was in no state to handle a mission.

He reminded himself that six hours from now things would get drastically simpler. He just had to hold out until that first train pulled into Union Station. He'd have Joey off his plate.

Then he'd run Van Sciver to ground and put a bullet through his skull.

The shower turned off, and a few minutes later Joey emerged, towel wrapped around her. She gestured at the rucksack. "Do you mind if I, uh . . ."

"You change out here. I'll clean up."

They passed awkwardly, giving each other a wide berth. In the bathroom he leaned close to the mirror and studied his face, nicked in several places from the shattered windshield. The sterile light caught a dab of dried blood at the corner of his mouth. Only then did he become aware of a throbbing above his right incisor. He lifted his upper lip, saw that the tooth was outlined in crimson. Above it a dot of safety glass speckled in his gum line. He worked it free with his fingers, dropped it in the trash.

Then he rinsed out his mouth and nose, brushed his teeth using Joey's toothpaste and his finger, and went back into the room.

She was in bed, facing away, her breathing already slow and steady. She'd left a pillow on the floor for him.

He lay down on the carpet near the door and closed his eyes.

He awoke to movement in the room. Stayed perfectly still. Kept his eyes veiled, mostly closed.

Joey continued to ease out of bed, moving so slowly she didn't even creak the hair-trigger coils.

Two silent steps, and then she hunched over her rucksack, reaching for something. She rose, turned. He watched her approach. Her hand passed through a fall of light from the window.

She was holding her fixed-blade combat knife.

She moved well, floating on bare feet. He read her posture. Her shoulders were hunched, her head lowered on her neck.

Nothing in it registered aggression.

Just fear.

She leaned over him.

He made the call to let her.

He felt the carbon-steel blade press against his throat.

He opened his eyes all the way.

Her own eyes were so large, the light coming through them from the side turning the irises transparent. The vivid green of them jumped out of the dark, the eyes of a great cat that no longer knew itself to be great.

"Don't hurt me ever," she said. "Please."

"Okay." He felt the word grind against the knife edge.

She nodded and then nodded again, as if to herself.

The pressure eased.

She withdrew as silently as she'd approached.

He lay there and stared at the water-stained map of the ceiling, the whole world laid out in its darkness and complexity.

16

The Turn to Freedom

A four-sided Romanesque Revival clock tower adorned with lit signage staked Portland Union Station to the west shore of the Willamette River. Evan hustled Joey beneath the GO BY TRAIN flashing sign and into the glossy Italian-marble waiting room, where he bought her a ticket under an alias on a train heading for Ashland, Kentucky, because the choice struck him as sufficiently random. The route ran through Sacramento and Chicago. Between travel time and layovers, that would keep her on the move for nearly three days.

He steered her out onto the chill of the platform, handed her the Amtrak tickets and a wad of cash.

"My email address is the.nowhere.man@gmail.com," he told her. "Say it back to me."

She did, her first words in nearly twenty minutes.

He took her gently by the arm, hustled her down to the far end of the platform. "When you get to Ashland, log into my account." He told her the password. "Type a message to me in the Drafts folder. Do *not* send it. I will log in, leave you instructions in the same unsent email. If it doesn't ever travel over the internet—"

"I know the protocols," she said.

She turned and waited for the train. A limp wind fluttered her hair, and she hooked it behind an ear, exposing a swath of the shaved area.

Frustratingly, his feet kept him rooted there.

"Watch your back better," he said. "Use windows as mirrors— like there or there. The reflections off passing trains. Watch your visibility, too. You should be noting where surveillance cameras are, minding their sight lines, head down."

Her lower jaw moved forward, and he heard a clicking of teeth. "I know the protocols."

"Then move four inches back behind this post," he said.

She stepped beneath the metal overhang and shot him a glare.

He said, "If you don't know what you don't know—"

" '—how can I know what to learn?' " she said. "Jack told me that one, too. Like I said. The protocols? I know them."

"Okay," he said.

"Okay," she said.

He left her on the platform. Staying alert, he carved his way back through the waiting room, scanning the crowd. His nose looked okay, but the break had left thumbprint bruises beneath his eyes, so he preferred to avoid looking anyone directly in the face. With each step he sensed the distance widening between him and Joey, between him and Jack's final, ill-considered wish. His boots tapped the cold, shiny marble. It felt like walking through a tomb.

He came out the front, hustled across the hourly-pay parking lot to a Subaru with a MY CHILD IS STUDENT OF THE MONTH bumper sticker. He'd swapped out vehicles early that morning in an office garage, taking advantage of a parking attendant's bathroom break to snatch a set of keys from a valet podium. Assuming the proud parent worked a full day, that gave Evan until five o'clock before the car would be reported missing.

He'd backed into the parking spot, giving him privacy by the rear bumper. He knelt down now and removed the license plate, switching it out for that of the Kia in the neighboring slot.

The Turn to Freedom

One more layer of protection before he hit the road, free and clear to resume his pursuit of Van Sciver.

He got into the car and pulled out of the parking lot, eyeing the freeway signs.

He was just about to make the turn to freedom when he checked the rearview and saw the HILLSBORO HOME THEATER INSTALLATION! van turn into Union Station.

17

A Single Hungry Lunge

A Hertz rental sedan moved in concert with the van. They parked side by side at the outer edge of the parking lot, reversing into the spots to allow for a quick getaway.

Three husky men emerged from the van. They wore commuter clothes, Dockers and button-ups. Muscle swelled the fabric. There was no way around that. Loose-fitting jackets to conceal their builds and their pistols. They entered the waiting room and spread out immediately, fighter jets peeling out of formation.

The driver in the sedan stayed put, his head rotating as he scanned the parking lot and roads leading to the train station. The lookout.

The men streaked through the waiting room, sidling between passengers and heavy oak benches. They stepped out of three different doors onto the platform and into the shade of the overhang. In the distance a freight train approached, *woo-wooing* a warning, rumbling the ground.

The whistle would provide good audio cover for a gunshot.

A Single Hungry Lunge

The men looked through the clusters of waiting passengers on the side platform and the two island platforms beyond. One of the men spotted a rucksack tilting into view from behind a wooden post at the end. And part of a girl's leg.

His head swiveled, and he caught the eye of the man in the middle, whose head swiveled in turn to pick up the last man. They shouldered their way along the platform, closing the space between one another.

Woo-woo.

The freight train wasn't slowing. It would blow right through the station, giving even more sound cover. The girl was isolated there at the end of the platform. That provided relative privacy to get the job done.

Woo-woo.

They converged on her, now shoulder to shoulder, linemen coming in for the sack.

Fifteen yards away.

Woo-woo.

She saw them only now. Alarm flashed across her face, but even so she stepped back into a fighting posture, hands raised, jaw set.

The man in the middle reached inside his loose-fitting jacket.

They swept forward.

Ten yards away.

Behind them a form swung down from the metal overhang and crouched on the landing to break his fall, one hand pressed to the concrete.

Soundless.

Evan couldn't fire his ARES. Not with Joey in the background. But that was okay. He was eager to use his hands.

Joey spotted him through the gap between the advancing men. They read her eyes, the change in her stance.

They turned.

Three men. One pistol drawn, two on the way.

Evan moved on the gun first.

A jujitsu double-hand parry to a figure-four arm bar, the pleasing *snap-snap* of wrist and elbow breaking, and—

—Jack sways in the Black Hawk, hands cuffed behind him, wind blasting his hair when—

—the pistol skittered free across the tracks, the guy on his knees, his arm turned to rubber. The second man gave up on the draw and came at Evan with a haymaker, but Evan threw a palm-heel strike to the bottom of his chin, rocking his head back. He firmed his fingers, drove a hand spear into the exposed throat, crushing the windpipe. The man toppled, crashing through a trash can, and made a gargling sound, his access to oxygen closed now and forever and—

—Jack reeled back, a parachute rip cord handle clenched in his teeth, his eyes blazing with triumph, when—

—the third man's gun had cleared leather, so Evan grabbed his wrist, shoved the pistol back into the hip holster, hooked his thumb through the trigger guard, and fired straight down through the tip of the holster and the guy's foot. The man was still gaping at the bloody mess on the end of his ankle when Evan reversed the pistol out of the holster, spun it around the same thumb, and squeezed off a shot that took off half the guy's jaw. Evan blinked through the spatter and the image of—

—Jack's parting nod to the men pinballing around the lurching Black Hawk, a nod filled with peace, with resignation, before he stepped out into the abyss.

People were screaming now, stampeding off the platform, the express train bearing down. Two corpses on the concrete, a glassy puddle of deep red spreading, smooth enough to reflect the clouds in the sky. The first man remained on his knees, straddling the yellow safety line on the platform, gripping his ruined arm as the hand flopped noodlelike on the broken stalk of the limb. Despite all reason he was trying to firm it, to make his wrist work again, when Evan wound into a reverse side kick, driving the bottom of his heel into the edge of the man's jaw and sending him flying over the tracks just in time to catch the—*woo-woo*—freight train as it blasted through, flyswatting him ahead and grinding him underneath in what seemed like a single hungry lunge.

A Single Hungry Lunge

Joey stared at Evan across the expanding puddle and the sprawled legs of the third man. Furrows grooved the skin of her forehead. She had forgotten to breathe.

The engagement had lasted four seconds, maybe five.

The other man had landed to the side, propped against the toppled trash can, one hand pawing the air above his collapsed windpipe. The motion grew slower and slower.

Joey looked at him and then back at Evan, her eyes even wider.

"He's dead," Evan said. "He just doesn't know it yet."

She cleared her throat. "Thanks."

"Grab your rucksack. Let's go."

She did.

They barreled through the doors into the waiting room. Chaos reigned. People shoved and elbowed to the exit. A homeless man was bellowing to himself, stuffing his bedding into a shopping cart. Workers cowered behind counters.

There were sirens outside already, flashing lights coloring the parking lot. Lead responders spilled through the front entrance, bucking the stream of humanity.

"This way." Evan grabbed Joey's arm, ushered her up the corridor to the bathrooms.

They were halfway there when a service door swung open and two cops shouldered through. Their eyes lasered in on Evan and Joey, Glocks drawn but aimed at the floor.

Evan swung her around, reversing course. They didn't get three steps when, up ahead, responding cops filled the waiting room.

They were trapped.

18

Short on Time and Short
on Crowbars

Behind them one of the cops shouted, "Wait! Stop right there!"

Evan and Joey froze, still facing away. The corridor was empty, squeaky clean save for a dropped newspaper and fresh plug of gum stuck to the wall.

"What now?" Joey said to Evan out of the side of her mouth.

"We don't kill cops."

Ahead, PD started locking down the big hall. Behind them the cops' boots squeaked on the marble as they approached cautiously.

"I know," Joey whispered. "So what do we do?"

"Get arrested. Face the consequences, whatever they are. We go down before we break a Commandment."

The cops were right behind them. "Turn around. Right now."

Joey reached up and flipped her hair over, exposing the shaved side of her head in its entirety. She brushed against Evan as she pivoted around, and when he followed her lead, he saw that she had his RoamZone in hand.

"This is totally not fair," she said. "Some big guy ran past us, all freaking out, and *whammed* into me. I dropped my phone and it's, like, *ruined*."

Her posture had transformed, shoulders slumped, twisty legs, head lolling lazily to one side, a finger twirling a tendril of hair—even her face had gone slack with teenage apathy.

And she was chewing gum. With teenage vigor.

Evan shot a look at the spot on the wall where the fluorescent green plug had been a moment before.

Joey yanked on Evan's arm. "Dad, you are buying me a new phone. Like, *now*. There's no way I'm going to school with the screen all cracked."

Evan cleared his throat. "I'm sorry, Officers."

The cops looked behind them. "A big guy ran past you? This way?"

"Yeah. You, like, *just* missed him."

The cops exchanged a look and bolted back down the corridor to the service door.

Joey called after them, "If you find him, tell him he's paying for my new phone!"

The door banged shut after them. Joey swept her hair back into place, blanketing the shaved side. "'Adapt what is useful, reject what is useless, and add what is specifically your own.'"

"Odysseus?"

She took the gum out of her mouth, stuck it back on the wall. "Bruce Lee."

He nodded. "Right."

They moved swiftly out through the service door, skating the edge of the parking lot just before more cops swept in, setting a perimeter around the building.

Evan peered across to the outer fringe of the lot. Even through the windshield glare, he could discern the outline of the man in the rent-a-car. He was trapped for now; the cops had blockaded the exits.

Joey took note of the man. "The lookout?"

"Yes."

Evan hustled her away from the commotion and into an employee parking lot shielded from view by a flank of the building.

"Is the car this way?" she asked.

"No. I parked it a block to the south."

"Then why are we here?"

He stopped by a canary-yellow Chevy Malibu.

"Evan, this isn't the time to swap cars again. We can't drive out of here anyways. You saw the exits."

Dropping to his back, he slid under the Malibu. He unscrewed the cartridge oil filter and jerked it away from the leaking stream.

He wiggled back out from under the car.

She saw the filter and said, "Oh." And then, "*Oh.*"

He shook the filter upside down, oil lacing the asphalt at his feet. Then he examined the coarse threading inside. "Give me your flannel."

She took it off. He used it to wipe oil from the filter and then his hands. It wasn't great, but it was the best he was going to do. Holding the filter low at his side, he stepped over a concrete divider onto the sidewalk and started arcing along the street bordering the station, threading through rubberneckers.

"Why are we risking this?" Joey asked. "Right now?"

"Given their response time, these guys have some kind of headquarters in the area. We saw at least seven more men at your apartment building, including the Orphan. We find the HQ, we get answers."

"You think the guy's just gonna tell you? This place is swimming with cops. It's not like you can beat it out of him."

"Won't have to."

They came around the fringe of the parking lot. The lookout's car was up ahead, backed into its spot, the trunk pressed to a row of bushes. The majority of cops were at the main exits or across the lot at the station proper, scurrying around, gesticulating and talking into radios.

Evan removed his slender 1911. He knew that the threading of the oil filter would be incompatible with the threading of the barrel, so he tore a square of fabric from the flannel, held it across the mouth of the filter, and snugged the gun muzzle into place.

A makeshift suppressor.

They skated behind a group of looky-loos who had gathered by the main entrance and vectored toward the rise of juniper hemming in the parking lot.

Evan said, "Wait here."

He sliced through the bushes. Three powerful strides carried him along the driver's side of the sedan. The lookout picked up the movement in the side mirror and lunged for a pistol on the passenger seat. Evan raised his 1911 to the window, held the oil filter in place at the muzzle, and shot him through the head.

The pop was louder than he would have hoped.

Between the flannel patch, the oil, and the muzzle flash, the filter broke out in flames. Evan dumped it onto the asphalt and stomped it out.

He squatted by the shattered window and watched, but no one seemed to have taken notice.

He opened the door, releasing a trickle of glass. The lookout was slumped over the console. Evan wiggled the guy's wallet and Samsung Galaxy cell phone from his pocket. Then he lifted his gaze to the object of his desire.

The Hertz NeverLost GPS unit nodded from a flexible metal stalk that was bolted to the dashboard.

Evan tried to snap it off, but the antitheft arm required a crowbar.

He sank back down outside the car, reshaped the flattened cartridge oil filter as best he could, and firmed it back into place over the muzzle. The sound attenuation of the first shot had been far from spectacular, and he knew that a makeshift suppressor degraded with every shot. But he was short on time and short on crowbars.

He took a few breaths. Juniper laced the air—bitter berry, pine, and fresh sap undercut by something meatier.

He leaned into the car, aimed at the spot where the stalk met the dashboard, and fired.

The unit's arm nodded severely to one side. He glanced through the blood-speckled windshield, saw some of the cops' heads snap up. They were looking around, unable to source the sound. As Evan worked the metal arm back and forth, several cops moved into the parking lot, Glocks drawn.

They were moving row by row.

The stalk proved stubborn. He sawed it back and forth harder, polyurethane foam swelling into view on the dash.

A female cop worked her way up the line of vehicles directly ahead of Evan. In a moment she'd step around the end car and they'd be face-to-face.

The unit finally ripped free of the molded plastic above the glove box. Evan backed out of the car, already powering down the GPS so it couldn't be accessed remotely. Staying low, he reversed through the juniper. He saw the cop come clear of her row and spot the windshield an instant before the foliage wagged back into place, enveloping him.

He popped out the other side onto the sidewalk, bumping into Joey. He handed her the NeverLost, unscrewed the filter from the tip of the pistol, and dumped it into a trash can. Then he holstered his 1911 beneath his shirt, took Joey's hand like a doting father. She understood, folding her clean fingers around his, hiding the oil smudges.

They crossed at Irving Street, blended into a throng of pedestrians, and headed for the family car.

19

More Than a Mission

November was a pleasant month in Alabama.

Van Sciver sat in a rocking chair, sipping sweet tea. On his knee rested an encrypted satphone, the screen dancing with lights even when it was at rest.

The plantation-style house wasn't so much rented as taken over. Though relatively humble compared to some of the mansions in the region, the place still showcased classic white woodwork, a formidable brick chimney, and an impressive pair of columns that guarded the long porch like sentries. It was a National Historic Landmark. Which meant that it was under federal jurisdiction—the Department of the Interior, to be precise.

The Orphan Program had a special relationship with the Department of the Interior. When the DoD required cash for Program operations, they made use of the bureaucratic machinery of Interior, figuring correctly that this was the last place that any inquiring mind would look for Selected Acquisition Report irregularities.

The money itself came straight from Treasury, shipped immediately after printing, which made it untraceable. And which meant that Van Sciver could quite literally print currency when he needed it. The life of an Orphan was not without hardships, but those hardships were cushioned by secret eight-figure bank accounts sprinkled throughout nonreporting countries around the world.

When forced to leave his data-mining bunker, Van Sciver didn't generally pull strings with Interior. But this mission was more than a mission.

It was a celebration.

So he'd made a single phone call, the effect of which had rippled outward until he found himself here, sipping sweet tea on the veranda, waiting for mosquitoes to stir to life so he could swat at his neck with a kerchief just like they did in the movies.

One of his men circled, his bushy beard and sand-colored FN SCAR 17S battle rifle out of place here among the weeping willows and lazy breeze.

"Perimeter clear," he said as he passed, and Van Sciver raised his iced tea in a mock toast.

Jack Johns had been the number two on Van Sciver's list. But killing him was not what had given Van Sciver his current glow of contentment. It was the fact that killing him had made Orphan X hurt.

That alone was worth the cost of a Black Hawk and six men.

Van Sciver's history with Evan stretched back the better part of three decades to a boys' home in East Baltimore. Their rivalry at Pride House had been nearly as vicious as it was now. Van Sciver had been a head taller, with twice the brawn. He'd been the draw, the one they'd scouted for the Program, the one they wanted.

And yet Evan had squirmed himself into position, had gotten himself picked first. Now Van Sciver held the keys to the kingdom and Evan was a fugitive. Van Sciver had played the long game.

And he had won.

Yet even here, rocking soporifically on a centuries-old porch at a mansion requisitioned on a whim through the federal government, even surrounded by ranks of trained men ready to do his bidding, even with the levers of power awaiting the slightest twitch of his fingers, he knew that it wasn't enough.

It would never be enough.

The phone chimed, the call routing in through Signal, an encryption app developed by Open Whisper Systems. Every call, made over a Wi-Fi or data connection, was end-to-end protected, the only encryption keys controlled by app users. As he did with all security measures, Van Sciver had gone above and beyond, tweaking the code slightly, altering the protocols.

He eyed the screen, which displayed two words: ADDER LUSTFUL.

He thumbed to answer. "Code," he said.

He heard a rustle as Orphan R eyed the words displayed on his end. " 'Adder lustful.' "

The matching code verified that the call was secure; no man-in-the-middle attack had occurred.

Van Sciver said, "Is the package in hand?"

Orphan R said, "We didn't get her."

"Because?"

A hesitation spoke to Thornhill's dread. "X showed up. Took out four of my men."

Van Sciver found himself actually using his kerchief to mop sweat off his neck. "How many men did you have at the train station?"

"Four."

Van Sciver had no response to that.

"We thought it was just the girl. The surveillance cameras picked up only her. Alone. We thought it'd be a quick snatch-and-dash, and then we could use her to lure him in."

"Instead he lured you in."

"Seems that way."

Van Sciver leaned forward in the rocking chair, set his glass down on the uneven planks of the porch. "We have unfinished business here. I want you back."

"Shouldn't we stick around in case X rears his head?"

"Leave your team in place there. But you won't find him. He and the girl are gone. You missed your shot."

There was an even longer pause. "I'm on a plane."

Van Sciver hung up.

He picked up his glass and tossed the remaining tea into the hydrangeas.

The time for celebrating was over.

20

Wayward Pieces

It took some doing, but Evan found a motel on par with the beauty in Cornelius. Stale cigarette smoke oozed from the bedding, the towels, even the popcorn ceiling. The toilet was missing the tank lid. A pull-chain table lamp with a yellowed shade threw off a jaundiced glow. The comforter sported a stain the color of dried blood, which Evan hoped it was, given the less appealing alternatives. He'd rented the room for three hours, which explained everything worth explaining.

Now he sat cross-legged on the floor, the Hertz NeverLost GPS unit before him. Still attached to the metal stalk, it resembled a dismembered antenna. The lookout's wallet and Samsung were laid on the floor beside the stalk, parallel to each other, edges aligned.

Order helped him think.

Joey leaned her shoulders against the bed, her hand working what seemed to be a steroidal Rubik's Cube that she'd produced from her rucksack. She spun it with the speed and focus of a squirrel stripping a walnut.

Wayward Pieces

Evan opened the lookout's wallet. It contained four crisp hundred-dollar bills and nothing else. All the slots and crevices were empty. He set it back in its place.

Then he turned on the Samsung and checked the contacts. There were none. E-mail was empty, as was the trash folder. No recent calls. No voice mail.

The clacking of Joey's Rubik's Cube continued, grating on his nerves. Without looking up, she said, "No luck, huh?"

He ignored her, powering on the NeverLost GPS. When he searched the settings, he saw that everything had been deleted from this device as well. No saved locations, no last destinations, no evidence that the unit had ever been used.

Clack-clack-clack-clack—

"Can you please stop that?"

She halted, cube in her hands. The thing had exploded outward into different planks and beams, an architectural scribble.

He frowned at it. "What *is* that thing?"

"This?" She turned the monstrosity in her hands, showing off its various dimensions. "It's a three-by-three-by-five. Cubers call it a shape-shifter."

"What does it do?"

"Gives you a headache."

"Like you."

She flashed a fake grin. Let it fall from her face.

She returned her focus to the cube. Her hands moved in a flurry, whipping the various planes around. "You have to solve the shape first. Wait, wait—see?" She held it up. She'd wrangled it back into form. It looked like a miniature tower. "Then you solve the colors. This part's easier. There are algorithms, sequences of steps. . . ."

To him it was just a blur of primary colors.

"You have to look for the wayward pieces, find the patterns that make them fall into place. Like so."

She held it up, finished, gave it a Vanna White wave with her free hand.

"Impressive."

"They say girls suck at geometry, but they forgot to tell me that."

"You would've ignored them anyway."

She tossed the cube into her rucksack, flicked her chin at the GPS unit. "How's it going with that?"

"They wiped everything. Can I use your laptop? I need to get into this thing."

She shrugged. "Sure." She retrieved her laptop and a USB cable, watched him plug in the NeverLost. "Whatcha doing?"

"Even if they deleted everything, the GPS still has coordinates, destinations, and deleted routes stored internally somewhere." He set to work. "First step of a forensic recovery is to image the data. It's called mounting the file-storage system. Then you make a copy of the device's internal memory in your computer but contain it so it can't infect your own data. Then I'm gonna wade through it, determine the data structures, see where and how the data's stored, what kind of encryption I'm dealing with. Like jailbreaking a phone. Understand?"

She tilted her head at the screen, taking in his progress, then looked at him with an expression he couldn't read. "What grampa taught you to hack? You learn that when COBOL and IBM S/370 were state-of-the-art?"

This joke seemingly amused her.

He said, "What?"

"Maybe you could use a dial-up modem. Or, like, we could get a bunch of hamsters on wheels to power the software."

He stopped, fingers poised above the keys. "You have a better approach?"

"You're using a memory-dumper program," she said. "Why don't you spin up a new local virtual machine like any idiot would, image and then boot the virtual device inside it, use the Security Analysts desktop code to do the heavy lifting?"

Blowing hair out of her eyes, she spun the laptop around to face her. Her fingers moved across the keyboard, a virtuoso pianist hammering through Rachmaninoff. Then she flicked the laptop back around to him.

The screen was doing lots of things and doing them speedily.

She settled back against the bed again, as bored as ever. He read the coding here and there, catching up to it well enough to start directing the software.

"Lemme see the phone," she said.

"I already checked it. It's been wiped."

"Two sets of eyes are better than one. Especially when the second set is mine."

"Trust me. There's no point."

She plucked up the Samsung, started thumbing at it.

The laptop spit out some results. It took Evan a moment to decipher them.

"Shit," he said.

"Hmm?" The phone made little tapping noises, its glow illuminating her round face.

"Looks like they used a secure erase tool," he said. "Layered over the data with twelve hours of alternating ones and zeros."

"There is a shortcut, you know."

He closed the laptop a touch harder than necessary. "What's that?"

"Oh, I don't know, maybe the Waze app on his phone." She held up the Samsung to show the nav application lighting up the screen. "It shows where the cops are, accidents, traffic jams. You know, useful stuff for lookouts and getaway drivers. Why did you think he had a phone?"

Heat rose beneath Evan's face. "To make calls."

"To make calls," she said. "That's so cute."

"The app—it has all the routes?"

"Yeah. But we don't need them."

"Why not?"

"Because look what happens when you touch the smiley car." She pressed the icon. A column of recent destinations came up. The second one down, an address in Portland's Central Eastside, was labeled HQ.

"That's what we in the spy business refer to as a clue," she said.

Evan rubbed his eyes.

"You really need to watch your nonverbal tells," she said.

He lowered his hands to his lap. "You have location services turned off on that phone, right?"

"Of course."

"Power it off anyway. Just to be safe."

She did. Then she tossed it back onto the worn network of threads that passed for a carpet. "When you said they could pick me up on the surveillance cameras at the train station, I thought you were being paranoid. But it's not paranoid when you're right, is it?"

"I need to get you far away from here before we put you on any kind of public transportation. I'm talking multiple states away."

"What about the headquarters?" She tapped the phone. "I mean, we're forty minutes away. You drive me to Idaho and come back, they'll be cleared out by then."

"What am I supposed to do with you?"

She just looked at him.

"No. No way."

"Give me your gun."

She stared him down, unblinking. Finally he unholstered the skinny ARES and handed it to her. She regarded the slender 1911 with amusement, turning it this way and that. "Nice gun. They make it in pink?"

"Only if you special order it."

"It goes well with your hips."

"Thanks."

"You should accessorize it with, like, a clutch purse. Maybe a string of pearls."

"Are you done?"

"Just about."

He waited.

She said, "If you pull the trigger, does a little flame come out the end? Or a flag that says 'Bang'?"

"Joey."

"Okay, okay," she said. "Go to the lamp."

He rose and walked over to the table lamp.

"Turn it off, count five seconds, then turn it back on."

He pulled the chain, the room falling into darkness. A five count passed, and he turned the light back on.

The 1911 rested in front of her crossed legs. It had been field-stripped. Frame, slide, bushing, barrel, guide rod, recoil spring,

spring plug, and slide stop. In a nice touch, she'd stacked the remaining four rounds on end on the magazine.

Her gaze held steel. "Again," she said.

He tugged the chain once more, counted to five, clicked the lamp on.

The pistol, reassembled.

She had a tiny dimple in her right cheek even when she wasn't smiling. She wasn't smiling now.

"You can be my lookout," he said. "But only because it's safer for you to be near me than on your own."

"Gee," she said. "Thanks."

She stood, twirled the gun on her palm, and presented him with the grip. He took the ARES and clicked it home in his high-guard Kydex holster.

"What if they're expecting you?" she asked.

"Even if they are," he said, "it won't help them."

21

Quick and Easy

Central Eastside was an industrial district checkered with low-rent housing. Evan coasted in the stolen Subaru with the switched rear license plate, watching a parade of radiator shops, commercial laundries, and wholesale construction-supply joints march by. The streets were pothole-intensive, shimmering with broken glass. A few spots had been taken over by brewpubs and distilleries, gentrification doing its cheery best, but they were out ahead of the curve here and—from the looks of the clientele and graffiti—in over their heads.

Joey took in the streets and seemed not uneasy in the least.

She wore a half squint, her taut cheeks striking, the youthful fullness of her face turned to something hard and focused. Evan found himself admiring her. She was a medley of contradictions, surprises.

They drove for a time in silence.

"I need a shotgun," Evan said.

"I'm sure we could rustle one up in these here parts."

Quick and Easy

"Last thing we need is to go down the rabbit hole dealing with local criminals and wind up with a rusty Marlin Goose Gun. We need something well maintained, and we need it quick and easy."

"Where you gonna find a shotgun like that on no notice?"

"The police."

"Of course. Quick and easy." She cast a glance across the console, did a double take. "You're not joking, are you?"

Evan pulled over beneath the green cross of a marijuana dispensary, fished out his RoamZone, and dialed 911.

The cruiser pulled up, and two venerable cops emerged, slamming the doors behind them. The driver hit the key fob, the car putting out a *chirp-chirp* as it locked.

Joey sat on the steps of the dispensary, holding Evan's phone and pretending to text. Her dark wavy hair fell across her face, blocking one eye, an artful dishevelment.

"What are you doing here?" the officer said. He had a dewlapped face, eyes gone weary from seeing too much shit for too many nights.

"My pops works here," Joey said.

The second cop, a tough-looking redhead with sun-beaten skin, stood over Joey. "We had an anonymous report of shots fired on this block."

"Oh, yeah?"

"You hear anything?"

"All the time."

An annoyance passed between the cops. "Care to elaborate?"

Joey sighed. Pocketed the phone. "C'mere." She brushed past the redhead, took the driver by the arm, walked him to the curb, and pointed across the street. "See that alley there? There's a auto-salvage yard at the end of it. That's where to go if you need a piece on the down-low. A shitty little .22, something like that. That's what everyone says around here. People test the goods before they pay up." She stood back, crossed her arms. "So yeah, I heard shots fired. Tonight and every night."

The redhead let out a sigh that smelled of coffee and cigarettes. "Let's go."

She and her partner headed across the street and disappeared up the alley.

Evan emerged from the darkness at the side of the store. Joey flipped him the keys she'd lifted from the driver's pocket.

Evan thumbed the fob, popped the trunk to reveal a mounted gun-locker safe.

Also remote-controlled.

He thumbed another button on the key chain, and the gun locker opened with a brief metallic hum.

Inside, cartons of shells and a Benelli M3 combat shotgun.

His favorite.

He grabbed two cartons, took the shotgun, then closed the gun locker and the trunk. He pointed at a spot on the sidewalk. "Drop the keys there."

Joey did.

They walked over to the Subaru and drove off.

22

Dead Man's Pocket

The headquarters were on Northeast Thirteenth at the very tip of Portland proper in a long-abandoned pest-control shop sandwiched between a trailer lot and a precast-concrete manufacturing plant. The drive over had been a descent into rough streets and heavy industry—truck parts, machining, welding. Gentlemen's clubs were in evidence every few blocks despite the absence of any actual gentlemen.

The small pest-control shop, no bigger than a shack, had been retrofitted as a command center. Evan recognized the make of steel door securing the front entrance—the kind filled with water, designed to spread out the heat from a battering ram's impact. A ram would buckle before it would blow through a door like that. That was incredibly effective.

When there wasn't a back door.

Which Evan watched now. At the edge of the neighboring lot, he'd parked the Subaru between two used trailers adorned with cheery yellow-and-red sales flags. He had the driver's window rolled down, letting through a chilly stream of air that smelled of tar and skunked beer. Joey sat in the passenger seat, perfectly silent, perfectly still.

Two cartons of different shotgun shells were nestled in his crotch, the shotgun across his lap. He had not loaded it yet.

A few blocks over, a bad cover band wailed an Eagles tune through partially blown speakers: *Some-body's gunna hurt someone, a'fore the night is through.*

Evan thought, *You got that right.*

A Lincoln pulled up to the rear curb of the building. Evan sensed Joey tense beside him. A broad-shouldered man climbed out of the sedan. He knocked on the back door—shave and a haircut, two bits. Even at this distance, the seven-note riff reached the Subaru through the crisp air.

A speakeasy hatch squeaked open, a face filling the tiny metal square.

A murmured greeting followed, and then various dead bolts retracted, the door swung inward, and the broad-shouldered man disappeared inside.

Now Evan knew how he wanted to load the shotgun.

One nine-pellet buckshot load for the chamber, two more on its heels in the mag tube. He followed those with three shock-lock cartridges and had a pair of buckshot shells run anchor.

He popped in the triangular safety so it was smooth to the metal, the red band appearing on the other side. When he pumped the shotgun, he felt the *shuck-shuck* in the base of his spine.

"Stay here," he said. He reached for the door handle, then paused. "You may not like what you're about to see."

He got out, swung the door closed behind him.

He walked across the desolate street, bits of glass grinding beneath his tread. The midnight-black Benelli hung at his side.

He could feel Jack fall into step beside him, hear Jack's voice, a whisper in his ear. *It's too late for me.*

"I'm sorry I wasn't there," Evan said quietly.

I want to know that I'm forgiven.

"You are." Evan quickened his stride, bearing down on the door.

He knocked out the brief melody and raised the shotgun, seating the butt on his good shoulder.

I love you, son.

The speakeasy hatch squeaked open, and Evan pushed the muzzle into the surprised square of face and fired.

There was no longer a face.

He shoved the shotgun farther inside, the muzzle clearing the door, and unleashed two buckshot rounds, one to the left, one to the right.

The three shock-locks were up next, copper-powdered, heavy-compressed centered shots that provided a total energy dump on one spot with no scatterback or frag.

Hinge removers.

He shifted the action to manual so he could cycle the low-powered breaching rounds and give them more steam. Then he stepped back and fired top to bottom—*boom-boom-boom.* The last slug knocked the door clear off the frame, sending it skidding across the floor.

Cycling buckshot into the chamber and toggling the switch back to autoload, he stepped through the dust into the metallic tang of cordite, shotgun raised.

The blow-radius effect of the initial blasts in the contained shop was biblical. With no air movement, the powdered smoke had stratified, hovering like gray mist.

Five men, either dead or in various stages of critical injury, shuddered on knocked-over folding chairs, tilted against bloodstained walls, sprawled over a central table. No sign of the Orphan. The broad-shouldered man was the only one able to do more than bleed out.

He bellied across the floor, dragging himself away with his forearms, a combat crawl. His right leg was a mottled fusion of denim and flesh.

He kept on, making for a rack of rifles and shotguns beside the steel front door.

Evan walked toward him, stuck a toe in his ribs, flipped him over.

The man tried to look away. "Oh, God," he said. "You're—are you—Orphan X? Oh, God."

Evan seated a boot square on his barrel chest, hovered the hot muzzle over his throat. "You killed Jack Johns."

The man's fine hair, so blond it was almost gray, was shaved in a buzz cut. His scalp showed through, glistening with sweat. "No—not me. I didn't go up in the chopper, man. There was a special crew."

"But you were there. On the ground in Alabama. You were all there."

"Yes."

Evan swung the shotgun to the side and blew off his hand.

The howl was inhuman.

But so was making a man in his seventies jump out of a Black Hawk with his wrists cuffed together.

Evan rotated the Benelli back to the man's head. "Van Sciver?" he said. "Where?"

Somewhere behind them, a final sputtering wheeze extinguished.

"I don't know. I swear. Never even met him."

Evan moved the Benelli over the guy's other hand.

"*Wait!* Wait! I'll tell you—tell you everything. Just don't . . . don't take me apart like this."

"How many freelancers did he bring in? Not including the helo crew."

"Twenty-five. He hired twenty-five of us."

Evan surveyed the wreckage, added it to the train-station tally. "Fifteen now," he said.

"*Sixteen.*" The man risked a look at his hand, failed to fight off a full-body shudder. "I make sixteen." And then, more desperately, "I . . . I still make sixteen."

"Who's running point here?"

The man looked over at the red-smeared linoleum where his hand once was and dry-heaved. His face was pale, awash in sweat. Evan put more pressure on his chest, cracking a rib, snapping him back to attention.

"Jordan Thornhill," the man said. "Orphan R. Nicest guy in the world. Until he kills you."

"What's he look like?"

"Black dude, all muscle. Could scale a cliff with his bare hands, he wanted to." The man started hyperventilating. "God, oh, God, I think I'm bleeding out."

"You've got enough for the next five minutes. Where is he?"

"Van Sciver called him home. I don't know where."

Evan twitched the barrel slightly.

"I DON'T KNOW WHERE! I don't know anything. I swear. They keep us in the dark about everything."

Evan let the weight of the hot barrel press into the hollow of the man's throat. The flesh sizzled. "Not improving your situation, hired man."

"Hang on! I overheard Thornhill saying something about a female Orphan. Candy something. Orphan V."

At this, Evan's face tightened.

"Please." Saliva sheeted between the man's lips. "That's all I know. I told you everything. Can I . . . will you let me live?"

"You were dead the minute Van Sciver told you my name." Evan pulled the trigger.

He heard a creak behind him and pivoted, dropping the empty shotgun and drawing his ARES.

He found himself aiming at Joey.

She stood in the doorway, surveying the wreckage. A flush had come up beneath her smooth brown cheeks. The shack smelled of blood iron and the insides of men. Through the lingering smoke, her emerald eyes glowed, unguarded, overwhelmed.

"I told you to stay in the car."

"I'm fine."

"Pull the car around. Hurry."

She stepped back and was gone.

He flung a corpse off the central table and rifled through the items beneath. Coffee cups, battery packs, a half-eaten sub. Useless. Beneath a pack of black gel pens, he found a red-covered notebook. Seizing it, he thumbed through the stiff pages. Nothing inside.

He tossed it, moved to the chipped counter em-dashing half of the east wall. Coffeepot, microwave, utility sink. The cabinet beneath held rusted pipes, water spots, a crusted bottle of Drano.

He turned in his crouch, giving the room a last, hurried scan.

Blood dripped from the edge of the table. A strip of duct tape shimmered beneath the lip.

A laptop, adhered to the table's underside.

He tore it free and turned for the door. As he stepped over what was left of the broad-shouldered man, something chimed. Evan paused to fish a familiar-looking Samsung Galaxy from the dead man's pocket.

He used the man's shirt to wipe a crimson smear off the screen. Location services were toggled off, GPS disabled.

Out front he heard the Subaru squeal to the curb.

Keeping the phone, he exited through the fortified steel door. As it swung open, he heard the faint slosh of water within.

It was a nice security measure, if you thought about it.

23

Damaged Goods

As Joey sped away, Evan checked out the Samsung. It appeared to be wiped of data, holding only the operating system and a single app.

Signal.

The encrypted comms software showed several incoming contact attempts.

Sirens wailed, a squadron of cop cars rocketing past one block over on Lombard Street, blues and reds lasering through the night air.

Joey had gotten them quickly away from the pest-control shop. She darted nervous glances at the seemingly endless procession. The cruisers were visible only at intersections and alleys, strobing into view behind warehouses and buildings.

"We're fine," Evan said. "Get on the 5."

"And then?"

"Head north."

Signal only worked over Wi-Fi, but—God bless Portland's waxed mustaches, artisanal beers, and municipal benefits—they remained under the umbrella of free citywide service.

The sirens reached an earsplitting pitch and then faded quickly.

Joey blew out a breath, letting it puff her cheeks.

Evan kept his eyes on the Samsung, waiting for it to chime.

Joey said, "What are you—"

It chimed.

Two words appeared: EVENTFUL AZURE.

Joey glanced over at him. Her eyes held the frantic alertness of cornered prey. "That's him, isn't it?"

Evan tapped the screen.

Van Sciver's voice came through. "Code."

"You don't need to bother with that anymore," Evan said.

A long, static-free pause ensued. Van Sciver finally spoke again. "How did you hack this connection?"

"I didn't," Evan said. "I hacked your men instead."

He let Van Sciver digest that fact. Forty percent of his manpower, gone. Freelancers were replaceable, sure, but getting them vetted, up to operational standards, and read in on an Orphan mission took time. And time was a luxury Evan wasn't going to allow him. Van Sciver had lit the fuse the instant he'd put Jack in that Black Hawk.

Evan checked to see if the Wi-Fi connection had dropped, but they were still in range.

Van Sciver finally replied. "X."

"Y."

"I didn't figure you'd hang around the area. After you surface, you always go to ground."

"Things are different now."

"Ah, right. The old saw—'This time it's personal.' I thought you were better than that."

Evan let the line hum.

"Jack jumped out of that helo himself," Van Sciver said. "You watched it with me. We didn't push him."

"But you were going to."

"Yes," Van Sciver said. "We were."

Evan pointed through the windshield, and Joey veered up the on-ramp, accelerating onto the 5.

"Can't blame me, can you?" Van Sciver said. "Hell, I learned it from you. To be ruthless."

"From me?"

"You had to be. You were never the best. Everyone loves a thoroughbred, sure. But they root for the underdog."

"Who's rooting, Charles?"

Van Sciver kept on. "Helluva move you pulled all those years ago back at the home. Beat me to the starting gate."

"That was long ago."

"It was the past, yes. And it's the present, too. You define me, Evan. Just like I define you."

Evan watched the headlights blur past on the freeway. He could sense Joey's gaze heavy on his face.

"The Mystery Man wanted me," Van Sciver said. "Not you."

"Yes," Evan said. "He did."

"We were so young. Remember when we thought he was important? Remember when he held all the power in the world?"

"I remember."

"Now he works for me. The Program's pared down, way down, but when I decided to recruit a little fresh blood . . . well, he's still the best. Though even *he* makes a mistake now and again. Like the girl. I'm sure she's told you all about it."

Joey's hands tightened on the wheel. Van Sciver's voice, deep and confident, was carrying from the receiver.

"A mistake," Evan echoed. "I asked her how to find you. She couldn't tell me anything. She's not even bait. She's useless."

Joey looked straight ahead, drove steady, but Evan could hear her breathing quicken.

"She's another stray mark we have to erase," Van Sciver said. "She knows my face."

"What's she gonna do? Hire a sketch artist? She doesn't have the skills. She's damaged goods. She's not even worth killing."

"Yeah, but Johns took her in, so I'm gonna kill her anyway. Because he took her in. Because that makes her important to you."

"Your call to make," Evan said. "If you think you can afford not to concentrate on me."

Van Sciver sounded amused. "You have no idea, do you? How high it goes?"

"What does that mean?"

He laughed. "You still think it's about me and you."

"That is all it's about," Evan said. "From the minute you took Jack."

The reception weakened and then came back, the Subaru skirting the edge of the Wi-Fi hot zone.

"For years I'd reconciled myself to living off the radar," Evan said. "I was content to hide in the shadows. To leave you alone. Not anymore."

Joey had inched above the speed limit, and Evan gestured for her to slow down.

"Evan," Van Sciver said. "That's what we're counting on."

The connection fizzled into static, then dropped.

Evan turned off the Samsung and pocketed it. He leaned to check the speedometer. "Keep it at sixty-five."

Joey's chest rose with each breath, her nostrils flaring. " 'Not worth killing?' " She shot his words back at him.

"Everything's strategic, Joey."

"Didn't seem that way to me."

"We don't have time for this," he said.

"What?"

He tore the dangling duct tape off the laptop and popped it open. "Your feelings."

They drove in silence.

24

A Teaching Moment

Given the events at Portland Union Station, Evan decided to get Joey safely out of the state before parting ways. In the past he'd had a few near misses with Van Sciver around Los Angeles, so Van Sciver likely knew that Evan had a base there. Putting himself in Van Sciver's shoes, Evan figured he'd bulk up surveillance on routes leading south from Oregon. So rather than head for California, Evan and Joey rode the bell curve of the I-90, routing up through Washington and cutting across the chimney stack of Idaho.

They swapped seats at intervals, Evan driving the current leg. His attempts to access the laptop had been unsuccessful. The Dell Inspiron had proved to be heavily encrypted. Breaking in would require time, focus, and gear, none of which he could get until he had Joey off his hands.

Van Sciver's words returned, a whisper in his ear: *You have no idea, do you? How high it goes? You still think it's about me and you. No* matter how many ways Evan turned the conversation over in his head, he couldn't make sense of it. Van Sciver was working off an agenda unknown to Evan.

That scared him.

It felt as though Van Sciver were sitting at the chessboard and Evan was a pawn.

It was ten hours and change to Helena, Montana, a destination chosen for its unlikeliness and because they had to cross three state lines to get there. His stomach started complaining in hour six. It had been nearly eighteen hours since he'd eaten.

Joey had finally dozed off, slumped against the passenger window, a spill of hair curled in the hollow of her neck. It was good to see her sleeping peacefully.

Evan pulled off at a diner, braking gently so as not to wake her. He parked behind the restaurant, out of sight from the road, and reached to shake her awake.

She jolted upright, shouting and swinging. "Get off me! Get *off*—"

Awareness came back into her eyes, and she froze, backed against the door, fists raised, legs pulled in, ready to kick.

Evan had leaned away, giving her as much space as possible. He'd taken the brunt of her fist off the top of his forehead. If he'd been a second slower, she would have rebroken his nose.

Her chest was still heaving. He waited for her to lower her shoulders, and then he relaxed his.

She unpacked from her protective curl, looked around. "Where are we?"

"I thought we'd get some food."

She straightened her clothes. "This isn't a thing, okay? Like some big window into me."

"Okay."

"You don't know anything about me. You don't know what happened to me. Or *didn't* happen to me."

"Okay."

"I just have a temper, is all."

Evan said, "I'd noticed."

A Teaching Moment

They sat in a booth in the far back of the empty diner, Evan facing out. Despite the stuffing peeking through the cracked vinyl benches, the restaurant was clean and tidy and appealed to his sense of order. The aroma of strong coffee and fresh-baked pies thickened the air. A Wall-O-Matic jukebox perched at the end of their table, the Five Satins "shoo-doo 'n' shooby-doo"–ing in between hoping and praying. Salt and pepper shakers, syrup bottles, and sugar jars gathered around the shiny chrome speaker like children at story time.

From the old-school baseball pennants to the inevitable Marilyn poster, the manufactured nostalgia made the place seem like a location from a TV show, a faux diner set decorated to look like a real diner.

Evan ate egg whites scrambled with spinach and dosed heavily with Tabasco. Joey picked at a stack of pancakes, furrowing the pooled butter with the tines of her fork.

Conversation had been in short supply since the incident in the car.

Evan set down his fork, squaring it to the table's edges. A few drops of coffee formed a braille pattern next to his plate, remnants from the waitress's lazy pour. He resisted for a few seconds and then caved, wiping them clean with his napkin.

Joey remained fascinated with her pancakes. Her rucksack rested next to her, touching her thigh, the closely guarded life possessions of a street dweller.

Evan searched for something to say. He had no experience when it came to matters like this. His unconventional upbringing had turned him into something sleek and streamlined, but when he collided with the everyday, he felt blunt, unwieldy.

Then again, he supposed she wasn't very good at this either.

He watched her eviscerate her short stack.

"If you're fighting off an attacker—a *real* attacker—go for the throat or eyes," he finally said. "Up and under. If you swing for the head, he can just duck, protect his face, take the blow off the top of the forehead where the skull is thickest."

Her mouth gaped, but for once no words were forthcoming.

He sensed he had said something wrong.

"Are you seriously turning this into a *teaching* moment?" she said.

The best course of action, he decided, was to consider the question rhetorical.

But she pressed on. "Everything doesn't have to be some learning experience."

He thought of his upbringing in Jack's farmhouse, where every task and chore held the weight of one's character—making the bed, drying the dishes, lacing your boots.

How you do anything is how you do everything.

"Yes," Evan said. "It does."

"You've seen me fight," she said. "I know how to fight. That wasn't about fighting. It was just . . . a startle response."

"A startle response."

"Yes."

"You need a better startle response."

She shoved her plate away. "Look. I just got caught off guard."

"There is no 'off guard,' Joey. Not once you get on that bus in Helena. Not for a second. That's how it is. You know this."

She collected herself. Then nodded. "I do." She met his stare evenly. "Throat and eyes."

Though the sky still showed a uniform black, a few early-hours patrons filtered in—truckers with stiff hats, farmers with worn jeans and hands that rasped against their menus.

"You'll be okay," Evan said. "The farther you are from me, the safer you'll be."

"You heard him. He's not gonna let me go."

"He's gonna have his hands full."

"I think we're safer together."

"Like at your apartment? The train station? That pest-control shop in Central Eastside?"

She held up her hands. "We're here, aren't we? And they're not."

The sugary scent of the syrup roiled his stomach. "This isn't—can't be—good for you."

"I can handle it."

"You're sixteen."

A Teaching Moment

"What were *you* doing at sixteen?" She glared at him. "Well? Was it good for you? Or is that different? Because, you know, I'm a girl."

"I don't care that you're a girl. I care that you're safe. And where I'm going? It's not gonna be safe."

A patter of footsteps announced the waitress's approach. "I just started my shift, and already I'm winded trudging all the way to you two back here." She grabbed her ample chest, made a show of catching her breath.

Evan managed a smile.

"Anything else I can get you or your daughter, sweetie?"

Evan touched her gently on the side, not low enough to be disrespectful. "Just the check, thanks."

"It's really nice, you know, to see. A road trip. I wish my daddy spent time with me like that."

As she dug in her apron pocket, Joey gave her a look that bordered on toxic.

The waitress pointed at her with the corner of the check. "Mark my words, you'll appreciate this one day."

She spun on her heel, a practiced flourish, and left them.

The bill had been deposited demurely facedown. Evan laid two twenties across it, started to slide out.

Joey said, "I didn't do it."

He paused. "What?"

"The duffel bag. The guy. I didn't do it. I couldn't pull the trigger."

Evan let his weight tug him back into the seat. He folded his hands. Gave her room to talk. Or to not talk.

She took her time. Then she said, "I stood there with the gun aimed, Van Sciver at my back. And I couldn't."

"What did he do?"

"He took the gun out of my hand. And showed me . . ." Her lips trembled, and she pressed her knuckles against them, hard. "The mag was empty. It was just a test. And I failed. If I'd done it, if I'd passed the test, I could've been like—" She caught herself, broke off the thought.

"Could've been like what?"

"Like you."

Silence asserted itself around them. Kitchen sounds carried to their booth, pots clanking, grills sizzling. In a booming voice, the short-order cook was telling the staff that he hadn't had much luck with the rainbow trout but he had a new spinning lure that just might do the trick.

"Van Sciver unzipped the duffel, let the guy out. He was acting all along. Probably some psyops instructor. Van Sciver said he was gonna walk him out, that I should wait there for him. But the thing is?" Her voice hushed. "I noticed something standing there, look-ing down at the duffel bag. It had a smudge of blood on the lining. And I knew that I hadn't just failed the test. I'd failed Van Sciver. And at some point it would be me in that duffel bag and another kid outside it. And when *that* happened? The gun wouldn't be empty."

She sat back, breaking the spell of the memory. "That raised of-fice in the hangar, it had a window with a shitty lock. I kept a hair-pin hidden in my hair. I thought it'd be wise to GTFO before he got back. So I did. I was on the run eleven months until Jack."

"How'd Jack find you?"

The distinctive ring sounded so out of place here among the retro candy-apple-red vinyl and Elvis clocks and display counter up front stocked with Dentine. It was a ring from another place, another life, another dimension.

It was the RoamZone.

Someone needed the Nowhere Man.

25

Honor-Bound

The RoamZone's caller ID generated a reverse directory, autolinking to a Google Earth map of Central L.A. Evan zoomed in on a single-story residence in the Pico-Union neighborhood.

The phone rang again. And again.

Evan's thumb hovered over the TALK button.

He could not answer this call. It was out of the question. He had a girl to unload. A laptop to hack into. A death to avenge.

Jack's murder had sent Evan's life careening sharply off course. His dying message had shattered any semblance Evan retained of order, routine, procedure. He should be home right now, concerned only with his vodka supply and his next workout. Instead he was in a diner outside Missoula, stacking his proverbial plate higher and higher until everything on it threatened to topple.

Why hadn't Jack made arrangements for Joey? Why had he saddled Evan with her? Jack had known that Evan had his own honor-bound obligations as the Nowhere Man. Jack had known that being a lone wolf had been drummed into Evan's cells—hell, Jack had done the drumming himself. Jack had to have known that Joey would be an inconvenient aggravation at the very moment that Evan's universe would compress down in the service of a single goal—the annihilation of Charles Van Sciver.

An unsettling thought occurred. What if there was some design behind the plan? Jack's teachings always carried a hint of back-alley Zen to them.

If you don't know what you don't know, how can you know what to learn?

But why this? What could Evan possibly have to gain from this disruption?

Everything doesn't have to be a learning experience.

And Jack answered him, as clearly as if he'd been facing him across the breakfast table in that quiet farmhouse in the Virginia woods.

Yes. It does.

Evan banished the thought. There was no design. No artful master plan. Jack had found himself at the end of the road and had sent up a flare because he'd been desperate and needed Evan to clean up his mess.

It was nothing more.

Joey was staring at him. "You gonna answer that?"

Another ring.

He clenched his teeth, gave Joey a firm look. "Do not speak."

Her nod was rushed, almost eager.

He answered as he always did. "Do you need my help?"

"Yes. Please, yes."

The man's gravelly voice had a tightness to it not uncommon for people calling the number for the first time. Like he was forcing the words up and out. A heavy accent, Hispanic but not Mexican. It was just past four in the morning. Evan imagined the man pacing in his little house, clutched in the talons of late-night dread, working up the courage to dial.

Joey had gone bolt upright, her elbows ledging the table, darkly fascinated.

"What's your name?" Evan asked.

"Benito Orellana. They have my son, Xavier—"

"Where did you get this number?"

"A girl find me—her cousin is friend with my cousin's boy. She is called Anna Rezian. She is from good Armenian family."

Evan had never—not once—conducted a Nowhere Man call in the presence of someone else. Though he trusted Joey sufficiently to answer the phone in front of her, her presence felt intrusive. He wondered if this was what intimacy felt like. And if so, why anyone would want it.

Evan said, "Describe her."

"She have the thin face. Her hair, it have missing patches. She is sweet girl, but she is troubled."

"Who has your son?"

"I cannot speak the name." The deep voice fluttered with fear.

"They kidnapped him?" Evan asked.

"No," the man said. "He has joined them. And he cannot get out."

"A gang?"

A silence, broken only by labored breathing.

"If you don't talk to me, I can't help you."

"*Sí*. A gang. But you don't know this gang. Please, sir. My boy. They will turn him into a killer. And then he will be lost. I'm going to lose my boy. Please help me. You're all I have left."

"Sir, if your son joined a gang of his own volition, I can't help him. Or you."

Beneath the words Evan sensed the pulse of his own relief. He couldn't take this on as well. His focus was already maxed, the plate stacked too high. The Seventh Commandment—*One mission at a time*—blinked a red alert in his mind's eye.

Evan pulled the phone away from his face to hang up. His finger reached the button when he heard it.

The man, sobbing quietly.

Evan held the phone before him against the backdrop of his wiped-clean plate, the sounds of hoarse weeping barely audible.

He blinked a few times. Joey was like a statue, every muscle tightened, her body like an arrow pointed over the table at him. Breathless.

Evan drew in a deep inhalation. He brought the phone back to his cheek. Listened a moment longer, his eyes squeezed shut.

"Mr. Orellana?"

"*¿Sí?*"

"I see the location you're calling from. I'll be there tomorrow at noon."

"Thank God for you—"

Evan had already hung up. He slid out of the booth, Joey walking with him to the back door. She shot glances across at him, her face unreadable.

He pushed through the chiming door into the parking lot, the predawn cold hitting him at the hands and neck. He raised the set of keys he'd lifted from the waitress's apron and aimed at the scattered cars, clicking the auto-unlock button on the fob. Across the lot a Honda Civic with a rusting hood gave a woeful chirp.

The waitress's shift had just started, which gave them six hours of run time. Even so, he'd steal a license plate at the first truck stop they saw, from a vehicle boondocking in an overnight lot.

He and Joey got into the Civic, their doors shutting in unison.

She was still staring at him. He hesitated, his hand on the key.

He said, "This is what I do."

"Right, I get it," she said. "You help people you *don't* know."

26

How Can You Know You're Real?

Dawn finally crested, a crack in a night that seemed by now to have lasted for days. Evan pushed the headlights toward the golden seam at the horizon, closing in on Helena. In the passenger seat, Joey had retreated into a sullenness as thick and impenetrable as the blackness still crowding the cones of the headlights.

By the time he reached the Greyhound bus station, a flat, red-roofed building aproned with patches of xeriscaping, the morning air had taken on the grainy quality of a newspaper photo. Frilly clouds fringed a London-gray sky.

He drove twice around the block, scouting for anything unusual. It looked clear. The three-state drive had served them well.

He pulled into the parking lot and killed the engine.

They stared at the bus station ahead. It looked as though it had been a fast-food restaurant in the not-too-distant past. A few buses slumbered in parallel, slotted into spots before a long, low bench. There was no one around.

Evan said, "They start leaving in twenty minutes. I'll pick one headed far away. When you get there, contact me as we discussed. I can send you money and IDs—"

"I don't want your money. I don't want your IDs."

"Think this through, Joey. We've got three Orphans and fifteen freelancers circling. How are you gonna make it?"

"Like I always have. On my own." She chewed her lower lip. "These last few months with Jack? They were a daydream, okay? Now it's back to life."

A band of his face gazed back from the rearview. The bruises beneath his eyes had faded but still gave him the slightly wild, insomniac look of someone who'd been down on his luck for too long.

"Listen," he said. "I have to honor Jack's last wish—"

"I don't give a shit. Honestly. I don't need you." She reached into the backseat and yanked her rucksack into her lap. "What? You think I thought you were my friend?" She gave a humorless laugh. "Let's just get this over with."

She got out, and Evan followed.

She headed for the bench outside while he went in and bought her a ticket, a routine they'd established at the train station in Portland. He tucked a thousand dollars into the ticket sleeve and stepped back outside.

She was sitting on the bench, hugging her rucksack. Her jeans were torn at the knees, ovals of brown skin showing through. He handed her the ticket.

"Where am I going?" she asked.

"Milwaukee."

She took the bulging ticket. "Thank you," she said. "For everything. I mean it."

Evan nodded. He shifted his body weight to walk away, but his legs didn't listen. He was still standing there.

She said, "What?"

Evan cleared his throat. "I never knew my mom," he said. "Or my dad. Jack was the first person who ever really *saw* me." He swallowed, which was harder than he would have expected. "If no one sees you, how can you know you're real?" He had Joey's complete attention. He would have preferred a little less of it. It took him a moment to get out the next words. "Van Sciver took that from me. I need to set it straight. Not just for Jack. But for me. And I can't have anything or anyone in my way."

She said, "I get it."

He nodded and left her on the bench.

He got back into the Civic and drove off.

One distraction down.

If he stopped only for gas, he'd make it home in seventeen hours. Then he could hack into the laptop belonging to Van Sciver's muscle and follow where it led. Tomorrow at noon he'd see about helping Benito Orellana. He still had plenty to do and an unforgiving timeline.

The Honda's worn tires thrummed along the road. The windows started to steam up from his body heat. He pictured Jack's writing scrawled there.

GET PACKAGE.

Jack's final words.

His dying wish.

Evan cranked on the defroster, watched the air chase the fog from the panes.

He said, "I'm sorry."

He's the best part of me.

Again he remembered waking up in that dormer bedroom his first morning in Jack's house, the crowns of oak trees unfurled beyond his window like some magical cloud cover. He remembered how trepidatious he'd been padding down the stairs, finding Jack in his armchair in his den. And Jack's gift to him on that first morning of his new life: *My wife's maiden name was Smoak. With an a in the middle and no e on the end. Want that one?*

Sure.

Evan screeched the car over onto the shoulder of the road. Gravel dust from the tires blew past the windshield. He looked for patterns in the swirling dust, saw only chaos.

He struck the steering wheel hard with the heels of his hands.

Then he made a U-turn.

He parked in the same spot, climbed out. A bus was pulling in, blocking the bench. For a moment he thought she was already gone.

But then he stepped around the bus, and there she was, sitting in precisely the same position he'd left her in, hugging the rucksack, her feet pressed to the concrete.

She sensed his approach, looked up.

"Let's go," he said.

She rose and followed him back to the car.

27

Never Been and Never Was and Never Will Be

The man was ill. That much was easy to see. A tic seized his face every few seconds, making him shake his head as if clearing water from an ear.

He'd once been a paragon of excellence, one of the finest weapons in the government's arsenal. And now this.

He clutched a rat-chewed sleeping bag. Dirt crusted his earlobe. He wore sweatpants over jeans to ward off the cold.

He jittered from foot to foot, then halted abruptly and screwed the toe of his sneaker into the earth, back and forth, back and forth. He was mumbling to himself, spillage from a brain in tatters. Gray hair, gray stubble, gray skin, a face caving it on itself.

Jack had come to Alabama to find him.

But locating a homeless man was like trying to find a glass cup in a swimming pool. Hard to know where to start and easy to miss even when you're looking right at it.

Yet Van Sciver had resources that Jack didn't.

It had taken some time, but now here they were, in the shadow of the freeway overpass. Commuters whizzed by above them, an ordinary Birmingham morning in ordinary motion, but down here among the puddles and heaps of wind-blown trash, they might've been the last humans on earth. Nearby a fire guttered in a rusted trash can, the stench of burning plastic singeing the air.

The man convulsed again, one shoulder twisting up, plugging his ear. Van Sciver reached out and clamped the man's jaw, the hand so big it encircled the lower half of his face.

The man stilled. Van Sciver stared into his mossy brown eyes. Saw nothing but tiny candlelight flickers from the trash-can fire behind him.

Van Sciver said, "Orphan C."

The man did not reply.

Around the concrete bend, Van Sciver could hear Thornhill shooing away the last of the homeless from the makeshift encampment. They were skittish and tractable and had good reason to be. There'd been a rash of attacks against the community of late, a neo-Nazi group curb-stomping victims in the night, lighting them on fire.

Van Sciver snapped his fingers in front of the man's nose. The man jerked away. The tic seized him once more, the skin of his cheeks shuddering beneath Van Sciver's hand. Van Sciver squeezed harder, firming the man's head.

"Do you remember Jack Johns?" Van Sciver asked.

"I'm dead Orphan dead man walking never knew never never knew."

"Back in 1978 Jack Johns conducted your psyops training. Nine sessions at Fort Bragg. Have you been in touch with him since?"

"The woman's head like an open bowl it was an open bowl and I did it used to kill people for a living you know used to kill them and poof I'd be gone and no one ever knew no one ever knew anything ever knew me I never knew me never did."

"Did Jack Johns ever mention Orphan X?"

The man's eyes widened. His tongue bulged his lower lip. "Don't know don't never he's a ghost he's never been and never was and never will be."

"Do you know anything about Orphan X?"

Never Been and Never Was and Never Will Be

The man's eyes achieved a momentary clarity. "No one does."

Van Sciver released the man, and he staggered back. Van Sciver knew from Orphan C's file that he was fifty-seven years old. He could've passed for eighty.

The last medical tests before he'd retired and dropped out of sight had shown the beginnings of traumatic brain injury, likely from a rocket-propelled grenade that had nearly gotten him in Brussels. Since then he'd deteriorated further, PTSD accelerating what the physical trauma had begun, taking him apart piece by piece. It made him unsafe, a glitchy hard drive walking around unsecured.

"R!" Van Sciver called out.

Thornhill ducked back through a sagging chain-link fence and jogged over, sinew shifting beneath his T-shirt. He wasn't wearing his usual shoes today.

He was wearing steel-plated boots.

"I'm done here," Van Sciver said. "He's got nothing for us." He regarded the man again, felt something akin to sadness. "There's nothing left to get."

The man's face seized again, and he tweaked forward, facial muscles straining. "People taking and taking like bites little piranha bites until there's nothing left until they've nibbled you down to the bone and you're dead a skeleton held together by tendons just tendons."

"I got this," Thornhill said, putting his arm around the man and walking him to the drain. "Come on, buddy. You're okay. You're good."

The man shuddered but went with him.

Van Sciver folded his arms across his broad chest and watched.

"I'm sorry you've had a rough time," Thornhill told the man. "It's not your fault. None of this is your fault. You can't help what you are. Hell—none of us can."

The man nodded solemnly, picked at the scruff sprouting from his jaundiced neck.

Thornhill removed a can of spray paint from his jacket pocket, gave it a few clanking shakes, and started to spray something on the concrete by the drain. The man watched him nervously.

"I knew a guy," Thornhill said, the sprayed lines coming together to form a giant swastika. "Loved dogs. Had a whole raft of them taking over his house, sleeping on his couches, everywhere. Well, one day he's out driving and sees a sign on the road. Someone's giving away baby wolves."

He pocketed the can of spray paint, set his hands on the man's shoulders, and turned him around. Then he knocked the back of the man's leg gently with his own kneecap and steered him down so he was kneeling before the drain.

"So he figures what the hell. He takes this baby wolf home, raises him just like a dog. Feeds it, shelters it, even lets it sleep on his bed. The wolf gets bigger, as wolves do, grows up. And one morning just like any morning, this guy, he's building a shed, fires a nail gun right through his shoe."

Thornhill tilted the man forward toward the raised strip of concrete running above the drain. "There you go. Just lie forward on your chest." He positioned the man. "So this guy comes limping through his backyard, scent of blood in the air. His dogs are all frantic, worried. Can sense his pain, right? They're worried for him. But that wolf? The wolf doesn't see a problem. He sees an *opportunity*."

Thornhill reached down, opened the man's jaw, set his open mouth on the concrete ridge. "So he tears out his owner's throat." The man was trembling, his stubble glistening with trapped tears, but he did not resist. He made muffled noises against the concrete lip. Thornhill leaned over him, mouth to his ear. "Because that wolf was just biding his time. Waiting, you see, for his owner to show the tiniest vulnerability." Almost tenderly, he repositioned the man's head. "No matter how docile it seems, a wolf will always be a wolf."

Thornhill reared back to his full height, his shadow blanketing Orphan C. Thornhill firmed his body, raised one of his steel-plated boots over the back of C's head.

Van Sciver climbed into the passenger side of the Chevy Tahoe. Even with the armored door closed, he heard the wet smack.

That was okay. Yesterday had given them a pair of solid leads. C had been the least promising of the two.

Never Been and Never Was and Never Will Be

On to the next.

Van Sciver opened his notebook and peered at the address he'd written inside. This one held his greatest hope.

Outside, Thornhill tugged off his boots and threw them into the trash-can fire.

Van Sciver removed his phone from the glove box and called Orphan V.

28

Her Version of Normal

In a McMansion in the impressively named and decidedly unhilly gated community of Palm Hills, Candy McClure strode through the kitchen wearing two oven mitts patterned with cartoon drawings of the Eiffel Tower.

Classy.

Her fuck-me lips, which would be her best feature if there weren't so many to choose from, were clamped around a candy cane. Sucking. She'd plumped them out further with lip liner and tinted gloss, which made things entirely unfair for anyone with hot blood in his—or her—veins. This was by design.

She had more assets than the other Orphans, and she was unafraid to deploy them.

Contour-fitting Lululemon yoga pants and a muscle tank gripped her firm body, showing off everything she had to show off while hiding everything she needed to hide.

Such as the scar tissue that turned her back and shoulders into an angry, swirling design better suited to pahoehoe lava than to human skin.

She leaned forward and removed a fresh apple pie from the oven. It smelled wonderful. On the counter rested a bag of powdered sugar, a tub of shortening, and a flask of concentrated hydrofluoric acid, effective at dissolving flesh and bone.

She was a domestic goddess.

On the easy-care quartz-topped island, her phone chimed. She flung off the mitts, leaned beneath the hanging copper pots, and picked up.

Her boss's voice came through. "Code."

She glanced at the screen. "'Iridescent motor,'" she said. "My nickname in high school."

"Are you still undercover?"

Steam rose lazily from the pie. A lawn mower started up somewhere outside. Curlicue writing on her apron read *Kiss The Baker!*

She said, "*Deep* cover."

"Target identified?"

She smiled, felt the peppermint seep between her teeth, cool and tingly. "Yeppers."

She pulled her red notebook over from its place by the salt and pepper shakers, tapped it with a Pilot FriXion pen. The notebook held her extensive and detailed mission notes. And a new recipe for delicious shortbread cookies.

For nearly two weeks, she'd been living here in this steamy slice of Boca Raton paradise, drawing the attention of the men and the ire of their wives. She'd been tasked with identifying who in the upscale community was on the verge of bundling $51 million in a super PAC opposing Jonathan Bennett. Van Sciver had backtracked bank records and data comms and found that someone in Palm Hills had masterminded the operation from a rogue cell-phone tower. Given that the negative campaign threatening to hit the airwaves was the start of a push for post-election impeachment, it was no wonder the mastermind was doing his best to keep his machinations—quite literally—off the grid.

So Orphan V had moved into the neighborhood and was doing

a suburban divorcée hot-as-fuck desperate-housewife routine, renting the house for a few weeks as her post-signing-of-the-papers "gift to herself." She mingled with the denizens and took plenty of night walks, surveilling who might be in their backyard or on the roof, erecting or disassembling a ghost GSM base station.

Last night she'd watched him through the slats of a no-shit white picket fence as he'd toiled red-faced over a tripod and a Yagi directional antenna.

"Neutralize now," Van Sciver said. "I need you on X."

Her expression changed. Orphan X always took priority.

"Something rang the cherries," Van Sciver continued. "It requires your feminine wiles. Finish now, get clear, contact me for mission orders."

She said, "Copy that."

The call disconnected.

Time to clean up.

She placed the notebook on the rotating glass turntable of the microwave and turned it on. Pocketing her flask of hydrofluoric acid, she cast a wistful gaze at the apple pie. She'd grown oddly fond of this house and her time here in Stepfordia, nestled into real life—or at least a simulation of it. Living among families, privy to their hidden resentments and petty squabbles. Yesterday at the country-club pool, she'd witnessed a disagreement over sunscreen application escalate into a battle worthy of the History Channel. She enjoyed her neighbors' small triumphs, too. Billy learning to ride a two-wheeler. A husband rushing out to the driveway to help his wife carry in her groceries. Teaching the new puppy to heel.

Candy had made a home here. A new wardrobe displayed on hangers in the walk-in. Essential oils by the bathtub to soothe her burns. Microfiber sheets on the bed, so soft against her aching skin. Satin sheets worked, too, of course, but they always seemed too porny.

The microwave dinged. She removed the notebook and, on her way out, dumped it into the trash atop a confetti heap of apple peelings.

She paused in the foyer, taking in the sweep of the staircase.

Her Version of Normal

How odd to have grown fond of this place.

Was it a sign of weakness? Since Orphan X had inflicted the hydrofluoric-acid burn on her, Candy sometimes woke up late at night gasping for air, her back on fire. In those first breathless moments, she swore she could feel her deficiencies burrowing into her, seeping through her flawed, throbbing flesh, infecting her core. The sensation had worsened since last month. In an alley outside Sevastopol, one of Candy's colleagues had turned a beautiful young Crimean Tatar girl into collateral damage.

Candy didn't mind killing. She thrived on it. But this one had been unnecessary and the girl so sweet and lost. She'd come up the alley and seen something she shouldn't have. Right up until she was stabbed in the neck with a pen, she'd been offering to help.

Her name had been Halya Bardakçi. She visited Candy in the late hours, her sweet, almond-shaped face a salve for the pain. She could have been fifteen or twenty—it was hard to tell with these too-attractive-for-their-age streetwalker types—but Candy had felt her death differently.

Like a part of herself had died in that alley, too.

A craven sentiment, unbefitting an Orphan.

She shuddered off the notion, turned her thoughts to stepping through her faux-Tuscan iron front door. She loved heading out into the community. She got so much attention here.

She stretched down and touched her toes, feeling the tight fabric cling to her, a second skin more beautiful than her own. Then she walked outside, putting on her best divorcée prance and twirling her tongue around the sharp point of the candy cane.

The entire street alerted to her presence. The snot-nosed fifteen-year-old across the street rode his hoverboard into a tree. Long-suffering Mr. Henley swung to chart Candy's course to the driveway, watering no longer the begonias but his wife's comfortable shoes.

Candy reached the RYNO one-wheel motorcycle she'd parked in the driveway. Before putting on the helmet, she took the candy cane's length down her throat and held it there. She was good like that.

She straddled the electronic bike and motored down to the club.

It took a bit of balance, but not as much as you'd think. It moved at the pace of a stroll, ten miles per hour.

Whereas all the other Orphans strove to blend in, Candy preferred to stand out. When people looked at her, they weren't really seeing her. They were seeing their fantasy of her. At a moment's notice, she could bind her chest, change her hair, alter her dress, and transform into someone else. And all those gawkers would realize—they'd never really seen her at all.

Right now she was interested in creating an alibi. Which meant being noticed.

At that she excelled.

She parked the RYNO at the country club between a yellow Ferrari and the tennis pro's beleaguered Jetta. She unscrewed her head from the helmet and shook her honey locks free. The curve of the candy cane rested snug against her cheek. She produced the red-and-white-striped length from her throat and got back to sucking.

The towel boy did a double take, his jaw open in mid-chew, the dot of his gum glowing against perfect molars. An elderly foursome paused on the facing tennis court, the ball bouncing untouched between two of the partners. A trio of wattle-necked women sipping iced tea tsk-tsked to one another as Candy blew past.

Three seconds, eight eyewitness.

Not bad.

Candy entered the club, breezing by reception, and walked down a rubber-matted hall into the eucalyptus-scented women's locker room. She locked herself in the spacious handicapped toilet stall.

A toilet stall that happened to have a window overlooking the back of the golf course's little-used eighteenth hole.

She squirmed out the window, hit the grass silently. Moved twenty yards behind the building to a familiar white picket fence.

She hurdled it.

She walked up to the rear sliding door, her luscious lips making an O around the stalk of the candy cane.

Her target sat at a sun-drenched workstation off the kitchen.

He was shirtless, horizontal parentheses of untanned skin delineating the paunch of his hairy belly.

She leaned toward the glass. "Knock-knock."

She didn't want to touch the pane and leave prints.

He caught sight of her and found his feet in a hurry, fumbling at the lock.

"Hi, hello, welcome," he said. "Wow."

She floated inside. "Wow yourself."

She glanced at his workstation, where two monitors ran stock-price tickers, an endless stream of industry. A financial titan like him would have so, so many enemies, which meant so, so many convenient investigative trails.

"You're renting the house on Black Mangrove Street," he told her.

She leaned close. "You've been keeping tabs on me?"

He was sweating. She had that effect on men.

"Why are you in my backyard? I mean—don't get me wrong—I'm delighted, but . . ." He lost the thread of the sentence.

She had that effect, too.

She slid the candy cane out of her mouth. "It's more *private*," she said, shaping her lips around the word, making it something dirty.

He blinked several times rapidly. His own meaty lips twitched. He scratched at a shoulder. "Okay. Um. That's nice. Private's nice."

A billion-dollar hedge-funder reduced to a teenager at a school mixer.

She placed a hand on his cheek, which was sticky with sweat. A breath shuddered out of him. He closed his eyes. She moved her hand up to his hair, grabbed his thinning curls, and tugged back his head.

He gave a little groan of pleasure.

Then she rammed the sharpened candy cane into his jugular.

The first gush painted the monitors. Arterial spurts were always mesmerizing. He went down fast, hand clamped to his neck, legs cycling on the cool tile floor. Then they stopped cycling.

She stared down at him. Dead people looked so common.

She removed her flask, poured hydrofluoric acid into the wound, the familiar scent rising as it ate through flesh. That would take care of any DNA from her saliva. She crossed to the kitchen sink, dropped the candy cane down the disposal, and ran it, pouring in a dose of hydrofluoric acid for good measure.

She picked up the cordless phone, called 911, wiped the buttons clean with a wet dish rag, and set it on the counter. The coroner would reach a precise time of death eventually, but why not help him out?

She walked out the open back door, hopped the white picket fence, and jogged along the rear of the clubhouse, breathing in the fresh-cut grass of the golf course. She'd miss it, being here, being normal. Her vacation had come to an end, but she had another "gift to herself" in mind.

Catching Orphan X and making him feel every ounce of pain that she lived with day and night.

She crawled through the window back into the toilet stall, walked out of the bathroom, turned left into the crowded gym, and mounted the StairMaster.

Beneath her shirt her ruined skin itched and burned, but she blocked out the pain. She'd keep at it for two hours, time enough for the cops to arrive and find Mr. Super PAC back-floating in a pool of his own blood.

So many residents could say precisely where the fetching divorcée had been since the moment she stepped out of her rented house this morning.

The gym was mirrored from wall to wall, and in the countless reflections, she could see every eye on her.

After all, Candy could work a StairMaster.

29

End-Stopped

As they barreled along the freeway, Joey reached into the backseat to retrieve the laptop that Evan had taken from the headquarters in Portland. She fired it up, then flexed her fingers like a gymnast about to tackle the uneven bars.

Evan glanced over from the driver's seat. "Careful you don't trip an autoerase—"

"Yeah," she said. "I got it."

He drove for a while as she clicked around. The late-morning sun beat down on the windshield, cooking the cracked dashboard. A pine-tree air freshener long past expiration spun in circles from the rearview. Above the speedometer a hula girl bobbed epileptically on a bent spring.

"Finding anything?"

Joey held up a wait-a-sec finger. "This is some heavy-ass encryption."

"Can you break it?"

"I don't know."

" 'I don't know' isn't an answer."

"Thanks, *Jack*." Her fingers skittered across the keyboard. It was like watching someone play an instrument. "I'll tell you this, *you* certainly couldn't."

"Yes or no, Joey."

"There are maybe a handful of people in the world who could hack this," she finally said, " 'n' I'm one of them. But it'll take some time. And a fast Internet connection."

"Van Sciver knows you're with me. So we have to assume he knows you can get to whatever information's guarded in there. He trained you."

"Please. I was better than him to begin with. It's the only thing I had, growing up. We're talking sixteen, eighteen hours a day online, checking out 2600, using the darknet and stuff. I put in lots of private IRC hacker chat-room time, too, like, browsing the chans, vulns, and sploit databases, fooling around with Scapy, Metasploit, all that. It was one of my selling points. Back when I was, you know, a wanted commodity. Before I was useless." She grinned and closed the lid. "He knows I'm good but has no idea *how* good."

"Once we hit L.A., I'll set you up in a safe house. I want what's in that laptop as quickly as possible."

"I'm gonna require a crate of Red Bull and a Costco tub of Twizzlers."

"You'll have what you need."

"And Zac Efron. I want Zac Efron."

"Who's Zac Efron?"

"God, you're old." She smiled, and it was like turning on a light, her face luminous. She observed him observing her. "What?"

"I haven't seen you smile."

She looked back at the road. "Don't get used to it."

As the Civic filled with gas, Evan scanned the parking lot and the freeway. Joey climbed out and stretched like a cat, slow and luxurious.

"Want any road food?" she asked.

"Road food?"

"Corn nuts, Slim Jims, Mountain Dew?"

"I'm good."

She brushed past him, heading inside. "Don't leave me here."

He looked at her. "Why would I leave you here?"

She shrugged, not breaking stride.

They were heading south on the I-15, Idaho ten exits away. Borders were always tricky—choke points, easy to surveil. So far it had been smooth sailing, but so far hadn't been long.

The gas pump clicked off, and Evan got back into the car to wait for Joey. Her rucksack tilted in the passenger-side foot well. Another greeting card had fallen out.

Evan leaned over and picked it up.

A cartoon of a nervous-looking turkey against a backdrop of orange and yellow leaves. Fresh concern pulled at Evan. He opened the card.

Sweet Girl,

I hope you have lots to be thankful for this Thanksgiving of your 16th year! Know that even though we're apart, I miss you and hold you in my heart.

Xoxo, M.

Again it seemed that Joey had read the card many times. Creases, wrinkled corners, a patch of ink worn off where she'd held it.

Thanksgiving. Your 16th year.

That was troubling.

He set the card on her seat and waited.

She approached, chewing gum, and opened the door. She spotted the card, hesitated, then picked it up and climbed in slowly. She stared straight through the windshield at the air pump. She smelled like Bubblicious.

"Why are you going through my stuff?"

"It fell out of your rucksack."

"Answer my question."

"There are more important questions. Like who is M and how did she have your address?"

"What do you mean 'my address'?"

"This is a Thanksgiving card. Thanksgiving was last Thursday. You were in the apartment Jack had set up for you. And Jack was in Alabama. No one should have known how to reach you."

"No one did know how to reach me."

"Joey, what if this is how they found your apartment?"

"Look, I promise you, it's okay."

"Who is M?"

Scowling, Joey grabbed her hair in a fist and pulled it high, showing the shaved side of her head.

"Joey, we have to have total trust. Or none of this works."

She took in a lungful of air, let it out slowly. "She's my maunt."

"Your maunt?"

"My aunt, but more like a mom. Get it?"

"Yes."

"She raised me until she couldn't, okay? Then I went into the system for a lotta years. Until Van Sciver's guy pulled me out."

"How did she know where to send you this Thanksgiving card?"

Joey's eyes filled with tears. It was so sudden, so unexpected that Evan's breath tangled in his throat.

She said, slowly, "It's not a risk, okay? I promise you. If we have total trust, trust me on this."

"They can track anything, Joey."

She tilted her head back, blinked away the tears. Then she turned to him, fully composed. It was a different face, stone cold and rock steady, the face of an Orphan. "I am end-stopped there. Completely end-stopped."

He stared at her a moment longer, deciding whether or not he believed her. Then he fired up the engine and pulled away from the pump.

Evan's focus intensified as they neared the border. He kept it on rotation between the mirrors, the on-ramps, the cars ahead. He changed speeds and lanes.

Meanwhile Joey changed channels on the radio, responding with enthusiasm or disgust to various songs that Evan found indistinguishable from one another.

End-Stopped

Despite everything, she was still sixteen.

A hunter-green 4Runner had been behind them for a while now. White male driver, wispy beard. Evan pulled to the right lane and slowed down, timing it so another car shielded them from view as the 4Runner drove past. The driver did not ease off the gas or adjust his mirror. Which meant he was either not interested or well trained.

Ensuring that passing drivers didn't get a clean look at them was no easy task on a seventeen-hour road trip. Van Sciver's people would be looking for a man traveling with a teenage girl—not an uncommon combination but not common either. The Honda's windows had been treated with an aftermarket tint, which helped decrease visibility. The sun was near its peak, turning the windshields into blinding sheets of gold, another momentary benefit.

A truck pulling a horse trailer sidled up alongside them. Evan tapped the brake, tucking into the blind spot.

"Hold on," Joey said, cranking up the volume. "Listen—this is my jam."

He listened.

It was not his jam.

The horse trailer exited. He watched it bank left and amble up into the hills.

At last the billboard flashed past: WELCOME TO IDAHO! THE "GEM STATE."

While Joey bounced in the passenger seat, the Gem State flew by in a streak of brown. Scrubby flats, a few twists carved through hills, more scrubby flats.

The gas needle had wound down to a quarter tank by the time he pulled off. The service plaza was at the top of a rise, a mini-golf bump in the terrain with good visibility in all directions.

A single strip of parking lined the front of the plaza, which made for easy scouting. Of the vehicles only a blue Volvo pinged Evan's mental registry, but when it had passed twenty miles back, he'd noted three children quarreling in the back.

After he'd filled the tank, he and Joey went into the plaza, splitting up as was their protocol. Joey drifted up the junk-food aisle while Evan dumped four bottled waters and a raft of energy bars before the register. As the woman rang him up, he caught sight of his reflection in the mirrored lenses of a pair of cheap sunglasses on the counter display.

The bruises beneath his eyes made him conspicuous. Memorable.

He snapped off the price tag, laid it on the counter, and put on the glasses. They'd be helpful for the moment, but he'd require something less obvious. He remembered Lorilee in the elevator, how she'd concealed the finger marks where her boyfriend had grabbed her.

"Just a second, please," he told the lady at the register.

One aisle over he found a cheap beige concealer.

Joey appeared, pressing a bag of Doritos to his chest. She took in his sunglasses with amusement. "Nice look," she said. "Did you misplace your fighter jet?"

"Don't worry. I'm getting this." He held up the concealer wand. "I'd ask to borrow yours, but I didn't figure you for the makeup type."

"I wouldn't exactly call our last few outings makeupworthy," she said. "But you couldn't use mine anyways. I'm browner than you. Thank God."

He headed back to the counter and laid the concealer and chips on top of the energy bars.

The woman gave a smile. "Picking up some makeup for the missus?"

"Yes, ma'am."

She handed him the plastic bag.

Joey was waiting outside, her arms crossed, staring through a patch of skinny trees down the long ramp to the freeway.

"What?" Evan asked.

She flicked her chin.

A hunter-green 4Runner exited the freeway and started up the slope toward the service plaza.

30

Do Your Business

Evan pulled Joey around the side of the building. They stood on the browning grass beneath the window of the men's room, peering around the corner at the travel plaza's entrance. A good vantage.

"That truck," she said. "Kept time with us for at least forty miles."

He thought of her bobbing in her seat, singing along to the radio. "I didn't think you were paying attention."

"That's my superpower."

"What?"

"Being underestimated."

The men's-room window above them was cracked open, emitting the pungent scent of urinal cakes. Through the gap they heard someone whistle, spit, and unzip. Evan set the shopping bag on the ground.

They waited.

The 4Runner finally came into view, cresting the rise.

It crept along the line of parked vehicles, slowing as it passed the

Civic. The driver eased forward, closer to the pumps, and stopped with the grille pointed at the on-ramp below.

"Hmm," Joey said.

Evan leaned closer to the building's edge, Joey's hair brushing his neck. They were thirty or so yards away from the 4Runner.

Leaving the truck running, the driver climbed out, scratching at the scraggly blond tufts of his beard. Cowboy boots clicking on the asphalt, he walked back to the Civic, approaching it from behind. As he neared, he untucked his shirt. His hand reached back toward his kidney, sliding under the fabric. He hooked the grip of a handgun, slid it partway out of the waistband.

It looked like a big-bore semiauto, maybe a Desert Eagle.

Not a law-enforcement gun.

The man approached cautiously, peering through the windows, checking that the car was empty. Then he let his shirt fall back over the gun and entered the travel plaza.

"He didn't see us," Evan said. "Not directly, not from behind us on the freeway. At best he could tell that we were a man and a young woman. He's trying to confirm ID."

"So what do we do?"

"*You* don't do anything."

"I could handle that guy."

"He's bigger than you," Evan said. "Stronger, too."

In the bathroom a toilet flushed, the rush of water amplified in the cinder-block walls. A moment later they heard the creak of hinges and then the hiss of the hydraulic door opener. A sunburned man waddled into sight around the corner and headed off toward his car.

Joey snapped her gum. "I could handle him," she said again.

"We're not gonna find out," Evan said. "Stay here."

"You're going into the plaza?"

"Too many civilians. We'll let him come to us. He'll check the bathrooms next."

Sure enough, the driver emerged from the plaza and started their way. They pulled back from the corner.

Evan moved his hand toward his holster. "Don't want to use the gun," he whispered. "No suppressor. But if I have to—"

Do Your Business

She completed the thought. "I'll have the car ready."

A crunch of footsteps sounded behind them. Was there a second man? Evan put his shoulders to the cinder block, flattening Joey next to him, and switched his focus to the rear of the building.

A Pomeranian bobbed into view, straining a metal-link dog leash. It sniffed the grass, its rhinestone-studded collar winking.

Evan came off the wall.

The little dog pulled at its chain, producing an older woman clad in an aquamarine velour sweatsuit. She frowned down at the dog. "Do your business, Cinnamon!" She looked up and saw Evan. "Oh, thank God. Excuse me. Can you watch Cinnamon for me just for a second? I have to use the ladies' room."

Evan could hear the driver's boots now, tapping the front walkway behind him, growing louder. "I can't. Not now."

Creak of hinges. Hiss of hydraulic door opener.

The woman said, "Maybe your daughter, then?"

Evan turned around.

Joey was gone.

He tapped his holster through his shirt.

Empty.

He hissed, "Joey!" and leaned around the front corner.

He caught only a flicker of brown-black hair disappearing through the men's-room door as the hydraulic opener eased it shut.

The woman was still talking. "Teenagers," she said.

Evan stood at the corner, torn. If he shouted Joey's name, he'd give her away. If he barreled in after her, he could alert the driver and get her killed. As it stood, she had Evan's gun and the element of surprise.

On point, he strained to listen, ready to charge.

The woman misread his agitation, her face settling into an expression of empathy. "I raised three of them," she went on, holding up three fingers for emphasis. "So believe me, I know. It's hard to learn to let them go."

The dog yapped and ran in circles.

"What with the driving and drinking," the woman said. "Making choices about their bodies."

Through the cinder-block walls, Evan heard a thud. A grunt. In the window just over the woman's shoulder, a spatter of blood painted the pane, and then the man's face mashed against the glass, wisps of beard smudging the blood.

The woman cocked her head. "Do you hear that?"

"I think they're cleaning the bathroom," Evan said.

Another pained masculine grunt and the snap of breaking bone.

"*Deep* cleaning," Evan said, as he shot around the corner.

He shouldered through the men's-room door.

The first thing he took in was Joey facing away, her tank top slightly twisted, arms raised, shoulders flexed. He couldn't see her hands, but his ARES pistol was tucked in the back of her pants.

The man was on his knees, his cheek split to the bone, his front teeth missing, his chest bibbed with blood. One arm dangled loosely at his side, broken. The other hand was raised palm out, fingers spread. Evan took a careful step forward, bringing Joey into full view. She was standing in a perfect Weaver stance, aiming the man's own Desert Eagle at his head, the long barrel made longer by a machined suppressor.

Joey's finger tightened on the trigger.

Evan held out a hand calmly, stilling the air. "Joey," he said.

The man ducked his head. Blood dripped from his cheek, tapped the floor. The acrid smell of his panic sweat hung heavy.

"Lower the gun," Evan said. "You don't want to cross this line."

"I do." Her eyes were wet. "I want to prove it."

"There's nothing to prove."

The barrel trembled slightly in her grasp. Evan watched the white seams of flesh at her knuckle.

"It's just one more ounce of trigger pressure," Evan said, "but it'll blow your whole world apart."

"What's the difference?" she said. "If I do it or you do it?"

"All the difference in the world."

She blinked and seemed to come back to herself. She inched the gun down. Evan stepped to her quickly and took it.

He faced the man. "A directive came from above to have me killed. I want to know *where* it came from."

The man sucked in a few wet breaths. He didn't answer.

Do Your Business

Evan took a half step closer. "Who's Van Sciver taking orders from now?"

The man spit blood. "He keeps us in the dark, I swear."

Evan shot a glance at the bathroom door. Time was limited. "How'd he find you? Are you former military?"

The man tilted his face up to show a crooked smile, blood outlining his remaining teeth. "Now, that would give away too much, wouldn't it? But it's your lucky day, X. I can help you. I'll send a message to Van Sciver."

"Yes," Evan said. "You will."

He shot the man in the chest. The suppressor was beautifully made, reducing the gunshot to a muffled pop. The man jerked back against the tiles beneath the window and sat in a slump, chin on his chest, head rocked to one side.

Eleven down.

Fourteen to go.

Evan dropped the gun, took Joey's arm, and walked out. No one at the gas pumps had taken notice.

He flipped Joey the keys to the Honda. "Get your rucksack and the laptop."

She jogged off to the right, and he veered left.

When he stepped around the corner to check on the woman, she was bent over the dog, scolding it. "Do your business, Cinnamon. Do your business!"

She sniffed at him. "You know, there was a time when strangers helped each other."

"I'm sorry, ma'am," he said, picking up his shopping bag. "It's the teenager. Unpredictable."

Her face softened. She returned her focus to the Pomeranian.

Evan walked swiftly past the gas pumps to the 4Runner, which waited for them, motor still on, already angled downslope for a quick getaway. Joey met him there, climbing in as he did, tossing her rucksack ahead of her.

She was still winded from the fight and the adrenaline rush, her clavicles glistening with sweat.

He said, "You are a powerful young woman."

He pulled out onto the freeway and headed for home.

31

Sprint the Marathon

By the time they arrived at Evan's Burbank safe house twelve hours and twenty-nine minutes later, they were driving a Prius with the license plates of a Kia. Bottlebrush and pepper trees shaded the street of single-story midcentury houses. Evan's sat apart at the end of the block behind a tall hedge of Blue Point juniper. When he'd bought it, one of a half dozen he kept at the ready, the neighborhood had been affordable, the houses charming if slightly ramshackle. But owing to Burbank's fine schools and proximity to the studios, the block's gentrification had reached a fever pitch; now remodels perennially clogged the quiet street. He'd been planning to unload the place and would do so as soon as he and Joey were done with each other. He maintained a labyrinthine and impenetrable network of shell corporations that allowed him to shuffle and discard assets without fear of being traced.

He parked in the garage next to a decade-old Buick Enclave that had served him loyally. The garage door shuddered down, and then he and Joey were cocooned in darkness, safe.

He started to get out when she said, angrily, "What does it matter?"

"What?"

"Whether I kill someone?"

He took a moment to consider. "It changes you in ways you can't understand. You'd never be able to have a normal life."

"A normal life? So I can . . . what? Hang out at the mall? Go to prom? Take a thousand fucking selfies?"

Her voice held an anger he did not understand.

"Yeah," she said. "I'd fit right in."

"It's about more than that," he said. "We've talked about the Tenth Commandment. 'Never let an innocent die.' But maybe there's another part to it: 'Never let an innocent kill.' "

"I'm not an innocent."

"No. But maybe we could get you back there."

She did not seem satisfied with that.

She made no move to get out of the car. Sitting in the Prius, they stared through the windshield at nothing.

"I'm weak," she said.

Her face cracked, contorting in grief, a flicker so fast that he'd have missed it if he'd blinked.

"Why do you think that?"

"I couldn't pull the trigger on the guy in the duffel bag. I couldn't do it at the rest stop either."

"That's not because you're weak," Evan said. "It's because you're stronger."

"Than who?"

He hadn't seen where the words were headed, not until now. He set his hands on the wheel, breathing the dark air.

"Than me," he said.

For Evan, maintaining the safe houses was a part-time job. Every few days he watered the landscaping, cleared flyers off the porch, took in the mail, programmed the lighting-control systems. Each location had what Jack called "loadouts"—mission-essential gear and weapons.

He entered the Burbank house, disarming the alarm system. The interior was dark, hemmed in by trees, the backyard shaded by a steeply sloped hillside. The house always smelled slightly damp, moisture wicking up through the foundation.

Joey walked from room to room, mouth gaping. She came back into the living room, let the rucksack drop on the thick brown carpet along with a bag of junk food he'd bought her at the last gas station. Twizzlers and Red Bull, as promised, as well as instant ramen packs, Snickers bars, and sandwiches in triangular plastic containers.

"You just have houses everywhere?"

"Not everywhere."

"Where do *you* live?"

"That's off-limits."

She held up her hands. "Whoa, cowboy. I got it. X's place—off-limits. But how do you have so much money?"

"When I was operating, they set me up with an excess of resources. They wanted me to have no reason ever to be heard from. It was a huge investment, but it paid well."

"Paid well?"

"How much is regime change worth?" Evan said.

Joey pursed her lips.

He said, "A well-placed bullet can change the direction of a nation. Tip the balance of power so a country's interests align with ours."

She shook her head as if shaking off the thoughts. "How has Van Sciver not tracked you down through your bank accounts?"

"He's tried."

"But you're too good."

"No. *Jack* was too good. He set everything up, taught me what I needed to know about keeping it untraceable."

"But things have changed since then."

"Right. I've refined the practices. After an unfortunate event last month, I diversified a little more. Bitcoin mining."

She smiled. "Because it's delinked from government regulation and oversight."

"That's right."

"So. That's why you can afford to have safe houses everywhere."

"Not everywhere."

She spun in a full circle, taking it all in. "And I can stay here?"

"Yes. And work." Evan fired up the Dell laptop, set it on a round wooden table that, along with a mustard-colored couch, passed for the living-room furniture. "I need what's in here. Getting Van Sciver? It's a marathon, not a sprint. But we want to sprint the marathon. Understand?"

She folded her arms. "Let me explain to you what we're looking at here. This Dell Inspiron is using a crazy strong encryption algorithm."

"So you can't brute-force the key?"

She gave a loud, graceless guffaw that was almost charming. "We're talking a substitution-permutation cipher with a block size of sixty-four bits and key sizes up to two hundred and fifty-six bits. So no, we can't brute-force the key unless you've got like a hundred or so years."

"What's the best way to get the key?"

"With a hammer from someone who knows it."

"Joey."

She sigh-groaned, sat down, and pulled the laptop over to her. "What's your password to get online?"

He told her. Waited. Then asked, "What are you doing?"

Her fingers blurred. "Downloading the tools I need."

"Which are?"

"Look," she said, "going up against the algorithms could take weeks. We have to figure out the key. Which in all certainty will be composed—at least in part—of words or specific numeric sequences that are familiar to these guys in some way. So I need lists. I'm talking every name in the English language, European names, nicknames, street addresses, phone numbers, combinations of all of the above. Did you know there are only one and a half billion phone numbers in North and South America?"

"I did not."

But she was barely listening. "There's this newish thing from Amazon? Called an AMI—an Amazon Machine Image. Basically it runs a snapshot of an operating system. There are hundreds of them, loaded up and ready to run."

Evan said, "Um."

"Virtual machines," she explained, with a not-insubstantial trace of irritation.

"Okay."

"But the good thing with virtual machines? You hit a button and you have two of them. Or ten thousand. In data centers all over the world. Here—look—I'm replicating them now, requesting that they're geographically dispersed with guaranteed availability."

He looked but could not keep up with the speed at which things were happening on the screen. Despite his well-above-average hacking skills, he felt like a beginning skier atop a black-diamond run.

She was still talking. "We upload all the encrypted data from the laptop to the cloud first, right? Like you were explaining poorly and condescendingly to me back at the motel."

"In hindsight—"

"And we spread the job out among all of them. Get Hashkiller whaling away, throwing all these password combinations at it. Then who cares if we get locked out after three wrong password attempts? We just go to the next virtual machine. And the one after that."

"How do you have the hardware to handle all that?"

She finally paused, blowing a glossy curl out of her eyes. "That's what I'm telling you, X. You don't buy hardware anymore. You rent cycles in the cloud. And the second we're done, we kill the virtual machines and there's not a single trace of what we did." She lifted her hands like a low-rent spiritual guru. "It's all around and nowhere at the same time." A sly grin. "Like you."

"How long will this take?"

"Not sure. I have to oversee the control programs, check results, offer the occasional loving guidance. After all, they *are* just machines."

"Okay. I have to get back. Towels in the bathroom. The fridge is stocked with food."

"Wait—you're leaving me here?"

He crossed to a cupboard, pulled out a burner cell phone, and fired it up for the first time. "Only call me. You know the number?"

"Yeah, 1-855-2-NOWHERE. One digit too long."

"Yes."

"So that's it?" She looked around at the blank walls, the mustard-colored couch. "This is my life?"

"For now."

"Is there a TV?"

"Nope."

"What do I do?"

He picked up the keys to the Enclave from a dish on the kitchen counter. He'd left his Ford F-150 in a long-term parking lot at Burbank Airport; he'd do one last vehicle swap before going home. "Get into that laptop."

"Okay," she said. "And when I do?"

He headed for the garage. "Then I follow the trail."

"No—I mean, what happens to *me*?"

He spun the keys around a finger once and caught them in his fist. He started out. "Just crack it, Joey."

"So what? We'll just figure out me later?"

"This isn't about you, Joey. It's about Van Sciver. You understand what I need to do here. That's my only concern."

He held her eye contact. She gave a little nod.

And he left her.

32

Cleaning Agent

Home.

Evan nudged the big Ford pickup into his spot between two concrete pillars, killed the engine, and released a sigh. Castle Heights' subterranean parking level was vast and gloomy and more pristine than any garage had a right to be. A pleasing whiff of oil and gasoline lingered beneath the aggressive lemon scent of environmentally friendly floor cleaner. The cleaning agent, part of the HOA's "go green" initiative, had passed by a narrow margin after a heated debate at the monthly meeting, a debate that Evan—as the resident industrial-cleaning-supply expert—had been roped into. His tie-breaking vote for the more expensive ecological product had drawn the ire of some of the older, fixed-income residents.

That was life in the big bad city.

At times he found the inner workings of Castle Heights—the rivalries, squabbles, and bureaucratic maneuverings—to be more exhausting than eluding teams of hit men.

He stayed in the truck. It was so quiet here in the garage.

Cleaning Agent

He took a moment to inventory his body. His broken nose looked passable but still ached across the bridge. The cut in his gums from the exploded windshield had mostly healed, but it gave an angry throb when he ran his tongue across it. Lower back, still stiff from the collisions with police cruisers on the road outside Hillsboro. A sharp pain under his armpit, maybe a cracked rib. His hands, scuffed from swinging off the metal overhang on the train platform. His shoulder injury, exacerbated by the recoil of the Benelli shotgun. All of which he could cover up.

But his eyes were still sufficiently bruised to elicit inquiries.

Turning on the dome light, he took out the concealer wand and dabbed a bit of beige makeup on his lower eyelids. As he smudged it with his fingertip, he couldn't help but grin a bit.

He'd let down his guard and a sixteen-year-old had broken his nose. Joey had played him perfectly. Crouched against the wall to hide her combat knife, that wounded-bird glance over her shoulder. *Can you help me?*

He got out of the truck and climbed the steps to the lobby. As he passed the mail slots and headed to the elevators, he spotted Lorilee outside in the porte cochere, waiting for the valet to bring around her car. She was arguing with her boyfriend, a fit man with long hair who looked to be in his late forties. He grasped her biceps, making a point. Evan's focus narrowed to the fingers curled around Lorilee's arm. He didn't like the laying on of hands in a dispute.

But this was none of his business.

Joaquin sat cocked back in an Aeron at his security desk. He was pretending to monitor the bank of security screens, but his eyes were glazed and Evan saw that he had one earbud in, hidden beneath his cap.

Evan said, "Twenty-one, please, Joaquin."

The guard bounced forward in his chair, tapping the control to summon the elevator and specify its destination, an old-timey Castle Heights security convention. "Got you, Mr. Smoak. How was your business trip?"

"Another day, another airport lounge. But I got a lot done."

"That's good."

"What's the score?"

Joaquin colored slightly. "Twenty-six–fourteen. Golden State."

"Sorry."

" 'Member when the Lakers used to be good?"

Before Evan could respond, Joaquin pulled out his earbud and straightened up abruptly. Ida Rosenbaum, 6G, walked through the front door, shuffling along. She was bent forward, oversize purse pinned beneath one elbow as if it were at risk of fluttering away.

Evan turned to face the elevator, praying it would arrive before she made it across the lobby. In the dated brass doors, his reflection came clear.

Thanks to the unforgiving light of the lobby, he saw now that his nose was still out of alignment. Not much, but it was shifted a few millimeters to the left, noticeable enough for the sharp eyes of Ida Rosenbaum.

As she neared, presaged by the smell of old-lady violet perfume, he reached up and cracked his nose to center.

It stung enough to make his eyes water.

"You again," she said, sounding less than delighted.

He stayed facing forward, blinking back the moisture; if he made his concealer run, that would provoke another conversation entirely. "Good morning, ma'am."

"Again with the 'ma'am,' " she said. "Call me Ida, already."

"Okay," Evan said.

The elevator arrived, and he got on, holding the door for Mrs. Rosenbaum. He felt heat building up in his sinuses and prayed his nose wouldn't start bleeding. The pain of the rebreak radiated out beneath his cheekbones.

"This weather," Ida said as the elevator started to rise. "It's playing games with my allergies. You wouldn't believe the aggravation. Feels like I'm snuffling through hay."

The blood was coming now—he could feel the warmth inside his nose. He didn't want to reach up and pinch it, so he tilted his head back slightly and gave a sharp inhale. The floor numbers ticked by in slow motion. His eyes no longer watered, but moisture still welled at his bottom lids, threatening to spill and wreak havoc with the concealer.

"And my hip. Don't even get me started." Ida waved a dismissive hand at him. "What would you know about it? My Herb, may he rest in peace, always said that no one in your generation learned how to handle pain. Everyone's off to get a massage or smoke medical marijuana."

He tried to compress his nostrils. "Yes, ma'am."

The elevator at last reached the sixth floor, and she stepped out, casting a final look back at him. "Slow learning curve, too," she observed.

As the doors glided shut, the bumpers blocking out Mrs. Rosenbaum, Evan tilted his face into his hand just in time to catch the blood.

In Evan's freezer drawer, one bottle of vodka had remained untouched for several years.

Stoli Elit: Himalayan Edition.

Evan opened the walnut chest and beheld the Bohemian hand-blown glass bottle.

Made with the finest variety of winter wheat from the Tambov region and water tapped from reservoirs buried beneath the famed mountain range, the vodka underwent a sophisticated distillation process, after which it was frozen to minus-eighteen degrees Celsius to segregate any additives or impurities. It came accompanied by a gold-plated ice pick. Given the price of the bottle, the best use for the pick was presumably to defend oneself against would-be vodka bandits.

Evan cracked the seal and poured two fingers over a spherical ice cube.

He lifted the tumbler to admire the clarity of the liquid. It smelled of ice and nothing more. The mouth feel was velvety, and the aftertaste carried a surprising hint of fruit.

Vodka's original purpose was to cleanse the palate after eating fatty foods. But Evan loved it for its quiet ambition. At first glance it looks as plain as water. And yet it strives to be the purest version of what it is.

He set the tumbler on the poured-concrete surface of the kitchen island, leaned over it, and exhaled.

An image came to him unbidden, the wind tearing through the Black Hawk, fluttering Jack's shirt, his hair. He'd taken a wide stance, steady against the elements.

Always steady against the elements.

Evan lifted the glass halfway to his mouth, set it back down.

His cheeks were wet.

"Goddamn it, Jack," he said.

He closed his eyes and dropped into his body. Became aware of its shape from the inside. Felt the pressure of the floor against the soles of his boots. The coolness of the counter beneath his palms. He stayed with his breath, feeling it at his nostrils, in his windpipe, his chest. Drew it into his stomach, belly-breathing a count of ten.

Right now, in this moment, there was no Nowhere Man mission, no Van Sciver, no sixteen-year-old stashed in a safe house. There was no past or imagined future, no bone-deep ache of grief, no figuring out how to live in a world without Jack.

There was only the breath. Inhale, exhale. His body doing what it did twenty thousand times a day, except this time he was mindful of it.

And this time.

And this time.

The brief meditation and the vodka sent warmth through his veins. He felt decontaminated.

He opened his eyes and headed to the Vault.

33

A Lot of Variables

Benito Orellana.

That was the name of the man who had called the Nowhere Man for help, the man Evan was to meet tomorrow at noon.

At least that's what the caller had claimed his name was.

Evan approached each pro bono job with the same meticulous mission planning with which he'd once plotted the assassination of high-value targets. The First Commandment: *Assume nothing.*

Including that the client is who he says he is.

Or that he might not be planning to kill you.

Evan had parked himself behind his sheet-metal desk in the Vault, sipping vodka in the pale glow of the monitors neatly lined up before him. From here he could access hundreds of state and federal law-enforcement databases. This required only a single point of entry: a Panasonic Toughbook laptop hooked to the dashboard of any LAPD cruiser. Because officers rotated through a squad car with every shift change, the laptop passwords were generally straightforward, often simply the assigned unit number:

LAPD_4012. Over the years Evan had broken into various cruisers from various stations and uploaded a piece of reverse-SSH code into their dashboard laptops. Firewalls face out to keep people from breaking in. They don't regulate outgoing traffic. When Evan needed to access the databases remotely, he initiated his hidden code, prompting the police computer to reach out through its firewall to him. Then he could sail right through the open ports and browse wherever he liked.

He'd already learned much about Benito Orellana.

An undocumented worker from El Salvador, he'd received amnesty in 1986 under the Immigration Reform and Control Act. His tax records showed Benito holding down three jobs—a dishwasher at an Italian restaurant downtown, a valet parker, and an Uber driver. Over the years he had diligently reported cash tips. If the information Evan was collecting was real, it revealed an honest, hardworking man.

Benito's wife had died in February. Medicaid test results from last year showed black spots on a chest CT scan, and the L.A. County death certificate listed lung cancer as her cause of death. It had been fast. Benito had one son, Xavier, who had taken a few courses at East Los Angeles College and then dropped out around the time of his mother's diagnosis. No other information on Xavier was to be found. Benito's financials seemed to be clean until recently; he'd racked up debt in the form of credit-card charges to Good Samaritan Hospital. The house in Pico-Union was leveraged, a second mortgage with a predatory lending rate gaining momentum by the month.

Evan looked over at Vera II. "The guy seems legit."

Vera II said nothing.

Evan took the last expensive sip of vodka, fished out what was left of the ice cube, and rested it in her serrated spikes. An ice cube a week was all the watering the fist-size aloe vera plant required.

He removed the Samsung cell phone from his pocket—the one he'd stolen from Van Sciver's man in Portland—and turned it on. No messages. There was a single coded contact. Push the button and it would ring through to Van Sciver. That would prove useful at some point. Evan turned the phone back off and charged it.

A Lot of Variables

He started to get up, but Vera II implored him.

"Okay, okay," he said.

He called up feeds from the hidden security cameras in the Burbank safe house.

He found Joey at the wooden table, chewing on a Twizzler, tapping at the keyboard. She had her own laptop set up next to the Dell now, connected with a cord. After a time she got up, fished in her rucksack for something, and retreated to the couch.

He couldn't see what she was staring at.

Finally she shifted, and he caught a vantage over her shoulder. She was reading the Thanksgiving card again, tracing her finger across the handwriting as if it were braille.

She looked forlorn there on the couch, leaning against the arm, her legs tucked beneath her.

Evan glanced at Vera II.

"Fine," he said.

He called Joey's burner phone. He watched her start, and then she crossed to the table and picked up.

"X?"

"How are you doing?"

She glanced at the laptops. "Making headway."

She'd misunderstood what he was asking about. It seemed awkward to backtrack now.

He said, "Good."

She went into the kitchen and slid a pack of ramen noodles into a bowl.

"Do we have an ETA?" he asked.

"We're dealing with ten thousand virtual machines," she said, filling the bowl with water and shoving it into the microwave. "There are a lot of variables."

"We need to—"

"Sprint the marathon," she said. "Right. Consider me chained to the laptop. When I'm done with this, maybe I could stitch some wallets for you."

An unfamiliar ring sounded deep in the penthouse, and Evan stood up abruptly. It had been so long since he'd heard it that it took a moment for him to place what it was.

The home line.

When he'd moved in, he'd had it installed so he could have a number to list in the HOA directory. Aside from a telemarketer three months ago, no one had called it in years.

"I'll check in on you in the morning," he said to Joey, and hung up.

He raced out of the Vault, through his bedroom, down the hall to the kitchen, and snatched up the cordless phone. "Hello?"

"Hi."

Hearing her voice caught him completely off guard.

34

The Job to End All Jobs

"I know we decided not to be in touch," Mia said, her voice light and nervous over the phone. "But, I don't know, you seemed messed up when I saw you in the parking garage last week."

Evan cleared his throat.

"And . . ." she said. "I know you were gone for a while. I saw your truck back in your spot tonight and figured . . . I guess I figured maybe you could use a home-cooked meal."

In the background he could make out some Peter-related commotion. She muffled the receiver. "Put the lid back on that!" she shouted. Then she was back. "Anyway, it was just a thought."

He heard himself say, "I'd like that."

"Really?"

He was asking himself the same thing. He'd responded before thinking. What part of him had that answer teed up, ready to deploy?

"Yes," he said.

"Okay. Well, come down in twenty?"

"Okay." He was, he realized, pacing nervously. There was something else he was supposed to say here, something he'd heard people say on movies and TV shows. The words sounded clunky and robotic in his mouth, but he forced them out. "Can I bring anything?"

"Just yourself."

That was how the script went. He'd watched it dozens of times but now he was inside it, saying the lines.

There was some other rule, too. Her job was to say no, but his job was to bring something anyway. Except what did he have to bring? Cocktail olives? An energy bar? A Strider folding knife with a tanto tip for punching through Kevlar vests?

Ordinary life was stressful.

He said, "Okay," and hung up.

Jack had trained him for so many contingencies, had made him lethal and worldly and cultured.

But not domestic.

Checking the adjustment of his nose, he padded back to shower.

Mia yanked open the door, a blast of too-loud TV cartoons hitting Evan in the face along with the smell of cooking garlic and onion. "Hi, welcome. Wow—vodka."

He stood nervously, holding a frost-clouded bottle of Nemiroff Lex, which was neither too expensive nor too cheap, not too showy nor too understated, not too spicy nor too citrusy.

There had been deliberations over the freezer drawer.

Feeling decidedly unmasculine, he'd also touched up his makeup on the bruises beneath his eyes. The discoloration was nearly gone; he hoped he could forgo the concealer come morning.

He hoisted the bottle. "It's Ukrainian," he said, sounding disconcertingly rehearsed. "Wheat-based and aged in wood for six—"

"Hi, Evan Smoak!" Peter blurred by, juggling oranges, which seemed mostly to involve dropping them.

Mia whipped around. "I am taking this house back! That's what I'm doing! So help me—"

A crunch punctuated a sudden pause in Peter's movement.

He looked down at his feet. Remorse flickered across his face. "The remote got broken," he announced in his raspy voice, and then he bolted over the back of the couch and resumed his not-juggling.

Mia seemed to register the afterimpression of her son. "'Got broken,'" she said. "That's what we call a strategically passive sentence construction."

She turned and hurried back into the kitchen, Evan following. With a pasta ladle, she scooped out a piece of linguine and tossed it against the cabinet. It stuck beside various strands that had previously dried and adhered to the wood. She caught Evan's expression and held up a hand, swollen by an oven mitt to inhuman proportions. "That means it's ready," she said, raising her voice over the blaring TV. As she dumped the pot's contents into a colander, rising steam flushed her cheeks.

The smoke alarm began bleating, and Mia snatched up a dish towel and fanned the air beneath it. "It's fine. It'll just . . ."

The rest of her statement was lost beneath an orchestral change in the intensity of Bugs Bunny's adventure.

In the midst of the chaos, Evan took a still moment. He set down the vodka bottle on the counter. Grabbing a steak knife from the block, he headed into the living room, sidestepping a toppled barstool. He found the remote on the carpet by the couch, the buttons jammed beneath the plastic casing, as he'd suspected.

He sat and worked the tiny screws with the tip of the steak knife. Three oranges tapped the couch cushion, light footsteps approached, and then Peter sat opposite Evan, cross-legged.

"What are you doing?" the boy asked.

Evan extracted the first screw, went to work on the second. "Unscrewing."

Peter said, "Why are you using a steak knife?"

"Because that's what I've got."

"But knives are for eating."

"Among other things." The screw popped up, and the top casing of the remote lifted, the rubber buttons jostling back into place beneath it. Evan fastened the faceplate back on, then touched the POWER button.

The TV mercifully silenced just as the smoke alarm stopped bleating. A moment of perfect, blissful quiet.

Mia said, "We are ready to plate."

While Peter disappeared to brush his teeth, Mia and Evan sat at the table, empty dishes between them. In the background, singing softly from an iPod speaker dock, Linda Ronstadt was wondering when she'd be loved.

Mia took a sip of vodka. "This *is* good. It tastes . . . aged in wood."

Evan said, "You're making fun of me."

"I'm making fun of you."

She held up her glass, and they clinked.

From the depths of his bathroom, Peter yelled, "Done!" and Mia shouted, "That wasn't two minutes!"

It was cold, and she had her sweater sleeves pulled over her hands. Her hair was a rich mess of waves and curls. The glow of the overhead light spilled through it, showing off all the colors, chestnut and gold and auburn.

Evan remembered that he was supposed to comment on the food. "That was delicious."

"Thank you." She leaned forward, cupped a hand by her mouth, gave a stage whisper. "I blend spinach in the marinara sauce. It's how I get him to eat vegetables."

Unexpectedly, Evan found himself thinking of Joey dining alone in the safe house, Twizzlers and ramen in the dead blue light of the laptop. A sensation worked in his chest, and he gave it some space, observed it, identified it.

Guilt.

That was interesting.

He looked across at the kitchen, where a new Post-it was stuck above the pass-through.

Remember that what you do not yet know is more important than what you already know.—Jordan Peterson

Mia left quotations around for Peter, rules to live by. As she'd once remarked to Evan, it took a lot of work to raise a human.

"Peter's lucky to have you," Evan said.

"Thanks." She smiled and peered into her vodka, her fingers peeking out of the sweater cuff to grip the glass. "I'm lucky to have him, too. It's the predictable response, but it's true."

"*Really* done now!" Peter yelled. "Can I read?"

"Ten minutes!"

"Tell me when time's up!"

"Okay! I'll be in to tuck you in!"

Evan looked at the freshly folded laundry, still in the basket on the floor. The homework chart above the kitchen table, bedazzled with puffy stickers. "It's so much work," he said.

"Yes. And that's on a good week. Then there's the strep-throat week, the getting-bullied week, the cheating-on-the-simplifying-fractions-test week."

"Fair enough," he said. "Fractions."

She laughed. "Kids turn your life upside down. But maybe that's where anything matters. In the big fat mess of it all. Of course, I'd like to do more. Travel. Relax." She hoisted the glass. "Drink." Her grin faded. "Sometimes parenting, it feels like . . . an anchor." Her expression lightened. "But that's the good part, too. You have this anchor. And it holds you in the world."

Evan thought, *Like having Jack.*

"God," she said. "Sometimes I miss Roger so much. It's never the big stuff like you'd think. Candlelight dinners. The sex. Wedding veils and vacations. No. It's coming home when you're at the end of a brutal day and there's someone there. Consistency. You know?"

Evan said, "No."

She laughed. "Your bluntness, it's refreshing. It's always yes and no with you. Never 'I'm sorry' or 'I get it.'"

He thought, *That's because I don't get it.*

"This personal thing you're dealing with," she said. "What is it?"

He took another sip, let the vodka heat his throat. "It is," he said, "the job to end all jobs."

"Truly?"

"I think so."

"If that's the case," she said. "Maybe a DA and a . . . whatever you are can be friends."

"Friends."

She rose from the table, and he followed her cue.

"Maybe we could do this," she said. "Just this. Maybe again Friday? Peter enjoys it. I enjoy it."

Evan thought of Jack, stepping silently into space, giving his life to protect Evan's. Joey, working furiously to get him back on Van Sciver's trail. Benito Orellana, besieged by debt, his wife dead, his son in danger. *Please help me. You're all I have left.*

Evan didn't deserve to have something this nice on a regular basis.

Mia was staring at him.

He said, "What?"

"This is where you say you enjoy it, too."

Evan said, "I enjoy it, too."

They were at the door. Mia was looking at his mouth, and he was looking at hers.

"Can I kiss you?" she asked.

He drew her in.

Her mouth was so, so soft.

They parted. She was breathless. He was, too. An odd sensation—odder even than guilt.

He said, "Thank you for dinner."

She laughed as she closed the door after him.

He had no idea why.

35

Patron Saint of
Dispossessed Orphans

It was a new look.

Chocolate-brown hair, cut in a power A-line bob with razor-blade bangs. Cat-eye glasses. A B-cup bra tamping down her voluptuousness beneath a professional white blouse. A fitted wool skirt curving her lower assets, delivering the package neatly into rich-girl riding boots.

Candy made sure the back view was on full display, leaning into the trunk of her car, struggling with the spare tire.

Her just-past-warranty Audi A6 quattro had blown a tire, you see, conveniently right beside the rear parking lot of the New Chapter Residential Recovery Center.

Candy was going for young Georgetown junior associate at a white-shoe firm, successful but not yet arrived, dressing and living beyond her means in hopes that she was on the verge of that next promotion. Few things were less threatening to men than a woman trying slightly too hard to make up professional ground.

She kept pretending to wrestle the tire, making sure that her face was getting a nice damsel-in-distress flush. It was 6:58 A.M., New Chapter unlocked its doors at seven o'clock sharp, and her target—from the intel Van Sciver had given her—would be jonesing for his early-morning hit of nicotine.

Orphan L's smoking habit was the one thing he wasn't currently faking. And the one thing he couldn't suppress even if his life depended on it.

Which, of course, it did.

Find what they love. And make them pay for it.

She heard the clunk of the dead bolt unlocking, footsteps, the snick of a lighter.

She stayed buried in the trunk, let the view do the talking. The skirt, sexy-conservative as was befitting the town, strained a bit at the seams.

She made exasperated sounds.

Oh, dear me. If only there were a strapping man who could—

"Excuse me?"

She extricated herself from the trunk, blew out an overwhelmed breath, pressed a hand to her sweaty décolletage.

He was walking toward her already, salt-and-pepper stubble, tousled hair. He looked convincingly like shit—she'd give him that—but he would've been handsome were he not playing addict. "Need a hand?"

In the Orphan Program's prime, Tim Draker had been one of the best. But he'd recently broken with Van Sciver, taken early retirement, and blipped off the radar. Then he'd found out there was no retiring from the Orphan Program.

Not with Van Sciver.

"God, yes. The tire went out, and I don't really know how to change it. I'm late for work—my boss is gonna *kill* me."

He drew nearer, flicking his cigarette aside with a practiced flourish. A broad smile, full of confidence. Too much confidence for a recovering heroin addict. It was too tantalizing—*she* was too tantalizing—for a trained Orphan to keep his tongue in his mouth, hold his distance, act his legend.

Her ass alone could do the work of a full team of Agency spooks.

Patron Saint of Dispossessed Orphans

Draker wore a T-shirt, a wise choice since it showed off the scabs and dark, wilted bruises at the crooks of his elbows. Terrific visuals, likely produced from a mixture of vitamin-C powder, Comet, and Visine shot just beneath the epidermis. Then you wolf down enough poppy seeds and Vicks cough syrup to ding the intake opiate-drug tests. After that it's just about theatrics. Rub your eyes with soap, slam Red Bull, Vicks, and Sudafed, and you have your basic amped, twitchy, rheumy-eyed, nauseated, sweating addict. Claims of suicidality buy you more time off the streets, out of the system, protected under that umbrella of total patient confidentiality offered by a drug-treatment facility.

A plan worthy of Jack Johns, Patron Saint of Dispossessed Orphans.

Van Sciver would never have known.

But for a single eyelash.

That had put him on the scent of anonymous treatment facilities. But what a bitch to search them. Had it been anyone but Van Sciver with his MegaBot data-mining lair, it never would've happened. Draker would've lain low, undergone another three-month fake treatment in another facility, and then skipped off into the wide world once the heat died down.

Draker sidled up, pretended not to eye her cleavage. "Let's take a look, shall we?"

"Oh, my God," Candy said, all breathy like. "Thank you so much."

Draker leaned into the trunk, reaching for the tire, his T-shirt straining across his muscular back. Candy withdrew a syringe from the top of her riding boot, popped the sterile plastic cap, and sank the needle into his neck.

He went limp immediately.

She flipped his legs into the trunk after him.

That was a nice feature of the Audi A6.

Good trunk space.

She slammed the trunk shut, got in, and drove away. The snatch-and-grab had taken three seconds, maybe four.

Men were so easy.

They had a single lever. You just had to give it a tug.

183

Van Sciver and Thornhill pulled the armored Chevy Tahoe through the tall chain-link gate and parked alongside the humble single-story house. Weeds had overtaken the backyard, and a BBQ grill had tipped over, rusting into the earth.

Van Sciver got out, the sun shining through his fine copper hair, and rattled the gate shut on stubborn wheels, sealing them in. Thornhill opened the back door.

They started to unload the Tahoe.

Padlocks and plywood.

Nylon ropes and boards of various lengths.

A decline bench press and jugs of water.

Mattresses and drop cloths.

Rags and a turkey baster.

Duct tape and a folding metal chair.

Thornhill whistled a tune the entire time. Van Sciver wondered what it would take to wipe that permanent smile off the guy's face.

When they finished, Van Sciver's cheeks and throat had gone blotchy pink from exertion. His shirt clung to the yoke of his shoulders. He had an Eastern European peasant's build—arms that barely tapered at the wrists, thighs stretching his cargo pants, a neck too thick to encircle with both hands. In another life he would've been a 60 gunner, hauling the massive, belt-fed pig for a platoon, a one-man artillery unit.

But this life was better.

He grabbed the last of the supplies, closed up the Chevy, and came inside.

Thornhill was doing handstand push-ups in what passed for the kitchen, his palms pressed to the peeling linoleum. The forks of his triceps could have cracked walnuts.

Van Sciver's phone alerted. He juggled the items he was holding and picked up. "Code."

" 'Potluck chiaroscuro,' " Candy said. "They're getting arty on us."

"Is the package in hand?"

"What do you think?"

"*V.*" He packed the syllable with impatience.

"Yes," she said. "It is."

He walked to the chipped counter. Set down a dog collar next to a galvanized bucket.

"Good," he said. "We're just getting ready."

36

Fresh Air

Joey answered the front door of the Burbank safe house. She looked like hell—swollen eyes, gray skin, her hair mussed.

Evan moved past her off the porch, swung the door shut. "Did you check the security screen before opening?"

"Nah. I figured I'd play door Russian roulette. You know, maybe it's you, maybe it's Van Sciver."

"It's increasingly hard to get a direct answer out of you," Evan said.

"Yeah, well, sprinting the marathon means not a lot of sleep."

He glanced immediately at the laptops, code streaming across both screens, progress bars filling in. "So nothing yet." He failed to keep the impatience from his voice.

"I would've called."

He took in the bare-bones house, wondering if it felt similar to the hangar in which Van Sciver had kept her. Or the apartment Jack had hidden her in. That familiar feeling compressed his chest again. He thought about her reading that Thanksgiving card last night, her legs tucked beneath her on the couch.

"How are you doing?" he asked.

"How do you think I'm doing? I've been either running for my life or staring at a screen for longer than I can remember. What kind of bullshit existence is that?"

She went to the kitchen counter, cracked another Red Bull.

He had a few hours before his meeting with Benito Orellana in Pico-Union. "Let's go for a walk," he said.

"Great. A walk. Like I'm a dog. You're gonna take me around the block?" She stopped herself, rubbed her face, heaved an exhale through her fingers. "Fuck. I'm sorry. I'm being a bitch."

"You're not," Evan said. "Come on. Fresh air."

She gave a half smile, swept her hair to one side. "I remember fresh air."

She followed him out. The invigorating smell of Blue Point juniper reminded him of the parking lot in Portland. They'd had a lot of close calls already, a lot of hours together in the trenches.

They turned left and headed up the street, Evan keeping alert, scanning cars, windows, rooftops. Wild parrots chattered overhead, moving from tree to tree. Their calls were loud and strident and somehow lovely, too. As Evan and Joey walked, they watched the birds clustering and bickering and flying free. Evan thought he detected some longing in Joey's face.

"You still haven't told me your full first name," Evan said.

"Right. Let me think. Oh, that would be . . . none of your business." She gave him a little shove on his shoulder, pushing him into the gutter.

"I'll tell you my full first name," he said. "I've never told anyone."

"It's not just Evan?"

"It's Evangelique."

"Really?"

"No."

She laughed a big, wide laugh, covering her mouth.

A pair of guys came around the corner ahead, one riding on a hoverboard, the other a longboard, the wheels skipping across the cracks in the sidewalk. They wore hoodies with skater logos and throwback checkered Vans.

The hoverboard hit a concrete bump pushed up by a tree root and the guy fell over, skinning his hands.

Evan was about to tell Joey to keep walking when she called out, "You okay?"

The guy picked himself up as they approached. "All good."

His friend, a burly kid, stepped on the tail of his longboard and flipped it up, catching it by the front truck. He looked to be in his late teens, maybe twenty. His hair was cropped short on the sides, the top gathered tightly in a man bun.

Evan didn't like him.

And he didn't like how he was looking at Joey.

"Hey, I'm Connor. You guys live around here?"

"No," Evan said. "Visiting a friend."

"Well," the guy said, directing his attention at Joey, "if you're around again, we hang at the old zoo most nights." He pointed up the street toward Griffith Park. "To chill. You should come."

Evan mentally graphed the angle of uppercut that would snap both hinges of his jaw.

"She's busy," he said.

"When?"

"Forever."

As they passed, Connor said in a low voice, "Dude. Your pops is intense."

Joey said, "You have no idea."

They left the guys behind, turning the corner for their street.

"Think he's a plant?" Joey asked.

"No. I think he's a useless reprobate. Loose body language. The stoner nod. He's not good."

"I thought he was kinda cute."

Evan said, "You're grounded."

"Like, locked-in-a-safe-house-and-forced-to-hack-an-encrypted-laptop grounded?"

Evan said, "Yes."

Fresh Air

A smile seemed to catch her by surprise. She looked away to hide it.

He gave her a little nudge on the shoulder, tipping her into the gutter.

37

Blood In, Blood Out

Benito Orellana twisted his hands together, shifting his weight back and forth, anguish throttling through him. He wasn't crying, but Evan could see that it was taking most everything he had not to. His stained dishwasher's apron was slung over a chair back; before Evan's arrival he had changed into an ironed white T-shirt. No money, but proud.

"A parent, they are only as happy as their least happy child," Benito said. "*Mi mamá* used to tell me this. You understand?"

Not at all, Evan thought. He said, "Tell me what happened to Xavier."

In the square front room of the tiny house in Central L.A., Evan stood across from Benito, facing the picture window. The view looked out onto a massive empty lot razed by bulldozers and the top floors of a tall building being constructed beyond. Workers were visible clinging to the steel skeleton, steering in I-beams as if they were planes on the tarmac.

In Pico-Union any direction you went, you hit a thoroughfare—

the 110 Freeway to the east, Normandie Avenue to the west, Olympic Boulevard up top, and the Santa Monica Freeway below.

A lot of getaway routes. Which meant a lot of crime.

Evan had safed the block, the surrounding blocks, and the blocks surrounding those. A three-hour undertaking, wholly necessary before the approach in case Benito was the bait in a trap.

On these initial forays, Evan used to bring a briefcase embedded with all sorts of operational trickery, including signal jamming if digital transmitters happened to be in play. But the briefcase had been unwieldy.

Also, he'd had to detonate it.

Now he used a simple portable RF jammer in his back pocket, no bigger than a pack of cigarettes.

Within minutes he believed that Benito was not an undercover agent for Van Sciver and that his plight was real.

Benito swallowed. "When my wife pass, I don't know how to cook, how to do anything."

"Mr. Orellana. I'm here about Xavier."

"She would have known how to talk to him. But I am working so hard. Even right now my friend, he cover for me at the restaurant. I have too much month at the end of the paycheck. I am working three jobs, trying to provide for Xavier. But I lose track of him. There just wasn't the time to earn and to also . . . also . . ."

He was at risk of breaking down.

"Mr. Orellana," Evan said. "What did Xavier do?"

Benito swayed on his feet, his eyes glazed, far away. "There is a gang where I come from. They kill anyone. Women, children. They are so bad that the government, they make a prison just for them in San Salvador. The police do not even go in. Instead they keep an army outside. The gang, they run this prison on their own. They are . . ." He searched for the right words. "They are the people you would least want to anger in the entire world."

"MS-13," Evan said. "Mara Salvatrucha."

Benito closed his eyes against the words, as if they held an evil spell.

"It is the most dangerous country in the world," Benito said. "For a young man, there is nothing but gangs and violence. A hand grenade, it sells for one dollar there. When Xavier was born, we came here for a better life." Now tears fell, cutting tracks down his textured cheeks. "But it turn out they came, too."

"And Xavier joined them?"

"He hasn't been initiated yet," Benito said. "I know this from my friend. His son, he is one of them. There is still hope."

"Initiated?"

"Blood in, blood out. You kill to get in. They kill you before they will ever let you leave." Benito wiped at his cheeks. "I am running out of time."

"Where is the gang's headquarters?"

"I don't know."

"Where do I find Xavier?"

"I don't know. We fought last week. He run away. I haven't seen him since. I lost my wife, and now I can't lose him. I promised her. When she was dying, I promised her I would take care of him. I did my best. I did my best."

"I don't understand," Evan said. "What do you want me to do?"

"Don't let them make my boy a killer."

"No one can make someone a killer." The words were out of Evan's mouth before he saw the irony in them.

"Yes," Benito said. "They can. They will."

The philosophical point was lost on Benito and not worth arguing.

"I promised I would meet with you," Evan said. "But there's nothing I can do here."

"Please," Benito said. "He is a good boy. Help him."

"I'm not a social worker."

"You can convince him."

"Convincing people isn't part of my skill set."

Benito walked over into the kitchen and pulled a photograph off the refrigerator, the magnet skittering across the floor. He returned to Evan, held up the picture in both hands.

Evan looked at it.

It had been taken at a backyard barbecue, Xavier in a wife-beater undershirt and too-big olive-green cargo shorts, a tilted beer raised nearly to his mouth. Raw-boned but handsome, clear brown eyes, carrying a trace of baby fat in his cheeks despite the fact that he was twenty-four. His smile made him look like a kid, and Evan wondered what it felt like for Benito to watch this human he raised transform into a confusion of opposing parts, menacing and sweet, tough and youthful.

Had Jack felt that way about Evan?

He's the best part of me.

"When he lose his mother," Benito said, his hands trembling, "he lose his way. Grief makes us do terrible things."

Evan saw himself in the pest-control shop in Portland, his foot pinning a man's chest, shotgun raised, the wreckage of a hand painting the floor red.

He gritted his teeth and took the photo.

38

Steel Bones

The construction workers drifted away from the site, heading upslope where an old-fashioned roach coach competed with an upscale food truck featuring Korean tacos. Three vast parking lots had been torn up to make way for a low-rent retirement community, which was portrayed in idyllic watercolors on the massive signage. Pinning down the southern end of the six-acre drop of cleared land were the steel bones of a five-story building, the first to go vertical in the new development. It backed on the high wall of the 10 Freeway, making it an oddly private spot in the heart of the city.

Which made it useful for Evan's purposes now.

A yellow tower crane was parked haphazardly among piles of equipment and supplies. Cement mixers and steel pedestals, hydraulic torque wrenches and bolts the size of human arms.

Way up above, the workers reached the trucks, their laughter swept away by the wind. And then there was only stillness and the white-noise rush of unseen cars flying by on the other side of the freeway wall.

A wiry man with orange hair darted into sight, shoving a wheelbarrow before him, his muscular arms shiny with sweat. He reached a mound of copper plumbing pipes and started loading them into the wheelbarrow, shooting nervous glances at the workers upslope.

Evan stepped out from between two Porta-Potties and came up behind him.

"Excuse me," Evan said.

The man started and whirled around, a length of pipe gripped in one fist. He looked street-strong, his muscles twitching from uppers, which would make him stronger yet. He had a face like a pug's—underbite, bulging eyes—and his complexion was pale and sickly.

"The fuck you want?"

"A couple of answers."

They were in the shadow of the freeway wall, and not a soul was in view all the way up to the trucks above. No one could see them down here.

A fine place to steal copper.

"You're local," Evan told the man. "Clearly you've cased the place, timed the workers. I have a few questions I need answered by someone who lives here."

"I'm gonna give you two seconds to walk away. Then I'm gonna cave in your fucking head."

The man inched forward. Evan did not move.

"Your first instinct is to escalate," Evan said. "That shows me you're a punk."

The man ran his tongue across jagged, rotting teeth. "Why's that?"

"Because you've spent your life around people it's feasible to escalate against."

"I'm not some West Coast pussy, okay? I'm from Lowell, Mass, bitch. I grew up street-fighting with boxers who—"

Evan daggered his hand, a basic *bil jee* finger jab, and poked him in the larynx.

The man's windpipe spasmed. His mouth gaped.

The man dropped the pipe, took a step back, sat down, and

leaned over. Then he lay flat on his back. Then he sat back up. His mouth gaped some more. Then he managed to suck some oxygen in with a gasp. He coughed and then dry-heaved a little.

Evan waited, staring up the erector-set rise of the structure. From the fourth floor, you could see Benito Orellana's house. From the fifth you'd be able to see most of Pico-Union. For all the crime, this was a small neighborhood. Intimate. People who lived on these streets would know things.

The man finished hacking and drew in a few deep lungfuls of air. "Fuck, man," he said, his voice little more than a croak. "What'd you do that for?"

"To speed up the conversation."

The man still couldn't talk, but he waved his hand for Evan to continue.

"MS-13," Evan said. At this the man's eyes darted up to find Evan's. "I need to know where their headquarters are here."

"I can't tell you that, man."

Evan took a step forward, and the man scrambled back, crab-walking on hands and heels until his shoulders struck the top flange of an I-beam. Evan shadowed his movement.

"Wai-wai-wait. Okay. *Okay.* I'll tell you."

He cowered against the steel, Evan standing above him.

He kept one hand clamped over his throat, the other raised defensively. "Just lemme catch my breath first."

39

Visions of the Occult

A reinforced steel door gave the first indication that the abandoned church was not what it seemed. The half dozen men on guard outside, smoking and bickering, were a more obvious second. Their heads were shaved, their faces and skulls covered with tattoos. Devil horns on foreheads. The numbers 1 and 3 written in roman numerals rouging each cheek. Dots in a triangle at the corner of the eye, showing the three destinations for Mara Salvatrucha members after they're recruited—hospital, prison, or grave.

To a one, the men wore Nike Cortez sneakers, blue and white for the flag of their home country. One shirtless bruiser had the monkeys of lore inked across his torso—see no evil, hear no evil, speak no evil.

Evan walked past on the far side of the street, then cut around the block and took his bearings. The church was north of Pico along the 110 Freeway, surrounded by buildings in steep decline. A textile plant. A bodega with plywood replacing the glass of one front window. Graffiti everywhere, covering Dumpsters, parked cars, walls. On the corner a shrine of flower wreaths and sanctuary candles remembered a young boy who peered out of a framed school picture with bright, eager-to-please eyes.

A street vendor hawked knockoff Nikes on a ratty bedspread, the swooshes positioned suspiciously low. They, too, were blue-and-white Cortezes, fan paraphernalia for residents who wanted to be seen rooting for the home team.

Evan headed up an alley and scaled a fire-escape ladder to the roof of a crack house. He walked across the rotting shingles toward the spire rising from the neighboring building and crouched by the rusted rain gutter, peering through a shattered stained-glass window into the church below.

The pews had been shoved aside, gang members congregating in the nave. A pistol on every hip, submachine guns leaning in the corners, at the ready. They weren't a gang.

They were an army.

The men exchanged rolls of cash, sorted baggies of white powder, collected from street-worn hookers. Electronic scales topped table after table like sewing machines in a sweatshop. Pallets of boxed electronics lined the far wall, fronted with heaps of stolen designer clothes. A hive, buzzing with enterprise.

Evan searched the milling crowd for Xavier. The tattoos were overwhelming. Pentagrams and names of the dear departed. Crossbones, grenades, dice, daggers, machetes. And words—words in place of eyebrows, blue letters staining lips, nicknames rendered across throats in Old English letters. Other tattoos coded for crimes the men had committed—rape, murder, kidnapping.

Their rap sheets, inked right on their faces.

Xavier was nowhere to be seen.

A broad-chested man descended from the sanctuary, and the body language of the others changed. Everyone quieted down, their focus drawn. The man had MS in a Gothic font on his forehead, showing him to be a high-ranking member; it was an honor to display the gang's initials above the shoulders. But that wasn't what drew Evan's attention first.

It was his eyes.

They were solid black.

For the first time in a long time, leaning over the eaves of the crack house, Evan felt a chill. It took a moment for him to recalibrate, to pull himself out of visions of the occult.

The man had tattooed the whites of his eyes.

He had a lean, lupine face, a crucifix running down the bridge of his nose, unfolding its wings across his cheeks. Twinned rows of metal studs decorated his cheeks, and his lower lip bore shark bites, double-hoop piercings on either side. Block letters spelling FREEWAY banded his chin like a drooled spill of blood.

Freeway hugged one of his lieutenants, a hand clasp to shoulder bump, and headed out. The army parted for him.

Benito's words came back to Evan—*They are the people you would least want to anger in the entire world*—and he shivered against the wind.

Walking along the edge of the roof, Evan watched Freeway clang out through the steel door. The guards quieted instantly and stepped aside. Evan mirrored Freeway's movement from above, walking along the rim of the roof as Freeway turned the corner.

A few men threw heavy-metal devil's-head signs at him from the alleys, their fingers forming an inverted *M* for the gang name. Freeway did not return the signs.

When passersby saw him coming, they averted their eyes and stepped off the sidewalk into the gutter to let him pass.

Still no sign of Xavier.

Freeway entered the bodega. Through the remaining window, Evan saw the store owner stiffen. He scurried over and turned the sign on the front door to CLOSED.

Freeway walked through the aisles, grabbing items off shelves, and disappeared into a back courtyard without paying. The owner waited a few moments, catching his breath, and then followed.

Evan's RoamZone rang, the piercing sound startling him. He hadn't noticed how tense he'd grown while watching the gang leader.

The burner cell's number registered in the RoamZone's caller ID.

Evan answered, "Go."

Joey said, "I cracked it."

Evan took in a breath of crisp rooftop air.

"You'd better get over here," she said. "It's worse than we thought."

40

Enhanced Interrogation

Candy pulled the Audi through the side gate, released Tim Draker from the trunk, and marched him in through the rear door. She stayed five feet behind him, pistol aimed at the back of his head. She'd zip-tied his hands at the small of his back, but you couldn't be too cautious. Not with an Orphan.

Draker stepped into the living room, blinking as his eyes adjusted to the gloom. Mattresses covered the windows and walls, soundproofing the space. An array of implements were spread out on a drop cloth. Across the room stood Charles Van Sciver, his log-thick arms crossed.

Candy couldn't help but smirk a bit when she saw Draker sag at the sight of him, as if someone had put slack in the line.

Van Sciver stared over the ledge of his arms, one eye sharp and focused, the other dilated, a dark orb. "Let me tell you what we know," he said. "Jack Johns has long been aware of the directive from above to neutralize washouts, dissenters, Orphans who tested high-risk for defiance. But the shadow file? He knew of its existence before I did. And he knew it was only a matter of time before I got my hands on it. So he reached out to anyone he could and hid those people any way he knew how. He got to a few before we got to him. You were one of them. After you left the Program, he helped you hide. He also took care of the asset you'd recruited for me. David Smith. Twelve years old. Now thirteen."

Van Sciver paused, but Orphan L gave no reaction.

At the mention of the boy, Candy felt cool air across the back of her neck. An uncomfortable sensation, like when she thought about that alley outside Sevastopol, Halya Bardakçi with her baby-giraffe legs and that almond-shaped face. East Slavic through and through, beautiful and alluring, cheaply had and cheaply dispatched. After she'd been stabbed in the neck and dumped in the back of the car, she was still alive. Rattling against the hatch as she bled out.

Van Sciver took a step toward Draker. "We know Jack hid the boy here in Richmond. We know that you helped him before you went to ground. I want to know where the boy is."

Draker said, "Even if I did know anything about this, why would you want the boy? You think he can lead you to X?"

"No," Van Sciver said. "I think he can bring X to me."

Draker said, "I don't know anything about this."

"Is that so," Van Sciver said.

The men regarded each other solemnly.

Then Van Sciver took a step back and tapped on the wall lightly with his knuckles.

A moment later Thornhill entered from the next room. He was holding the turkey baster. He walked a casual arc in front of Van Sciver.

"Enhanced interrogation," Thornhill said, with that broad, easygoing grin. "It's such a well-considered term. Gotta hand it to the Agency. They do know their marketing." He gazed into the middle distance, tapping the baster in his palm. "You know another one I like? Rectal rehydration. It sounds so . . . therapeutic." His stare lowered. "When your intestines are all swollen up with fluid and you get a steel-toed boot in the gut, do you have any idea how much it hurts?"

Draker said, "I do."

"That's just the start," Van Sciver said. "Have a look around."

Keeping her gun raised, Candy watched Draker take in the items arrayed on the floor.

There were padlocks and plywood.

Nylon ropes and boards of various lengths.

A decline bench and jugs of water.

Mattresses and drop cloths.

Duct tape and a folding metal chair.

A sheen of perspiration covered his face now, and it was no longer a fake-addict sweat. He lifted his head again. Set his jaw.

He said, "Let's get to it, then."

41

Borrowed Time

Joey chewed her thumbnail, leaning over Evan's shoulder as he sat before the Dell laptop, staring at a list.

Five names.

One of them was Joey Morales.

Morales. All this time he didn't know her last name. He'd been unable even to get her full first name out of her.

The hillside crowded the back windows of the safe house, shadows making the interior dismal. That ever-present moisture had taken hold in the trapped air, turning the place dank. It smelled of microwaved food and girl's deodorant. Evan ran his eyes across the screen once again.

"So much encryption," Evan said, "for five names."

She paused from chewing her thumbnail. "Not just five names. It's a list of people in the Program who were associated with Jack in some way. Look." She shouldered him aside, taking over the keyboard. When she hovered the cursor above the top name, a hidden file appeared. She clicked it, and a host of images proliferated.

"This guy? Jim Harville? He was Orphan J. One of the original guys. Jack was his handler way back when. It says it was Jack's first Program assignment."

Evan scanned the files. "How the hell did Van Sciver get his hands on this? This is intel that isn't supposed to *exist*." He scrolled down the page. "And it's from channels *outside* the Orphan Program. Look here. See, this is NSA/CSS coding."

"What does that mean?"

"It means someone else in the government is watching Van Sciver and the Program—keeping tabs. Van Sciver didn't oversee this intel collection, and he doesn't control it."

"Well," Joey said, "till he *got* control of it."

Dread crept into Evan's stomach, digging in its nails. Van Sciver's cryptic comments looped through his head once again: *You have no idea, do you? How high it goes? You still think it's about me and you.*

Evan said, "What happened to Orphan J?"

"They caught up to him in Venice." She brought up a crime-scene photo of a man lying in a flooded piazza, the back of his head blown off. Another red spot bloomed below one of his shoulder blades. Blood ribboned the water around him. The picture had been taken moments after he was shot, a cell-phone snap.

Evan noted the time stamp on the photo. "Van Sciver's updating the initial files, building on the intel pieces he got his hands on. He's taken these five names and turned them into active hit missions."

"That's right. Like Orphan C." She brought up a picture of an older man, half in shadow, moving through the concourse of a shopping mall in Homewood, Alabama. He was dressed shabbily, toes showing through one of his sneakers. "Now look at this." She'd dug up an article about an unidentified homeless man murdered beneath a freeway ramp in Birmingham. A picture from a local shelter accompanied the article, showing the man at a soup kitchen.

Evan sank back in the chair. "That's why Jack was in Alabama. He knew this was coming, that this file could leak."

"And that's why he found me," Joey said. "Why he moved me to Oregon and hid me."

Evan stared at the name, bare on the screen: *Joey Morales.*

"It's beyond creepy." Joey slid the cursor over her own name, and a surveillance grab from a 7-Eleven security camera popped up, showing her walking through the aisles, baseball hat pulled low. But the angle was sufficient to capture her face. It was dated nearly a year ago, an address listed in Albuquerque. Same faded NSA/CSS stamp at the bottom of the page.

"This is from a week after I took off from Van Sciver," Joey said. "But it was enough to get them on my trail. And lead them here."

She tapped another link, and zoom-lens surveillance photos of the Hillsboro apartment populated the screen. Joey through a rear window, brushing her teeth. Joey shadowboxing, no more than a silhouette in the unlit apartment. Joey in the open doorway, casting a wary eye as she paid for a take-out order. She minimized the windows, exposing a report beneath that listed sixty-three nodal points of facial recognition and the same Oregon address that Jack had scrawled on his truck window right before he'd been forced aboard that Black Hawk and lifted sixteen thousand feet in the air.

"You were right," Joey said. "They had someone sitting on me. Waiting for you."

Evan looked at the remaining two names.

"Tim Draker," he said. "Jack told me about him. Orphan L. He was one of Van Sciver's guys until they fell out about a year ago. Is he dead, too?"

"Probably," she said.

Evan put his finger on the trackpad, targeted Draker's name. A streetlight camera had caught him exiting an anonymous drug-rehab center in Baltimore ten months ago. The imagery featured the NSA/CSS stamp.

A newer surveillance photo caught Draker smoking outside a facility in Bethesda, Maryland. It was dated November 28, two days ago, the time stamp showing 8:37 P.M. Minutes before Evan had blasted through the door of the pest-control shop, killed everyone inside, and taken the laptop. Van Sciver's update must have just come in. This second photo had no stamp or coding of any kind.

"The NSA intel put Van Sciver on the trail of drug-treatment places," Joey said. "From there it was only a matter of time."

Evan stared at the date on that surveillance photo and knew in his gut that Draker was lost.

"Which means that we're down to one little Indian," Joey said.

Evan stared at the last name: *David Smith*. Moved his fingertip a few inches. The ghost file opened.

A photo of a twelve-year-old boy. A birth certificate. A file painting a familiar story, various foster homes in various poverty-stricken counties. And then it showed a recruitment report from two years ago, listing Tim Draker as David's handler.

Evan looked for more information, but there wasn't any to be had. "That's it?"

"That's it."

"Won't Van Sciver have found him by now?"

"There are 33,637 people named David Smith in the country," Joey said. "And believe me, with how well Jack's been stashing people? The kid ain't using that name anymore." She jabbed a finger at the screen. "These people are hidden as well as it is possible to hide someone. Everything I know—hell, everything *you* know about being invisible? We learned from Jack. So I think Van Sciver's still searching for this kid. I think he's chasing him down now. And if we don't find him first, he's gonna kill the kid like he killed everyone else."

Evan stood up. Laced his hands at the back of his neck and breathed. "All this . . ."

Joey completed the thought. "All this is because of you."

He looked at her.

"Van Sciver's killing his way to you right now," she said. "All of us—these five names and however many more Van Sciver doesn't have yet? We're *all* on borrowed time."

"How do we help that kid?" Evan said.

"We find him."

"We can't compete with Van Sciver's resources. I have access to databases, but he's at a whole other level."

"You're right." Joey was chewing her thumb again, drifting

behind the table, her eyes intense. "When it comes to David Smith we have an absence of data."

"Right," Evan said. "How do you look for an absence of data?"

"Deep-learning software," she said. "Believe me, that's what Van Sciver's using."

She looked over at Evan, saw that he wasn't following.

"It's machine learning using advanced mathematics," she said.

"That doesn't help."

She leaned over the table, peering at him from above the laptop screen. "It finds patterns you don't even know you're looking for." She took another turn around the table, passing behind Evan. "Between the name David Smith, potential fake names befitting a thirteen-year-old white kid, facial characteristics, his birth-certificate information, physical developmental changes, purchase patterns for foster kids fitting his analytics, past locations, receipts, meds, and thousands of other factors we're not aware of but can be extrapolated from on the basis of that thin file"—she jabbed a finger at the screen—"let's say that there are five billion combinations of data. Being conservative."

"Conservative."

"Yes. Without a machine learning system, it would be impossible to correlate all that data, let alone zero in on David Smith under his new name in his new hiding place."

"Okay," Evan said. "So what's the best way for us to do that?"

She paused long enough to flick a smile his way. "Someone who knows where he is—"

"—and a hammer," Evan said. He stood up. "Seriously, Joey. Can we break into somewhere that has these capabilities and run the data?"

"No. This kind of processing takes time. Days even."

"What equipment do we need?" he said.

"A pile of hardware," she said. Mutual exasperation had given the discussion the tenor of an argument. "And like, say, a shit-ton of common graphics-processing unit chips. The mathematics involved in machine learning take advantage of the massive parallelism of the thousands of cores in those things. We'd need giant-ass GPU arrays, computer towers stuffed full of graphics cards, linked together with a high-speed InfiniBand network, running at eighty gigabits and—." She stopped, looked at him. "More stuff I'd explain to you if I thought you could understand."

"So how do we do that? Right now?"

"Raid the computer-graphics lab building at Pixar." She studied his expression. "Joking."

Frustration mounting, he drifted over and leaned against the couch. The cushions and pillows had been rearranged for her to sleep there, a T-shirt balled up for a pillow.

He stared across at an old-school photograph of David Smith on the screen. He wore a dated bowl cut and a collared three-button shirt with a frayed shoulder. Lank blond hair with a cowlick parting his bangs, hazel eyes, pleasingly even features. His gaze was lifted from the camera, as if the photographer's last directive had caught him off guard. He looked lost. They always did.

"I'm not gonna let Van Sciver get to that kid," Evan said. "So give me an answer for how to find you what you need to figure this out."

"It's complex shit, X," she said. "It's not like we can just drive through a Best Buy. Your average person doesn't have—"

She stopped, mouth slightly ajar. She bowed her head, pinched her eyes at the bridge of her nose.

"Joey?"

"Don't talk."

"Joey—"

She held up a hand. He silenced. She stayed that way for thirty seconds. Thirty seconds is longer than it sounds.

And then, with her face still buried in her hand, she said, "Bitcoin mining."

"What?"

"You do bitcoin mining." She lowered her hand, and her face held something more than joy. It held triumph. "No government regulation, no oversight."

"Yes."

"Which means you have a 2U rackmount computer bay."

"Two of them."

Borrowed Time

Her eyes were shining. "I could kiss you. Figuratively. Each rack has sixteen graphics cards. At four chips per card and 2,048 cores per chip, that gives us 8,192 graphics cores per card. We have thirty-two cards, which makes"—she closed her eyes again, her lips twitching—"262,144 graphics cores." She looked up. "That's a lotta horsepower."

"So I can just use my bitcoin-mining setup?"

"No." Her irritation flared again. "Everything has to be reconfigured."

Evan looked at the Snickers wrapper on the kitchen counter, the T-shirt pillow on the couch. "Pack up your stuff," he said.

"What? Why?"

"I just came up with a new Commandment."

At this her eyebrows rose. "A new Commandment? What is it?"

" 'Don't fall in love with Plan A.' "

42

Undone by Target

Joey stood in the great room of Evan's penthouse in Castle Heights, staring at the tall ceiling, her mouth gaping. After the places she'd lived, it probably seemed like the Serengeti to her.

Watching her, Evan felt discomfort beneath his skin, an awareness of his posture, how he was holding his arms. He could count on his fingers the number of people who had been inside 21A, and not one of them had known Evan's real identity.

"By bringing you here, I am giving you my absolute trust," he said. "Trust I have given no one before. Ever."

Joey was taking a pass through the kitchen, trickling a finger across the countertops, the island, the Sub-Zero, like a housewife at an open house. But at his words she paused and looked over at him. The weight of the moment was potent enough that it quieted the air between them.

"What if I don't deserve it?" she said.

"If you didn't deserve it, I wouldn't give it to you."

"This place," she said. "It's like something made up."

"What did you expect?"

"Judging by your taste in motels and your lovely safe-house decor, I thought you lived in . . . I don't know, a shoe."

"A shoe."

"Yeah. But this? This is like a Louboutin."

"What's that?"

"A fancy shoe they talk about on TV."

"Oh."

"Where do I stay?" She looked around. "I guess I could sleep on the dumbbell rack."

He hadn't thought about it. "There's a couch in the reading loft."

"The reading loft. Of course."

He pointed at the steel spiral staircase. "Full bathroom, too."

She gestured tentatively. "May I?"

"Yes."

She twisted up the stairs and disappeared.

Another human. Out of sight. Inside his place. Doing whatever humans did.

He looked over at the vertical garden. It looked back. He wondered if the plants were as uncomfortable as he was.

"This might be a very bad idea," he told them.

He thought again of David Smith in his frayed school shirt and swallowed his own discomfort.

After a moment Joey came back downstairs, running a hand along the curved handrail as if she wasn't sure it was real.

"Is it okay?" he asked.

"It is," she said, "more than okay."

"Let's get to work."

"Okay. Quick question: Where are the extra sheets? And pillows?"

He looked at her.

"Like for guests," she said.

"Guests," Evan repeated. He gave a nod. "We'll figure that out later."

Joey turned to the east-facing windows, gawking at downtown in the distance. The discreet armor sunshades were raised, the glass tinted. She took a step closer. The entire wall was transparent. At least in one direction.

She said, "You can see into so many apartments from here."

Evan said, "Yes."

She set her palms against the Lexan pane. He made a note to wipe off the smudges later.

"Did Jack teach you about the Mangoday?" she asked.

"Genghis Khan's cavalrymen."

"Yeah." She laughed, her breath clouding the glass. "He said they were the first elite special-operations force. They fought without fear, beyond the limits of the human body. Know how Khan trained those warriors?"

"Built a regimen based on starving wolves."

"Yeah," she said. "The hungrier a wolf is, the braver and more ferocious he gets."

"You're saying that's what we are."

"Yes. That's what we are. And this place? This place looks like the home of someone who's always hungry."

"For what?"

She looked back at him, her hair flicking over one shoulder. Her hands remained on the window. "For everything out *there*."

Evan broke off her stare, heading down the hall to the master suite. "Let's get to work," he said again.

He could hear Joey jogging to catch up. He opened the door and stepped into his bedroom. She crossed the threshold and halted.

"Um," she said. "Your bed is floating."

"Yes."

"You have a bed," she said. "That floats."

"We've covered that."

"Why?"

Evan blinked at her. "Can we please just get to work?"

She looked around. "Where?"

When they stepped through the hidden door into the Vault, Joey actually gasped. She circled the cramped space, checking the equipment, noting the monitors. "Is this . . . ? Am I in . . . ? This is heaven."

She picked up Vera II in her glass bowl. "Cute."

"Put her down."

"Her?"

Before he could respond, Joey spotted the 2U rackmount computer bays and beelined over to them. "Good. Good. This is good." She checked the setup. "You already have an InfiniBand cable, so you're not entirely useless, but we have to pick up some basic Cat 6 cables."

"This is a state-of-the-art system. Why do we need Ethernet cables?"

"What we're building? It's basically a bunch of graphics cores tied together. We need to hook up the machines, and the best way to do that is using plain old GigEthernet." She studied his blank expression. "People today. You know how to work everything, but you don't know how anything works."

She breezed past him, heading out. "Come on. Let's go to Target."

"Target?"

"Yeah, we can grab the cables there. Plus, I need stuff."

"Like what?"

She faced him, filling the doorway. "There's no soap. Or shampoo. Or conditioner. Or sheets. Or pillows. And I need some other stuff."

"I can get it for you."

"Girl stuff."

Oh.

"Target it is," he said.

Red signs blared 50-percent-off discounts. A kid stutter-stepped past, trying on a pair of sneakers still connected by a plastic loop while his mom shouted, "How's the toe? Is your heel slipping?" A cluster of girls modeled sunglasses, checking themselves out using their iPhones as mirrors. A stern-looking father was saying, "Read the ingredients. There's no food in food anymore." A husband and wife were having a heated debate over detergent. "No, the *lavender* scent is the one that gives you the rash!"

Evan stood frozen in the wide aisle of the second floor next to Joey.

She did a double take at his stunned expression. "You okay?"

A worker wheeled a pallet piled with jumbo diaper packs, nearly clipping Evan's knee.

He swallowed. "I'll wait outside," he said.

Evan stood in the parking structure just past Target's sliding glass doors, breathing the night air, catching his breath. Brimming shopping carts rattled past concrete security posts, shoved by flustered parents in sweatpants. Evan kept his hand near his hidden pistol and his eyes on the circuslike surroundings. Parking disputes proliferated. Car horns blared. Remote-controlled minivan doors wheeled open. By the shopping-cart rack, kids fought over coin-operated kiddie rides.

Exclamations crowded in on him.

"—not gonna buy you a toy every single time we go to the—"

"—I was already backing up! I saw the reverse lights before I was past the—"

"—not the kind your mom uses, thank God, or the powder room would smell like the potpourri Olympics—"

And then, mercifully, Joey was there. A few bags dangled from either arm. She was regarding his face with what seemed to be amusement.

"Let's go," Evan said.

"Aw. You're all uncomfortable like. That's so cute."

"Joey."

"Okay, okay."

"You got the cable."

She smacked her forehead with her palm. "Shoot. I knew I forgot something."

He felt himself blanch. "Really?"

"No." She smiled that luminous smile. "Of course I have it. Let's get you away from the big, scary discount retailer."

He gritted his teeth and turned for his truck.

That's when he saw Mia and Peter climbing out of Mia's Acura.

He stiffened. Turned back to Joey. Her face grew serious. "What's wrong?" she said.

"Nothing. Someone I can't see here. Now. With you. Go there. Pretend you're . . . I don't know, playing on the ride."

Joey took in the coin-operated kiddie rides. "The choo-choo train?"

"Yes."

"I'm sixteen."

"I don't care."

"You don't know much about kids, do you?"

He put a hand on her side, hustled her toward the front of the store.

"Lemme help you out," Joey said. "I'll just pretend I'm playing on my phone."

"Okay. Fine. Good."

From behind him he heard Peter's raspy voice: "Evan Smoak!"

He turned as Mia and Peter approached.

Mia said, *Evan?*

"Hi."

"Wait. I didn't think you knew where Target was. Lemme guess—there's a sale on vodka?"

"Just needed some . . . things."

"Is that girl with you?"

"Who?" Evan said. "No."

Joey remained immersed in her phone. For all their collective tradecraft, the ruse was paper thin.

"Yes," Evan said.

Joey looked up, gave a flat smile.

Mia's head cocked. Her gaze narrowed—the district-attorney gaze.

"She's sort of . . . my niece." Evan said. "Staying with me awhile. She needed some . . ." He winced. "Girl things."

"I thought you didn't have any family."

"She's the closest to it, I guess. Kind of a . . . a second cousin's kid. Through a marriage. But then her parents died. Sort of thing."

He took a deep breath, let it burn in his lungs. All his impeccable training, living his cover, becoming his legend. Never a skip, a stutter, a false move. And here he was.

Undone by Target.

"It's a weird situation," he conceded.

"Indeed." Mia's glare softened only when she looked over at Joey. "Hi, honey. I'm Mia."

Joey came over and shook her hand. "Joey."

"Super-cool girl name," Peter said.

Mia's ringtone sounded—the theme to *Jaws*, which signaled a call from her office. She said, "Gimme a sec," and stepped away to answer.

Peter blinked up at Joey and Evan. "I was in class today? And Zachary had an egg-salad sandwich? And he took it out right before lunch, and it totally smelled like someone farted, and it was on my side of the classroom, so everyone was looking at *me*, and what am I gonna say? Like, 'I didn't fart'? I mean, who believes that?"

Joey looked over at Evan. "Does it have an off button?"

Standing a few paces away, Mia paused from her call to glance across at Evan, her displeasure clear.

Was she mad at him for having a sort-of niece? For being at Target? For not introducing her to Joey right away?

Peter had cornered Joey against the choo-choo ride. "What's your favorite color?"

"Matte black," Joey said.

"What do you like to play?"

"I don't."

"What do you like to play *with*?"

"The entrails of children."

"What's an entrails?"

"Guts."

"Really?"

"Yes."

Peter processed this behind his charcoal eyes. "Really they're the guts, or really that's what you like to play with?"

Evan cleared his throat. "Time we get going."

Mia wrapped up her phone call and stepped back over, ruffling Peter's hair.

"Mom," Peter said, "Evan Smoak's niece person is *awesome*."

"I'm sure she is," Mia said. "It was nice to meet you, sweetheart."

She shot Evan a look that seemed to code for murderous rage, put her arm around Peter's shoulders, and disappeared through the automated glass doors.

Evan exhaled a breath he hadn't known he was holding.

"Well played," Joey said. "Orphan X."

Evan started for his truck, not caring if she kept up.

43

Grown-Man Problems

Evan crouched gargoyle-still at the edge of the crack-house roof, peering through the shattered stained-glass window into the church next door.

Freeway sat on the carpeted steps leading to the altar, a king on his throne. A series of kids entered, each slinging a giant zippered bag at his feet. They looked no older than Evan had been when he was taken from the Pride House Group Home.

Indoctrination—best started early.

The boys entered the church with swagger, but all signs of confidence evaporated by the time they reached the altar. They kept their heads lowered, afraid to meet Freeway's stare.

It was a hard stare to meet.

He cast his solid black eyes over his spoils, giving a faint nod to dismiss each child in turn.

Evan scanned the other gang members clustered in groups around the tipped-over pews, searching for Benito's son. But just like this morning, there was no sign of Xavier. Evan had left Joey in the Vault, hard at work reassembling his hardware. The thought of her in his sanctuary unattended, pulling cords and handling his possessions, caused a discomfort that was physical, insects running beneath his skin. He couldn't think about it right now and keep his focus.

And given that he was surveilling the deadliest gang in the world, he needed to keep his focus.

A commotion at the front door drew his attention. A group of women were corralled into the vestibule. Bright makeup, torn stockings, stiff hair. One was missing the heel on one of her red pumps.

Evan was surprised to see that the men who had brought them were not yet visibly tattooed. Lowly initiates, given the lowly task of gathering the street girls.

As the newcomers shuffled through the sporadic falls of light from the overheads, Evan caught a glimpse of a young man in the back. Xavier. He helped herd the women through the nave toward the altar. He wore a flannel shirt with the sleeves ripped off, the gym-toned muscles of his shoulders rippling.

The women rotated before Freeway, handing over wads of crumpled cash that he eyed and then handed to one of his lieutenants. None of the women met Freeway's eyes. Several seemed to hold their breath until they scurried away to gather by the bags of stolen goods.

The last woman in the group, the one with the broken heel, stepped forward and offered up a few tattered bills. Freeway examined them, clearly unimpressed, then let them fall to the floor.

He stood up.

The effect was momentous.

All the gang members went on point. The woman started trembling, shaking her head. Evan couldn't hear her beg, but he knew that she was.

Freeway gripped her chin, squeezing her cheeks. He flicked out a straight razor, which gleamed in the low lights from the altar.

She cowered, her back to Evan, blocking his view. Freeway towered over her. Evan saw his hand rise and move across her face, two strokes, each punctuated with an artistic flair of the wrist. Her shriek was clear, even above the wind rushing over the rooftop.

Evan moved his gaze away from Freeway and the woman, finding Xavier. Benito's son stood in the half shadows to the side of the altar. The other gang members looked on with reverence, but Xavier's arms were crossed uncomfortably. His face was pale, blood draining away, and his blink ratio had picked up—signs of an anxiety reaction.

Freeway flung the woman aside. She landed on her belly with her torso twisted, bringing her face into view, and Evan saw the damage inflicted on it.

Matching slashes across both cheekbones, red streaming like war paint.

Freeway hadn't just punished her. He'd marked her for life.

She sat on the floor, hands cupping her face, blood spilling through her fingers.

All the gang members were watching Freeway.

Except Xavier.

He watched the woman.

Noteworthy.

Freeway dismissed his men with a flick of his fingers and headed back to the sanctuary to attend to other business. They streamed out. Xavier got halfway to the door, then paused and looked back at the woman, on her knees before the altar.

His jaw shifted with discomfort. He looked torn.

One of the other initiates said something to him, and he snapped to, exiting the church.

Evan watched the woman unsteadily find her feet. The other women finally broke out of their paralyzed trance by the bags of stolen goods and rushed to her. The injured woman collapsed into their embrace.

They helped her out a side door.

Evan backed away from the edge of the roof.

He caught up to Xavier four blocks north as he said good-bye to two fellow initiates at a street corner. Xavier peeled off, heading up a dark block alone, ignoring the invitations of the street girls: "Hey, Big Time, wanna get warm?"

Evan shadowed him, keeping a half block back. After a quarter mile, Xavier cut up the stairs of a dilapidated house that had been diced into a fourplex. From across the street, Evan waited and watched. Most of the windows of the apartment building behind him were open, *banda* radio music and the smell of charred meat streaming out.

After a moment a light clicked on in a window on the fourplex's second floor.

Evan waited as a low-rider scraped past and then he crossed the street. The front door's lock was a joke, the metal guard bent back from previous B&Es. Evan pulled out his fake driver's license, used the edge to slide the turtle head of the latch bolt level with the plate, and eased the door open.

He took the stairs up to a tiny entry between two facing doors. The floorboards, though battered, looked to be oak, probably the surviving section of a study from before the house had been carved up.

He rapped on the door to the left.

Footsteps. The peephole darkened.

"Who the hell are you?"

"Your father sent me."

"Go away. You're gonna get yourself hurt."

"Open the door."

"You threatening me, fool? Do you have any idea who the fuck I am?"

"Why don't you open the door and show me?"

The door ripped open. Xavier stood there holding a crappy .22 sideways, like a music-video gangsta. His head was drawn back, chin tilted up.

Evan stood there staring at him over the barrel.

Xavier cleared his throat, then cleared it again. Apparently the gun was not having the effect he'd hoped.

"Your throat's dry," Evan said.

"*What?*"

"Because you're scared. Adrenaline's pumping. It acts like an antihistamine, lessens the production of saliva."

Xavier stuck the muzzle in Evan's face.

Evan regarded it, a few inches before his nose. "You're holding your weapon sideways."

"I *know* how to hold my *goddamn*—"

Evan's hands blurred. He cranked Xavier's arm to the side, snatched the .22 neatly from his grasp, and stripped the gun. Pieces rained down on the floor. Slide, barrel, operating spring, magazine, frame.

Xavier stared at his empty hand, the red streak on his forearm, his dissected gun littering the floor around his Nikes.

"Step inside," Evan said.

Xavier stepped inside.

Evan followed, sweeping the remains of the gun with his boot, and closed the door behind him.

It was a run-down place, sleeping bag on the floor, flat-screen TV tilted against the Sheetrock, floor strewn with dirty clothes. An add-on kitchenette counter bulged out one wall—hot plate, microwave, chipped sink. An exposed snarl of plumbing hung beneath the counter like a tangle of intestines.

"Life's not fair," Evan said. "Your mom died. You pulled a dumb move and joined a gang. The wrong gang. I think you're scared. I think you're in over your head and you don't know how to get out."

The sleeveless flannel bulged across Xavier's chest. Veins wiggled through his biceps. He was a big kid.

"You don't know nuthin' about me, *baboso*."

"You sure you want me to work this hard to like you?"

"I didn't ask you to come here."

"No. Your father did."

"That old man don't know shit."

Evan cuffed him, an open-handed slap upside the head. The sound rang off the cracked drywall. When Xavier pulled his face back to center, his cheek bore the mark of Evan's palm.

"Make whatever choices you want to fuck up your life," Evan said. "But don't disrespect that man."

Xavier touched his fingertips to his cheek. Down near the elbow, his forearm had a tattoo so fresh it was still scabbed up. An elaborate *M*—the beginning of *Mara Salvatrucha*.

He stared at Evan. And then he nodded. "Okay."

"We both know you're not a killer," Evan said. "But they're gonna make you one."

Xavier's face had softened, his cheeks full, his eyes as clear as in that photograph Benito had shown Evan. He looked much younger than twenty-four.

"I know," he said.

Evan recalled the tremble in Benito's voice when he discussed his son. This boy he'd taught to put on socks, ride a bike, throw a baseball. Countless hours of loving attention, late nights and early mornings, and then your son winds up here, with grown-man problems. And you—the father who once held the answers to the universe—you're helpless.

A memory flash penetrated Evan's thoughts: *Jack squinting into a handheld camera at sixteen thousand feet, wind whipping his hair.* Evan banished the image.

"I *am* out of time," Xavier said. "I swore the oath." He held up his arm, showed the tattooed *M* at his elbow. "It's written on my flesh. Know why they do that?"

"It's good business," Evan said. "Once you're marked, you can't ever join another gang. They own you. Which means they can treat you however they want and you can never leave."

Xavier looked confused at that. "It's to show allegiance. For *life*, get it?"

"Nothing is for life. We can remake ourselves in any image we want. One choice at a time."

"I'm out of choices."

"We're never out of choices."

"Know what their motto is? *'Mata, viola, controla.'*" Xavier snarled the words, suddenly the raw-boned gang member again. "'Kill, rape, control.'"

"*Their* motto," Evan said.

"What?"

"You said, 'Their motto.' Not 'Our motto.'"

"I already robbed a store. I stole stuff from a truck. They make me collect from the *putas*. I brought one in today, and she . . . she got her face cut open." Xavier put his hand over his mouth, squeezed his lips. "I'm already one of them."

"Does anyone beyond this chapter know about you?"

"No. I'm just getting jumped in."

"No one back in El Salvador?"

Xavier's eyes shone with fear. "No."

"You've got one chance to get out."

Xavier paced a tight circle by the kitchenette, came back around to face Evan. "Why do you care?"

"I got into something when *I* was young," Evan said. "I'll never get out. Not clean. You still can."

"What about them?"

"I can handle them."

"You can't do that. No one can do that."

Evan just smiled.

Human engineering had been part of Evan's training, no less than savate and marksmanship and endurance. He had been trained to disappear into a crowd and fire three-inch clusters at a thousand yards. He had been trained to intimidate, to make grown men afraid. He could convey breathtaking menace when he had to.

So he just smiled, and that was enough.

"You decide what you want," Evan said. "And call if you need me: 1-855-2-NOWHERE. Say it back to me."

Xavier said it back.

Evan started for the door. He'd stepped over the stripped gun and set his hand on the doorknob when Xavier spoke.

"This girl today, her face . . ." Xavier lowered his head. "There's a point you cross where you can't get yourself back. Where you can't find, I don't know. Redemption."

"Every choice holds redemption."

Xavier lifted his eyes to meet Evan's. "You really believe that?"

Evan said, "I have to."

44

Running the Same Race

A half-drunk glass of milk rested on the kitchen island. Standing just inside his front door, keys still in hand, Evan stared across the open stretch of floor at it.

There was filmy white residue up one side where Joey had sipped.

He unlaced his boots and then crossed to the kitchen.

He picked up the glass. It had left a circle of milk on his counter. Beside it a pile of crumbs rested next to a torn-open box of water crackers. The inside bag was left open, the crackers exposed to the air, growing stale.

What kind of feral creature ate like this?

The rest of the world could be filthy and chaotic and lawless. But not in here. After scraping through the underside of society, Evan needed to return to order.

He washed the glass by hand, dried it, and put it away. There was another glass missing from the cupboard, an empty spot leaving the left row incomplete. It occurred to him that two glasses had never been out of the cupboard at the same time. He nudged the clean glass into place, the set of six still down one soldier.

Maybe she needed another glass upstairs.

Maybe that's how people did things.

Joey could have used more time with Jack. The Second Commandment: *How you do anything is how you do everything.*

Evan put away the box of crackers, swept the crumbs into his hand, dumped them into the garbage disposal. He waved his hand beneath the Kohler Sensate touchless kitchen faucet, turning on the clean blade of water so he could run the disposal. There were smudges on the polished chrome.

Who touched a touchless faucet?

He cleaned off the smudges and then got out a sheet of waxed paper and used it to wipe down the chrome. It prevented water spots. When he was done, he sprayed and paper-toweled the counter, washed his hands, got an ice cube for Vera II, and headed across the great room and down the brief hall.

The door to his bedroom was open.

He didn't like open doors.

The bedspread on his Maglev floating bed was dimpled where someone had sat and not bothered to smooth it back into place.

The door to his bathroom was open.

One of Joey's sweatshirts was tossed on the floor by the bathmat. One corner of the bath mat was flipped back. With a toe he adjusted it.

The shower door was rolled open.

The hidden door to the Vault left wide.

He took five deep breaths before proceeding.

"Joey," he said, stepping into the Vault. "The milk glass—"

The sight inside the Vault left his mouth dry. An adrenaline antihistamine reaction.

Various monitors had been yanked off the wall and rearranged on the floor, data scrolling across them. The computer bays had been dissected, torn from their racks. Cables snaked between hardware, connecting everything by no evident design.

Joey lay on her back like a car mechanic, wearing a tank top, her sleek arm muscles glistening with sweat. She was checking a cable connection. She rolled over and popped to her feet.

"Check this shit out!"

"I am. Checking this shit. Out." Evan picked Vera II up off the floor, nestled an ice cube in her serrated spikes, and eyed her accusatorily: *I left you in charge.*

Joey breezed past him, using her bare foot to swivel a monitor on the floor so she could check the screen. The scent of girly soap tinged the air, lilac and vanilla, anomalous here among the weapon lockers and electronic hum.

She laced her fingers, inverted her hands, cracked the knuckles. "You are looking at a beautifully improvised machine learning system—262,144 graphics cores devoted to a single cause. Tracking down David Smith."

Evan figured maybe he could forgive the milk. And the crumbs. And the smudges on the faucet.

He set Vera II back on the sheet-metal desk. She was now the only item in the Vault in the proper place.

He looked at the open door to the Vault and the rolled-back shower door beyond and bit his lip. Managed the words "Good job."

She held up a hand, and they high-fived. "At least now you and Van Sciver? You're running the same race."

45

A Bit More Incentive

Listening to all that gurgling and choking wore on a man.

Van Sciver set down the watercooler jug of Arrowhead and wiped his brow. Enhanced interrogation was hard work.

Orphan L was strapped onto a decline bench, a soaked towel suctioned onto his face. Van Sciver had been pouring a steady stream of fresh springwater through the towel and into L's sinuses, larynx, oropharynx, trachea, and bronchi. It didn't actually reach the lungs.

It just felt like it.

Van Sciver had been waterboarded as part of his training. All Orphans were.

The discomfort almost defied explanation.

He'd been drownproofed as well, and by comparison that was a breeze. Bound at the bottom of a swimming pool, breathing in water, the head going hazy as in a dream.

But this felt like having a water hose opened up inside your skull. The more you gasped for air, the further you pulled the towel into your mouth, an octopus clutching your face, expelling an endless stream of fluid through your orifices.

Van Sciver nodded at Thornhill, who lifted the soaked towel from Orphan L's face. For a time Draker bobbed on the bench, bloodshot eyes bulging, mouth guppying. He didn't make a noise.

When the upper respiratory tract filled, water obstruction prevented the diaphragm from expanding and contracting to produce a suitable cough. You had to fight to earn your oxygen.

Five seconds passed as Draker contorted, clutching for air.

Thornhill gazed down at him with empathetic eyes. "I feel you, pal. I feel you."

Candy leaned against the mattress cushioning the far wall, examining her fingernails. They looked freshly painted. Aubergine.

Van Sciver looked back at Thornhill, nodded again. Thornhill undid the straps around L's chest and thighs, and L rolled off the bench onto his side. When he struck the floor, the impact loosed his lungs, his head seeming to explode with jets of water.

He coughed, heaved, coughed some more.

Thornhill slapped his back a few times, encouragingly. "There you go."

Draker whipped up in a violent sit-up, driving his forehead at Thornhill's nose. Thornhill wheeled back, nearly losing his footing. He looked down at his shirt, darkened by the spray from Draker's wet hair. Draker's head butt had missed him by inches.

"Whoa, cowboy," Thornhill said, seemingly pleased by the effort. "That was close."

Draker collapsed flat on the floor, spent.

Van Sciver squatted beside him, knees cracking, alert. "The boy," he said. "The address."

Draker gagged a few times. Van Sciver pressed two fingers into his solar plexus, and Draker vomited a water-clear stream so calmly and steadily that it was like opening up a tap. When he was done, he took a few seconds to catch his breath. Then he said, "What boy?"

"Right on," Candy said. "Gotta admire the grit."

She peeled herself from the wall and tested the plywood covering one of the rear windows. It was screwed in tight but not too tight. Which was perfect.

Van Sciver said to Thornhill, "Get the dog collar on him."

The next technique, walling, was a Guantánamo Bay special. There they slipped a rolled towel around the detainee's neck and used it to slam him into a semiflexible wall. The shoulder blades hit first, snapping the head. The collision gives off a sound like a thunderclap, like someone banging cymbals in the space between your ears.

Van Sciver preferred to use an actual collar. They were more durable, and his meaty hand never slipped. Plus, when he squeezed tight, he'd found, his knuckles shoved into the larynx, which added a bit more incentive.

Thornhill secured the collar around L's neck.

"I don't know about this, bud," Thornhill said, flashing that carefree smile. "I was you, I'd just talk to the man."

L lay there, curled on his side, panting. Van Sciver knew how it was. You had to enjoy the respites when you had them.

It was tough work from both sides.

"Get him on his feet," Van Sciver said.

Draker was limp, his muscles turned to rubber. Candy and Thornhill juggled him up, holding most of his weight. He'd gone boneless.

Van Sciver seized the collar and dragged L over to the plywood sheet.

"Where is David Smith?" he asked again.

Draker couldn't speak, not with the knuckles, but he managed to shake his head.

"Damn," Van Sciver said, setting his feet and firming his grip. "You must really love the kid."

46

Menu of Even More Specialized Services

At the edge of an industrial park in Northridge, through two security doors, past a warehouse humming with painters and restorers reviving valuable vintage movie posters, down a back hall tinged with the smell of petroleum and cleaning surfactants, Melinda Truong stood in a dark-walled photography room, fists on her slender hips, regarding Evan and Joey.

Melinda wore yoga pants and spotless robin's-egg-blue Pumas that looked to be limited-edition and pricier than most vehicles. Straight black hair fell to her waist, which was gripped by a construction worker's tool belt that required freshly awled holes so it could be cinched tighter in order to accommodate her tiny frame. The tool belt held an Olympos double-action airbrush, a 000 paintbrush, and various sizes of X-Acto blades, their grips padded with pink tape to discourage her workers from borrowing them.

She was the sole woman in the building. She was the owner of the operation. She was also the finest forger Evan had ever encountered.

HELLBENT

One of her fists still gripped a retrofitted insecticide atomizer. Evan had interrupted her at the wet table over a *Frankenstein* one-sheet from 1931, cleaning a coffee spot off Boris Karloff's cheek. The restored movie poster would be worth hundreds of thousands of dollars. But that was far less than she made from her menu of even more specialized services, conducted here in the photography room with its windows blacked out, ostensibly to prevent reflections during shooting.

She ticked the muzzle of the atomizer at Evan now, a show of mock annoyance. "It's a good thing I have a secret crush on you," she said. "Or I'd never let you stomp in here with this child and interrupt my work."

"I'm not a child," Joey said.

Melinda did not look over at her, instead holding up a finger. "Seen but not heard."

Joey zippered her mouth.

Evan said, "Apologies."

Melinda swept back her hair, a gesture that was at once concise and sensuous, and tapped her cheek. Evan complied, moving forward to kiss it. At the last minute, she turned, catching his lips with hers.

She lingered a moment, then shoved him back. "Now. What do you want?"

Joey took this in speechlessly.

"I need full papers for her," Evan said. "Multiple IDs, Social, driver's, birth certificate, travel visas, a backstopped history. Make her eighteen."

"When?" Melinda asked.

"Now."

Melinda looked over at her cobbler's bench covered with etched metal plates, embossing tools, letterpress drawers holding passport stamps. She sighed.

Then she snapped her fingers at Joey, who stepped forward as if jabbed with a cattle prod. Melinda took her chin in hand and turned her face this way and that, assessing the face behind which she was going to build a new identity.

Menu of Even More Specialized Services

"Beneath all that scowling and the weird haircut, you are a very pretty girl," she finally conceded.

"Thank you."

"It's not a compliment. It's an observation."

The sounds of the workers in the warehouse carried up the hall—suction tables roaring, equipment racks wheeling from station to station, exclamations rising above the din.

Melinda released Joey's face, picked up a phone on the desk next to an AmScope binocular microscope, and punched a button. Then she said in her native tongue, *"Be quiet. I can't hear myself think in here, and when I can't think, I act on emotion."*

The entire building silenced immediately. She hung up the phone. When she turned back, Joey's mouth was slightly ajar.

Joey said, "You are one badass lady."

"Yes, honey," Melinda said. "I am sure."

47

The Language of Comfort

Before bed Evan showered, dressed, and then finished tidying up the Vault as best he could. He found himself trying to align the monitors on the floor and finally gave up.

Chaos was a small price to pay when a thirteen-year-old boy's life was at stake.

He stared at the various progress bars, all that software dredging the Web for signs of David Smith. "Work faster," he said.

As he turned to leave, a rapid-fire series of beeps chimed from the alarm system, indicating an intruder at the windows or balconies. His eyes darted around the Vault, searching the rejiggered monitors to find the one holding the appropriate security feed. He was two steps to the gun locker when he found it and relaxed.

On the screen he watched a dark shape hover outside his bedroom window, bumping the glass.

He sighed and stepped through the shower and the bathroom.

As he emerged into his bedroom, Joey entered from the hall. She was wearing pajama bottoms and a loose-fitting T-shirt.

She said, "What's that noise?"

Evan pointed to the window. An old-fashioned diamond kite flapped in the breeze, smacking against the pane.

Peter's bedroom was directly below Evan's, nine floors down.

"A kid's kite?" Joey said.

Evan opened the window and pulled in the yellow kite. Scotch-taped to the underside was a small freezer bag containing a folded piece of loose-leaf paper and a pencil. He removed the note.

Written in blue crayon: *"Yor neece person is cool. Does she like me to? Check Yes or No. Your friend, Peter."*

There were two boxes.

He handed the note to Joey.

She took it, her eyebrows lifted with surprise. As she read, a microexpression flickered across her face, gone as soon as it appeared. But he'd noticed. She was charmed.

When she looked up at Evan, she'd fixed her usual look of annoyance on her face. "Nice spelling," she said.

He handed her the pencil.

She sighed. "Seriously?"

"Seriously."

She held the paper, tapped the pencil against her full bottom lip, as if contemplating. Then she checked a box, not letting Evan see. She stuffed the note back into the little bag and tossed the kite out the window.

It nose-dived from view.

He knew which box she'd checked.

She said, "You going to bed?"

"After I meditate."

"Meditate?"

"Jack never taught you?"

"No. We didn't have time for that." She wet her lips, seemingly uncomfortable. "Why do you do it? Meditate?"

He contemplated. Jack had taught him this along with so much else. How to find peace. How to embody stillness. How to punch an eskrima dagger between the fourth and fifth ribs, angling up at the heart.

It struck Evan anew how Jack had embodied so many contradictions. Gruff but gentle, insistent but patient, firm but hands-off. He'd known how to raise Evan, how to push him further than he wanted to go.

Joey was watching him expectantly, slightly nervous, a flush rouging her smooth cheeks. Her question touched on the intimate, and that put her out over her skis.

He remembered telling her that Jack was the first person who ever really saw him. *If no one sees you, how can you know you're real?*

Evan tried to imagine how Jack might see Joey.

"Your Rubik's Cube," he said. "From the motel—the shape-shifter with all the different planes?"

She nodded.

"You told me that to bring it into alignment you solve one dimension at a time. Shape first, then color. You said you look for the wayward pieces, find the right patterns to make them fall into place. Right?"

"Right."

"That's what meditating is. Finding the wayward pieces of yourself, bringing them into alignment."

"But *how*?"

He went to the bed, sat crossed-legged, pointed to a spot opposite him. She climbed on the bed and mirrored his pose. Hands on thighs, straight spine, shoulders relaxed.

"What now?" she asked.

"Nothing."

"So I just breathe?"

"Yes."

"Just sit here and breathe?"

"If you want to."

Her eyes shone.

"Focus on your breath," he said. "And nothing else. See where it leads you."

He let his vision loosen until Joey blurred into the wall behind her. He tracked the cool air through his nose, down his windpipe, into his stomach. Beneath his skin he sensed a turmoil, blood rushing through his veins. His thoughts cascaded, cards in a shuffled deck. Jack in free fall, a cup of half-drunk milk, the frayed shoulder of David Smith's shirt—

Joey's words slashed in at him. "This is fucking stupid."

He opened his eyes fully. She'd come out of the pose, slumping forward, at once lax and agitated. He watched her twist one hand in the other.

"Okay," he said.

"We done?"

"Sure."

She didn't move. She was glaring at him. "It didn't do anything."

"Sure it did," Evan said. "It led you to anger."

"That's real useful. What am I supposed to do with that?"

"Ask yourself, what are you angry about?"

She got off the bed and stood facing the door. He watched her shoulders rise and fall with each breath.

"Do you want to talk about it?" he asked.

She wheeled on him. "Why would I tell you shit? You'll just leave anyways. Once you're done with me and we're done with this." She gestured to the bathroom and the Vault beyond. "Won't you."

"That doesn't sound like a question," Evan said. "It sounds like a dare."

"Don't turn it around on me," she said. "It's the only outcome."

"There's never only one outcome."

"Yeah? How do you see it working? You're gonna what? Drive me to school? Bake muffins for the PTA? Help me with my fucking calculus?"

"I think you'd probably help me with *my* calculus."

She didn't smile, barely even paused. "You're just using me, like everyone else. You don't get it. Why would you? You *chose* to leave the Program. You don't know what it's like to just be *discarded*. They threw me away 'cuz I was"—her lips pursed as she searched out the word—"deficient."

"You're not deficient."

"Yeah, I am. I'm broken."

"Then let's unbreak you."

"Oh, it's that easy."

"I'm not saying it's easy. I'm saying it's worth doing. Pain is inevitable. Suffering is optional."

"Easy for you to say." She wiped her nose, pigging it up. She looked so young. " 'Suffering is optional.' "

"Yes. Let me know when you're ready to start giving it up."

"I'll fucking do that."

She walked out.

He listened to her feet tap up the brief hall and across the great room, the noise echoing off all those hard surfaces. Then her steps quickened up the spiral stairs to the loft.

Evan exhaled, rubbed his eyes. When he was younger, Jack had always known what to do. When to answer, when to leave a silence for Evan to fill.

Right now Evan felt adrift. He reached for the Commandments, but none were applicable. He'd gone down the path and arrived at a wall.

Another Jack-ism: *When you're at a wall, start climbing.*

There he was, still pushing Evan from beyond the grave. Maybe that's what this final mission was, placing Joey in his care, a living, breathing package. Maybe this was just another version of Evan walking behind Jack, filling his footsteps.

But this was a different trail. It required different rules. Evan thought of the Post-it note Mia had put up in her kitchen: *Remember that what you do not yet know is more important than what you already know.*

He tried to meditate again. Couldn't.

Then he was up on his feet. Moving silently along the hall. Keying off the alarm and slipping out the front door. Riding the elevator down, still pinching his eyes, shaking his head.

Walking up to 12B. Raising a fist to knock. Lowering it. Walking away. Coming back.

He tapped gently.

There. Now it was too late.

The door opened. Mia looked at him.

"I know you're angry with me," he said.

"You told me you didn't have any family," she said. "Either you lied before. Or you're lying now."

"It's complicated."

"Save it for Facebook."

She started to close the door.

"Wait," he said. "Joey is from . . . my job. I'm trying to help her. And I wanted to keep you and Peter clear of anything that's related to that world. So I tried to cover it up. I was dumb enough to think I was being helpful."

"That's even more alarming."

He held his arms at his sides, considered his blink ratio, resisted an urge to put his hands in his pockets. "I'm not sure what you would have preferred me to do. At Target."

"God," she said, more in wonderment than anger. "You really don't get it."

"No."

"How about 'Hey, Mia. I'm in an unusual situation and I'm not sure how to talk about it with you.' How 'bout that? Actually just being honest and trusting that we'll figure it out? Was that an option you considered?"

He said, "No."

She almost laughed, her hand covering her mouth. When she took her hand away, the smile was gone. "Okay. I'm angry. But I've also learned not to trust my first reaction. To *anything*. So. Let me figure out my second reaction before we talk about this anymore."

She started to close the door again.

"I need advice," he said, the words rushed.

It had taken a lot to get them out.

"Advice?" she said. "You're asking me. Advice."

"Yes."

She pulled her head back on her neck. Blew out a breath. Let the door swing open.

Evan entered, and they sat on her couch. She didn't offer him wine. The door to Peter's bedroom, bedecked with Batman stickers, a pirate-themed KEEP OUT! sign, and a Steph Curry poster, was open a crack. The heat was running, the condo toasty, a few candles casting gentle light. They were grapefruit-scented—no, blood orange. A burnt-red chenille throw draped one arm of the couch. So many things he would never have thought of, the things that turn a house into a home. They were words from a different language, the language of comfort, of knowing how to belong.

Evan kept his voice low. "How do you talk to a teenage girl?"

"Very carefully," Mia said.

"That much I've figured out."

"She seems like a great kid. But she's had it tough."

"How do you know that?"

"I'm a DA." Mia set her hands on her thighs, tilted her head to the ceiling, took a breath. "Don't push. Just be there. Be steady."

He thought of Jack's even pace through the woods, not too fast, not too slow, his boots stamping the mud, showing Evan where to step.

Mia pointed at Evan. "When it comes to kids, honesty matters. And consistency. That's why I thought, you know, you coming for dinner once a week. It's important to Peter. Stuff like that's a clock they set their hearts to."

He nodded.

"At the end of the day, all they *really* want to hear?" Mia ticked the points off on her fingers. "You're okay. You're gonna be fine. You're worth it."

He nodded again.

She studied him. "What?"

"*Are* they worth it?"

"Yes." She rose to see him out. "But if you're ever gonna say it, you better believe it first." She shot him a loaded look. "Because she'll know if you're lying."

Evan paused halfway up the spiral stairs to the loft. A clacking sound carried down to him, and it took a moment for him to place it: Joey working a Rubik's Cube. Lifted halfway between floor and ceiling, he had a glorious view of downtown. The shimmering blocks, a confusion of lights shivering in the night air. Overhead, the cube clacked and clacked. He heard Joey cough.

It felt so odd to have another moving body in the penthouse.

He continued up to the reading loft. Joey sat in a nest of sheets on the plush couch. Her head stayed down, that rich chocolate hair framing her face, which was furrowed with concentration. The cube, smaller than the previous one he'd seen, was a neon blur in her hands.

She'd turned off the overheads and pulled the floor lamp close. It was on the lowest setting, casting her in a dim light. The cube alone was bright, glow-in-the-dark colors radiating in the semi-dark. Chewing-gum green and fluorescent yellow. Safety-cone orange and recycling-can blue.

At the second-to-top step, he halted.

"Can I come in?" he asked.

"It's your place."

"But it's not my room."

Her deft fingers flicked at the cube, transforming it by the second. "Yeah it is."

He noticed that she wasn't trying to solve the cube; she was alternating patterns on it, the colors morphing from stripes into checkers and back to stripes.

He said, "Not right now."

Her eyes ticked up. But her hands still flew, the cube obeying her will. It changed into four walls of solid color, and she let it dribble from her hands into her lap.

"Yeah," she said. "You can come in."

He stepped up into the loft and sat on the floor across from her, his back to one of the bookshelves. By her knee was the worn shoe box from her rucksack. The lid was off and one of the greeting cards pulled out. She'd been reading it. He remembered what Mia had told him and said nothing.

Joey picked up the cube. Put it down again.

"It's such a big world," she said. "And I don't want it to just be this."

"What?"

"My life. My whole life. Kept here, kept there, always hiding. There's so much out there. So much I'm missing out on."

Evan thought of the burnt-red chenille throw draping the arm of Mia's couch.

"Yeah," he said. "There is."

Joey put the card into its envelope, slipped it into her shoe box, and set the lid back in place.

"Sorry I'm such an asshole sometimes," she said. "My maunt used to say, *'Tiene dos trabajos. Enojarse y contentarse.'* It doesn't really translate right."

Evan said, " 'You have two jobs. Getting angry. And getting not angry again.' "

"Something like that, yeah."

He said, "You were close to her."

Joey finally looked up and met his stare. "She was *everything.*"

It was, Evan realized, the longest they had ever held eye contact.

Joey finally slid off the couch. "I have to brush my teeth," she said.

She lifted the shoe box from the sheets. As she passed, she let it drop to the floor beside him.

A show of trust.

She entered the bathroom, closed the door. He heard water running.

He waited a moment and then lifted the lid. A row of greeting cards filled the shoe box from end to end. He ran his thumb across the tops of the cards. The front two-thirds had been opened. The rear third had not.

And then he understood.

He felt his chest swell, slight pressure beneath his cheeks, emotion coming to roost in his body.

He used his knuckles to push back the stack so he could lift out the first card. Flocked gold lettering read:

It's your ninth birthday
A most happy day
A time to sing
And a time to play . . .

The Language of Comfort

He opened the card, ignoring the rest of the printed greeting. An iris was pressed inside, already gone to pieces. Familiar feminine handwriting filled the blank page.

My sweet, sweet girl,
The first one without me will be the hardest. I'm sorry I'm not there with you. I'm sorry I got sick. I'm sorry I wasn't strong enough to beat it. Let my love for you be like a sun that warms you from above.
Forever and always, M.

Evan put the card back. He flicked through the ones behind it.

New Year's. Valentine's. Easter. Birthday. First day of school. Halloween. Thanksgiving. Christmas.

He took a wet breath. Let the next set of cards tick past his thumb.

New Year's. Valentine's. Easter. Birthday. First day of school. Halloween. Thanksgiving. Christmas.

The last opened card was Thanksgiving, the one that had fallen out of her rucksack in the foot well of the stolen car yesterday.

He pulled out the one behind it, sealed in an envelope that said *"Christmas."*

He scrolled ahead, the labels jumping out at him. *"Easter."*

"Halloween."

"Your 18th Bday."

And then they stopped.

In the bathroom the sink water turned off.

He closed the shoe box, set it back on the couch, and returned to where he'd been sitting.

Joey emerged, wiping her face on a towel. She slung it over the couch back and sat again on the cushions and sheets. She noted the shoe box's return and then stared at her lap.

Finally she said, "That's when I went into the system."

"I'm sorry."

"The cards, they're gonna run out when I turn eighteen," Joey said. "Then what'll I have?"

He showed her the respect of not offering an answer.

"After I ran away from Van Sciver, that's where Jack found me.

Visiting her grave." She looked down, gave a soft smile. Her thick mane was swept across, the shaved side exposed, two halves of a beautiful whole. "He was smart like that. He knew how my heart worked."

Evan nodded, not trusting his voice. *Yes, he was. Yes, he did.*

After a time Joey slid down into the sheets and curled up, her head on the pillow. "I never fall asleep with anyone in the room," she said.

"Should I leave?"

"If you want to stay, it's fine."

Evan said, "I do."

He sat and watched the curve of her shoulder, the tousled hair on her cheek. Her blinks grew languorous. And then her eyes closed. Her breathing grew regular, took on a rasp.

He rose silently and eased from the room.

48

Something Akin to Pride

After checking the deep-learning software in the Vault before sunrise the next morning, Evan meditated, showered, and then walked down the hall to the kitchen.

Joey was up early as well, digging in the freezer, an ice pack in one hand, the bottle of Stoli Elit: Himalayan Edition in the other.

She heard him coming and looked over her shoulder. "Don't you have any frozen burritos or whatever?"

"Careful with that," Evan said, nodding at the Stoli. "It's three thousand dollars a bottle."

Joey appraised it. "Is it worth it?"

"No vodka is worth three thousand dollars."

"Then why do you have it?"

"What else am I gonna spend it on?"

She stared into the pristine white void of his freezer. "I don't know. Food."

He came around the island.

"Out of my way," he said.

———

Two eggs dropped in the frying pan with a this-is-your-brain-on-drugs sizzle. Joey sat on a stool, leaning over the island counter, chin resting on her laced fingers. Fascinated.

"You know how to cook?" she asked.

"I'd hardly call this cooking."

"How'd you learn?"

"Jack."

"You fit it in between drownproofing and close-quarters combat?"

"Yes."

"Mr. Humor."

The toaster dinged, and Evan flicked two pieces of sourdough onto a plate. "Butter?"

"Duh."

He buttered the toast and slid the eggs atop the two slices. "Go snap some parsley off the living wall."

"Living wall?"

"The vertical garden. There."

She walked over. "Which one's the parsley?"

"Upper left quadrant near the edge. No. No. Yes."

She tore off a piece, brought it over as he twisted pepper from the mill onto the sunny-side-ups.

He halved the sprig, laid a piece on each yolk. Then he set the plate before her, nudging it so it was precisely between knife and fork.

She stared down at the plate, not moving.

"What?" he said.

"Just appreciating it," she said.

"Eat."

She looked up at him, cleared her throat. "Thank you."

Before he could reply, a chime sounded over the wireless speaker system. His head snapped up.

"What's that?" she asked.

He was already heading back. "Software just hit on David Smith."

Something Akin to Pride

They stood side by side within the damp concrete walls of the Vault, staring at the monitors. The interconnected web of metadata on display was fascinating.

From the scant information on David Smith and a few photos, the software had made height and weight projections, assessed facial-structure changes, checked hospital intakes, flight and bus records, school registrations, and foster-home placements in targeted regions on the East Coast. These criteria correlating space, time, visuals, database entries, and events had been dynamically created so the machine would heuristically improve itself, learning as it went, ever evolving. Strange algorithms tracked online purchase orders, grouping vehicular-themed *Star Wars* Lego sets costing $9.95 or less, industrial-strength drain cleaner, bulk-ordered Little Hug Fruit Barrel drinks, Lavex Janitorial brown paper towel rolls, and dozens more items, narrowing the scope even further. These results were paired with Instagram photos and other social-media posts clustered around specific neighborhoods.

A YouTube video of a schoolyard fight at Hopewell High in Richmond, Virginia, posted in September of the previous year had caught a wink of a passing car in the background. Despite the midday glare off the passenger window, a freeze-frame had captured the ear of the boy in the passenger seat, which had been picked apart using precise distances and ratios, measuring the upper margin of the ear canal's opening to the tip of the lower lobe and the flap of the tragus. It gave an 85-percent probability that the ear belonged to their David Smith.

Two days previous a girl had been adopted out of McClair Children's Mental Health Center in Richmond's Church Hill neighborhood, opening a spot in what had previously been a steady forty-bed population. No new child showed to have been committed at the center since, the population seemingly remaining at thirty-nine. However, a bill from a local health clinic the following week showed a new patient-intake exam, and the number of flu shots administered the next month remained a steady forty.

A child taken into the center under a false claim of domestic violence would have been kept off the books.

The deep-learning software gave a 99.9743-percent likelihood that the mystery patient was the boy previously known as David Smith.

Joey jotted down the address, biting her lower lip, frowning with concentration. The light of the monitors played off her smooth cheeks. Evan watched her, feeling something akin to pride.

She caught him looking. "What?"

He said, "Nothing."

All you could hear was the man's panting.

Blood flecked the floor, the plywood over the windows, the mattresses on the walls. A molar rested on the plastic tarp. The room stank of vomit, body odor, and worse.

Two of the three Arrowhead watercooler jugs were empty. That was ten gallons of fluid forced through Orphan L's face holes.

Draker lay on the floor curled up in a ball. His head was ducttaped, a slit left open for the nostrils.

Van Sciver squatted, waiting.

Thornhill was balanced on his hands again, doing inverted push-ups.

The guy was the friggin' Energizer Bunny.

Candy had left to organize the freelancers Van Sciver had called up from Alabama. Things were about to get busy.

Van Sciver finally rose with a groan. He was feeling it in his back.

"Thornhill," he said.

Thornhill's boots hit the ground with a thump. He started unwinding the duct tape from L's head. As he did, a faint tinny music became audible, growing louder with each loop of tape unstripped. At last he got to the final layer, which he tore free, ripping out clumps of L's hair and splotching his flesh with broken capillaries. The Beats headphones adhered to Draker's head were now laid bare, Josh Groban blaring "You Raise Me Up" at top volume.

Thornhill turned off the music, tugged off the headphones. He stroked Draker's hair, pushing the sweat-pasted bangs out of his eyes.

"You did good," Thornhill said. "Better than Jack could have asked. But this will continue forever."

Draker managed a single hoarse syllable. "No."

"You know it's gotta go this way," Van Sciver said. "It is what it is and that's all that it is."

Draker squeezed his eyes shut and panted some more. He'd developed a tic at the top of his left cheek, the skin spasming, tugging the eyelid into a droop.

"Okay," Van Sciver said. "Get him back on the bench."

Thornhill started for the Arrowhead jug.

Draker began to sob.

Van Sciver held up a hand, freezing Thornhill.

This was the glorious moment right before they broke. He let Draker weep. The sound was gut-wrenching, dredged up from the depths.

Thornhill petted his hair. "It's okay," he said. "You did good. You did so good."

Draker keened and keened. Finally he quieted. Van Sciver waited for his breathing to slow. After all L had been through, he deserved a few moments of rest before the end.

Draker looked up through bloodshot eyes. "I'll tell you," he said. I'll tell you where he is."

49

Good Isn't Enough

"You missed him by an hour, Mr. Man," the charge nurse said.

A broad woman packed into navy-blue polyester pants and a billowing white nurse coat, she conveyed warmth and authority in equal measure. A sunshine logo on her coat accompanied equally cheery canary-yellow lettering, which read MCCLAIR CHILDREN'S MENTAL HEALTH CENTER.

Evan put away his forged Child Protective Services credential, flapping closed the worn brown billfold. The wallet, in addition to his frayed Dockers and Timex watch, were props that screamed Ordinary Guy on State-Employee Salary.

Tapping his clipboard against his thigh, he hurried to accompany the nurse as she ambled down the hall.

"Missed him?" Evan said. "What do you mean missed him? His caseworker visitation is overdue."

"Baby doll, the only things here that *ain't* overdue are the late notices on the bills. We are bailing out a rowboat with a Dixie Cup."

Good Isn't Enough

In one of the rooms, a kid was thrashing against the wall and bellowing. Two orderlies restrained him, one for each arm.

The nurse stopped in the doorway. "C'mon now, Daryl," she said. "Act like you got some sense in you."

The boy calmed, and she kept on.

A few perfunctory posters were gummed to the bare walls, tattered and ripped. Lichtenstein apple. Picasso face. A faded *Starry Night*. Stacked on a service cart were dining trays filled with half-eaten meals. Watery green beans. Cube of corn bread. Hard-crusted grilled-cheese sandwiches. The place smelled of industrial detergent, bleach, and kids of a certain age kept in close proximity.

Evan knew this place, knew it in his bones.

He cleared his throat as if nervously, adjusted his fake glasses. "You said I missed Jesse Watson?"

Joey's additional online machinations had confirmed that this was the name David Smith had been living under at the Richmond facility. Joey was outside now in the rented minivan, a block away in an overwatch position near the intersection.

The nurse paused and heaved a sigh that smelled of peppermint. "He ran away."

"Ran away? When?"

"Like I said, he was gone before seven-o'clock bed check. So call it a hour, maybe a hour and a half. Musta slipped out the back door during the commotion." Her mouth tweaked left, a show of sympathy. "Girl in six had a grand mal at mealtime."

Evan shoved his glasses up his nose, a cover for the actual dread he felt rising from his stomach into his throat.

She registered his concern. "We already filed the police report. I'm sorry, but it's in their hands now."

"Okay. I'll just do a living-conditions check and be on my way."

"We do the best we can do here with the state funds shrinking all the time."

"I understand."

"Do you?"

"I do."

She stopped and took his measure, the raised freckles bunching high on her copper-colored cheeks. Then she blew out a breath, deflating. "Look at us, acting like we on different sides. I'm sorry, Mr. . . . ?"

"Wayne."

"Mr. Wayne. I know you're just trying to do the best you can, too. I guess it's . . ." Her not-insignificant bosom heaved. "I guess I'm embarrassed we can't do better by them. I use my own salary for Christmas and birthday gifts. The director, too. He's a good man. But good isn't enough sometimes."

"No," Evan said. "Sometimes it's not. Which room was he in?"

"Fourteen," she said. "We group the kids with less severe conditions in the C Hall. We're talking ADHD, dyslexia, visual-motor stuff."

"And Jesse's condition was . . . ?" Evan flipped through the pages.

"Conduct disorder."

"Of course."

She waved a hand adorned with hammered metal rings. "C'mon, I'll walk you."

The walk took longer than Evan would have liked, but he held her pace. They passed a girl sitting on the floor picking at the hem of her shirt. Her fingernails were bitten to the quick, leaving spots of blood on the fabric.

"Hi, baby doll, be back for you in a second, okay?" the nurse said.

The girl turned vacant eyes up toward them as they passed. She had beautiful thick hair like Joey's, a similarity Evan chose not to linger on.

The nurse finally arrived at Room 14, knocked on the door once briskly, and opened it. The three boys inside, all around the age of thirteen like David Smith, lounged on bunk beds, tapping on cheap phones.

In another time, in another place, Evan had lived in this room.

"This is Mr. Wayne," the nurse said.

The oldest-looking kid shot a quick glance at Evan and said, "Lucky-ass us. Another social worker."

"Respect, Jorell, or I'll notch you down to red on the board again."

Evan asked, "Did any of you see Jesse Watson run away?"

They all shook their heads.

"He didn't talk about it before? No planning? Nothing?"

"Nah," Jorell said. "That fool was *bent*. For a skinny white boy? He was nails. Could fight like a mofo. He had things his *own* way."

"Jorell," the nurse said wearily.

It wasn't the first time she'd said his name like that. Or the hundredth.

"Where were you guys before bed check?" Evan said.

"Still in the caf," another kid said. "Mindin' our bidness. Jesse come back to the room early, do push-ups and shit. He say he gonna be a marine."

Evan stepped inside, pointed. "This his bunk?"

"The very one," Jorell said.

Jorell was a smart kid. Smart kids in places like this tended to have worse outcomes. A nice dumb boy could toe the line, graduate with C's, get a steady job at a fast-food joint, live to see thirty.

On the radiator by the empty lower left bunk rested a Lego version of a *Star Wars* rebel commanding a Snowspeeder. Evan recognized it from one of Peter's comic books. He picked it up. "This was Jesse's?"

"Yeah. Ain't that some white-boy shit?"

All three kids laughed, even the Caucasian one.

The charge nurse said, "You just dying for me to level you down tonight, ain't that so, Jorell?"

He silenced.

Holding the Snowspeeder, Evan stepped back to her, said quietly, "I'm guessing this was one of the gifts that came out of your salary."

She nodded.

Evan said, "It's probably the only thing in the world he has that's actually his."

Her mocha eyes held the weight of all forty lives she'd been charged with. "That's probably right."

"I doubt he'd run away and leave it behind."

"What are you saying, Mr. Wayne? The boy broke out. Happens all the time."

Evan set the Lego rebel back on the radiator and stepped toward the sash window. It rattled up arthritically. He leaned out, noted the fresh gouge marks in the paint on the sill.

"They usually break out from the outside?" he said.

The charge nurse came over and looked at the window, and her hand pressed against her neck. Seeing her expression, he regretted his phrasing.

"I'll call the police again," she said quietly.

The boys had silenced; even Jorell had sobered up.

Evan started for the door. "Like you said, it's in their hands now."

As he hustled out, he passed that girl in the hall, forgotten, picking at the hem of her shirt with bloody fingernails. In his mind's eye, he pictured Joey sitting in her place.

He blinked away the image, banishing it from his thoughts, and kept on.

50

The Best Hat Trick

Evan sat in the passenger seat of the minivan, the Virginia sun pounding the windshield. Joey had taken the news of David Smith's kidnapping stoically, though he'd noticed her fists whiten on the steering wheel as he'd filled her in.

"One hour," she finally said. "One hour earlier and we could've saved him."

"We don't know that he's dead," Evan said.

"Orphan J. Orphan C. Orphan L. All the other names on that file are dead. Except me. If Van Sciver kidnapped David Smith, he already killed him."

They stared up the block at the crumbling façade of the McClair Children's Mental Health Center. It radiated a kind of despair that resonated in Evan's cells. He thought of the boys he'd grown up with in Pride House. Andre and Danny and Tyrell and Ramón. Every so often Evan checked in on them from the safe remove of the Vault, searching them out in the databases. Danny was serving a dime for armed robbery at the Chesapeake Detention Facility, his third stint. Ramón had overdosed in a by-the-hour motel in Cherry Hill. Tyrell had finally managed to join the army, KIA outside Mosul on his first deployment.

Any one of their fates should have been shared by Evan. He was them and they were him.

Until Jack.

Searching for hope here on this block was hard, but Evan tried. David Smith was owed that much.

"If Van Sciver wanted him dead, why didn't they just shoot him in the room?" Evan said.

"Because that would be a big public thing," Joey said. "A runaway's just another story."

"When a kid gets killed in a neighborhood like this, it's not a big public thing. It's two lines of print below the fold. Everyone would think it was gang retribution. Remember, no one in the world knows who David Smith is."

"Except Van Sciver," Joey said. "And us."

Evan felt it then, the first ray of hope, straw-thin and pale, not enough to warm him but enough to lead the way. "The smart move isn't to kill him. The smart move is to use him for bait."

"So what do we do?" Joey asked.

"Swallow the hook. Let them reel."

"And if he's already dead?"

Evan stared at the sign above the security gate of the facility's front door. A number of the letters were smashed or broken.

He said, "It's a chance I have to take."

"That sounds less than strategic."

"The Tenth Commandment."

" 'Never let an innocent die,' " she quoted. "So where do we start?"

Evan took out the Samsung Galaxy cell phone he'd lifted off the dead man in Portland. He called up Signal, the encrypted comms software that led directly to Van Sciver. He was about to press the icon to call when he realized that his emotions around this place and these foster kids were infecting him, making him reckless.

He thumbed the phone back off.

"We need to gather more intel before I make contact," he said.

The Best Hat Trick

"There's an ATM at the gas station two blocks that way, facing the street. Maybe we can get the security footage, see what we see."

Joey made a sound in her throat. Unimpressed.

"What?"

"*If* they drove that route," she said. "*If* we know who we're looking for." She was leaning forward, straining the seat belt, seemingly peering up at the telephone wires overhead.

"You have a better suggestion?" Evan asked.

"As a matter of fact, I do." She pointed through the windshield. "See those streetlights?"

"Yes."

"They're not just streetlights." She reached into the backseat, retrieving her laptop. "Those are Sensity Systems lights. We're talking thermal, sound, shock, video—they continuously gather information and suck everything into the cloud." She ran her fingers through her hair, flipped it over so the shaved strip showed above her right ear. "'Member how Van Sciver got onto Orphan L?"

"A surveillance photo of him smoking."

"Taken from a streetlight," she said. "We're gonna use Van Sciver's game against him."

Evan stared at the streetlights, but they looked ordinary to him. "You sure those are the kind you're talking about?"

She gave him a look, then booted up her computer.

He said, "How can they afford something like that in a broke neighborhood like this?"

Her fingers were already working the keys in a fury. "Federal funding. It's part of the Safe Cities initiative. Detroit got a hundred mil off the government, and if Detroit can get it . . ." She glanced over. "You don't keep up on this stuff, do you?"

"No."

"The streetlights are all LED. The whole system gets paid for by the money cities save from the reduction in electricity costs. How 'bout that? A government plan that *isn't* a total cluster. Not that it started with the government. The software was developed to track foot traffic at shopping malls, see what stores people go into, what they look at, how they respond to sales announcements, coupons, all that."

"Can you hack it?"

She kept her head lowered, her fingers moving. "I'm gonna pretend you didn't ask me that."

He cast an eye toward the facility's front door. "The cops are gonna be here soon."

"Well," she said, "then it's a good thing I'm fast."

"Turn left up there. No, the *next* intersection. Good. Now run it straight for a half mile."

Evan was driving the minivan, Joey in the passenger seat, directing him through traffic and simultaneously hammering away at the laptop. He felt increasingly like her chauffeur, an observation that, he was chagrinned to note, Mia had once made in regard to Peter.

Evan was becoming just another suburban dad.

Joey had what looked like a dozen windows open on the screen. He risked a glance over. On one of them she seemed to be reviewing footage angled on the eastern flank of the McClair Children's Mental Health Center.

"Anything?" he asked.

"Patience, young Padawan." The laptop was humming. "Wait. You were supposed to turn left back there. Hang on." She popped another window to the fore, this one featuring a GPS map. "Go left, left, right."

He obeyed. Focusing on the road and the rearview mirrors rather than on Joey's active laptop screen took some discipline.

"Okay. Just—pull over here. We're in range."

He looked around. A fenced park. A courthouse. A McDonald's.

"In range of what?" he said.

She ignored the question. "Let's get you up to speed." She punched a button, swiveled the laptop on the minivan's roomy center console. Evan watched the exterior of C Hall, the image so steady that save for a few leaves blowing past and the sound of out-of-frame traffic it might have been a photograph.

At last a pair of shadows darkened the bottom of the screen. Two men approached the window of Room 14. One held a crowbar, the other a pistol lengthened by a suppressor. The guy holding the pistol moved aggressively, sweat glistening on his bald head. The men flattened to either side of the window.

Evan told his heartbeat to stay slow and steady, and it obeyed.

He didn't recognize either man; Van Sciver had sent more free-lance muscle. The gunman raised a black-gloved hand, his ridged, shiny skull gleaming as he did a three-finger countdown. The other guy jammed the crowbar beneath the sash window and slid it up. The bald man spun into the open frame, pistol raised, his mouth moving.

Issuing orders.

The streetlight sensor was too far away to capture the words, but a moment later David Smith appeared at the sill, holding his hands before him, showing his palms. He looked more shocked than scared. The bald man grabbed the boy's shirt and ripped him through the window. As he manhandled the kid away from the building, another figure emerged at the edge of the screen, her back to the camera.

Her face wasn't visible, but Evan recognized her form.

Orphan V.

Candy McClure pointed at the gunman, clearly issuing an admonition, and he lightened his grip on the boy. The freelancers kept David between them, hustling him away. An instant later the frame was as empty and serene as before.

The snatch-and-go had taken six seconds.

Evan looked at Joey across the console. "Seems like they want to keep him."

"Or kill him off site."

"No," Evan said. "You saw the way Orphan V spoke to that guy. Van Sciver wants the kid unharmed."

"Or *she* does. She might have to duke it out with Van Sciver."

"She can be convincing," Evan said.

Joey read something in his face and let the point drop. She leaned over, bringing up a freeze-frame of the men standing on both sides of the window before the break-in. Reference points littered their heads, a digital overlay.

"I go with Panasonic FacePro Facial Recognition," she said. "It's the best. Two for two."

"Two for two?"

"Fast *and* accurate. They use it at SFO."

"When do we get the results?"

"We have them."

Another window, another revelation. The two men, identified as Paul Delmonico and Shane Shea. Delmonico was the one who'd jimmied the window and Shea the gunman. Shea had a bony build, his forehead prominent, the grooves of his cranial bones pronounced on his shiny bald skull. Their records had recently been classified top secret, which put their backgrounds and training out of reach for the time being. Evan figured they were dishonorably discharged recon marines, Van Sciver's favorite source of renewable muscle. For now Evan and Joey had faces and names, and that was all they needed.

Next Joey pulled up a United Airlines itinerary she had unearthed. "They came in on a flight this morning from Alabama."

"Where Van Sciver killed Orphan C." And where Jack had plowed into the dirt from sixteen thousand feet.

"Right. And they rented this at the airport." *Click.* "A black Suburban. I know, inventive, right? License plate VBK-5976."

She paused to check if he was impressed.

He was.

"The same credit card was used to get another matching Suburban, license plate TLY-9443. So I'm thinking four men."

"Looks like it," Evan said.

"You know what ALPR is?" she asked.

"Automated license-plate recognition," Evan said, relieved to be back on familiar turf. "Police cruisers have sensors embedded in the light bars that scan the plates of all surrounding vehicles. They can swallow numbers eight lanes across on cars going in either direction up to eighty miles per hour. They process the plates for outstanding warrants in real time and store them for posterity."

"Gold star for the old guy," Joey said. "I already input the licenses into the ALPR system and coded the system to send me and only me an alert when one of the light-bar sensors picks up either Suburban. We're gonna use Virginia's Finest to track down these guys for us." Her grin took on a devious cast. "In more ways than one."

Evan followed her gaze up the street to the courthouse. It was a beautiful Colonial Revival building—weathered brick, white columns, hipped roof. A trickle of men and women scurried across the front lawn, some black, some white, some in suits, others in overalls, each of them moving with a sense of purpose. A sign in front read CRIMINAL GENERAL DISTRICT COURT.

"Oh," Evan said. *"Oh."*

Already Joey was pulling up the courthouse's private Wi-Fi network reserved for judges, DAs, and clerks. Hashkiller's 131-billion-password dictionary required only twenty-seven seconds to get her on. The Records Management System took two and a half minutes. And then there it was before them on the screen, glowing like a holy relic.

A bench warrant.

Evan and Joey smiled at each other.

"First move," Joey said. "Get the bad guys off the street. Or at least the two we have names for."

"You're kind of a genius."

"I agree with everything but the 'kind of.' " She wiggled her fingers in glee and then typed in a phony case record.

If the cops brought in the men, red-tape confusion would tangle them up for days.

"What should we have them arrested for?" Joey asked. "Home-grown terrorism is always good, gets the local constabulary all hot and bothered."

"Terrorism?" Evan said. *"Delmonico* and *Shea*?"

"You have a point."

"Let's make them pedophiles," Evan said.

She typed, her smile growing broader as she warmed to the idea. "And prison escapees."

"Who are also wanted for killing a police officer."

"That is *so* the best hat trick," she said. "It's like making a list for Santa."

She finished filling out the arrest warrant, issued a statewide

HELLBENT

BOLO, and fed the forms into the legal and law-enforcement machinery of greater Richmond.

Then she held up her palm.

He slapped it.

51

Push a Little More

Candy's back was on fire, but she granted her skin no concessions when on a mission. She refused to scratch it, even resisted tugging at her shirt so the fabric would rub against the ruinous flesh and soothe the burn. Candy had pulled Van Sciver into the hall of the safe house to talk to him privately.

Van Sciver was as unyielding a man as she'd ever encountered, but he was still a man, which meant she had a shot at getting what she wanted from him. He'd pulled his pistol out of his underarm tension holster.

An FNX-45 with a threaded barrel and holographic red-dot sights.

A lot of firepower for the skull of a thirteen-year-old.

"The hard part's over," Van Sciver said. "We have him now. X knows it or will soon enough. The kid's served his purpose."

Van Sciver's eyes twitched across the threshold to where David Smith sat on the decline bench, a pillowcase cinched over his head, hands pressed between his knees. He hadn't made a noise since

Delmonico and Shea had delivered him. The two men stood by the rear door, guarding it with M4s in case the skinny thirteen-year-old kid went Dwayne "The Rock" Johnson on them. The other pair patrolled the front of the house as if working perimeter duty at a presidential inauguration.

L's corpse had been removed, the spillage from his body more or less cleaned up, though the smell of vomit lingered.

Over in the kitchen, Thornhill stirred something in a pot, humming to himself. It smelled delicious and spicy, and Candy wondered where Thornhill was from, how he'd learned to cook and who for. It brought back a memory from high-altitude SERE training in her seventeenth year. She'd summited a tree-blanketed rise in the Rockies, nearly stumbling onto a family of four picnicking out of the back of their Range Rover. The mom had laid down a blanket, and there were sliced apples in bowls and cold fried chicken and thermoses of hot cider. The daughter was around Candy's age. Candy had hidden behind the tree line, staring down at the exotic sight before her, scarcely breathing lest she spook them. She'd remained long after they'd driven off, her boots embedded in a film of snow, trying to loose the tangle of emotions that had knotted up her throat.

Thornhill lifted the wooden spoon for a taste, smacked his lips at a job well done. In a holster snugged to his hip, he had an FNX-45 that matched Van Sciver's. He was so disarming that it was easy to forget how lethal he was. With Thornhill it was a pleasant conversation right up until the minute the bullet entered your brain.

Candy refocused on Van Sciver, keeping her voice low. "I'm saying let's not have a failure of imagination here."

"Which means what, precisely?"

"L took the kid out of circulation. And Jack kept him off the books after that. David Smith has got no real record—no files, no fingerprints, nothing. Aside from a few kids in a loony ward, no one knows his face." She paused for dramatic effect. Pursed her distractingly plump lips. "Which means he's a blank check."

Van Sciver's fair-complected face was mottled from the exertion of the past twenty-four hours, splotches of red creeping up from his shirt collar. That blown pupil was like a void. Candy felt that if she stared long enough, she might fall into it and keep tumbling.

She thought of the beautiful young woman locked in a car trunk in an alley outside Sevastopol. The rattle of her fists against the metal as she bled out. The scraping of her nails.

Candy shuddered off the thought, looked away from Van Sciver's lopsided gaze so he couldn't read anything in her face. The pillow-case fluttered in the spot where the boy's mouth was, the fabric pulsing like a heartbeat, surprisingly steady.

"L acquired him for you initially," she said. "Now you have your asset back."

"What if Jack Johns turned him?"

"Jack Johns only had him a few months before dumping him at that facility. Not enough to fully indoctrinate him. But the kid did get the benefit of Johns's training. Johns is good at that. Maybe the best."

Van Sciver gritted his teeth, neither confirming nor denying. "What are you suggesting?"

"After we get X, we pick up with the kid where L and Jack left off."

"I don't have the time or interest to train some boy myself."

"I'll do it. Assuming he's the right material."

The dilated pupil pegged her where she stood, that weird, hazy starfish floating in the depths. She wasn't sure where to look.

Van Sciver said, "This have to do with Sevastopol? Dead girl in the alley?"

"Of course not." She hoped she hadn't rushed the words. "We need more arrows in our quill." She pointed into the living room. "And that could be one of them."

Van Sciver's jaw shifted to the side and back. He holstered his .45.

Candy did not let him see her exhale.

He tugged a red-covered notebook from one of his wide cargo pockets and flipped it open. Inside were various intel scribblings and the list of five names.

Orphan J. Orphan C. Orphan L.

All crossed out.

Then Joey Morales, circled twice.

And David Smith.

Van Sciver removed a Pilot FriXion pen from the fold and erased the boy's name. He lifted that bottomless stare to Candy. Then he tossed the notebook onto a side table and walked into the living room. The former marines stood at attention the way former marines did.

Thornhill pulled the pot off the stove to cool, came around to confer with Candy and Van Sciver.

Van Sciver said, "You got the propofol?"

Thornhill flashed that million-dollar grin. *"Now* it's a party."

He went to a black medical kit and came up with a syringe filled with a cloudy white liquid. They didn't call it "milk of amnesia" for nothing. The medication provided a quick knockout and a rapid, clear recovery. Push a little, it was an anesthetic. Push a little more and you had a lethal injection.

In all matters Van Sciver strove to have a full range of choices.

How the boy responded in the next few minutes would determine how much pressure Thornhill's thumb applied to the plunger.

Candy found herself biting the inside of her cheek.

Van Sciver walked over to the boy and tugged off the pillowcase.

David Smith blew his lank bangs off his forehead and took in the plywood-covered windows, the empty jugs of water, the fresh plastic tarp on the floor. Then he squinted up at Van Sciver.

"Is this a test?" he asked.

52

Chess-Matching

Evan didn't want to risk checking in to a motel, not when he and Joey were this close to Van Sciver. Not when Van Sciver knew he was coming.

Instead he used a false Airbnb profile to book a room for forty-nine dollars a night. The owner, who listed several dozen apartments in seedy sections of greater Virginia, seemed to be a digital slumlord who oversaw his holdings from afar. The key waited inside a Realtor lockbox hooked around the front doorknob. The neighbors would be accustomed to high turnover, lots of renters coming and going. Which was good, since Evan's profile represented him as Suzi Orton, a robust middle-aged blonde with a forceful smile.

The L-shaped complex had seen better days. Paint flaked on the fence around the pool out front, which had algaed itself to a Gatorade shade of green. A cluster of shirtless young men wearing calf-length charcoal denim shorts smoked blunts on strappy lawn chairs. Several of the doors remained open, women—and one fine-boned young man—lingering at the thresholds in off-the-shoulder tops, offering more than just a view. The thrumming bass of a remix rattled a window on the second floor. Pumping music, paired with the scattered regulars at the fringes, gave the place the woeful feel of a sparse dance floor at a club that couldn't get up steam.

It was dusk by the time Evan had completed his second drive-by and parked the minivan several blocks away. He and Joey moved unnoticed up the sidewalk and then the corridor. Evan punched in the code to free the keys. He handed one to Joey, turning the other in the lock, and they stepped into a surprisingly clean small room with two freshly made twin beds.

He tossed his stuff onto the mattress closer to the door as Joey plugged in her laptop and then checked her phone for the fiftieth time for updates. She grabbed a change of clothes from her bag and went to shower as Evan worked out—push-ups, sit-ups, dips with his heels on the windowsill and his hands ledging the seat of the solitary chair. Joey came out, sweeping her hair up into a towel, and he turnstiled past her in the tight space.

When he finished showering and emerged from the bathroom, she was at the laptop again, chewing her lip. He checked his Roam-Zone to see if Xavier had called. He hadn't. Evan used the wall to stretch out the tendons of his right shoulder. Almost back to full range of motion.

It occurred to him that neither he nor Joey had uttered a word in the preceding forty-five minutes and yet the silence had been comfortable. Pleasant, even.

It reminded him of when he was a kid, walking around the farmhouse with Jack, wiping the counters, taking turns on the pull-up bar by the side of the house, filling Strider's water bowl. At times Jack and he cooked, ate, and cleared an entire meal without a word passing between them.

They were so in sync that they didn't need to speak.

Joey looked over from the bluish screen, saw Evan watching her. That dimple floated in her wide cheek.

She said, "What are you thinking about?"

"Nothing," he said.

Chess-Matching

They blinked at each other for a moment.

"What are you doing over there?" he asked.

"Catching up on the latest and greatest. There's a disposable, disappearing chat room for black-hat hackers."

"I won't ask if it's secure."

"No," she agreed. "That would be condescending."

"Do you want to try meditating again?"

She gave a one-shouldered shrug. "I seem to suck at it."

"Meditating?"

"Being out here." She made a halfhearted gesture at the laptop. "Easier to be online. I feel real in there."

"But it's not," he said. "Real."

"What is?"

"Trauma."

Her lips tensed until they went pale. "What's that supposed to mean?"

"I don't ever have to know what happened to you in those foster homes," he said. "But you've got it inside you. It's holding on in your body."

"Why do you say that?"

"Because it's waiting when you close your eyes and get quiet."

"Bullshit. I just don't like sitting still."

He went over to his bed and sat with his back to the headboard. He stayed very still.

"Fine," she said. "Fine."

She logged out, bounced from chair to bed. Crossed her legs.

"Get relaxed but not too relaxed," he said. "Become aware of any tightness or tingling. Rest your tongue on the roof of your mouth, your hands on your knees. Focus on the breath moving through you. Follow it and see where it takes you."

He straightened his spine, pulled his shoulders back into alignment, made a two-millimeter adjustment to the column of his neck. Slowly the laughter and music from outside faded. He became acutely aware of the pressure of the mattress beneath him, a twinge in his right shoulder, the scent of laundry detergent. He started to constrict his focus, the outside world irising shut. But he sensed an unease inside the room.

Joey, rocking from side to side. She rolled her neck.

"Try not to squirm," he said.

"I'm not squirming."

"Just keep coming back to your breath. And to sitting still."

She remained motionless, but her agitation grew, a physical force clouding the air between them.

She exhaled sharply and flopped back. She stared at the ceiling. When she blinked, tears streamed down her temples. She was breathing hard.

Then she got up violently, the mattress springs whining, her bare feet hitting the floor with a thud. She rushed out, slamming the door behind her.

Evan stared at the door. She'd caught him off guard, perhaps even more than when she'd broken his nose.

He uncrossed his legs, stood up, hesitated.

She wanted to be alone. Should he respect that? In *this* neighborhood?

He reminded himself that she could take care of herself just fine.

Somewhere outside, a car horn blared.

He noted the concern swelling in his chest with each breath. An odd sensation. She was fine.

But he wasn't.

Already he was walking to the door and then moving swiftly through the outside corridor. The other apartment doors were closed now, the denizens busy inside from the sound of it. He swept around the other arm of the complex—no sign of Joey. He circled back around the pool, the same young men telling the same stories, smoking different blunts, not noticing him or anything else. His chest tightened even more as he cut between the cars in the parking lot.

Still no Joey.

He jogged up the block. A pimped-out Camaro drove past, windows down, rap booming from the radio. Eminem was cleaning out his closet and doing a damn fine job of it.

She wasn't at the minivan.

She wasn't visible from the next intersection or the one after that.

He checked the RoamZone. She hadn't called. Nor had Xavier. His worry compounded when he considered what he'd do if Xavier decided to contact him now. *Sorry about your gang situation, but I'm busy running around Virginia trying to prevent a boy's execution, chess-matching with the world's most lethal assassins, and my sidekick just went missing.*

Sidekick.

The word had tumbled naturally into his thoughts.

He cut over one block, walked back across cracked sidewalks, pit bulls gnashing at him from behind fences. Activity swirled inside an abandoned house, unsavory customers visible through the missing windows and front door. Evan strode across the gone-to-seed front lawn and through the rectangular hole where the front door used to reside. His boot crushed the shards of a dropped crack pipe. Half the back wall was missing, bodies milling ten deep in the packed living room. A couple was having sex on a couch shoved against one wall, their pale skin nearly glowing in the darkness.

Evan shoved through toward the backyard.

"Hey, fucker, you'd best watch where you're—"

Palm—jaw—floor. The guy dropped as if brought down with a lasso, and Evan broke through the remaining fringe of bodies. More faces, more hands clutching crinkled brown paper bags, more glass pipes. A fire leapt inside an enormous clay pot, casting irregular light across bare midriffs, shaved skulls, a guy with glasses missing one lens.

No Joey.

Evan cut up the side yard, jogged back to the apartment complex, his stress quickening. The guys remained on the lawn chairs, the smell of weed contact-high thick in the corridor.

The door to the rented room was open.

Evan jogged forward, hand resting on the grip of the skinny ARES shoved into his waistband. He came around the doorway, stepping inside, ready to draw.

Joey stood in the middle of the room, shoulders hunched, her face in her hands. Her back shuddered.

He heeled the door shut behind him. "Joey?"

She wheeled on him. "Where were you?" She came at him, striking blindly. "Why'd you leave me here? I got back, and you . . . you weren't here. Why weren't you here?"

He retreated, but she launched at him again, pounded with her fists, not like a trained operator but like an angry sixteen-year-old. "You left me. I thought . . . I thought . . ."

He tried to gather her in, but she shoved him away. She slammed the closet door off its tracks, kicked the chair across the room, threw the lamp against the wall, knocking a divot through the paint.

He moved to get out of her way, sat on the floor, and put his back to the door.

She ripped the hanger pole off its mounts in the closet, kicked the bed hard enough that the metal feet gouged marks in the carpet, drove her hand through the drywall.

Finally she finished.

She was facing away from him, her body coiled, her hands in loose fists at her sides. Blood dripped from a split knuckle.

She walked over. She sat across from him, facing away from his bed. Her huge eyes were wet, her shoulders still heaving.

"Where were you?" she said.

"I went to look for you."

"You weren't here."

He swallowed. *"Tiene dos trabajos. Enojarse y contentarse."*

She pressed both hands over her mouth. Tears ran over her knuckles, but she did not make a sound.

They sat on the floor together for a very long time.

53

My Breath on Your Neck

The next morning Evan and Joey sat on their respective beds spooning gas-station-bought oatmeal into their mouths from Styrofoam cups. He'd told Joey to put the room back together, and she'd done her best, but still the closet door was knocked off its tracks, the lamp shattered, the walls battered. The wreckage of the chair was neatly stacked in the corner, a pyre of kindling. It was a foregone conclusion that Suzi Orton, cheery Airbnb patron, was going to have to retire her profile after they cleared out.

"Look," Joey said. "Sorry I kinda freaked out last night. It's just . . . I was—"

Her phone gave a three-note alert, a bugle announcing the king.

She thumped her Styrofoam cup down on the nightstand, oatmeal sludge slopping over the brim, and swung off the bed into a kneeling position before her laptop at the desk.

"A police cruiser hit on the plate," she said, her voice tight with excitement.

He leaned over her shoulder, saw a screen grab of the black

Suburban captured by the light bar of a passing cop car. The SUV was parked in a crowded Food Lion grocery-store lot, the GPS specifics spelled out below.

"Damn it." Joey nibbled the edge of her thumbnail. "By the time we get there, they'll be gone."

"No," he said. "This is good. No one drives across town to get groceries."

She caught his meaning, nodded, and snapped her laptop shut. They threw their stuff together in less than a minute.

Before heading out, Evan left ten crisp hundred-dollar bills on the floor beneath a fist-size hole punched through the drywall.

He started at Food Lion and drove in an expanding spiral, creeping through increasingly rough neighborhoods. A few miles along their winding path, he pulled abruptly to the curb.

Joey said, "What?"

He pointed at a ramshackle single-story house a half block up that looked like most every other house they'd passed. A chunk of missing stucco on the front corner, planters filled with dirt, over-stuffed trash cans at the curb. A tall rolling side gate had been turned impenetrable by green plastic strapping interwoven with the chain-link. One of the gutters had come loose and dangled from the fringe of the house like a coal chute.

"I don't get it," Joey said.

"The trash cans," he said. "See those green plastic strips poking up?"

She leaned toward the dash, squinting through the windshield. "They match the fence filler."

"Right. Someone cut and installed that privacy screen on the gate this week." He unholstered his ARES and opened the door. "Wait here."

He crossed the street, darted through front yards, hurdling hedges. He slowed as he came up on the house, keeping his arms firm but not too firm, the pistol pointed at a spot on the ground a few feet ahead of the tips of his boots.

The gate was lifted two inches off the concrete to accommodate the wheels. Easing onto the edge of the driveway, Evan dropped to his stomach and peered through the gap.

The driveway continued past the gate to where the yard ended at a rotting wooden fence. Parked halfway there at an angle was a black Suburban. Weeds pushed up from cracks in the concrete, brushing the vehicle's flanks. But they weren't dense enough to cover the license plate.

VBK-5976.

Next to it on the baked dirt of the yard were the second rented Suburban and a Chevy Tahoe.

Evan withdrew.

Jogging back up the street, he flicked a finger for Joey to get out. She climbed from her perch in the driver's seat, locking the vehicle behind her.

"It's there?" she asked.

"It's there."

As they circled the block, he could hear Joey's breathing quicken.

They cut through a side yard next to a partially burned house. The frame of an Eldorado rested on blocks in a carport that sagged dangerously on heat-buckled steel beams. They stepped carefully, moving into the backyard. A rear patio had served as a firebreak, preserving a yard filled with dead, waist-high foxtails. Evan and Joey waded into the weeds, their shoes crunching as they headed for the rotting wood of the rear fence. Though the fire looked to be a few days old, ash still scented the air, the smell just shy of pleasing.

The warped fence had plenty of cracks and crevices that provided a ready vantage across the target house's backyard. On what was left of the lawn, an old-fashioned round barbecue grill melted into a puddle of rust. The reddish tinge on the earth brought a host of associations to Evan, which he pushed aside, focusing instead on the house beyond.

Plywood covered two of the living room's three windows. One sheet had been removed and set to the side, presumably to let in light. The high kitchen window over the sink had been left exposed, and the rear door was laid open.

Paul Delmonico and Shane Shea, Van Sciver's freelancers, stood at semi-attention, focused on someone in one of the blind spots. Evan assumed the other two freelancers were holding down the front of the house. In the kitchen window, Thornhill's head was visible. A moment later a woman stepped beside him, facing mostly away from Evan.

Midlength hair, confident posture, athletic shoulders that tapered to a slender but not-too-slender waist—Evan would recognize her bearing anywhere.

Orphan V turned around.

In the shaft of light falling through the kitchen window, she looked quite striking. As she murmured something to Thornhill, she reached over her shoulder and scratched at a spot on her back. Evan thought of the burned flesh beneath her shirt and felt a jagged edge twist inside him.

Palms pressed to the splintering fence, he breathed the rot of the wood and watched the freelancers watching whoever was in that blind spot, two attack dogs waiting for a command. Beside him Joey shifted her weight uncomfortably, rolling one sneaker onto its outer edge. She was humming with nervousness.

The person in the blind spot stepped out of the blind spot and into view.

That broad form, the thin copper hair, the muscular forearms and blocky wrists. But it wasn't just Van Sciver who made Joey's breath hitch audibly in her throat; it was what he was carrying.

David Smith's frail form draped across his arms.

Van Sciver dumped the body onto a tarp on the floor. His arms were swollen with exertion, bowed at his sides. The lines on the right side of his face caught the shadows differently—perhaps scarring, perhaps a trick of the light. Evan hadn't laid eyes on him, not directly, since they'd shared a tense drink in Oslo nearly a decade ago.

Seeing him now in the stark light of day, Evan felt emotions shifting along old fault lines. They'd spent so many years circling each other from the shadows that some small piece of Evan wondered from time to time if he'd conjured Charles Van Sciver entirely.

But there he was, in the flesh.

And the body of the boy who used to be David Smith.

"He's dead," Joey said. Despite the cool December air, sweat sparkled across her temple, emotion flushing her cheeks.

Staring at the motionless, slender form on the tarp, Evan felt heat pulse in his windpipe, fired by a red-hot coal lodged in his chest.

He pushed away from the fence, looked down at the tips of his boots. He pictured the crowded bunks of Room 14 at McClair Children's Mental Health Center. A Lego rebel riding a Snowspeeder across a rusting radiator. Jorell, too smart for his own good. In another life Jorell would be a lawyer, a philosophy professor, a stand-up comedian. In another life David Smith would be sitting down to dinner with a real family. In another life Jack was still alive and he and Evan had plans on the books to share a meal in a two-story farmhouse in Arlington.

"Wait," Joey said. "Evan—he's breathing."

Evan's head snapped back up. He watched as the boy stirred and rolled onto his side.

Evan's jaw had tightened. That red-hot coal singed the inside of his throat, fanned with each breath. "We have to get him."

"There are three Orphans and four muscleheads in that house," Joey said. "Armed to the teeth. And we're out here in the weeds with your girly gun."

"Yes."

"So how do you plan on getting to him?"

Evan fished the Samsung Galaxy from his pocket. "By telling Van Sciver where we are."

He thumbed the Signal application.

A moment later a xylophone chime of a ringtone carried to them on the breeze. Evan put his eye to a knothole and peered into the house.

Van Sciver lifted the phone from his pocket and looked down at the screen. Candy and Thornhill alerted to his expression and went to him, the three of them standing in a loose huddle by the kid's body.

They were in close enough proximity that a tight grouping of nine-millimeter rounds could take them down.

If they weren't Orphans, Evan might consider hurdling the fence and rushing the house to get within range. But he knew he wouldn't get three steps past the rusting barbecue before they alerted to him.

Van Sciver's thumb pulsed over the screen, and he lifted the phone to his face. Evan watched his lips move, the familiar voice coming across the line on a half-second delay; there was a lot of encryption to squeeze the single syllable through. "X."

"Now you're catching on."

"I suppose you're calling about the boy."

From the remove of one backyard and a disintegrating fence, Evan watched Van Sciver turn. Through the phone he heard the rustle of the big man's boots on the tarp. Candy had one hip cocked, directing the two freelancers to keep eyes up. Thornhill's muscles coiled, thrumming with energy, ready to go kinetic. He walked to the front of the house to alert the others.

Van Sciver said, "You took one of mine . . ."

Joey must've heard the words from the receiver, because she stiffened at the mention of herself.

". . . so I took one of Jack's," Van Sciver continued. "But he doesn't have Joey's weaknesses. He's like you and me. Tabula rasa. Jack found him and tucked him away somewhere safe. Now we have him. Like a gun without a serial number."

"Disposable," Evan said. "You'll train him up, spend him when you need to."

"That's what we're for, Evan, remember?"

"Orphan J. Orphan C. Orphan L. Jack. Joey. And now this boy. All to get to me."

"That's right."

Candy was close at hand, hanging on Van Sciver's words, her lips pursed into a shape evocative of a kiss. But the eyes told a different story, of dark appetites unsatiated.

Van Sciver's stare picked across the backyard and snagged on the rear fence. His eyes looked lopsided even from this distance, and it took Evan a moment to realize that it was because the right pupil was larger. Evan could have sworn Van Sciver was looking through the knothole right at him. It was impossible, of course, and yet Evan still pulled back a few inches from the wood.

He knew that look, the same one Van Sciver used to issue when they gathered on the cracked asphalt of the basketball courts across from Pride House, a group of punk-ass kids with nothing to do and nowhere to go.

A look like he was trying to see inside you.

Evan took a breath, eased it out. "How 'bout you get around to telling me what makes me so special?"

Again he watched Van Sciver's lips move, the dubbing off from the voice coming through the line. "You really haven't put it together?"

Evan didn't reply.

Van Sciver laughed. "You don't really think this is *just* personal?"

Evan didn't indulge him. Their earlier conversation played back in his head. *You have no idea, do you? How high it goes?*

"It's amazing," Van Sciver said. "You don't even know how valuable you are."

He pivoted slightly, meeting Candy's loaded gaze. She was clearly read in on whatever reason had escalated the hunt for Evan.

Van Sciver's shoulders rose, his neck corded with muscle, his blocky hand firming around the phone. "They sent me to the Sandpit a few times, needed to pick another name off that deck of playing cards. I caught up to him in Tikrit. Shitty little compound in Qadisiyah, jungle-gym bars and rusty Russian munitions. We'd already rained down with aerial munitions, but Habeeb's still strolling around his little fenced-in yard, lord of his domain. I was set up with my .300 Win Mag on a rooftop at twelve hundred meters, ready to shoot the dick off a mosquito. And Habeeb comes around the yard into sight. I have the head shot, clear as day. But at the last minute, I move the crosshairs from his face to his arm, take it off at the shoulder." His breath came as a rush of static across the receiver. "He'll bleed out, right? But I wanted it to be slow. Guess why."

Evan said, "To draw out the other targets."

"No," Van Sciver said, his voice simmering with latent rage. "Because I wanted him to *know*."

Evan let the silence lengthen.

Van Sciver said, "When I catch up to you, Evan, you're gonna have time also. To know. All your questions? I'll fill you in at the very end. When you're bleeding out on the ground at my feet."

His whole body had tensed, but Evan watched him try to relax his muscles now, a snake uncoiling.

"I am hot on your trail," Van Sciver said.

"And I'm hot on yours," Evan said, the Samsung pressed to his cheek. "Can you feel my breath on your neck?"

Van Sciver's expression turned uneasy. He walked into the kitchen, peered out the window into the backyard once more. "Is that so?"

"Yeah," Evan said. "We've got a lock on the kid."

Next to him Joey bristled. Her hands flared wide—*What are you doing?*—but he held focus on the house.

Van Sciver muffled the phone against his shoulder and snapped his fingers. The freelancers readied M4s and spread around the interior, taking up guard positions. Thornhill drew an FNX-45 from his hip holster and ambled out of sight.

Van Sciver kept his pistol in his underarm tension holster. He moved the phone back to his mouth. "If you want him," he said, "come and get him."

Evan said, "Okay," and hung up.

"What the hell?" Joey hissed. "Now they're on high alert. If they come back here—"

Evan pulled out his RoamZone, pressed three buttons, held up a finger to Joey while it rang.

A feminine voice came over the line. "911."

"Yeah, hi," Evan said. "I work at the McClair Children's Mental Health Center in Church Hill. A man and a teenage girl have been lingering around the building all morning. One of our nurses said she saw that the man had a gun. Can you please get someone here right away? Hang on—*Shit.* I think they're approaching."

He hung up.

Joey gestured for him furiously, pointing through the gap. Crouching, he peered again through the knothole.

Candy swung through the kitchen, heading for the rear of the house. He couldn't see her body until it filled the doorway to the backyard.

She held an M4.

She moved swiftly across the porch and strode out to recon the yard.

Joey backpedaled, her sneaker tamping down the foxtails loudly. She cringed at the noise, wobbled to avoid landing her other foot. Evan shot out a hand and grabbed her arm. She was frozen with one leg above the dead weeds. The brittle foxtails stretched all around them, an early-warning system that would broadcast to Candy any move they made.

Firming his grip on Joey's biceps, Evan swung his head back to the fence. He peered through the knothole, now a foot away. The perspective had the effect of lensing in on the yard.

Candy, twenty yards away and closing.

With his free hand, Evan reached down and tugged his ARES 1911 from the holster. He kept his eyes locked on the knothole.

Candy passed the rusted barbecue, the bore of the M4 facing them, a full circle of black.

She swept toward the fence.

Evan lifted the pistol and aimed through the silver-dollar-size hole.

54

Illegal in Police Departments from Coast to Coast

Evan's torso twisted, pulled in two directions, Joey's weight tugging him one way, his drawn ARES aimed the other. He felt a pleasing burn across his chest, ribs unstacking, intercostals stretching.

If he pulled the trigger, he'd drop Candy but the sound would alert Van Sciver and his men. Then he'd be in retreat with a sixteen-year-old and eight in the mag, pursued by six trained men armed with long guns.

Not ideal.

But he'd handled not-ideal before.

Candy neared the rear fence. He sighted on the hollow of her throat. Her critical mass filled the knothole, blocking out everything else.

His finger tightened on the trigger.

"V!"

Van Sciver's voice from the house halted her in her tracks. She pivoted, M4 swinging low at her side.

She was no more than four feet from the fence line.

The gun was steady in Evan's hand, aimed at the fabric of her shirt fluttering across her back. He'd punch the round through her marred flesh, two inches right of her spine beneath the blade of her shoulder.

Despite Evan's grip, Joey wobbled on her planted foot, her other arm whipping high as she rebalanced herself. In Evan's peripheral vision, he sensed her raised boot brush the tips of the foxtails.

"We just picked up a 911 call!" Van Sciver shouted across the yard. "Armed man and a teenage girl at McClair Children's Mental Health Center."

"They're one step behind," Candy said.

"Let's meet them there."

Candy jogged back toward the house, her figure shrinking in the telescope lens of the knothole. As she receded, Evan released Joey's arm. Joey eased her other foot down to the ground, the weeds crackling softly. She came to Evan's side to watch through the fence.

At the house Van Sciver swung out of the rear door, keys in hand. Thornhill and Candy flanked him across the yard, Delmonico and Shea in their wake.

The two other freelancers had been drawn onto the back porch by the commotion.

"Hangebrauck—wipe the notebook," Van Sciver called out to the bigger of the two, a hefty guy with an armoring of muscle layered over some extra girth.

"Yes, sir."

"Bower, eyes on the front."

Bower, a lanky man with sunken eyes, scratched at his neck. "Yes, sir."

Across the yard Delmonico slid back the gate, the rusty wheels screeching. Van Sciver and Candy hopped into the Tahoe, Shea and Thornhill into the nearest Suburban, and they backed the SUVs out. The Suburban idled in the driveway, waiting on Delmonico as he closed the gate, wiping himself from view.

There was a moment of stillness, Hangebrauck's head tilted back as he sniffed the ash-tinged air. And then he went into the house again.

Bower met him in the kitchen with a red notebook.

It looked just like the notebook Evan had found in the Portland headquarters.

Hangebrauck carried it into the kitchen. Then he placed it in the microwave. The lit carousel spun, rotating the notebook.

Joey looked over at Evan, her brow furled.

Bizarre.

As Bower disappeared once again to the front of the house, Hangebrauck walked into the living room and stared down at David Smith. The boy lay quietly, half off the tarp, his cheek smashed to the floorboards, his thin shoulders rising and falling.

Hangebrauck slung his M4 and sat on the high end of the decline bench, a bored expression on his face. He dug something out from beneath a thumbnail.

Joey leaned toward Evan, her sneakers crackling in the weeds. "There are still two of them," she whispered.

Evan smiled.

Evan didn't have a suppressor. A gunshot would alert the neighbors. He would have to use his hands.

He moved silently along the side of the house and came up on the open back door. Hangebrauck remained on the decline bench, gazing blankly through the sole uncovered rear window into the yard. A dark hall led to the front of the house and to Bower.

Evan waited.

After a time Hangebrauck stood and stretched his back, his shirt tugging up and showing off a pale bulge of flesh at the waistband. He gave a little groan. Resting his hand on the butt of the carbine, he walked to the window.

Over his shoulder Evan's reflection ghosted into sight in the pane.

Evan's right elbow was raised, pointing at the nape of Hangebrauck's neck.

The big man's eyes barely had time to widen before Evan reached over his crown, grabbed his forehead, and yanked his head back into his elbow.

The bony tip of Evan's ulna served as the point of impact, crushing into the base of Hangebrauck's skull, turning the medulla oblongata into gray jelly.

A reinforced horizontal elbow smash.

The man didn't fall so much as crumple.

Evan stripped the M4 cleanly from Hangebrauck as he dropped out of the sling.

The thump made a touch more noise than Evan would have liked.

He tilted the M4 against the wall and moved quickly down the hall. He got to the entryway just as Bower pivoted into sight, rifle raised.

Evan jacked Bower's gun to the side, the man's grip faltering. He spun Bower into the momentum of the first blow and seized him from behind, using a triangular choke hold made illegal in police departments from coast to coast. Evan bent Bower's head forward into the crook of his arm, pinching off the carotid arteries on either side. Bower made a soft gurgling sound and sagged, heavy in Evan's grip.

Evan lowered him to the floor.

Thirteen down.

Twelve to go.

Evan walked back to David Smith. Crouching, he found a strong pulse on the boy's neck. He noticed a slit on the forearm, recently sutured, but otherwise the kid looked fine. He'd probably gotten sliced during the snatch and Van Sciver had patched him up.

The room looked to have been recently cleaned, but despite that a bad odor lingered. Sporadic water spots darkened the walls, the plaster turning to cottage cheese. Scrub marks textured the floorboards. The bristles had left behind a thin frothed wake of bleach, the white edged with something else not quite the shade of coffee.

Evan knew that color.

HELLBENT

He stepped into the kitchen. The glass plate was still spinning inside the microwave. He stopped the timer, grabbed the red notebook from inside, and shoved it into his waistband.

He went back to David Smith, slung him over his shoulder, and walked out the front door into broad daylight.

Joey had the minivan on the move already, easing to the front curb, the side door rolled back. Evan set the boy down gently inside, climbed in, and they drove off.

55

Vanished in Plain Sight

They were halfway across Richmond when the kid woke up.

Puffy lids parted, revealing glazed eyes. David Smith lifted his head groggily, groaned, and lowered it back to the bench seat of the minivan.

Joey peered down from the passenger seat, concerned. "He's up. Pull over."

Evan parked across from a high school that stretched to encompass the entire block. He killed the engine and checked out the surroundings. On the near side of the street, magnolias fanned up from a verdant park, their crooked branches bare and haunting. A man-made river drifted beneath the low-swooping boughs, white water rushing across river stones to feed an elaborate fountain at the center. There were speed walkers and young couples and dogs chasing Frisbees—a good amount of activity to get lost in.

Evan leaned around the driver's seat to peer back at the boy.

"You're okay, David," he said. "You're safe now."

The boy blinked heavily. "That's not my name."

"We know it is. We know you were trained by Tim Draker, that you had to go on the run, that Jack Johns hid you in that mental-health center until you were kidnapped yesterday."

"Is this another mind game?" the boy asked.

"What?"

"You know, like SERE stuff. You take me, mess with my head, see what I'll give up."

Evan said, "Not even close."

A bell warbled, and kids started streaming from the school, pouring down the front steps, zombie-mobbing the minivan on their way to the park. The added movement was good, even easier to blend into.

Joey pointed to the sutured slice on the back of David's left forearm. "What happened there?"

The boy regarded the cut and his arm as if he'd never seen them before. "I don't . . . I don't remember."

He tried to sit up, wobbled, finally made it. His face was pale, his lips bloodless. He shook his head. "I don't feel so good."

"Let's get him some fresh air," Evan said, already stepping out into the sea of high-schoolers.

He slid back the side door, and Joey helped David out.

"Off the street," he said, and she nodded.

They joined the current of kids flowing through the magnolias and across the park. Kids clustered to take phone pics and compare the results. Braying laughter, deafening chatter, a cacophony of ringtones. Evan led Joey and David, cutting between cliques. They stopped at the fountain. Students rimmed the encircling concrete. The air smelled of chlorine, hair spray, the skunky tinge of pot. A family of black ducks paddled across the still water at the fountain's edge. Buried treasure glimmered beneath, copper wishes waiting to be fulfilled.

No one took note of the three of them; they'd vanished in plain sight.

Color crept back into David's cheeks, his lips pinking up. He sat on the rim of the fountain, poked at the sutures.

"Looks like you were drugged," Joey said.

His head bobbled unevenly. "But why? I woulda done whatever."

To one side a crew of girls crowded around a ringleader with gel nails and green-and-white Stan Smiths. "Loren's totally gonna uninvite her from her sweet sixteen, because—get this—she posted a pic of herself with Dylan in his backseat. They were just sitting there, but still. Hashtag: trashy."

This doubled the girls over. Leaning on each other, weak with laughter, retainers gleaming. Their sneakers matched. Their haircuts matched. Their backpacks were mounded at their heels, different shades of the same Herschel model.

Joey regarded them as one might a herd of exotic animals.

"Where's that guy?" David asked. "The big guy?"

Joey refocused. "We got you from him."

"But he was gonna put me in that program. The one Tim was training me for." David's gaze sharpened. "Wait—where's Tim? What happened to him?"

Evan said, "They killed him."

David's mouth opened, but no noise came out.

Evan crouched and set his hands on David's knees. "We're gonna make sure you're taken care of."

"Evan," Joey said. "*Evan.*"

She'd clocked something at the park's perimeter. He picked up her gaze, spotting a black Suburban flickering into view behind clusters of students and the skeletal branches of the magnolias. It turned at the corner, creeping along the front of the high school.

Shea at the wheel, Delmonico in the passenger seat, Jordan Thornhill in the back, bouncing his head as if to music.

Joey somehow had one of the Herschel backpacks at her feet, unzipped. She'd already taken out an iPhone hugged by a rubber Panda case. She tapped in 911. When she put the phone to her ear, her hand was trembling.

They watched the Suburban prowl.

Evan popped the bottom two magnetic buttons of his shirt, creating an unobstructed lane to his hip holster. The breeze riffled the fabric, tightened his skin. Thornhill and the two freelancers would try to flush Evan, Joey, and David from the park. Presumably

Candy and Van Sciver were in the surrounding blocks somewhere, lying in wait.

There were at least two hundred kids on scene—a lot of flesh to catch stray bullets.

"I just spotted two fugitives," Joey said into the phone. "Paul Delmonico and Shane Shea."

As she named the high school and the park, paranoia bubbled up in Evan. He looked down at the slit on David's arm.

Dried blood at the seam. Fresh sutures. Good placement.

David blinked up through bleary red eyes. "What? What is it?"

"Come," Evan said. *"Now."*

As the Suburban drifted around the block, Evan circled to the far side of the fountain, keeping the spouting water between them and their pursuers.

Joey brought the stolen backpack, still talking into the phone. "There's kids all over here, and those guys are armed, and they're gonna start shooting people."

The Panda phone case undercut the gravity of her tone, lending a surreal touch to the situation.

Youthful movement churned all around. Two skinny kids sat cross-legged at the base of a tree, testing each other with math equations on flash cards. An older kid in an artfully torn flannel snickered with his compatriots. "Dude, I am *so* gonna hit that this weekend." One of the girls on the far side of the fountain had produced a selfie stick, and she and her friends were leaning together, making pouty lips, adjusting wisps of bangs. A half block away, three assassins glided down the street.

Joey hung up, pocketed the ridiculous Panda phone. "Let's see how long it takes PD to respond to prison-escapee pedophile cop killers in a park full of children."

David said, *"What?"*

She shushed him.

Through a jetting arc of water, they watched the Suburban ease into a parking spot a half block behind their minivan. Evan did a full 360. Nothing but kids on the grassy expanse, the weaving faux river, more trees. Van Sciver and Candy weren't showing themselves.

They didn't have to.

All around the park's periphery, parents were picking up their kids, the Suburban just another SUV. Its doors opened, and the three men got out. They stood at the curb, scanning the park.

Joey said, "How?"

"His forearm," Evan said.

She looked down at the four-inch seam sliced through David's flesh.

"Wait," David said. "What do you mean?"

"They chipped you."

Thornhill's stare moved to the fountain.

And locked onto them.

He rocked back on his heels, a small display of delight, and said something to Delmonico and Shea. All three sets of eyes pegged them now.

They were about a quarter mile away. The spray beneath the bent spurt of fountain caught the fading sunlight, suspending a rainbow in its web of drops. Evan glared through the gauzy veil of color. The men glared back. Except Thornhill.

Thornhill was grinning.

They stepped forward in unison, cutting through groups of students. Delmonico and Shea wore trench coats. With each step the barrels of their M4s nosed forward into view beside their knees. Thornhill angled away from them behind one of the gnarled tree trunks, opening up a second front.

Evan slid his hand through the gap of his shirt, clenched the grip of the ARES, and readied to draw.

56

Crimson Firework

As Delmonico and Shea started for the fountain, Thornhill sidled farther to the side, dividing Evan's attention. Even from this distance, Evan could see that his lips were pursed. Was he whistling?

Evan tightened his hand around the pistol. David bristled at his side. Though the men were still way across the park, Joey had instinctively slid one foot back into a fighting stance.

There were countless students before them. And countless behind them.

Evan would have to thread the needle.

Three times.

He unholstered the ARES, held it low by his thigh, let a breath out, tried to relax his clenched jaw.

All at once scores of cop cars erupted onto the block.

There was nothing gradual about it; one moment they were absent, the next a half-dozen units had morphed into existence on the street behind Delmonico and Shea, sirens screaming, lights strobing. Officers sheltered behind car doors and spread across the sidewalk, aiming shotguns and Berettas at the two freelancers—180 degrees of firepower.

The kids bucked and surged, going up on tiptoes, straining their necks, the murmur of their voices heating to a low boil.

A captain had a radio mike snugged beneath his gray mustache, barking orders over the loudspeaker.

Delmonico and Shea halted and raised their arms. Their trench coats gaped wide, revealing the slung M4 carbines.

A few of the kids screamed, those close to the action going skittish. Anxious excitement rippled across the park as a vanguard of cops pressed forward and took the freelancers down.

Evan barely watched them. He kept tabs on Thornhill, lingering by the perimeter of the cop cars, watching him right back.

Evan gave him a *What can ya do?* shrug.

Thornhill smiled good-naturedly and threw his hands up, like a magician tossing cards. The legion of officers faced the park, Thornhill mere feet behind them, unnoticed. He heeled backward across the street, which had been conveniently cleared for him, then turned and strolled up the wide steps of the school.

He started jogging as he reached the top stairs, building steam. Then he leapt from a planter onto a doorframe, pinballed his way up a crevice between a concrete pillar and a wall, and flipped himself onto the roof. His jacket flared like a cape, his powerful wrestler's build momentarily silhouetted against the sky.

"Holy shit," David said. "Did you see that? The guy's friggin' *Spider-Man.*"

Instead of fleeing, Thornhill took a seat at the lip of the roof above the school's entrance, legs crossed. He curled over his lap like weeping Buddha, the muscles of his shoulders undulating.

Across the park the cops hauled Delmonico and Shea onto their feet and steered them at a diagonal away from the high school. They angled across the grass to where a police van waited on the neighboring street, clear of the traffic jam of responding cruisers. The freelancers shuffled along compliantly, hands cuffed behind them. Though a good number of students had scattered, others remained, rubbernecking from what they considered a safe distance. Many of the parents were out of their cars, rushing to their kids, pulling them away.

Up on the roof of the high school, Thornhill straightened up, and Evan saw what he'd been doing.

Screwing a suppressor onto the threaded barrel of his FNX-45.

"How far away are we?" Joey said.

Evan squinted, assessing. "Just under five hundred yards."

"It's impossible for him to hit us."

"He's not aiming at us."

It took a beat for Joey to catch his meaning. "Jesus," she said. "Really?"

Thornhill popped onto his feet at the roof's edge, a single deft movement.

Evan said, "Van Sciver can't afford for them to be in custody."

David started to step up onto the fountain's basin so he could see, but Evan set a hand on his shoulder, firming him to the ground.

This the boy could skip.

The cops steered Shea and Delmonico farther into the park and away from the school, but Thornhill appeared unhurried. He took a supported position against an A/C unit, his off hand braced against the housing.

"He can't make that shot," Joey said. "Not through the trees. Not at that distance."

A black bulge rode the top of the gun—holographic red-dot sights. The suppressor stretched the barrel into something lean and menacing. Most common loadings for a .45 ACP kept the gun subsonic, so Thornhill could squeeze off both shots without making a sound signature loud enough for the cops to source.

Delmonico and Shea disappeared from view, temporarily lost in a cocoon of officers. They were at least two hundred yards from Thornhill. Maybe two-fifty. A few cops moved ahead, clearing the rest of the way to the police van.

Evan swept his view back across the park, the street, and up the stairs to the roof of the school. Shouldered into the A/C unit, Thornhill was so still he might have been part of the building.

Two hundred seventy-five yards, at least.

Crimson Firework

The clump of blue uniforms reached the intersecting street. Two transport officers emerged from the paddy wagon, laying open the rear doors.

The arresting cops jerked Delmonico and Shea to a rough halt and stepped forward to confer with the transfer officers. The other cops milled around, spreading out into the street.

Creating gaps.

On the roof, the .45 twitched in Thornhill's grip.

Delmonico fell, a crimson firework painting the side of the van.

Confused, the cops crouched and ran for cover.

Having his hands cuffed at the small of his back put Shea on a half-step delay. His head was cocked with confusion, the cloud-muffled sun gleaming off his bald dome. For an instant he stood wide open there in the street, twisted around, looking in the wrong direction. The cuffs yanked his shoulders back, nicely exposing the expanse of his chest.

A dark flower bloomed on his shirt. He staggered backward, his spine striking the side of the police van. His knees were bent, tilting him into the vehicle, physics momentarily holding him on his feet.

Then his heels slipped and he fell, landing with his legs splayed before him.

Evan turned to look again at Thornhill way across on the roof and was not surprised to see Thornhill looking back.

Fifteen dead.

Ten left.

Evan gave a respectful nod.

Thornhill placed one hand on his chest and flourished the other as if to accompany a bow, accepting the compliment. He holstered the pistol and stepped back from sight.

Gone.

Pandemonium swept across the park. The cops spread out, weapons drawn, eyes whipping across rooftops and vehicles in every direction. The remaining students stampeded out of the park, trampling abandoned backpacks. Pages of dropped textbooks fluttered in the breeze. One girl stood frozen, sobbing amid the chaos, fists pressed to her ears. Parents hauled their children away, one father sprinting with his son flopped over his arm like a stack of dry-cleaned shirts. Horns blared. Brakes screeched. Fenders crumpled. A girl had tripped near the fountain and was curled up, holding a bloody knee.

David yanked on Evan's arm. "What happened? What's going on?"

"We gotta move," Joey said. "Ride the chaos out of the park."

Evan took David's arm in his hands, turned it to show the slice. "This first."

He sat David on the wall of the fountain and moved his thumbs along the sides of the forearm scar, pressing gently. David winced. Behind him in the fountain, the black ducks glided by, unperturbed by the commotion.

Cops moved swiftly through the park, corralling stray students. Joey vibrated with impatience, her head swiveling from the approaching officers to the surrounding streets. "We don't have time for this."

Evan felt nothing unusual around the scar. He ran his fingers across the unmarred flesh up toward the boy's elbow.

Something hard beneath the flesh pressed into the pad of his thumb.

A thin disk, about the size of a watch battery.

"What is it?" David asked.

"A digital transmitter."

"Up there?" Joey said. "How are we supposed to get it out?"

The tiny bulge was about six inches up from the incision; it had been slid up toward the elbow to conceal it. Seventy-eight percent of Orphans were left-handed. Van Sciver had inserted the transmitter on the left side, Evan assumed, so that if David noticed it and tried to cut it out, he'd be forced to use his nondominant hand to do so.

Evan said, "We need a magnet. A strong magnet."

Two of the cops had closed to within a hundred yards of the fountain. Joey ducked behind its low wall. "We have to figure this out later."

"As long as this is in him, Van Sciver has our location."

Joey's wild eyes found Evan.

His hands went to his shirt buttons, but the magnets wouldn't be strong enough; they were designed to give way readily. He said, *"Think."*

Joey snapped her fingers. "Hang on." She reached for the purloined Herschel backpack and whipped a silver laptop out of the padded sleeve in the back. She smashed it on the lip of the fountain, dug around in its entrails, and tore out the hard drive. Gripping the drive in both hands, she hammered it against the concrete until it split open. She yanked out the spindle, revealing a shiny top disk, and then dug out a metal nugget to the side. With some effort she pried apart its two halves, which Evan was surprised to see weren't screwed together.

"Wa-la," she said. "Magnets."

Evan checked on the cops. The nearest pair were now thirty yards away, temporarily hung up with a sobbing mother. He reached into his front pocket for his Strider, raking it out so the shark-fin hook riding the blade snared the pocket's hem and snapped the knife open. He spun the blade around his hand, caught it with the tanto tip angled down.

David said, "Is this gonna—"

Evan slipped the knife beneath the sutures. With an artful flick of his wrist, he laid the four-inch cut open. David gaped down at it.

Evan held out his hand. "Magnet."

Joey slapped it onto his palm with a surgical nurse's panache.

Evan laid the magnet over the bulge in David's elbow and tracked down to the incision.

Joey's head flicked up. "Cops're almost here."

The transmitter followed the magnet down the forearm, tugging the skin up, and popped out through the wound, snicking neatly onto the magnet.

David expelled a clump of air.

One of the black ducks hopped up onto the concrete ledge, bobbing its head, its pebble eyes locked on a stray rind of bread by Evan's shoe.

From the far side of the fountain, a young cop shouted, "Stand up! Lemme see your hands!"

Evan peered across the fountain at the cop and his partner. The park was dense with officers. Two SWAT units rolled up in front of the high school, new cruisers screeching to block the intersections in every direction.

"Too late," Joey said under her breath.

Evan rose slowly, hands held wide, and stared into two drawn Berettas.

57

What He Thought He Knew

David stood on shaky legs between Evan and Joey. Across the dancing water, both cops aimed at Evan's head.

The entire block was now locked down by backup officers and SWAT.

Evan gauged his next move. The young cop stood in front of his partner, taking lead. He seemed capable, more confident than nervous.

Evan could work with that, play to the cop's ego. He let a worried breath rattle out of him. "Thank God. Is it clear, Officer? I was picking up my daughter, and . . . my son, he got knocked over. His arm's cut open, and—"

"Calm down. Sir? Calm down."

David cupped his hand over the wound, red showing in the seams between his fingers.

The officer's elbows stayed locked, but he swung the gun down and to the side. "Does he require medical attention?"

"I can take him to urgent care," Evan said. He put his arm around

Joey's shoulders, gathered her in. "I just want to get my kids out of here. I wasn't sure it was safe to come out yet."

The cop's partner, a tough-looking woman, said, "Where's your car?"

Evan pointed. "Minivan over there."

"Come with us."

The cops gave them an armed escort across the park, passing by dozens of officers, none of whom took notice.

They reached the curb, and the young cop gestured at the SWAT trucks to allow the minivan to pull out.

Evan rushed the kids into the van. "Thank you so much, Officer."

The cop nodded, and he and his partner jogged off to resume the search.

Evan pulled out of the spot, driving past the rows of police cruisers with flashing lights. Two units at the intersection, parked nose to nose, reversed like a parting gate to let the minivan through.

At the next street, Evan signaled responsibly and then turned. The flashing blue and red lights slid out of his rearview mirror.

Joey tilted her head back and shot a breath at the roof.

Evan waited until they'd cleared city limits to pit-stop. He parked behind a liquor store and wrapped David's forearm using gauze pads and an Ace bandage he'd pulled from the first-aid kit lodged beside the spare tire.

The alley behind them gave off the sickly-sweet odor of spilled beer. Flies swayed above an open Dumpster. Broken glass littered the asphalt around it; somebody had practiced empty-bottle free throws with a twelve-pack, showing all the accuracy one would expect from somebody who'd drunk a twelve-pack.

The hatch was raised, David sitting at the edge of the cargo space, his legs dangling past the rear bumper. Crouched before him, Evan smoothed down the bandage and snared the fabric with the metal clips to secure it.

Joey came around to check on their progress. "All good?"

David turned his arm this way and that. "Yeah. Can this be stitched once we get there?"

"Get where?" Evan asked.

"To the Program HQ or wherever."

Past the boy, Evan sensed Joey pull her head back slightly.

"We're not going to any HQ," Evan said. "You're not joining any Program."

David's tone hardened. "What are you talking about?"

"That's no longer an option," Evan said.

"No way. That big guy said I could be part of it."

"That big guy will dispose of you if you don't make the grade," Joey said.

David spun to face her. "I'll make the grade," he said. "It's all I ever wanted." He glared up at them. "I want a way out. I finally got it. And you want to take it from me?"

"These guys killed Tim," Evan said.

"Then Tim wasn't good enough."

"Watch your fucking mouth." Joey stepped forward, shouldering Evan aside, her intensity catching him off guard. "He died for you."

David's mouth pulsed as he fought down a swallow. But his eyes stayed fierce.

Joey leaned over him. "You don't even know what the Program is."

"I don't care what," David said. "I don't care. I want to go back with the guy who took me. I want something better than a shitty life in some shitty facility."

"Did Jack teach you anything?" Joey said.

"Yeah. To be better. I deserve better than this."

Joey said, "None of us *deserves* anything."

"Maybe so," David said, hopping to his feet and finger-stabbing at Joey. "But that's *my* choice. I'm not going with you if you're not part of the Program. You take me back to those guys, or the first chance I get, I'll tell that you kidnapped me."

His features were set with a bulldog stubbornness that seemed well beyond his thirteen years. Given the life he'd led up to now, that made sense. Hard years counted double.

Evan had been a year younger than David was now when he'd stepped off the truck-stop curb into Jack's car and never looked back. He thought about who he was then and what he thought he knew.

Evan said, "Is there anything we can say to dissuade you?"

David's face had turned ruddy. "No."

"Can we give you more information to—"

"*No.*" The boy was on tilt, his nose angled up at Evan, shoulders forward, fists clenched by his hips.

Evan looked at the boy calmly until he settled onto his heels. David shook his head, eyes welling. "I don't want to be a nobody."

Evan said, "You go down this road, that's all you'll ever be."

At that, Joey touched her hand to her mouth as if trying to stop something from escaping.

"Maybe so," David said. "But it's *my* road."

Evan watched him for ten seconds and then ten seconds more. Not a thing changed in his expression.

Evan said, "Stay here."

He walked over toward the Dumpster, Joey trailing him. They huddled up, facing the minivan to keep an eye on David.

Joey looked rattled. "We have to change his mind."

"It's not gonna happen," Evan said.

"So we just what? Leave him for Van Sciver to pick up again?" She took a few agitated breaths. "He'll kill him, you know. Sooner or later, directly or indirectly."

Evan said, "Unless."

"Unless what?"

Evan cleared his throat, an uncharacteristic show of emotion.

"Unless what?" Joey repeated.

"We take him public."

She gawked at him.

"He doesn't know anything yet," Evan said. "Not one proper noun in his head."

"He knew Tim Draker. And Jack."

"Both of whom are dead. Anything he has to say about them will sound like a foster-kid fantasy."

The words were so true that saying them out loud felt like a betrayal.

"There's safety in exposure," he said. "No one wants a spoiled asset."

"Then why didn't Jack just do it months ago?"

"Tim Draker was alive. I'm sure he wanted to get David back once it was safe."

Joey flipped her hair over, revealing the shaved band. She lowered her head, crushed shards of glass with the toe of her sneaker. "I don't know. It's a risk."

"Everything's a risk. We're juggling hand grenades."

She didn't respond.

Evan said, "With everything else going on, with us still out here, you really think Van Sciver's gonna burn resources and risk visibility for a screwed-up thirteen-year-old kid?"

She fussed with her hair some more. Then she pinched the bridge of her nose, exhaled. "Okay," she said. "Fuck. Okay."

When she looked up, all emotion was gone, her features blank.

She walked back over to David, her hand digging in her pocket. She came out with the phone in the stupid Panda case, held it four feet from David's face. The shutter-click sound effect was more pronounced than necessary.

She bent her head, a sweep of hair hiding her eyes, and clicked furiously with a thumb.

"What the hell?" David said. "What are you doing?"

She kept on with her thumb.

David grew more uncomfortable. "I said, what are you doing with my picture?"

" 'My cousin's best friend was kidnapped by the U.S. government,' " Joey read slowly. " 'Jesse Watson. Please retweet. Exclamation point.' " Now her eyes rose, and Evan was startled by how little they seemed to hold. "Twitter. Facebook. Instagram."

A few chirps came from the phone, notifications pinging in.

Joey frowned down at the screen. "Looks like BritneyCheer28's a popular girl. Lotta 'friends.' "

She held up the phone. David's face duplicated with each new post, a Warholian effect on the endlessly refreshing screen. The chirps quickened, reaching video-game intensity.

"You bitch." David's voice was so raw it came out as little more than a rasp.

"I don't expect you to understand," Joey said. "Maybe you'll get it when you're older."

"You just took away any shot of me being anything."

"No, you stupid little shit," Joey said. "We *saved* you. We just gave you a normal *life*. Where you don't have to spend all your time running away from . . . running away from yourself." Her voice cracked, and beneath the vehemence there was something wistful, something like longing. She swallowed hard and turned away to stare at the rear of the liquor store.

"Go back to the McClair Center," Evan said to David. "There's a charge nurse who'll be happy to see you."

"Fuck McClair." Tears streaked David's red cheeks. "Fuck the charge nurse."

"I'm going to give you my phone number in case you ever need my help."

"I'm never gonna call you. I'm never gonna ask for your help. I never want to see you again."

Evan took the first-aid kit out of the trunk and dropped it at David's feet. Then he walked to the driver's seat and got in.

Joey stayed in the alley, gazing at the cracked stucco wall, her arms folded. It took her a moment to start moving, but she did.

She climbed in, slammed the door louder than she needed to.

Evan said, "Look up the number of the McClair Children's Mental Health Center and tell them you spotted him here. I already called. It should be a different voice."

Joey said, "Gimme a moment."

David didn't move as Evan backed out. The side mirror passed within a foot of his shoulder. Evan hit a three-point in the cramped space and spun the steering wheel toward the open road.

They left him in the alley, staring at nothing.

58

An Ad for Domesticity

A few minutes past eight o'clock, the GPS dot finally stopped moving. In the passenger seat, Van Sciver pointed up a suburban street and said, "There."

Thornhill steered the Chevy Tahoe into a hard left. Van Sciver held his phone up and watched the blipping dot, finally at fucking rest. Candy hunched forward from the backseat, bringing a faint hint of perfume.

"Two houses up?" she said.

The muscles of Van Sciver's right eye ached from all the focus. He nodded. "Backyard."

They slowed as they passed a white Colonial house that had recently undergone a Restoration Hardware facelift. A family of four ate at a long wooden farm table, displayed in the picture window like an ad for domesticity.

Thornhill threw the gear stick into park.

Three doors opened. Three Orphans climbed out.

Van Sciver and Candy parted at the curb, each heading to a

different side of the house. Thornhill leapt from trash can to fence top to a second-floor windowsill, vaulting onto the roof. Inside, the family dined on, oblivious.

The Orphans converged on the backyard at the same time, Van Sciver and Candy crowding in with drawn pistols as Thornhill dropped down from the decidedly un-Colonial veranda, landing panther-soft on the patio.

The backyard was empty.

A family of black ducks bobbed in the swimming pool.

Van Sciver stared at them, his jaw shifting.

Then he sighted with the holographic red dot and pulled the trigger. The suppressor pipped once, a pile of feathers settling over the water. The ducks winged off vocally into the night. Van Sciver held the unit in one meaty hand and watched the blinking beacon fly away.

Candy said, "I told you GPS was sloppy."

Van Sciver's phone chimed, an alert muscling in on the GPS screen. He thumbed it to the fore and read the brief report. The visuals were distressing—David Smith's face propagating out through the Information Age.

Candy's phone had gone off, too, and she drifted over, reading the same update on her screen.

Thornhill gave them their space.

"Let's head back to McClair," Van Sciver said. "Put the kid down."

"Sure," Candy said. "That's strategic. A kid whose picture just went viral, let's turn him into a media event."

"He's a loose end."

As Van Sciver started back through the side gate, Candy stayed at his elbow. "Does he know your name?" she said.

"No."

"Does he know anything about the Program?"

"No."

"Then let him rot in a kid's mental ward, spin his delusions in group therapy with the rest of them." She shook her phone. "Taking him out after this is gonna bring press. Why add fuel for the conspiracy theorists?"

An Ad for Domesticity

Van Sciver halted in the cramped space at the side of the house. *"So X doesn't get what he wants."*

His eruption caught Candy by surprise. It seemed to have caught him by surprise, too.

He turned and continued on. As they neared the front yard, the door to the kitchen opened, the father leaning out in front of them, hands on hips. He was wearing a red-and-green Christmas sweater, seemingly without irony.

"Ex*cuse* me," the man said.

Van Sciver kept moving, eyes forward. But he lifted the .45 and aimed it at the man's nose. "Back inside. Call the cops and I'll come back and rape your wife."

Candy smiled. "Me, too."

The man jerked back as if yanked by puppet strings, the door closing with enough force to tangle the cutesy country curtains.

As Van Sciver and Candy stepped out into the driveway, he felt his nostrils flaring, and he tried to contain the rage in his chest. Thornhill dropped from the garage and sauntered up beside them.

Candy kept her focus on Van Sciver. "You're playing X's game. Don't let him trick you—"

He wheeled on her, grabbing her shirt with both hands. *"Don't try to manipulate me."*

Leaning over her, his face in hers, he was struck by just how much more powerful than her he was. If he slipped his hands up from the fabric, he could catch her chin in one palm, the back of her skull in the other, and twist her head halfway off.

Her expression remained impressively placid.

"I *am* trying to manipulate you," Candy said. "But I'm also right."

He observed the ledge of her chin, the thinness of her neck.

Then he released her and stormed for the Tahoe, his breath clouding in the night.

"I know," he said.

59

All Fucked Up

Evan kept one hand on the wheel of the stolen rig, a Toyota pickup with a leaf blower rattling around in the bed. Joey looked out the window at the passing night. Evan hoped that Van Sciver and what remained of his crew were still on their wild-duck chase, pursuing the partially digested digital transmitter Evan had smashed into the bread rind by the fountain.

He wasn't going to risk going out of any of the airports in neighboring states. Dulles International was too obvious, Charlotte and Nashville clear second choices. St. Louis, however, was just under twelve hours away and featured one-stop service to Ontario, California, an unlikely airport forty miles east of Los Angeles. Just before boarding time tomorrow morning at the airport, he'd purchase two tickets under their fake names for the first leg only. He'd buy the second set of tickets during the layover in Phoenix.

Joey finally broke the two-hour silence. "What do we do now?"

"Go home. Regroup."

"How?"

All Fucked Up

"I haven't figured that part out yet."

The highway this time of night was virtually empty. Dark macadam rolled beneath them like a treadmill belt. The headlights were as weak and pale as an old man's eyes.

Joey said, "You think that kid has a shot?"

"Everyone does."

"He was so stubborn. Refusing to go with us, refusing our help. It's like he's locking himself in his own prison."

Evan thought of the gunmetal grays and hard surfaces of his penthouse, such a contrast with Mia's throw blankets and candles.

He said, "A lot of people do."

Joey muffled a noise in her throat.

Evan said, "What did you want?"

"I don't know." Anger laced her voice. "To help him. More."

"You can't help people more than they want to help themselves."

He looked at her. Her eyes were wet.

She turned back to the window, shook her head.

"Stupid fucking kid," she said.

He and Joey sat in their parallel twin beds, Joey with her laptop across her knees, Evan sipping vodka poured over cubes from the motel ice maker. The front desk sold miniature bottles of Absolut Kurant, which Evan didn't buy because he wasn't a fucking savage. A twenty-four-hour liquor store five blocks away had a bottle of Glass, a silky vodka distilled from chardonnay and sauvignon blanc grapes. It had a tangy finish, unvarnished by added sugars or acids, and if he swirled it around his tongue enough, he could catch a trace of honeysuckle.

It wasn't Stoli Elit, but at four in the morning in a less-than-tony neighborhood adjacent to St. Louis International, he'd take what he could get.

He flipped through the red notebook he'd recovered from the microwave in the Richmond house. The pages were blank.

Baffling.

Joey looked over at his glass. "Can I have some?"

"No."

"Oh, I can help steal a shotgun from a cop car, fly on a fake ID, kidnap a kid from a safe house, but God forbid I drink alcohol."

Evan considered this a moment. He handed her his glass. The room was small enough that he barely had to lean to reach her.

She took a sip.

The taste hit, and she screwed up her face. "This is *awful*. You actually like this?"

"I tried to warn you."

She shoved the glass back at him.

"It always reminds me of my foster home," she said. "The smell of alcohol. And hair spray. Menthol cigarettes."

Evan set down his glass. He thought about how Jack used to leave silences for Evan to fill, room for him to figure out if he wanted to talk and what he would say if he did. He remembered Mia's advice: *At the end of the day, all they* really *want to hear? You're okay. You're gonna be fine. You're worth it.*

"She always smoked them," Joey said after a pause. "The 'foster mom.'" The words came with teeth in them. "We all called her Nemma. I don't know if that was her real name, but that's what everyone called her."

Evan cast his mind back to Papa Z sunk in his armchair, as snug as a hermit crab in a shell, one fist clamped around a Coors, the other commanding a remote with lightsaber efficiency as the boys swirled around him, fighting and shoving and laughing. Van Sciver always reigned supreme, the king of the jungle, while Evan slunk mouselike around the periphery, trying to get by unseen. It was a lifetime ago, and yet he felt as if he were standing in that living room now.

Joey kept her gaze on her laptop screen. "She was a beast of a woman. Housedresses. Caked-on blush. And her favorite phrase."

Evan said, "Which was?"

"This is gonna hurt you more than it hurts me." She laughed, but there was no music in it. "God, was she awful. Breath like an ashtray. Big floppy breasts. She had a lot of girls under her roof. She always had boyfriends rotating through. That's how she kept them."

All Fucked Up

She paused, wet her lips, worked the lower one between her teeth.

Evan remained very still.

"I don't remember much about them," she said. "Just the faces." The glow of the screen turned her eyes flat, reflective. "There were a lot of faces."

For a moment she looked lost in it, her shoulders raised in an instinctive hunch against the memories. Then she came out of it, snapped the laptop shut. "I don't want to talk about it."

Evan said, "Okay."

She wouldn't look over at him.

He got up with his glass and the bottle with its elegant clear stopper. He dumped his drink in the bathroom sink and poured out the rest, the vodka *glug-glugging* down the drain. He dropped the empty bottle in the trash can, came back to his bed, and returned to leafing through the red notebook.

He sensed her stare on the side of his face.

"That's why I'm all fucked up," she said.

"You're not any more fucked up than everyone else."

"I'm angry," she whispered. "All the time."

He risked a glance over at her, and she didn't look away.

"Those are the skills you learned to survive," he said. "They're what got you through."

She didn't reply. The thin sheets were bunched up beneath her knees, the folds like spread butter.

He said, "But you also have a choice."

She swallowed. "Which is?"

"To ask yourself, do they still serve you? You can keep them and be angry. Or let them go and have a real life."

"*You* can't," she said. "Let go and have a real life."

"Not so far," he agreed.

"I feel like I'm stuck," she said. "I hate the Program, and I hate that I wasn't good enough for it. And then I wonder—is that the only reason I hate it? Because I wasn't good enough?"

"You were good enough to get out," he said. "You know how many people have done that and are alive?"

She shook her head.

"For all we know, we're the only two."

She blinked a few times.

"You did that," he said. "On your own."

"Yeah, well, you never know what kind of strength you have until you have to have it." She reached over, clicked off her light, and slid down onto her pillow.

"Good night," Evan said.

He turned his light off as well. The blackout curtains left the room as dark as a crypt. He heard her shifting, burrowing into the sheets. And then a silence so pure that it hummed.

"Good night," she said.

Evan's RoamZone vibrated in his pocket. He drew it out and stared at caller ID, which sourced to a mobile with an area code in downtown L.A. He stood and took a few steps away from the final passengers waiting to get on the connecting flight in Phoenix. The flight attendant had just announced the last boarding group, so Evan waved for Joey to go ahead. He'd catch up in a second.

He clicked to answer. "Do you need my help?"

Breath fuzzed the connection.

"Yes," Xavier Orellana said. "I want out. I want out of the gang."

Evan said, "I'm coming."

He hung up and got on the plane.

60

Not Good

"Know any good your-mama jokes?" Peter peered up at Evan and Joey as the elevator doors clanked shut.

His charcoal eyes were dead earnest, as if he were asking for a physician referral.

Evan and Joey had pulled in to Castle Heights right behind Mia in her Acura, returning from picking up Peter at school. Peter had practically run circles around the two of them across the lobby and onto the elevator.

Standing beside his mom, Peter yanked the straps of his oversize backpack. It looked like it was loaded with bricks. How many textbooks could a nine-year-old possibly require?

Joey said, "What are you talking about?"

"Like: Your mama's so fat she jumped in the Red Sea and said, 'Take that, Moses.'"

Mia said, "Your public-education tax dollars at work."

Peter kept on, undeterred. "Your mama's so ugly she made a blind kid cry."

Mia said, "I like that one because it's offensive in two distinct ways."

"Your mama's so fat she can't even fit in the chat room."

Joey looked away to hide her grin.

They reached the twelfth floor, and Peter shot out, holding the elevator open with one skinny arm.

"See you for dinner tonight, right, Evan Smoak?"

Evan's face failed to conceal the fact that he'd forgotten.

Contacting Xavier upon touching down in Ontario, Evan had laid out a plan that required him to be in Pico-Union by ten o'clock. Dinner at seven put him clear by eight-thirty, which gave him time to get across town. As he ran this quick calculation, he felt the heat of Mia's gaze. The elevator door bumped impatiently against Peter's arm, retracting with an angry clank.

"Yes," Evan said.

Peter smiled and let the door go.

Evan pounded the heavy bag, the blows echoing off the floor-to-ceiling glass. He reached his count and stopped, drenched with sweat, breath heaving through him. He'd just started back to the shower when he heard Joey call his name with urgency.

He jogged across the empty expanse and up the winding staircase to the loft.

She was sitting on the couch, the open laptop discarded on the cushion beside her. She peered at him over the red notebook he had pulled from the microwave in Richmond.

"Pilot FriXion pens," she said.

He waited.

"Know how erasable ink works?" she asked.

"You use the eraser."

"Funny," she said, sans smile. "The ink they use is made of different chemical compounds. When you use the eraser, you create friction, friction creates heat, heat makes one compound activate an acid compound, which neutralizes the dye."

"The microwave."

"Right. They figured out how to use heat to make the ink disappear without friction. You can wipe out all your mission notes with a quick zap in the microwave."

"But that would leave behind—"

"Impressions," she said. "Unfortunately, it looks like the notebook pages are treated to, like, replump with heat to prevent that."

"Is 'replump' a word?"

She ignored him. "Know how they feel a little stiffer, like higher stock?"

By way of display, she rubbed a page between thumb and forefinger.

"So everything's wiped out?" he said.

"Almost. One page in the middle didn't quite get there. Like, you know the cold spot in the center of a frozen burrito?"

"No."

"Never mind. C'mere." She fanned the pages at him, and he could see that she'd shaded every single one with a pencil all the way to the margins. They were uniform charcoal except for one of the innermost pages, on which a snippet of writing had been brought into negative relief.

"*6-1414 Dark Road 32.*"

It reminded him of Jack's last message, the one he'd written invisibly on the driver's window of his truck.

"A partial address?" Evan asked.

"Would you believe there isn't a single address that includes '6-1414 Dark Road 32' in America?"

"How about not in America?"

"There isn't one in any English-speaking country. I checked translations, too. No, it's gotta be a code. Which got me thinking about what kinds of codes Van Sciver might be using with his men. Remember how Delmonico and Shea's files had top-secret classification?"

"'Had'? Past tense?"

"Check it out." She tapped her laptop screen, and Evan was surprised and not surprised to be looking at several documents emblazoned with the highest classified designation. "They were former marines, all right. That's why you got that read on them. But after they left the Corps? They became Secret Service agents."

Staring at the eagle-and-flag security stamp, Evan felt a weightless rise in his gut, the moment before a roller-coaster plummet. Van Sciver's taunt over the phone came back to him once more: *You have no idea, do you? How high it goes?*

Evan had once found himself hugging a cliff edge in the Hindu Kush in the dead of night, waiting for an enemy convoy to pass on the narrow road above. One of his boots had slipped from a thumb-size lip in the sheer face, sending a cascade of stones tumbling. He'd managed to cling to the wall and, looking down, he'd watched the stones vanish into darkness. It was a rare windless night, the mountain air chilled into silence, and yet he'd never heard them hit bottom.

He had the same sense now—holding on for his life with no sense of the greater terrain.

"What does that mean?" Joey asked. "That they used to be Secret Service, too?"

"I don't know for certain," Evan said. "But it's not good."

61

Unacceptable

Charles Van Sciver stood on his Alabama porch as the remaining freelancers loaded out of the plantation house behind him, hauling Hardigg Storm Cases filled with gear and ammo. Their work on this coast was done. It was time to reposition the pawns on the chessboard and stake out key positions so they'd be fast-strike-ready the instant Orphan X reared his head.

Van Sciver had his phone out, the number cued up, but was reluctant to press the button.

He gathered his will.

And he pressed.

Jonathan Bennett had a number of remarkable skills as you would expect from a man of the Office. The most valuable one the public saw almost every day without even noticing.

Impeccable body control.

He'd once slogged through a Louisiana heat wave for a four-day swing—twenty-seven stops from stump speeches to union rallies in humidity so high it felt like wading through a swamp. He'd flipped the state as promised, and never once had he broken a sweat. Not beneath the hot light of the campaign trail, not during the nine debates, not in the situation room contemplating an aerial bombardment to unfuck the rugged north of Iraq.

That's what had killed Nixon. The sweating.

But Bennett was different.

He was the un-Nixon.

Before law school in his early days as a special agent for the Department of Defense, he'd learned to exert control over functions of his body he'd previously thought uncontrollable. This skill had served him well, then and now. He'd never been photographed with a sheen across his forehead or sweat stains darkening a dress shirt. He didn't stammer or make quick, darting movements with his eyes.

Most telling, his hands never shook.

The American people required that in this day and age. A leader with a steady hand. A leader who knew how to sell image, his and theirs. They never noticed the minutiae that projected this competence, at least not consciously, but they registered it somewhere deep in their lizard brains.

That's what you appealed to. What you targeted. What you ruled.

The lizard brains.

Instinct. Survival. Fear.

He studied his staff through the wire-frame eyeglasses he'd selected to convey authority and a certain remoteness. Right now his people were at odds over a housing bill that was threatening to blow up in the Senate and, more importantly, on CNN. For the last five minutes, he'd listened with predatory repose, but now it was time to strike.

He cleared his throat pointedly.

The debate ceased.

Before he could render his judgment, one of three heavy black phones rang on his desk. When he noted which one, he rose from the couch, crossed the rug featuring his seal in monochromatic sculpting, and picked up the receiver with his notably steady hand.

He put his back to the room, a signal, and the murmured discussion resumed behind him.

"Is it done?" he asked.

Orphan Y replied, "No."

Bennett waited two seconds before replying. Two seconds was a long time in the life of a conversation, particularly when one half of that conversation was emanating from the Oval Office.

Bennett was out of earshot of the others, but he lowered his voice anyway. "This cannot get to NSA, CIA, or State. That's why I assigned you my own personally vetted men. It gets out of your hands, it could get out of mine. And that is unacceptable."

Van Sciver said, "I completely—"

Bennett took off his eyeglasses and set them on the blotter. "When I ran the DoD, we had a saying. 'It takes wet work to do a clean job.' I need this to be watertight. I cannot have him out there. He may not know why, but he's the only remaining connective tissue. Someone can connect the dots, and those dots lead through X. Without him they're just dots." Bennett allowed another two-second pause. "Clean out the connective tissue or I'll consider you part of it."

"Yes, Mr. President."

Bennett set the receiver down gently on the cradle that sat on the weighty Resolute desk. A quick internal inventory showed his pulse to be normal, his breathing as calm as ever.

He turned around to face his staff. "Now, where were we?"

62

Not Easy

Still cool from the shower, Evan stood before his dresser in his boxer briefs. He opened the top drawer. Identical dark Levi's 501s on one side and on the other, tactical-discreet cargo pants. They were sharply folded, stacked so neatly they looked machine-cut. He pulled on a pair of cargo pants and snugged the Kydex high-guard holster on the waistband, relieved to be wearing a normal-size pistol again. Then he slid two backup magazines into the streamlined inner pockets. They gave no bulge.

The next drawer down housed ten unworn gray V-neck T-shirts. He put one on, tucked it behind his hip holster. In the closet he grabbed the top shoe box from a tiered tower in the corner. He changed out his Original S.W.A.T. boots regularly, ensuring that he couldn't be tracked by microfibers or soil residue trapped in the tread. Nine Woolrich shirts hung in parallel, magnetic buttons clamped. They were straight from the shipping package, though he'd cut off the price tags and ironed out the wrinkles before hanging them. As he donned the nearest shirt and snapped the buttons shut, he thought about what he was planning to do just a few hours from now.

He was going to walk into the den of the world's most dangerous gang.

Innumerable variables, a risk level too high to assess. That was why he needed every other facet to be locked down, predictable, second-nature. He knew each contour, thread, and operation spec of his gear. Every magazine had been painstakingly validated on a desert range, tested to ensure that it dropped from the well without the slightest hitch.

A passel of fresh Victorinox watch fobs waited in a hinged wooden box. He'd just clipped one to the first belt loop on the left side when it occurred to him that he'd dressed for the mission and not for the preceding dinner at Mia's. He was due downstairs in twenty-three minutes.

Showing up to a DA's condo with illegally concealed firearms didn't strike him as the most prudent idea.

He went back into the bedroom, took off the hip holster, and then removed the magazines from his hidden pockets. The Victorinox fob seemed vaguely militaristic, so he unclipped it and set it aside. The cargo pants and S.W.A.T. boots were low-profile enough, but a wary eye might find them aggressive. He kicked them off, stood there in his boxer briefs and Woolrich button-up.

Now he was questioning the shirt. Tactical magnetic buttons— Mia couldn't possibly notice those. Could she?

He took the shirt off. Then the one under that.

Down to boxer briefs.

This wasn't going well.

There was a knock on his door. Joey called through, "Wanna try that meditating stuff before you go?"

Evan said, "Yes, please."

Evan and Joey sat facing each other in the loft. After Operation Getting Dressed for Dinner, he figured he needed to meditate more than she did. He'd thrown his clothes back on hastily and headed up to meet her in the loft.

She assumed an erect yogi's posture. "Back in Richmond you told David Smith, 'You can't help people more than they want to help themselves.'"

Evan said, "Yes."

He could see that it was taking everything she had to get the words out.

"I want to help myself," she said. "I want to wind up better."

"Okay."

"Clearly I suck at meditation."

"That's not clear. It might be doing exactly what it should be doing."

"Walk me through how to do it again?"

Jack had taught Evan proper procedures for everything from fieldstripping a pistol to readying for meditation. He started to haul out the directives now when he caught himself and thought of the new Commandment he'd invented for himself—and for Joey.

Don't fall in love with Plan A.

She was waiting on him, puzzled by his delay.

"You know what?" he said. "Maybe we've been approaching this wrong."

"What do you mean?"

"Sit however's comfortable. However makes you feel safe."

She gave a nervous laugh. "I don't know."

"Then figure it out."

She looked around. Then she rolled her shoulders. Cracked her jaw. She crossed her legs and uncrossed them. "Can I go to my couch?"

"You can do anything you want."

She got up on the couch, hugged her pillow, pulled her knees in to her chest. She took a cushion and pressed it against her shins. She put another against her exposed side, building a burrow. "Is this weird?"

"There's no such thing as weird."

"Okay," she said. "Okay."

"Does that feel all right?"

She nodded, two quick jerks of her head.

"Just focus on your breath now, and let your body talk to you."

He closed his eyes. As the first minute passed, he acquainted himself with the silence. He barely had time to narrow his focus when she broke. The first shuddering breath and then the storm.

She stayed hugging her knees, curled into herself, sobbing. He waited for her to get up and stomp out like before. She didn't. She rocked herself and cried until the pillow was dark with tears, until her hair stuck to her face, until he thought she'd never stop.

He sat still, being with her without being with her. After a time it occurred to him that might not be enough.

He said, "May I sit by you?"

She shoved tears off her cheeks with the heels of her hands, gave a nod.

He took a seat on the couch at a respectful distance, but she nudged the cushion aside and leaned into him.

He was surprised, caught off guard, unsure of what was expected of him.

At first his arms floated above her stiffly. She was shuddering, hands curled beneath her chin. He thought about what Jack might do and then realized that Jack might never have found himself in a situation like this.

So instead Evan asked himself what *he* might do.

He lowered his arms to comfort her.

He wasn't sure if his touch would elicit anger or flight, but she stayed there, her face buried in his chest.

She felt like an anchor to him, not dragging him down but mooring him to this spot, to this moment, locking his location for once on the grid. For the first time in his life, he felt the tug as something not unpleasant but precious.

Her legs flexed, jogging her back and forth ever so slightly. He held her, rocking her, as she wept. He brushed her hair from his mouth. Cleared his throat.

"You're okay," he said.

"You're gonna be fine," he said.

"You're worth it," he said.

———

Downstairs in his bedroom, he called Mia. When she answered, he took a deep breath.

"Hi, Mia. It's Evan. I know I was supposed to be there twenty minutes ago. But I can't come over for dinner with you and Peter. I'm sorry."

Joey had finally pried herself off the couch to wash her face, and Evan had told her he'd be right back up. He had to head to Pico-Union in an hour and change, and he wasn't willing to leave her alone until he had to. The imperative was as much for him as for her, the protective impulse spilling over into something more intimate, paternal.

It felt threatening and out of control, and he could afford neither at the moment. But he knew that if he left that sixteen-year-old girl alone after what she'd just gone through, he wouldn't forgive himself for it.

There was a brief, surprised silence. And then Mia said, "Okay. Can I ask why?"

He was torn between what he owed Mia and what he owed Joey. "Something personal came up."

"And you couldn't call to let us know? I mean, before?"

"I really couldn't. I'm sorry."

"Peter made place cards and set the table an hour ago. Wait— scratch that." Her breaths came across the receiver. "Sorry. I don't mean to guilt-trip you. And I don't mind that he learns to handle disappointment. That's part of life. But I guess I'm not sure how to handle stuff about you with him when *I* don't even have any answers. And that seems to come up more and more. No answers, I mean. Which I'm not sure is gonna work, Evan. I thought it might. But I don't think it will."

Something inside him crumbled away, brittle and dead. He thought about the dishes stacked on her counter, the smell of laundry, the instructive Post-its, and how they'd always seemed to be from some other life better than he deserved. Nine floors separated Evan from Mia and Peter, and yet they were out of reach. They always had been. But for a brief time, it had been lovely to pretend otherwise.

He said, "I understand."

Not Easy

"You understand." She made an unamused sound of amusement. "You know, I've never seen you upset. Never seen you get mad, flustered, lose it. At first I thought it was a kind of strength. But then I realized it's just a kind of . . . nothing."

Her words weren't just true. They were profoundly true. They landed on him with the tonnage of decades.

"Look," she said. "Even if this is our last conversation, I don't want to do this. I don't want to play the role of the one who cares. And you get to play the role of the wanted asset. We can't figure it out, whatever 'it' is. That's fine. We're both adults with complicated lives. But I wish you at least had the spine to say that you cared, too."

It exploded out from the core of him, a blinding heat, escaping before he could trap it. "You think I'm *pretending*, Mia? That this is some game to me? You think I don't want to just cook linguine and chat over dinner and be with you? I don't have the same choices you do. I lost someone very close to me, and I need to set that right, whether I'm stuck with some kid I don't know what to do with, whether I have other jobs I have to see through, whether you want me to come to dinner. It's what I have to do."

His head hummed. His vision felt loose, as if he'd had a drink. He wondered if he'd actually said the words out loud. It seemed improbable that he had.

"Okay," Mia said. "That's a start. Thank you."

There was not a trace of sarcasm in her voice. He was as stupefied by her reaction as he was by his outburst. He had no slot for any of this, no bearings to guide him into familiar shore.

Across the penthouse he heard the slam of his front door.

His pistol was already drawn, aimed at the open bedroom door, a familiar calm descending over him like a drape. He welcomed it.

"I have to go," he said, and cut the call.

He moved out into the hall, noted a crumpled piece of paper halfway to the great room. He eased past and emerged onto the concrete plain, swinging wide for the best vantage on the closed front door. The elaborate internal locks were unbolted.

Which meant it had been opened from inside.

He holstered the pistol, stuck his head out into the corridor. The elevator had already reached the lobby. He reversed and hustled across to the spiral staircase and up, confirming that, yes, the loft was empty. Joey's rucksack was still there, her treasured shoe box out on the sofa.

That was good. She'd have to come back for those.

With increasing chagrin he padded downstairs, walked to the end of the hall, and stared at the ball of paper ten yards from his open bedroom door. From this position his words to Mia would have been clear and crisp: *I'm stuck with some kid I don't know what to do with.*

He moved forward on numb legs. Crouching over the paper, he uncrumpled it. Fragile pieces of blue and yellow fell out—the remains of a pressed iris from Joey's maunt.

Joey had written a note of her own on the paper.

Thanks for being there for me. I know I'm not easy.

L, J.

63

Devil Horns

The night breeze cut straight through Evan's shirt. Outside the abandoned church, Mara Salvatrucha members clustered loosely in front of the reinforced steel door, their shaved heads making them look sleek and feral. Here on the street, they kept their weapons hidden, but their shirts bulged in predictable places.

When they noted Evan's approach, their skulls pivoted in unison. It was hard to distinguish their eyes from the ink spotting their faces. They flicked their cigarettes aside, shoved off the pillars fronting the church entrance, and presented a unified front that called to mind an NFL defensive line.

As Evan drew within reach, they tugged up their shirts to expose gleaming handguns.

A man with devil-horn tattoos rolled his head back, regarded Evan down the length of his nose. "I think you in the wrong neighborhood."

Evan said, "I want to talk to Freeway."

The men laughed. "A lotta folks want to talk to Freeway."

Evan let the breeze blow.

"Do you have *any idea* who we are, *gringo culero*? We are Mara Salvatrucha. I translate it for you. *Mara* means 'gang.' *Trucha* means 'fear us.'"

Evan stepped forward. The men drew their pistols but did not aim them. "Your tattoos are designed to elicit fear. You're probably used to scaring people when you walk down the street, into a store, a restaurant. Because you've written right on your face how little you care about how you're perceived. And that signals that you're capable of anything. I'm sure you're used to that working. So look at me. Look at me very closely. And ask yourself: Do I look scared?"

For a moment there was nothing but the white-noise hum of traffic in the distance. Devil Horns sniffed, rolled his lower lip between his teeth.

Evan said again, "Tell Freeway I'm here to see him."

The men cast nervous looks between them. Then Devil Horns said, "You packing?"

"Yes. One pistol. And I'm not giving it up. Ask your leader if he's afraid to meet me inside his own headquarters with fifty armed men."

"Be careful what you wish for, *cabrón*." He turned to his compatriots. "Watch this *hijo de puta*."

The steel door creaked open and shut heavily behind him.

Evan waited, keeping a level stare on the remaining men. They returned it, shifting on their blue-and-white Nikes.

At last the door opened again, and Devil Horns emerged. He held the door ajar for Evan. When Evan walked inside, he caught a whiff of incense and body odor.

Dozens of men waited in the nave, holding pistols and submachine guns. They folded behind Evan, encircling him. Freeway sat on the broad carpeted steps beneath the altar like a demon god, his hands clasped.

Tables rimmed the room, covered with baggies and electronic scales. Most of the pallets of boxed TVs had been moved out, but plenty of shoplifted iPhones, Xboxes, and Armani jackets remained.

Devil Horns

The smaller goods spilled out of booster bags—duffels lined with aluminum foil to thwart stores' electronic security detectors.

From the corner of his eye, Evan noted Xavier in the shadowed phalanx, but he made sure not to look at him directly. Evan walked up the aisle between the shoved-aside pews and stopped ten yards shy of Freeway. The man did not rise. Now that Evan was closer, he could discern the features beneath the ink. A pit-bull face—broad cheeks, near-invisible eyebrows, a snub nose that smeared the nostrils into ovals. He had a round head, a bowling ball set on the ledge of his powerful torso. The *MS* tattoo banded his forehead, an honor and a distinction.

Freeway spread his hands, clasped them again. An unspoken question. Ambient light glimmered off the steel studs embedded in his cheeks and lips.

"I have business with one of your men," Evan said. "I want to buy him out."

Freeway's eyes flickered in a blink. It was hard to tell, the tattooed lids blending with the tattooed sclera. "Which man?"

"That's between me and him. Once you agree."

"And if I lie to find out?"

Evan said, "I trust you're a man of your word."

Looking into those black eyes was like looking into death itself.

"Nobody takes what's mine," Freeway said. "I own these men. As much as I own the *putas* I run in the streets. Drugs and guns are good, *sí*. But with those? Everything is a onetime sale. A woman? I can sell ten, fifteen times a day. A man I can use a hundred different ways in the same week." He rose, and the stairs creaked beneath his weight. "There will be no sale. My men are my most valuable possessions."

"I understand. That's why I'm offering to pay you for him."

"If you move on one of my men," Freeway said, "I will kill him, his entire family, and you."

A wet breeze blew through the shattered stained-glass window above. Evan glanced through it at the rooftop where he'd perched just two nights before. He realized he was tired. Tired of the miles he'd put on the tread and tired for the road ahead.

"I don't want a war with you," Evan said. "But I'm not afraid of one."

Freeway showed his teeth. "You. A war. With us."

"I'll give you twenty-four hours to decide. I'll come back. I'll ask again. And either you'll let him leave. Or you will all die."

Some of the men laughed, but Freeway just stared at Evan.

"What are you planning to do?" he asked.

"I'll figure something out."

A rumbling stirred in the ranks.

"Kill this bitch now, Freeway!" a man called from behind Evan.

Freeway reached to the small of his back, came out with a straight razor. "What stops me from gutting you right here?"

"Nothing," Evan said. "But I assume you don't take orders from your underlings."

Freeway pulled the razor open a few inches, let it snick shut. "Why don't we handle this now?"

"It's inconvenient for me," Evan said.

"Inconvenient."

"Yes. I have other business to handle."

"You are an interesting man."

"Twenty-four hours. I'll come back. You give me your decision then." Evan stepped forward, and he heard movement behind him, guns clearing leather, slides being jacked.

Freeway held up a hand, and the gang members silenced.

Evan said, "Assuming you're not afraid to face me again."

The black orbs, sunk in Freeway's face, fixed on Evan.

"I like this game," Freeway said. "Twenty-four hours. I will look forward to this."

When Evan turned, he sensed Xavier somewhere in the back of the crowd. As Evan walked out, the men spread to let him through and then filled the space behind him, moving like a single living organism.

64

Steady as a Metronome

Joey had left the Uber car back at the vintage merry-go-round and asked directions to the old zoo from a group of high-school kids decked out in varsity jackets. She felt like she was inside a CW show. Everything outside was beautiful and night-lit. But inside she was a jumble of raw emotion.

Connor, the skateboarder she and Evan had bumped into outside the safe house, had said that he hung here most nights with friends. She wasn't sure why she'd thought to come here. She just wanted to be out.

To feel like she was normal.

She made her way up the hill, leaving the lights of Griffith Park behind. The farther she got upslope, the sketchier the surroundings. Homeless men rustled in bushes, and tweakers swapped crumpled bills for tinfoil squares. At last she reached the brink of the abandoned zoo.

An empty bear exhibit shoved up from the ground, a rise of Disneyesque stone slabs covered with spray-painted gang tags and fronted by a handful of splintering picnic benches. It looked haunted. She wound her way into the heart of the place, passing rows of cages, the bars vined with ivy. Stone steps led to fenced-off dead ends. A groundskeeper's shack had been turned into a squat house, laughter echoing off the walls, a campfire stretching dancing figures up the walls. She peeked inside but saw only druggies. She kept on, peering through the darkness. Syringes and used condoms littered the narrow path between the cages.

And then she heard the drawl of his voice.

He was inside one of the cages with his friend, the one who'd fallen off the longboard. A few skinny girls around their age were in there, too, their eyes glazed.

Connor looked up through the bars and saw Joey. "Hey."

Her smile felt forced. "Hey."

"Hold this, Scotty." Connor handed off the water bong to his friend and pointed to the back of the enclosure. "Go around. There's a hatch back here."

She circled in the darkness and ducked to squeeze through the narrow opening. As she entered the enclosure, Connor and Scotty held out their fists, and she bumped them.

"This is Alicia," Connor said. "Tammy and Priya."

Joey held up her fist, but the first girl just stared at it. Her lipstick was smeared. "Who's the little girl?" she drawled.

Her friends didn't laugh, but they shook their shoulders as if they were, the effect creepy and detached.

"Forget Alicia," Connor said. "She's fucking wasted." He gestured at Scotty. "Give her the bong. She needs a hit."

"I'm good," Joey said.

Connor smiled, his man bun nodding at the back of his head. Though he was clearly several years older than her, his handsome face was still padded with baby fat. His cheeks looked smooth and white, like he barely needed to shave. The smell of bud and Axe body spray wafted off his untucked shirt. "Okay. Give her a beer."

Scotty passed Joey a beer, and she cracked it and took a sip. It tasted skunky, but she didn't make a face.

"S'good," she said.

"Then tell your face," Alicia said.

Steady as a Metronome

Joey wondered what was wrong with her expression. She was too aware of it now, wearing it like a mask. The bottle suddenly felt large and silly in her hand, a prop. The girls seemed so much older, their frail frames and drugged high lending them an otherworldly aura, as if their feet were floating an inch above the dirt. Joey felt clumsy and common by comparison, a flightless bird.

Scotty enabled the light on his iPhone and rested it on a concrete ledge by a pile of rusted beer cans. Graffiti covered the walls and ceiling, the bubble letters and vulgar sketches made menacing in the severe light.

"Alicia," Connor said, "that was the last beer. Wanna grab the other sixer from the cooler?"

Alicia's lips peeled back in a smile. She ran her hand up her throat as if feeling her skin for the first time. "Sure, Connor."

She held up a pale fist to Joey. "I was just kidding earlier," she said. "C'mon, gimme knucks."

Joey lifted her hand, but Alicia lowered her fist and turned away, the other girls snickering in a matching low key. Alicia slid an anorexic shoulder along the wall to the hatch, the other girls trailing her, so pale and insubstantial they looked like shades. They slipped through the cramped space without slowing.

As soon as they vanished, Scotty stepped over, blocking the way out. Joey sensed Connor sidle up behind her.

Blocking her in.

All of a sudden, Joey felt her awkwardness lift. She was aware of the scuff of Connor's shoe in the dirt, the distance to the concrete walls around her, the latent power of her muscles. Her heartbeat ticked in the side of her neck, as steady as a metronome.

This part wasn't scary or intimidating, not like drinking beer or bumping fists or figuring out how to smile the right way.

This part felt like home.

As she started to turn, Connor grabbed her belt in the front and pulled her close. She let him. He was big enough to bow her lower back, her face uptilted to his. His breath smelled like tea leaves.

His hand curled over her belt, knuckles pressed into her lower stomach.

"You know why you came," he said.

Joey said, "Let go of me."

He kissed her.

She kept her mouth closed, felt his stubble grate her lips. Behind her she heard Scotty laugh. Connor pulled his face back but kept the front of her jeans clamped in his fist.

She said, "Let go of me."

Connor loomed over her. "I don't think I want to just yet."

She stepped away, but he tugged her buckle, snapping her back against his chest.

"Oh," she said sympathetically. "You think you're in charge."

Calmly, she chambered her leg high and pistoned her heel through his ankle.

The snap sounded like a heavy branch giving way.

Connor stared down at his caved shin in disbelief. His foot nodded to the side, ninety degrees offset from the ankle.

Joey said, "Three . . . two . . ."

He screamed.

Scotty yelled, "Crazy bitch!" and charged her, lowering his shoulder for a football tackle. Sidestepping, she took his momentum and redirected him into the wall. His face smacked the concrete. It left a wet splotch. He toppled over, his legs cycling against the pain, heels shoving grooves in the dirt.

Joey placed her hand on Connor's barrel chest and shoved. He fell hard, landing next to Scotty. He was still making noises.

She squeezed through the narrow hatch, emerging from the cage. As she stepped out, she sensed the world opening up all around her. Starting back down the hill to civilization, she felt a part of her flutter free from the trap inside her chest and take flight against the canopy of stars.

65

Not an Innocent

Joey stepped through the unlocked door of 21A and stared at the cavernous great room. All the lights were off, but the city shone through the giant windows, making the contours of the penthouse glimmer darkly.

A silhouette rose from one of the bar chairs at the kitchen island. Evan.

He said, "I made up your bed."

Joey stepped inside and shut the door behind her. "Thanks."

"I'm not very good at it," he said.

"What?"

He gestured from her to him. "This."

"You're better than you think."

"I didn't mean what I said on the phone. What you overheard."

"I know."

She came forward, and they stared at each other.

"I went to see that guy with the stupid hair," she said. "From outside the safe house?"

Evan nodded.

"He's a useless reprobate," she said. "You were right."

Evan said, "I don't want to be right."

She leaned into him stiffly, her forehead thunking against his chest, her arms at her sides. He hesitated a moment and then hugged her, one hand holding the back of her head, her thick, thick hair.

He said, "Rough night all around, huh?"

"Yeah." Her voice rose an octave and cracked. "I think I'm done pretending."

"Pretending what?"

"Acting like I didn't need anything from anyone. I started after my maunt died, because . . . you know, I wasn't gonna get it anyways." She straightened up. "But I was lying. Now and then I still think about what mighta been. Someone to tuck me in, maybe. You know, 'How was your day?' Cute boy in homeroom. A soccer team. All that normal shit. Instead. Instead." Her lips wobbled. "Do you think I ever could?"

"Yes."

"It's not too late?"

"No. Once we get Van Sciver, we'll find what comes next for you. It doesn't have to be this."

She blinked, and a tear glided down her flawless brown cheek. "How 'bout you?"

"It's not an option anymore for me. It's different."

She looked up at him. "Is it?"

He nodded.

"Even after you get Van Sciver?"

"There will always be Van Scivers."

"But what about Mia? And the kid?"

"There will always be Van Scivers," he said again.

She pursed her lips and studied him in the semidarkness. "I remember I was fourteen, bleeding from my ear. Van Sciver put me with a demolition breacher who let me get too close to a door charge. I thought it was a punctured eardrum. He took me back to town and dropped me at a park, you know, for pickup. Anyways, I was worse than anyone thought. I was stumbling along off the trail. And I came up behind a guy on a bench, rocking himself and murmuring. At first I thought he was injured, too. Or crazy. But then I saw he had a baby. His baby. And he was holding it so gently. I snuck up behind him in the bushes. And he was saying . . . he was saying, 'You are safe. You are loved.'" Her eyes glimmered. "Can you imagine?"

Walking behind Jack in the woods, placing his feet in Jack's footprints.

"Yes," Evan said.

"Maybe that's all anyone needs," Joey said. "One person who feels that way about you. To keep you human."

"It's a gift," Evan said. "It's also a weakness."

"Why?"

"Because it's a vulnerability they can exploit. Jack protecting me. Me protecting you. Us protecting David Smith. But we're gonna stop all that now. Instead of letting them use it against us, we're gonna start using it against them. The Ninth Commandment."

"'Always play offense,'" she said. "But how?"

"We have what they want."

She stared at him, puzzled.

He said, "Us."

Her eyes gleamed. "Use me as bait."

Evan nodded. "And we know where to drop the line."

They left at five in the morning, switched out Evan's truck for a black Nissan Altima he kept at a safe house beneath an LAX flight path. Seven hours and four minutes later, they reached Phoenix. They did a few hours of recon and planning before pulling over in the shade of a coral gum tree. The car windows were cracked open, and the arid breeze tasted of dust.

The downtown skyline, such as it was, rose a few blocks away. They were on the fringe of suburbia here, two blocks north of the 10 Freeway, a handful more to the 17. A tall-wall ad on the side of a circular parking structure proclaimed ARIZONA'S URBAN HEART and featured a cubist rendering of a heart composed of high-rises.

Evan and Joey had worked out a dozen contingencies and then a dozen more, charting escape routes, meet points, emergency scenarios. Because they'd driven from Los Angeles and didn't have to concern themselves with airport security, he'd brought a trunkful of gear and weaponry, a mission-essential loadout that left him prepared for virtually anything. But at the end of the day, when you went fishing, you never knew precisely what you'd get on the line.

As if reading his thoughts, Joey said, "Okay. So if they go to grab me. What do you do?"

"Grab them."

She shifted the bouquet of irises in her lap. "And then what?"

"Make them talk."

"How?"

Evan just looked at her.

"Right," she said. "And if we're not so lucky as to have *that* work out?"

"Don't fall in love with Plan A."

The sunlight shifted, and at the peak of the hill above, the arched sign over the wrought-iron gate came visible.

SHADY VALE CEMETERY.

This was where Jack had found Joey, visiting her maunt's grave. As she'd said, he knew how her heart worked.

Van Sciver knew, too, though not from the inside out. He understood people from a scientific remove, learning where the soft spots were, which buttons to push, where to tap to elicit a reflex.

He had kept Joey for eleven months, had trained, analyzed, and assessed her. Evan was counting on the fact that Van Sciver was strategically sharp enough to surveil a location that held this kind of emotional importance to her. Whether that surveillance took the form of hidden cameras or freelancers on site, he wasn't sure.

For Van Sciver vulnerability was little more than a precipitating factor in a chain reaction. Joey's maunt would lead to Joey. Joey would lead to Evan.

Evan thought about the GPS unit Van Sciver had planted in David Smith's arm and wondered how they'd plan to tag Joey if they caught her here.

He recalled the Secret Service background of at least two of the freelancers Van Sciver had hired. Van Sciver had never drawn operators from the Service before, and it was unlikely a random choice for him to do so now. Evan's train of thought carried him into unpleasant terrain, where the possibilities congealed into something dark and toxic.

Joey screwed in her earpiece and started to get out of the black car. Evan put his hand on her forearm to halt her. A memory flash hit him—the image of himself at nineteen years old climbing out of Jack's truck at Dulles International, ready to board a plane for his first mission. Jack had grabbed Evan's arm the same way.

It was the first time Evan had ever seen him worried.

Evan reminded himself that he wasn't worried now. Then he reminded himself again. Joey was looking at him in a way that indicated that his face wasn't buying what he was telling himself.

"What?" she said.

"The Tenth Commandment," Evan said. " 'Never let an innocent die.' " He paused. "This is a risk."

"I'm not an innocent," Joey said.

He nodded. For this mission she wasn't.

"Plus, they need me to get to you," Joey added. "Like you said, they want to snatch me, direct the action."

"That's our play, but it's still a guess. With former Secret Service in the mix, we don't know how far this reaches. But we know what they're willing to do."

"I'm fast," she said. "I'll stay in public, keep my head on a swivel."

"If we do this . . ."

"What, Evan?"

"Don't fuck up."

"What does *that* mean?"

"After what happened to Jack, nothing will stop me from getting to Van Sciver. Nothing. And no one." His throat was dry, whether from the dry desert air or the air-conditioning, he didn't know. "Don't put me in a position to make that choice."

She read his meaning, gave a solemn nod, and climbed out of the car.

66

Friction Heat

Lyle Green handed off the binoculars to his partner, Enzo Pellegrini, who raised them to his face and blew out a breath that reeked of stale coffee. They were sitting in a parked truck, focused on a particular headstone on a rolling swell of grass. It was a shade of green you only got from well-fertilized soil, which meant corpses or gardeners, and Shady Vale had an excess of both.

Enzo said, "Eyes up, south entrance."

Lyle said, "Right, like your 'eyes up' on the pregnant broad or the guy with the prosthetic leg."

"It was a limp."

"Because that's what you do when you have a prosthetic leg."

"Girl, midteens."

Lyle pulled the detached rifle scope from the console and lifted it to his face. The girl cut behind a stand of bushes and stepped into view. "Holy shit. That's her."

"Raise Van Sciver. Now."

Lyle grabbed his Samsung, dialed through Signal.

A moment later Van Sciver's voice came through. "Code."
Lyle checked the screen. "'Merrily dogwood.'"
"Go."
"It's her. It's the girl."
She drifted close enough that Lyle no longer required the scope. She set a bunch of flowers before the grave and paused, her face downturned, murmuring something to the earth.
"Do not approach," Van Sciver said. "Repeat: Do not approach. Track her at a distance in case X is watching. Pick your moment and get her tagged. Let her lead us to him."
Enzo dropped open the glove box. Inside were a variety of GPS tracking devices—microdots, magnetic transmitters for vehicle wheel wells, a vial of digestible silicon microchips.
The girl headed off, and Lyle tapped the gas and drifted around the cemetery's perimeter, keeping her in sight. "Copy that."

Twenty minutes later Lyle sat in a crowded taqueria, sipping over-cinnamoned horchata and peering across the plaza to where the target sat at a café patio table. Lyle had a Nikon secured around his neck with camera straps sporting the Arizona State University logo. Smudges of zinc-intensive sunscreen and a proud-alumnus polo shirt completed the in-town-for-a-game look.
He pretended to fuss with the camera, zeroing in with the zoom lens on the girl. Scanning across the patio, he picked up on Pellegrini inside the café, leaning against the bar and swirling a straw in his Arnold Palmer. A few orders slid across the counter, awaiting pickup. Pellegrini removed a vial of microchips, dumped them in a water glass, and used his straw to stir them in.
He'd just resumed his loose-limbed slump against the bar when the waitress swung past and grabbed the tray. As she carried the salad and spiked water glass over to Joey's table and set them down, Pellegrini exited the café from the opposite side and walked to the bordering street where they'd parked the truck.
Lyle kept the Nikon pinned on the water glass resting near Joey's elbow. From this distance the liquid looked perfectly clear, the tiny black microchips invisible. Once ingested, they would mass

in the stomach, where they'd be stimulated by digestive juices and emit a GPS signal every time the host ate or drank. The technology had recently been improved, no longer requiring a skin patch to transmit the signal, which made for easier stealth deployment. But with this upgrade came a trade-off; the signal's duration was shorter, remaining active for only ten minutes after mealtime. The microchips broke down and passed from the system in just forty-eight hours.

Van Sciver was banking on the fact that at some point within two days she'd be in proximity to Orphan X.

The girl poked at her salad, then rested her hand on the water glass. Lyle willed her to pick it up and drink, but something on her phone had captured her attention. She removed her hand, and he grimaced.

He had to put the camera down to avoid suspicion, so he took another chug of sugary horchata while he watched her thumb at her phone and not drink water.

His Samsung vibrated, and he answered.

"Code," Van Sciver said.

Lyle checked the screen. " 'Teakettle lovingly.' "

"Update."

"The table's set. We're just waiting on her to do her part."

"Mechanism?"

"Water glass."

"I'll hold on the line," Van Sciver said.

Lyle swallowed to moisten his throat. "Okay."

The silence was uncomfortable.

Enough time had passed that Lyle could fiddle with his Nikon again without drawing attention. He lifted it up, watched Joey chewing and gazing absentmindedly into the middle distance. The sun was directly overhead, warming the patio. They were in fucking Arizona. Why wouldn't she just take a sip of water?

At last she wiped her mouth. She reached for the glass. She lifted it from the table.

A figure loomed behind her, blurry in the zoom-lens close-up. A hand lifted the water glass out of the girl's hand.

Lyle adjusted the focus, found himself staring at Orphan X.

Friction Heat

How the hell did X know the water had been spiked?

Abruptly, Lyle was perspiring. The ASU polo stuck to the small of his back. X was saying something to the girl.

Lyle's breathing must have changed, because Van Sciver said, "What? What is it?"

Lyle started at the voice; he had forgotten about the phone pressed to his cheek. His mind whirled, assessing the best phrasing of the update. He opened his mouth, but dread prevented any words from exiting.

The girl rose to leave.

Orphan X paused by her chair, water glass still in hand.

Then he drank it down.

As X followed the girl out of the plaza, Lyle felt his mouth drop open a bit wider. A chime announced the GPS beacon going live on his Samsung.

Van Sciver said, "What happened?"

It took Lyle two tries to get the words out. "We just hit the jackpot."

Samsung in hand, Lyle ran across the plaza to where Pellegrini waited in the idling truck. Lyle jumped in, eyeing the GPS grid, gesturing madly for Pellegrini to turn right.

"There, there, there! We only have seven minutes left."

Pellegrini looked confused by Lyle's urgency. "We got the girl?"

Lyle said, "We got Orphan X."

Pellegrini's expression went flat with shock. The tires chirped as he pulled out. Lyle directed him around the block, following the blinking dot on his screen.

"Do we do this ourselves?" Pellegrini said. "Or wait for backup?"

Lyle held up the screen. As former Secret Service, they had a clear operational sweet spot, and that encompassed surveillance, prevention, and protection. When they had to be, they were proficient assaulters as well, but that wasn't where the critical mass of their training had been spent. That had been made all too apparent by the death count of their fellow recruitees.

"We have Orphan X tagged," Lyle said. "We can get the drop on him if we move right now."

Pellegrini nosed the truck around the corner, and they saw it up ahead, a black Nissan Altima with a spoiler, Orphan X in view behind the wheel, the girl in the passenger seat. Lyle texted the vehicle description and license plate to Van Sciver.

Van Sciver had access to satellites, and once they locked the car in from above, there was nowhere on God's green earth it could go that it wouldn't be found.

Van Sciver's text confirmed: BIRDS ONLINE NOW.

ARE YOU EN ROUTE?

ALMOST AT THE AIRPORT.

The Nissan wheeled around the corner. As it turned, Orphan X's face rotated slightly toward them.

"Shit," Pellegrini said. "Did he see us?"

"I don't know," Lyle said. "I don't think so."

"Tell Van Sciver."

Lyle texted: MIGHT HAVE BEEN MADE. UNSURE.

Van Sciver's reply: PROCEED. BE CAUTIOUS.

The Nissan kept driving, neither quicker nor slower. They stayed on its tail.

"Holy shit," Lyle said. "We're gonna be the ones. We're gonna be the ones."

"Calm down," Pellegrini said.

Up ahead the Nissan pulled into a six-story parking structure.

Lyle texted Van Sciver: ENTERED PARKING GARAGE.

The reply: BIRDS ARE UP. WE'LL PICK HIM UP WHEN HE EXITS. FLUSH HIM OUT BUT DO NOT PURSUE.

Lyle brought up the GPS screen, watched the dot rise and rise. "He's heading to an upper floor."

Pellegrini turned into the parking structure. As he slowed to snatch a ticket from the dispenser, Lyle pointed ahead. The black car, now empty, was parked next to the handicapped spots by the elevators.

The truck pulled through, and Lyle hopped out and circled the car, confirming it was empty. As he ran back to the truck, he was already keying in his next text to Van Sciver: CAR EMPTY, PARKED BY ELEVATORS ON GROUND FLOOR.

The last reception bar flickered, but the text sent just before the

Friction Heat

Samsung lost service. Lyle climbed into the truck. "Go, go, go. He went upstairs."

Pellegrini said, "Why?"

"If he's switching cars on another level, we have to get there to ID the new vehicle for the satellites. We've only got a few minutes before we lose GPS."

A circular ramp looped around a hollow core at the center of the parking structure. Pellegrini accelerated into the turn, centrifugal force shoving Lyle against the door as they rode up the spiral to the second level.

He watched the dot. It was way above them on six.

Pellegrini made a noise, and Lyle glanced up from the screen.

A black rope was now dangling down the center column of the parking structure.

Lyle's brain couldn't process the rope's sudden appearance. He looked back at the screen. The dot was no longer way above them. It was on the fifth level. Now the fourth.

Pellegrini was slowing the truck, reaching for his handgun.

Lyle looked back at the thick nylon cord dangling ten feet away from them.

A *rappelling* rope.

As they curved around onto the third floor, Orphan X zippered down the rope, a pistol steady in his gloved hand.

The driver's window blew out as he shot Pellegrini through the temple.

Even after the spatter hit Lyle, he hadn't caught up to what was happening. Orphan X rappelled down as the unmanned truck banged up the ramp to the third level, their fall and rise coordinated like the two sides of a pulley.

There was a suspended moment as the two men drew eye level, Lyle catching a perfect view of X's face over the top of the aligned sights.

He saw the muzzle flare and nothing else.

Evan hit the ground floor, coming off the fast rope and crouching to break his fall. He threw his gloves off with a flick of his wrists and they dangled from clips connecting them to his sleeves, the full-grain leather steaming with friction heat.

Seventeen men down.

Eight left.

Joey stepped out from the stairwell and ran across to meet Evan at the Nissan Altima. As he tore off the detachable spoiler and ran it over to a Dumpster, she stripped carbon-fiber wrap from the Altima, revealing the car's original white coat. Evan unscrewed the Arizona license plates, exposing the California plates beneath.

A few puzzled pedestrians gawked up the ramp at the rappelling rope. Near the third level by the smashed truck, horns blared. There was enough confusion that Evan and Joey went largely unnoticed. They stuffed the Arizona plates and fiber wrap in the trash container near the elevator, climbed into the now-white Nissan, and pulled out into the flow of traffic.

67

The Pretty One

As Orphan X, Evan had left behind a spaghetti snarl of associations, connections, and misery. Every high-value target he neutralized anywhere on the globe was a stress point in a vast web. The Secret Service's involvement meant that somewhere in his dark past a silken thread trembled, leading back to the heart of the District.

As he neared the freeway exit, Joey said, "Hang on."

Pulled from his thoughts, he glanced over the console at her. "We've gotta get back to L.A."

"There's something I want to do first."

The set of her face made him nod.

He followed her directions, winding into an increasingly shabby part of east Phoenix. Joey studied the passing scenery with an expression that Evan knew all too well.

"They call this area the Rock Block," she said. "Can't walk down the sidewalk without tripping over a baggie of crack."

Evan kept on until she gestured ahead. "Up here," she said.

He got out and stood by the driver's door, unsure in which direction she wanted to go. She came around the car and brushed against him, crossing the street. He followed.

Behind a junkyard of a front lawn sat a house that used to be yellow. Most of the cheap vinyl cladding had peeled up, curling at the edges like dried paint. An obese woman filled a reinforced swing on one corner of the front porch.

Joey stepped through a hinge-challenged knee-high front gate, and Evan kept pace with her through the yard. They passed an armless doll, a rusting baby stroller, a sodden mattress. Joey stepped up onto the porch, the old planks complaining.

Despite the cool breeze, sweat beaded the woman's skin. She wore a Navajo-print dress. Beneath the hem Evan could see that half of one foot had been amputated, the nub swaying above the porch. The other leg looked swollen, marbled with broken blood vessels. Evan could smell the sweet, turbid smell of infection. A tube snaked up from an oxygen tank to the woman's nose. The swing creaked and creaked.

The woman didn't bother to look at them, though they were standing right before her.

Joey said, " 'Member me, Nemma?"

Fanning herself with a *TV Guide*, the woman moved her gaze lazily over to take Joey in.

"Maybe I do," the woman said. "You were the pretty one. Little bit dykey."

Joey said, "I wonder why."

Air rattled through the woman's throat, an elongated process that sounded thick and wet. "There's nuthin' you can do to me the diabetes ain't done already. And that's just the start. They cut out the upper left lobe of my lung. Five, six times a day, I get the coughs where I can't even clear my own throat. I have to double over, give myself the Heimlich just so's to breathe. Bastards took away my foster-care license and everything."

Joey eased apart from Evan, putting a decaying wicker coffee table between them. She said, "You want me to feel sorry for you?"

The woman made a sound like a laugh. "I don't want anything anymore."

The Pretty One

Evan noticed that his hip holster felt light. Joey stood with her body bladed to him so he couldn't see her left side. The woman's gaze had fixed on something in Joey's hand. Evan recalled how Joey had brushed against him by the Altima after he'd parked. He didn't have to move his hand to the holster to know it was empty.

Joey had positioned herself nicely. The angle over the coffee table was tricky. He wouldn't get to her in time, not given her reflexes and training.

The woman gave a resigned nod. "You came to hurt me?"

Evan sidled back a step, but Joey eased forward, keeping the mass of the table between them. Her eyes never left the woman's face.

He stopped, and Joey stopped, too. He still couldn't see her hand, but her shoulder was tense, her muscles ready.

The only sound was the sonorous rasp of the woman's breathing.

Joey exhaled slowly, the tension leaking from her body. "Nah," she said. "I'd rather let life take you apart piece by piece. Like you did to all us girls. The difference is, I can put myself back together."

The woman didn't move. Evan didn't either.

Joey stepped forward and leaned over her. "You don't get to live in me anymore. You get to live in yourself."

She turned and walked off the porch. As she passed Evan, she handed his pistol back to him.

They left the woman swaying on the porch.

68

Locked-Room Mystery

Candy stepped up to the police cordon at the Phoenix parking structure. The cops had loosened up the crime scene by degrees, CSI coming and going.

An officer stopped her. "Are you parked inside, ma'am?"

"Yeah, I work at the PT office across the plaza, and—Oh my God, what happened?"

"We can't disclose that, ma'am. Please claim your vehicle and exit immediately."

She nodded nervously and stepped inside, scanning the cars on the ground level. Van Sciver had kept satellite monitoring on the garage all day, and there'd been no sign of a black Nissan Altima exiting.

The ramp was still blocked off, cops dispersed through the parking structure. Candy strode toward the elevators, taking in the remaining cars. No black Altima.

The car hadn't left the building. And it wasn't in the parking spot where Lyle Green's last text indicated.

Which made for the kind of locked-room mystery she wasn't in the mood for.

Her gaze pulled to the trash can beside the handicapped spaces. It was stuffed with what looked like black tarp. She drew closer.

She said, "Fuck."

She twisted the lid off the concrete trash container and looked down at the heap of stripped-off carbon-fiber wrap. Digging through the detritus, she pulled out the pieces, checking each one for distinguishing marks. Midway through the stack, she found a tiny copyright logo at the edge of a band of stiff carbon fiber: ©FULL AUTO WRAPATTACK.

She took a picture with her cell phone and texted the image to Van Sciver. As she shoved the material back into the trash, she noted the ditched license plates in the bottom of the container.

She exited the structure through a side door, slipped past a break in the cordon, walked across the plaza, and got into the backseat of one of two Chevy Tahoes waiting at metered spots. They were heavily armored, just like the one in Richmond.

Van Sciver and Thornhill occupied the seats in front of her.

Thornhill held up his phone with a location pin-dropped on Google Maps. "Full Auto WrapAttack," he said, "At 1019B South Figueroa. Los Angeles. One shop, they custom-make their own materials on site. What do you think?"

Van Sciver weighed this a moment. "It's not a sure thing," he said. "But it's the best bet. Let's move headquarters."

Thornhill said, "Good thing we're mobile."

Candy turned to look into the Tahoe parked one spot behind them. Through the tinted rear window, she could barely make out the outlines of the eight freelancers crammed into the bench seats. "Which one's the pilot?" she asked.

"Guy in the passenger seat," Van Sciver said. "I have a Black Hawk on standby. We'll set up downtown, striking distance to most points in the city. The minute X eats or drinks something, we'll have ten minutes to scramble to his location and put him and the girl down."

"You think the girl's worth killing?" Candy said.

"Why take the chance?" Thornhill said.

Candy said, "You pay him extra to answer for you?"

Van Sciver met Candy's stare in the rearview.

She knew she had overstepped her bounds, and she had no idea what might happen next.

Van Sciver said, "Step out of the car, Thornhill."

Thornhill obeyed.

Candy could feel the pulse beating in the side of her neck. "Let's skip the part where you beat your chest and I back down," she said. "Consider me backed down. Why don't we think about this. And by 'we' I mean you and I—the ones with brains. Thornhill's a blank space. A good body and a nice set of teeth. There's nothing there."

She pictured Van Sciver wheeling around in the driver's seat, his hand clamping her larynx, squeezing the air passage shut. But no, he remained where he was, a large immovable force, his eyes drilling her in the mirror.

"He's an extension of me," Van Sciver said. "He's a scope."

"And scopes have their use," she said. "But we're talking strategy. It's a surgical operation. We want clean margins. What is unnecessary brings with it unnecessary complications. We X out Evan, we leave no trace. We kill a sixteen-year-old girl, that makes a bigger ripple in the pond. Which means unforeseen ramifications. Then who do we have to kill to take care of those?"

That blown pupil in the rearview seemed to pull her in. She found herself leaning back to avoid tumbling down the rabbit hole.

"I don't care," Van Sciver said.

"But the man in charge might."

For the first time, Van Sciver looked away. His trapezius muscles tensed, flanking the neck. She was certain he was going to explode, but instead he gave a little nod. Then he gestured at Thornhill, who was waiting patiently at the curb. Thornhill climbed back in, started up the nav on his phone, and both Tahoes pulled out in unison.

The two-SUV convoy headed for Los Angeles.

69

A Drool Not of Saliva

By the time they returned to Castle Heights, Evan and Joey were ragged from the drive and the detour to switch vehicles. Evan pulled his trusty Ford pickup into his spot on the subterranean parking level, and they climbed out. He took a moment to stretch his lower back before heading in.

They heard the voice before they stepped through the door to the lobby.

"—just saying you should go easy on the carbs at your age. I mean, have you *seen* you? You could stand to tighten up."

As Evan and Joey came around the corner, Lorilee and her boyfriend came into view standing before the bank of mail slots. Her head was lowered, her cat eyes swollen. The boyfriend swept his long hair off his face with a practiced flick of his head and continued flipping through the stack of mail in his hands.

"And where's my new credit card?" he continued. "I thought you said you ordered it already."

As Evan came up on them, Lorilee wouldn't meet his gaze. Evan thought about what Joey had just confronted on that porch in Phoenix and how an argument like this would sound to her ears. He felt bone-tired and angry.

Lorilee's reply was soft, the voice of a little girl. "I did."

"Yeah, well, then is it magic that it's still not—"

Evan's elbow moved before he told it to, knocking the boyfriend's arm and dumping the sheaf of mail onto the floor.

"Oops," Evan said. "Didn't see you."

He crouched down to gather the envelopes, reading the boyfriend's shadowy reflection on the polished tiles.

"No worries, man," the boyfriend said, leaning to help.

Evan rose abruptly, shattering the guy's nose with the back of his head.

The boyfriend reeled back, leaning against the mail slots, hand to his face. Bright red blood streamed down his forearm.

"Oh, jeez," Evan said, "I'm so sorry."

Behind him Joey coughed into a fist. He saw something in Lorilee's eyes, something like a smile.

Evan gave an apologetic nod, patted the guy on the back, and started for the elevator. "Keep pressure on that and send me the bill."

Inside the Vault, Evan fed Vera II an ice cube. He hadn't watered her in a while, and the tips of her spikes were browning. Then he crossed to the gun locker, unclipped his holstered ARES from his waistband, and put it away.

Sitting on the sheet-metal desk, Joey watched him disarm. "This is so stupid. It's *way* too dangerous."

He removed the spare magazines from the hidden pockets of his cargo pants and set them aside as well. "Yes."

"You're just gonna walk in there? Confront the entire gang?"

"Yes."

They'd been having this argument for hours, and it was showing no sign of abating.

"You cannot go into that church unarmed," Joey said.

"I told them I was coming back to kill them all," Evan said. "There's no way they let me in with a weapon. Not this time."

A Drool Not of Saliva

He smoothed down his shirt, checked his Victorinox watch fob. It was almost time.

"If *every single thing* doesn't go exactly right—"

"Joey," he said. "I know."

"Why don't you wait until we figure out a better plan?"

"I told Freeway twenty-four hours. A guy like him will get restless if I don't show, start asking questions, exerting pressure. If he finds out Xavier's behind it, he'll kill him."

"You're really gonna do this? For some guy you barely even know?"

"Yes."

Unarmed, he started out.

She slid off the desk, put her palm on his chest. Her yellow-flecked green eyes were fierce. *"Why?"*

"Because he needs help. And I'm the only one who can give him this kind of help."

She implored him with her eyes.

"Joey," he said. "This is what I do. It's what I've always done. Nothing's changed."

"I guess . . . I guess *I* have."

"What do you mean?"

"Once you realize you want a life," she said, "it's a lot harder to risk it."

He thought of Jack stepping out of that Black Hawk, riding the slipstream, spinning through darkness.

He moved her hand off his chest and walked out.

The Mara Salvatrucha contingent outside the church had been beefed up, no doubt in anticipation of Evan's return. At 9:59 P.M. he emerged from the shadows and walked up to the crew of waiting men.

The handguns came out quickly, ten barrels aimed at Evan's face. He halted a few steps from the doors.

Devil Horns said, "Spread your arms. We need to make sure you ain't jacketed up like some Mohammed motherfucker."

Evan obeyed.

Two younger MS-13 members came forward and patted him down roughly from his ankles to his neck. Puzzled, they looked back at the others and shrugged. "He's clean."

Devil Horns smiled, shaking his head as he reached for the reinforced door. "You play one crazy-ass fool."

The hinges squealed as the door swung open. It seemed the rest of the gang was waiting inside, scattered among the overturned pews. Only a dim altar lamp illuminated the interior, falling across Freeway's shoulders, backlighting him.

Dozens of tattooed faces swiveled to chart Evan's progress through the nave. He didn't bother to look for Xavier; he'd contacted him earlier and told him to make sure he wasn't on site.

Xavier would not survive what was about to happen.

Evan reached the center of the church and paused. Freeway pressed one fist into the other palm, the knuckles popping one at a time.

"Twenty-four hours," Freeway said.

"That's right."

Freeway curled his lower lip, the piercings clinking on his teeth. "And now you've come to kill us all."

"That's right."

A few of the men laughed.

"How you gonna do that?" Freeway asked.

"With this." Evan reached for his cargo pocket. In the shadows countless submachine guns rose and countless slides clanked.

Freeway held up his arms for his men to calm down. Then he nodded at Evan to proceed.

The Velcro patch on Evan's pocket flap gave way with a tearing noise that sounded unreasonably loud in the quiet church. Evan stuck his hand in the pocket and came out with a Snickers bar.

There was a disbelieving silence.

Evan peeled the wrapper and took a bite. He chewed, swallowed. He couldn't remember the last time he'd eaten a candy bar.

He'd taken it from Joey's rucksack.

One of the men cracked up, a deep rumble, and then the laughter spread.

A Drool Not of Saliva

No amusement showed on Freeway's face. He skewered Evan with his black stare. "This *pendejo* is fucking *loco*."

"We should skin him," someone called out from the darkness.

Freeway flicked open his straight razor. "Not you. Me." He started down the carpeted stairs, those tattooed eyes never leaving Evan. "Big dog's gotta eat."

Evan took another bite. "I'm not done yet," he said through a full mouth.

"You want to finish your candy bar?" Freeway said.

Evan nodded.

Freeway kept the razor open, but he crossed his arms, the blade rising next to the grooved ball of his biceps. "Okay," he said. "Your last meal."

Evan chewed some more, then popped the last bite into his mouth. He crumpled up the wrapper, let it fall from his hand onto the floor.

Freeway started forward, but Evan held up a finger as he cleared the caramel from his molars with his tongue. He strained his ears but heard nothing. A spark of concern flared to life in his stomach. He was out of time.

And then he sensed it.

The air vibrating with a distant thrumming.

It grew louder.

Freeway took a half step back toward the altar, his eyes pulling up to the ceiling. The other men looked spooked, regarding the church walls around them. The thumping grew louder. A few shards of stained glass fell from the high frame.

From beyond the front door came the unmistakable sound of sniper rounds lasering through the air. Then the thud of falling bodies.

Evan said to Freeway, "You might want to go see about that."

The steel front door blew open, Devil Horns sailing back through the vestibule, the top of his head blown off. A Black Hawk whoomped down at the entrance, gusting wind through the nave. Operators in balaclavas spilled out with military precision, subguns raised, firing through the doorway, dropping the first ranks of gang members.

The inadvertent cavalry, right on time.

As the gang members scrambled to return fire, Evan walked to the side of the church where the stolen goods were stored. Ducking behind a head-high pallet, he dumped out a booster bag, emptying a load of RFID-tagged Versace shirts onto the floor. Then he climbed into the roomy duffel and zipped himself in. The inside, lined with thick space-blanket foil, crinkled around him.

His own miniature Faraday cage.

It would mute the GPS signal emanating from his stomach.

The sounds from the church nave were apocalyptic. Cracking rounds, panicked shrieks, crashing bodies, wet bellowing, splintering wood—a full-fledged urban firefight.

Two birds, one stone.

At last the frequency of gunfire slowed. A prayer in Spanish was cut off with a last report.

The smell of cordite reached Evan even here, hidden in the bag. He heard heavy boots moving through the nave, and then Thornhill said, *"Clear.* Jesus F. Christ. Who knew we were wading into Fallujah?"

Van Sciver's deep voice carried to Evan. "What a shitshow. How many did we lose?"

Candy's voice said, "Three. I count three."

In the darkness of the booster bag, Evan thought, *Twenty dead. Five to go.*

Van Sciver's voice came again. "Where's X?"

Thornhill again. "I don't know. The GPS signal, it vanished."

"Vanished? We had at least four more minutes by my count."

"I don't know what to tell you."

"How 'bout the blood trail there at the back of the altar?"

"One of the gang members. I saw him stumble out. It wasn't X."

"Get me optics on thermal signatures in the building. *Now."*

Shuffling boots. Then Thornhill said, "There's nothing on premises except the dead bodies, and we've looked under them." A beat. "I think homeboy played us."

A few seconds of silence. Then Van Sciver swore loudly, the sharp syllable booming off the walls.

Evan had not heard him lose his cool, not since their Pride

A Drool Not of Saliva

House days. In his booster bag tucked behind the pallet, he stayed perfectly still.

Van Sciver said, "Get our bodies out of here. We need to lay down a cover story. Gang violence, cartel involvement, whatever. We were never here."

Thornhill issued orders over a radio, and then more boots thumped in. The sounds of corpses being dragged.

The floorboards groaned as someone drew near. They groaned again, nearer yet. Evan felt faint tremors through the foundation.

Then Van Sciver's voice came, no more than ten feet away. "No," he said.

And then, "No."

And once again, with an undercurrent of worry, "No."

A phone call.

Van Sciver had stepped to the side of the church for privacy.

"Okay," he said. "We won't. Not a trace." A beat, and then, "I understand the Black Hawk is high-profile. We won't use it again. This was our best shot—" Another pause. "Not very well."

Van Sciver took another step, so close now that Evan could hear him breathing.

"I understand he's the only connective tissue. But 1997 is a long ways back."

Evan could hear the voice on the other end of the line now, not the words but the tone. Firm and confident, with a hidden seam of rage.

Van Sciver replied, "Yes, Mr. President."

The phone call terminated with a click.

Van Sciver exhaled through what sounded like clenched teeth. He shifted his weight, the floorboards answering.

Then his steps headed out.

A moment later Evan heard the Black Hawk rotors spin up and the helo lift off. The sound faded. There came an instant of peace.

And then sirens wailed faintly somewhere in the night.

Evan unzipped himself, releasing the humidity of the booster bag. He climbed out. The air tasted of smoke and blood.

Bodies covered the nave, folded over pews, sprawled on the floor, heaped against the walls.

No sign of Freeway.

The sirens were louder now.

Bullets riddled the old wooden altarpiece. Blood painted the Virgin Mary's forehead, an Ash Wednesday smudge. The arc of the cast-off spatter pointed to the right side.

Evan followed, mounting the carpeted steps.

A brief hall behind the altar led to a rear door.

He stepped out into the crisp night. Drops of blood left a fairytale trail out of the back alley. Evan followed them.

He came to the street and crossed it as a swarm of cop cars screeched up to the front of the church. A crowd had gathered, and he melted into its embrace.

More crimson drops on the sidewalk. The transfer pattern of a handprint on a streetlamp. A red dab stained a flyer by the bodega with the plywood-covered window.

The bodega sign was turned to CLOSED.

Evan slipped inside. The owner stood behind the cash register, trembling.

Evan said, *"Lárgate."*

The owner scrambled out through the front door.

The blood drops were thicker now on the floor tiles. Evan followed them up the aisle and into the back courtyard.

Freeway was leaning against a metal post, clutching a gunshot wound in his side. His other hand held the straight razor. He firmed his posture and held the blade to the side.

Those black eyes picked across Evan. "You're stupid to come here with no weapon."

"Maybe so," Evan said. "But I have one advantage."

Freeway bared his teeth. "What's that?"

"I don't have metal in my face."

He hit Freeway with a haymaker cross. The studs moored the skin. There was a great tearing and a drool not of saliva. The straight razor clattered to the concrete as Freeway hit his knees, the wreckage of his face pouring through his fingers.

Evan picked up the razor from the ground, looked down at Freeway.

"Look what I found," he said. "A weapon."

70

Negative Space

Sitting at his kitchen island, Evan fanned through Van Sciver's red notebook again. He stared at the scrawl standing out in relief from the pencil-blackened page in the middle.

"6-1414 Dark Road 32."

He'd returned to Castle Heights to make a few arrangements, laying the groundwork for the battle to come. In light of the conversation he'd overheard in the church, he needed to check the notebook again. Staring at the words now, he sensed the puzzle piece slide into place.

He walked past the living wall, catching a whiff of mint, and stepped through one of the south-facing sliding doors onto the balcony. He crouched before a square planter at the edge that held a variety of succulents and slid clear an inset panel. It hid a camouflage backpack, which he removed and carried inside.

He returned to the island, the notebook page looking up at him, the scrawl rendered clear in the negative space.

Joey came down from the loft, ready to go. She paused and took him in sitting over the notebook.

"You know what it means now," she said.

He nodded absentmindedly.

"You gonna share?"

Evan shut the notebook as if that could somehow contain the problem within. "Yeah. (202) 456-1414 is the main switchboard for the West Wing," he said.

She processed this. "And 'Dark Road'?"

"A code word. Presumably to kick the caller to a security command post in the White House."

"And the 32," she said. "That's an extension."

He nodded again.

"That goes to who?" she asked.

He looked at her.

"Holy hell," she said.

"Indeed."

"Why?" she said. "Why would he be involved?"

Evan rubbed his face. Again he pictured Jack dropping him off at departures at Dulles back when Evan was a nineteen-year-old kid. Jack's hand on his forearm, not wanting to let him go.

Evan said, "When I was in that booster bag, I heard Van Sciver reference 1997."

"And?"

"That was the year of my first mission."

"What was it?"

"I can't tell you that," he said. "But in 1997 President Bennett was the undersecretary of defense for policy at the DoD."

"And the Orphan Program existed under the Department of Defense's umbrella," Joey said slowly, putting it together.

All at once the rationale for the shift of the Program's aim under Van Sciver's leadership came clearer. So did the sudden push to exterminate Orphans—Evan most of all.

He didn't just know where the bodies were buried. He'd buried most of them himself.

Joey said, "So Bennett greenlit your first mission."

"Yes. And as the leader of the free world now, he wants to clean up any trace of his involvement in nonsanctioned activities. Any trace of me."

Joey set her elbows on the island and leaned over, her eyes wide. "Do you get what this means? You've got dirt on the president of the United States."

Evan spun back in time to his twelfth year, riding in Jack's truck, Jack describing the Program to him for the first time in that ten-grit voice: *You'll be a cutout man. Fully expendable. You'll know only your silo. Nothing damaging. If you're caught, you're on your own. They will torture you to pieces, and you can give up all the information you have, because none of it is useful.*

"I know the who," Evan said. "But not the what."

"What do you mean?"

"I know what I did in '97. But I don't know anything else. Or how it connects to Bennett." He looked down at the red notebook as if it could tell him something. "But someday when this is all over, I'm gonna find out."

"When *what's* all over?"

"Come and I'll show you." He shouldered the camo pack, grabbed the keys, and started for the door.

The Vegas Strip rose from the flat desert earth like a parade, a brassy roar of faux daylight. Evan kept on the I-15, let the bombastic display fly by on the right-hand side, Joey's head swiveling to watch it pass. For a few minutes, it was impossible to tell that it was nearly four in the morning, but as the glow faded in the rearview and the stars reasserted themselves overhead, it became clear that they were driving through deepest night.

Joey worked her speed cube without looking. Whenever Evan glanced over, he saw that she was once again spinning it into patterns from memory. The clacking of the cube carried them across the dark miles.

Once the grand boulevard was far behind them, Evan pulled over and wound his way through back roads. The pickup rumbled onto a dirt road that narrowed into a sagebrush-crowded trail. At last he pulled over at a makeshift range. Tattered targets

fluttered on bales of hay beneath the moonlight, Monet gone belli-
cose. When they stepped out of the truck, shell casings jingled underfoot.

"What are we doing here?" Joey asked.

"Planning."

"For what?"

"For the next time I eat something and light up the GPS in my
stomach."

"Now Van Sciver'll know it's a trap," she said.

"Right."

"So he'll spring a trap on our trap."

"And we'll spring a trap on the trap he's springing on our trap."

She squinted at him through the darkness. He felt a flash of af-
fection for this girl, this mission that had blown through his life
like an F5 tornado. He thought of his words to Jack in their final
conversation—*I wouldn't trade knowing you for anything*—but he
couldn't make them come out of his mouth now, in this context.
They stopped somewhere in his throat, locked down behind his
expressionless stare.

Far below, a solitary set of headlights blazed through the night.
Evan and Joey watched them climb the dune, disappearing at
intervals on the switchbacks. Then a dually truck shuddered up
beside Evan's F-150, rocking to a halt.

The door kicked open, and Tommy Stojack slid out of the driver's seat and landed unevenly. His ankles were shot from too many
parachute jumps, as were his knees and hips. The damage gave
him a loose-limbed walk that called to mind a movie cowboy.

"Shit, brother, I was way out at the ranch prepping for Shot Show
when you called. Just had time to wash pits and parts and haul ass
out, but here I is."

He and Evan clasped hands in greeting, and then Tommy looked
over at Joey, his biker mustache shifting as he assessed her.

"This the one you told me about?"

"It is."

Tommy gave an approving nod. "She looks lined out."

Joey said, "Thanks."

"For a sixteen-year-old broad, I mean."

Joey smiled flatly. "Thanks."

Tommy stroked his mustache, cocked his head at Evan. "Last we broke bread, I said if you needed me, give a holler. You hit a wall, and you figured what the fuck."

"I figured exactly that," Evan said.

"Well, I can't scoot like I used to, but I can still loot and shoot. I know you well enough to know if you're calling in air support, you're up against it."

"Yes," Evan said.

"Well, with what you're asking, I'm gonna need you to make more words come out your mouth hole."

"They're trying to kill me. And they're trying to kill her."

A long pause ensued as Tommy chewed on this. "*You* I understand," he said finally, his mustache arranging itself into a smirk. "But still, I suppose it'd be unsat for me to sit back and let a good piece of gear like you hit a meat grinder. So. What services of mine are required?"

Evan said, "Your research for DARPA . . ."

Tommy's eyes gleamed. "Before we get to puttin' metal on meat, I'd best know what we're looking at so I can see if it falls within my moral purview. So if you want me to put on the big boy pants and the Houdini hat, let's go back to the shop, I'll drink a hot cuppa shut-the-fuck-up, and you read me in on what's read-in-able."

"Wait a minute," Joey said. "DARPA?" She looked from Evan to Tommy. "What are you guys talking about?"

"What're we talking about?" Tommy smiled, showing off the gap in his front teeth. "We're talking about some Harry Potter shit."

71

Bring the Thunder

A cup of yerba maté tea and a plate of fresh-sliced mango, both lovingly served, both untouched, sat before Evan on the low coffee table of the front room. Benito and Xavier Orellana occupied the lopsided couch opposite him.

Benito said, "My son and I, we don't know how to express our—"

Evan said, "No need."

Xavier folded his hands. The forearm tattoo he had recently started, that elaborate *M* for *Mara Salvatrucha*, had taken a new direction. Rather than spelling out the gang's name, it now said *Madre*. The last four letters looked brand-new, hours old. They were interwoven with vines and flowers.

Xavier saw Evan looking and shifted self-consciously. "You said we can remake ourselves however we want. So I figured why not start here."

Benito's eyes welled up, and Evan was worried the old man might start to cry. Evan didn't have time for that.

He looked over their shoulders and out the front window to the brim of the valley of the vast razed lot. Sounds of construction carried up the slope. At the edge of the lot, way down by the 10 Freeway, the fifth story of the emergent building thrust into view. It had been roughly framed out now, workers scrambling in the cross section of the visible top floors. Their union shifts would end in two hours, and then the lot would be deserted for the night.

"How can we repay you for what you've done?" Benito asked.

"There is one thing," Evan said.

"Whatever you ask," Xavier said, "I'll do."

Beside him his father tensed at the edge of the couch cushion.

"Find someone who needs me," Evan said. "Like you did. It doesn't matter how long it takes. Find someone who's desperate, who's got no way out, and give them my number: 1-855-2-NOWHERE."

Both men nodded.

"You tell them about me. Tell them I'll be there on the other end of the phone."

Benito said, "The Nowhere Man."

"That's right."

As Evan rose, Xavier found his feet quickly. "Sir," he said, the word sounding ridiculous and old-fashioned in his mouth, "why do you do this?"

Evan looked at the floor. An image came to him, Joey standing in front of that house in the Phoenix heat, gun in hand, staring down a woman on a porch swing. And then handing the pistol back to him, unfired.

The words were surprisingly hard to say, but he fought them out: "Because everyone deserves a second chance."

Xavier extended his hand, that *Madre* tattoo bleeding and raw and beautiful. "I'll do it. I'll find someone else."

Evan shook his hand.

The front door banged in, Tommy shouldering through, gripping a Hardigg case in each hand.

Xavier and Benito looked at the stranger with alarm.

"Also," Tommy said, "we're gonna need to borrow your roof."

HELLBENT

At the base of the sloped lot, Evan and Joey stood between a tower crane and a hydraulic torque wrench, staring up at the five-story development. Beyond the tall concrete wall to their side, afternoon rush-hour traffic hummed by.

The workers had retired for the night. The six-acre blind spot provided an unlikely patch of privacy in the heart of Los Angeles. Upslope, the lot ended at a street, but the houses beyond, including Benito Orellana's, were not visible.

The construction platform's lift, an orange cage half the size of a shipping container, had been lowered for the work day's end. Joey stepped forward, rocked it with her foot. It didn't give. Then she leaned back and appraised the steel bones of the building-to-be.

"Which route?" Evan asked.

Joey squinted. Then she raised an arm, pointing. "There to there to there. See that I-beam? Third floor? Then across. Up that rise. There, there, and then up."

Evan visualized the path. "How do you know?"

"Geometry."

"Okay," he said. "Now you're done. Let's get you somewhere safe."

"You're kidding, right?"

"No," he said. "You're out. Me and Tommy will handle it from here."

"You and Tommy are gonna have your hands full. You need me. Any way you cut it, it's a three-man plan."

He knew she was right. Evan could handle five freelancers, skilled as they were. But not three Orphans on top of that.

He leaned against the blocky 1980 Lincoln Town Car they'd driven down the slope. Beside it the lowered claw of a backhoe nodded downward, a crane sipping from a lake.

Joey looked up to the top of the building, the breeze lifting her hair, a wisp catching in the corner of her mouth. "You laid it out yourself. Van Sciver won't deploy drones on U.S. soil. The president ordered him not to use choppers anymore. We can control some of the variables."

"This is different," Evan said.

"I'm not leaving you to this alone. And you only got a few more hours before those GPS chips break down in your stomach. You'd better eat something and throw a signal while you still can." She reached into her jacket pocket, pulled out a Snickers bar, and wiggled it back and forth.

He didn't smile, but that didn't seem to faze her.

"I'm not going anywhere," she said. "So quit wasting time."

"Joey. It's too dangerous."

"You're right. Anywhere I go, he'll find me. You know that. You know it in your gut. I will never be safe until he's dead. And you know you need me to make this plan work."

Evan studied her stubborn face. Then he came off the car and pointed at her, trying to keep the exasperation from his voice. "After this you're out."

"I'm out. Some other life." Her smile held equal parts trepidation and excitement. "Ponytails and white picket fences."

"The minute this operation goes live—"

"I'll just sail out of here," she said. "*I'll* be fine." She paused. "But you? I don't see you getting out of this."

He listened to the wind whistle through the I-beams overhead. Jack, paraphrasing the German field marshal and the Scottish poet, used to say, *Even the best-laid plan can't survive the first fired bullet.* Evan had taken his measurements, charted his course, laid his plans. He had escape routes planned and off-the-books emergency medical support on standby. Despite all that he knew Joey was right, that this man-made valley could well prove to be his grave.

"Maybe not." He placed a wire-thin saber radio in her hand; the bone phone would pick up her voice and allow her to listen directly through her jaw.

She said, "We could still get into that ugly-ass Town Car and just drive away."

A wistful smile tugged at his lips. He shook his head.

The breeze blew across her face, and she swept her hair back. "He's gonna come with everything he has. And he's gonna kill you like he has everyone else. You think Jack would want this?"

"It's not just about Jack anymore. It's about everyone else who Van Sciver's got in his sights." His throat was dry. "It's about you, Joey."

He'd said it louder than he'd intended and with anger, though where the anger came from, he wasn't sure.

Her eyes moistened. She looked away sharply.

For a time there was only the breeze.

Then she said, "Josephine."

"I'm sorry?"

"My name. You wanted to know my full name." Her eyes darted to his face and then away again. "There it is."

Beyond the concrete rise, vehicles whipped by on the freeway, oblivious people leading ordinary lives, some charmed, some not. On this side of the wall, there was only Evan and a sixteen-year-old girl, trying their best to say good-bye.

Joey lifted the forgotten Snickers bar from her side and tossed it to him. She took a deep breath.

"Okay," she said. "Let's bring the thunder."

72

Thin the Herd

The freelancers came in first, and they came by foot. The five men wound their way toward the valley in a tightening spiral, a snake coiling.

Former Secret Service agents, they brought the tools of the trade designed to protect the most important human on earth. Electronic noses for hazardous chemicals and biologicals, bomb-detection devices, thermal-imaging handhelds. Though it wasn't yet dusk, they had infrared goggles around their necks, ready for nightfall. After safing the surrounding blocks, they meticulously combed through every square foot of the valley, communicating with radio earpieces, ensuring that anything within view of the construction site below was clear.

Each man wore a Raytheon Boomerang Warrior on his shoulder, an electronic sniper-detection system. Developed for Iraq, it could pinpoint the position of any enemy shooter within sight lines up to three thousand feet away.

Two of the freelancers rolled out, hiking back up the slope, giving a final check, and disappearing from view.

Ten minutes passed.

And then two Chevy Tahoes with tinted windows, steel-plate-reinforced doors, and laminated bullet-resistant glass coasted down the slope. They parked at the base of the construction building in front of the porta-potties.

Van Sciver got out, swollen with body armor, and stood behind the shield of the door. Candy and Thornhill strayed a bit farther, the freelancers holding a loose perimeter around them, facing outward. The operators now held FN SCAR 17S spec-ops rifles, scopes riding the hard-chromed bores. Menacing guns, they looked like they had an appetite of their own.

Van Sciver cast his gaze around. "Well," he said. "We're here."

Thornhill scanned the rim of the valley. "Think he'll show?"

Van Sciver's damaged right eye watered in the faint breeze. He wristed a tear off the edge of his lid. "He called the meet."

"Then where is he?" one of the freelancers asked.

"The GPS signal from the microchips is long gone," Thornhill said. "It's up to our own selves."

The faint noise of a car engine rose above the muted hum of freeway traffic behind the concrete wall. The freelancers oriented to the street above.

The noise of the motor grew louder.

The men raised their weapons.

A white Lincoln Town Car plowed over the brim of the valley, plummeting down the slope at them. Already the men were firing, riddling the windshield and hood with bullets.

The Town Car bumped over the irregular terrain, slowing but still pulled by gravity. The men shot out the tires, aerated the engine block.

The car slowed, slowed, glancing off a backhoe and nodding to a stop twenty yards away.

Two of the freelancers raced forward, lasering rounds through the shattered maw of the windshield.

The first checked the car's interior cautiously over the top of his weapon. "Clear. No bodies."

Thin the Herd

The other wanded down the vehicle. "No explosives either. It's a test."

Twenty yards back, still protected by their respective armor-plated doors, Van Sciver and Candy had already spun around to assess less predictable angles of attack that the diversion had been designed to open up.

Van Sciver's gaze snagged on the side of the under-construction building, the platform lift waiting by the top floor. "He's there," he said.

"We would've picked up thermal, sir," the freelancer said.

Van Sciver pointed at the mounted platform's lift control. Thornhill jogged over to the base of the building, keeping his eyes above, and clicked to lower the lift.

Nothing happened.

The bottom control mechanism had been sabotaged.

All five freelancers raised their SCARs in concert, covering the building's fifth floor.

Van Sciver said, "Get me sat imagery."

Keeping his rifle pointed up, one of the freelancers shuffled over and passed a handheld to Van Sciver, who remained wedged behind the armored door of the Tahoe. Van Sciver zoomed in on the bird's-eye footage of the building, waiting for the clarity to resolve.

Stiff, canvaslike fabric was heaped a few feet from the open edge of the fifth floor.

"He's hiding beneath a Faraday-cage cloak," Van Sciver said. "The metallized fabric blocked your thermal imaging. It's not distinct enough to red-flag on the satellite footage unless you know to look for it."

"He's holding high ground," Candy observed. "And we've got no good vantage point."

Van Sciver stared at the concrete wall framing the 10 Freeway. Posting up on the fifth floor was a smart move on X's part. The open top level was in full view of the freeway and the buildings across from it. They couldn't come at him with force or numbers without inviting four hundred eyewitnesses every second to the party.

"What's he waiting for?" one of the freelancers asked through clenched teeth.

"For me to step clear of the armored vehicle and give him an angle," Van Sciver said. "But I'm not gonna do that."

With a gloved hand, the freelancer swiped sweat from his brow. "So what are *we* gonna do? We can't get up there."

Van Sciver's lopsided stare locked on Thornhill. An understanding passed between them. Thornhill's smile lit up his face.

Van Sciver said, "Fetch."

Thornhill snugged his radio earpiece firmly into place. Then he sprinted forward, leaping from a wheelbarrow onto the roof of a porta-potty. Then he hurtled through the air, clamping onto the exposed ledge of the second floor. The freelancers watched in awe as he scurried up the face of the building, frog-leaping from an exposed window frame to a four-by-four to a concrete ledge. He used a stubbed-out piece of rebar on the third floor as a gymnast high bar, rotating to fly onto a vertical I-beam holding up the fourth story.

Mere feet from the edge of the fifth floor, he paused on his new perch, shoulder muscles bunched, legs bent, braced for a lunge. He turned to take in the others below, giving them a moment to drink in the glory of what he'd just done.

Then he refocused. His body pulsed as he slide-jumped up the I-beam's length. He gripped the cap plate with both hands and readied for the final leap that would bring him across the lip to the top of the building.

But the cap plate moved with him.

It jerked free of the I-beam and hammered back against his chest, striking the muscle with a thud.

One of the high-strength carriage bolts designed to secure the cap plate to the I-beam's flange sailed past his cheek.

The other three bolts rattled in their boreholes, unsecured.

He clasped the cap plate to his chest, a weightless instant.

His eyes were level with the poured slab of the fifth floor, and he saw the puddle of the Faraday cloak there almost within reach.

The cloak's edge was lipped up, a face peering out from the makeshift burrow.

Thin the Herd

Not X's.

But the girl's.

She raised a hand, wiggled the fingers in a little wave.

"It's the girl," Thornhill said. His voice, hushed with disbelief, carried through his radio earpiece.

He floated there an instant, clutching the cap plate.

And then he fell with it.

Five stories whipped by, a whirligig view of construction gear, Matchbox cars drifting through fourteen lanes of traffic beyond the concrete wall, his compatriots staring up with horrified expressions.

He went through the roof of the porta-potty. As he vanished, one sturdy fiberglass wall sheared off his left leg at the hip, painting the dirt with arterial spray.

A moment of stunned silence.

Van Sciver tried to swallow, but his throat clutched up. One of his finest tools, a weaponized extension of himself as the director of the Orphan Program, had just been splattered all over an outdoor shitter.

Candy moved first, diving into the Tahoe. Van Sciver's muscle memory snapped him back into focus. Raising his FNX-45, he set his elbows in the fork of the armored door and aimed upslope. He said, "It's another decoy."

The freelancers spread out, aiming in various directions—up the partially constructed building, across the valley, at the freeway wall.

The lead man squeezed off a few shots, nicking the edge of the fifth floor to hold Joey at bay.

The wind reached a howl in the bare beams of the structure.

"Fuck," Van Sciver said. "Where is . . . ?"

Twenty yards away the trunk of the white Lincoln Town Car popped open and Evan burst up in a kneeling stance, a Faraday cloak sloughing off his shoulders.

He shot two freelancers through the heads before they could orient to the movement. The third managed to and took a round through the mouth.

The remaining pair of freelancers wheeled on Evan, their rifles biting coaster-size chunks of metal from the Town Car's grille. Evan spilled onto the dirt behind the Town Car and flattened to the ground. The big-block engine of the old Lincoln protected him, at least as well as it had on the car's descent into the valley, but time was not on his side.

The reports were deafening.

He clicked his bone phone on. "Joey, jump now and get gone."

She'd played bait one last time. Her only job now was to vanish.

Evan had set her up with the camouflage backpack he kept hidden in the planter on his balcony. The pack was stuffed with a base-jumping parachute. A running leap off the backside of the fifth-floor platform would allow her to steer across the immense freeway, land in the confusion of alleys and buildings across from it, and disappear.

Evan risked a peek around the rear fender. He spotted Candy rolling out of the Tahoe's backseat with a shotgun an instant before one of Van Sciver's bullets shattered out the brake light inches from his face. He whipped back, felt the Town Car shuddering, absorbing round after round as the freelancers advanced.

He spoke again into the bone phone. "Tommy, you're up."

Flattening against the car, he rested the back of his head to the metal, pinned down to a space the width of a rear bumper.

Tommy emerged from the umbra beside Benito Orellana's chimney and bellied to the edge of the roof where his two Hardigg cases waited, lids raised. The first held optical-sighting technology, and a half-dozen eightball cameras nestled in the foam lining.

He had no direct sight line onto the valley or the construction site below.

He plucked free the first eightball and hurled it across the street. It bounced once, disappearing over the lip and rolling downslope, its 360-degree panorama replicated on the laptop screen. The round camera landed behind a backhoe, providing him a view of the dirt slope beyond, the clear blue sky, and nothing else.

He threw the second and third eightball cameras in rapid succession. The second landed in a ditch, but the third stopped three-fourths of the way down the slope, providing a lovely perspective on the mayhem unfolding at the construction site below. Two freelancers stood in the open, but Van Sciver and Candy were wisely tucked away, using the armored SUVs for cover.

That was okay. Tommy could still thin the herd for Evan.

In front of the second Hardigg case, an assembled Barrett M107 awaited him. He'd chosen the self-loader for rapidity—once this shit went down, the boys below would be scrambling every which way, all asses and elbows.

Firming the .50-cal into position, he lay at the roof's edge. He would have preferred a spotter, but given the sensitive nature of the mission and Evan's wishes, no one else could be in the loop. It would be a helluva challenge to crank off two shots in rapid succession, especially since he had to steer the first one in. Microelectronics distorted the shape of the round after it left the barrel, changing its line of flight. As good as Tommy was and as state-of-the-art the technology, there was only so much guidance you could lay on a projo hurtling along at 2,850 feet a second. He checked the optics screen, using the eightball's feed to index locations for landmarks.

Then he set his eye to the scope and prepared to bend a bullet in midair.

Evan read the freelancers' shadows. That was all he could do. Braced against the rear bumper of the Town Car, he watched them stretch alongside him, upraised rifles clearly silhouetted. If he rolled to either side, he presented himself not just to them but to Van Sciver and Candy, who were posted up in the SUVs twenty yards beyond.

"We got you pinned behind the car and the little girl stuck up on the roof!" Van Sciver shouted. "Even if she has a rifle, she can't cover you, not from there. I've seen her shoot."

Tommy still hadn't announced himself. The technology was fledgling; Evan had always known that any help would be a literal and figurative long shot.

Cast forward, the shadows on the earth inched past his position crammed behind the Town Car. They advanced in unison. Any second now Evan would have to make the choice to move one way or the other.

He decided to expose his right side. He could shoot with either hand but was stronger with his left, so if an arm went down, better the right one.

If he was lucky enough to merely take a round to the limb.

He sucked in a breath, tensed his legs, counted down.

Three . . . two . . .

The whine of a projectile was followed by a snap on the wind. The shadow to Evan's right crumpled, a body falling just out of sight by the side of the Town Car. A bright spill oozed into view by Evan's boots, staining the dirt.

Twenty-four down.

One left.

The last freelancer pulled back. "Holy shit. How the fuck . . . ?"

Evan popped up to drop him, but Candy was waiting by the other Tahoe. She unleashed the shotgun, and Evan dropped an instant before the scattershot hit the trunk. The trunk slammed down, nearly sawing off his chin, and banged back up. The edge clipped his shooting hand, the ARES flying out of reach, landing ten yards in the open.

Slumped low at the rear fender, he panted in the dirt.

The bullet holes in the raised trunk cut circles of light in the shadow thrown on the ground behind Evan. He rose to reach for a backup pistol in the trunk, but Candy fired again, the slugs tearing through the metal, whistling past his torso. The trunk slammed down, banging his forearm. Evan hit the ground again, dust puffing into his mouth.

The freelancer was crawling away; Evan could see him for an instant beneath the carriage of the Town Car. Another of Tommy's rounds whined in and bit a divot from the dirt four inches from the freelancer's pinkie finger.

The man bellowed and rolled away, grabbing at the screen of the Boomerang Warrior unit mounted on his shoulder. A third round clipped the butt of the man's slung rifle, kicking it into a hula-hoop spin around his shoulder.

He dove behind a heap of gravel next to the tower crane, shouting, "How the hell does he see me? I'm showing nothing in our line of sight!"

Van Sciver's calm, deep voice rode the breeze. "Check for cameras."

A moment later, "The Boomerang Warrior's picking up a remote-surveillance unit in the valley with an angle on us."

Evan debated going again for the backup ARES in the ravaged trunk of the Town Car, but there were enough holes now that the raised metal no longer offered protection; it would be like standing behind a screen door. He got off a glance around the punctured rear tire, catching Van Sciver's thick arm reaching past the Tahoe's door to haul in a fallen FN SCAR 17S.

Even without an earpiece, Evan heard Van Sciver say, "Send me the coordinates."

The simple directive landed on Evan like something physical, the weight of impending defeat.

Twenty seconds passed, an eternity in a battle.

Then the rifle cracked, and Evan saw metal shards jump up from the earth upslope, glinting in the dying sunlight.

Van Sciver's voice carried, ghostly across the dusty expanse. "We are clear. Candy, haul ass up there and find who's behind that camera."

At the Town Car's rear bumper, Evan heard Tommy's voice come through the bone phone. "I'm blind."

"Fall back to the rally point," Evan said quietly. "Immediately. Do not engage any further."

Tommy was a world-class sniper, but past his prime. If he went head-to-head with Candy, an Orphan at the top of her game, she would kill him.

Evan heard one of the Tahoes screech away. It barreled upslope, giving Evan's position wide berth. He caught a glimpse of Candy's hair in a side mirror as the SUV bounced across the razed lot.

Through the radio Tommy's voice sounded scratchier than usual. "What about you?"

Evan stared at his ARES 1911 where it had landed in the dirt ten yards away. His backup was out of reach in the trunk behind him. Tommy neutralized. Van Sciver beaded up on the Town Car with his rifle.

"I got you covered," Van Sciver called to his freelancer. "Make the move."

A crunch of footsteps signaled the man's emergence from behind the gravel pile.

Evan realized what Van Sciver's countermove was, the genius of it turning his insides ice-water cold.

He heard the clang of footsteps on metal rungs. Then the door to the elevated operator's cabin of the crane hinged open and slammed shut.

Evan was finished.

He still owed Tommy an answer. He set a finger on the bone phone, said, "I'll be fine."

"You're clear?" Tommy asked.

Evan swallowed. "I'm clear."

"Falling back," Tommy said. "Call me for extraction?"

The Tahoe creaked as Van Sciver posted up and slotted a fresh twenty-round mag into the big rifle.

"Sure thing," Evan said. His mouth was dry. "And, Tommy?"

"What, pal?"

"Thanks for everything."

73

The Black Hereafter

Joey stood at the edge of the fifth floor, the poured-concrete slab solid underfoot, the base-jumping pack snug to her back, fist gripping the rip cord. The sound of gunfire carried up, pops muffled by the concrete wall and the roar of traffic beyond. She picked her spot across the fourteen lanes of traffic, a parking lot glistening with shattered glass. The city had started to granulate with dusk. Night wasn't far off, and blackness would aid in her escape.

From her perch she'd watched most of the action unfold. Tommy had rolled off the roof of the Orellana house and disappeared well before Candy McClure had forged upslope in the Jeep. Her pursuit would be in vain; Tommy had too much of a jump on her.

That left Evan pinned down without a weapon, facing off against Van Sciver and a freelancer. Last Joey had peeked, they'd taken up strategic positions at a ninety-degree spread, vectoring in at him from two angles he couldn't cover even if he had a gun.

But he was Orphan X, and Orphan X always found a way.

And so she'd donned the backpack and retreated to the far edge as promised.

Now she was here, freedom a single leap away.

A mural decorated the far wall of the freeway, visible to the eastbound passing cars. Cesar Chavez and Gandhi, Martin Luther King and Nelson Mandela. A cacophony of quotations and languages painted the drab concrete, but one sentence in particular stood out.

"If you've got nothing worth dying for, you've got nothing worth living for."

She read it twice, felt it pull at something deep inside her.

Pushing away the sensation, she took a few backward steps to allow herself a running start.

Then she heard another sound.

A large piece of machinery rumbling to life.

At the dead center of the uppermost slab, she hesitated.

Run.

Or turn.

She closed her eyes, took a deep breath, heard a voice that was part Jack's, part Evan's, part her own.

The Sixth Commandment, it said. *Question orders.*

She turned.

Easing to her former position, she had a perfect vantage on the scene below.

Van Sciver in the embrace of the armored Tahoe, rifle raised. Evan hidden behind the increasingly frayed Town Car, his 1911 well out of reach on the ground.

The slewing unit of the colossal crane below squealed, the horizontal jib lurching into motion. The freelancer had climbed up into the operator's cab and swiveled it into position directly below the orange cage of the raised platform lift.

Directly below her.

The freelancer worked the controls, getting the hang of the massive unit. The jib rotated unevenly and then halted, aligned with the Town Car. The massive steel lifting hook lowered, scooping up the carry cables of an I-beam.

The I-beam rose.

But only a few feet off the ground.

The trolley engaged, running the load out from the crane's center. The I-beam traveled a few yards, nosing the Town Car like a rhino checking out a Jeep full of safari-goers. The Town Car tilted up onto the tires of its left side, not quite high enough to expose Evan. Then it settled back down.

The load hadn't acquired sufficient momentum.

The crane screeched, the trolley pulling the I-beam away from the car toward the mast. It drew back and back, like the windup of a massive battering ram. The Town Car stood directly in its path, an empty can awaiting a mallet.

If you've got nothing worth dying for, you've got nothing worth living for.

Joey let the camo backpack slip from her shoulders. She stepped onto the platform lift and clicked the big red button to lower herself.

Evan knew what was coming, and this was not an instance where that was a good thing.

The crane hummed, its motor a low-grade earthquake that rumbled the ground. He stretched his neck, watched the I-beam reach the end of the track and pause, swaying mightily, preparing its journey back along the jib and into the side of the Town Car.

Once it went, the car would be swept away, laying Evan bare.

The I-beam stilled, readying to reverse course.

Evan calculated five possible moves, but they all ended the same way—with Van Sciver putting a tight grouping through his torso. When the time came, Evan would choose one of them. His instinct and training demanded as much.

But this time he already knew the outcome.

Riding the platform lift, Joey watched the I-beam dangling way below the jib. It had reached the terminus of its backswing. Her thumb jammed the DOWN button so hard her knuckle ached. She willed the orange cage to descend faster, but it kept its infuriatingly steady pace.

The freelancer was partially visible inside the operator's cab— a downward slice of forehead and one cheek. The noise of her descent was lost beneath the roar of the motor driving the slewing unit.

The platform lift inched lower, the operator's cab coming up below. The freelancer's hands were locked around two joystick-like controllers.

He threw his right fist forward.

The I-beam rocketed toward the Town Car an instant before Joey's orange cage struck the top of the cab.

It was too late.

Evan couldn't see anything, but he felt the rush of a forced breeze, the air shuddering as the I-beam swept for the Town Car.

Five seconds to impact, now four.

He had to go for the backup 1911 in the trunk even if it meant getting shot by Van Sciver.

He sprang up, painfully aware of the full presentation of his critical mass, and grabbed the ARES where it lay against the carpeted cargo space. Through the holes in the raised trunk, he could see Van Sciver twenty yards away, shielded by the armored door of the Tahoe.

He expected to be staring at the full-circle scope of the rifle, the last sight he'd ever see.

But miraculously, Van Sciver wasn't looking at him. He was aiming up at the lowering platform lift, firing round after round.

His shots sparked off the edge of the lift as it crushed into the top of the operator's cab. The freelancer leapt out of the cabin an instant before it crumpled and gave way. As the lift continued its descent, he began monkeying down the caged rungs, staying ahead of it.

Was that *Joey* riding the orange cage down?

Before Evan could react, the I-beam swept in, a massive blur in his peripheral vision.

He snatched the backup gun from the trunk and whipped down out of sight.

One instant the Town Car was at his back, solid as a bulwark.

The next it was gone, Evan alone on the open stretch of dirt.

The mass of metal had hurtled close enough to him that its wake spun him around onto one knee.

He achieved a single instant of clarity.

The freelancer at the base of the tower, jumping free of the rungs, a second or two away from being able to aim his rifle.

Van Sciver twenty yards away, his SCAR rotating back to lock on Evan.

In an instant Evan would have two targets on his head from two angles, a 7–10 bowling split.

Evan got off the X, throwing himself to the side, hitting a roll, elbows locked, ARES extended before him. He had nine shots to spend—eight in the mag, one in the spout.

Upside down, Evan aimed at the space beneath the Tahoe's door. One of Van Sciver's rounds flew past his ear, trailing heat across his cheek.

Evan kept rolling, lining the sights, the target spinning like a vinyl record. He fired one, two, three, four shots before a round clipped the back of Van Sciver's boot, tearing free a chunk of durable nylon and Achilles tendon.

Van Sciver grunted but kept his feet, cranking off another round that buried itself in the dirt two inches from Evan's nose, blowing grit in his eyes.

Evan shot at the armored door. The impact drove the door back into the frame, hammering Van Sciver with it. The blow disoriented him, the rifle joggling in his hands.

Evan used the pause to flip himself into a kneeling position.

The freelancer now stood in a sniper's standing pose, feet slightly spread, right elbow tucked tight to the ribs to support the rifle, butt held high on his shoulder to bring the scope into alignment.

Evan fired through the scope atop the rifle and blew out the back of the man's head.

He quick-pivoted to Van Sciver, who was hauling his weapon into position again, still protected by the armored door.

Evan advanced and shot the door again, slamming Van Sciver backward into the truck. The rifle spun free. Evan pressed his advantage, firing again into the door. Van Sciver banged into the Tahoe once more, this time spilling partially out from his position of cover.

Van Sciver's head was protected by the armored door, but his body, made bulkier by a Kevlar vest, sprawled in full view. Night was coming on, but Evan was close enough that visibility was not a problem.

He had one shot left.

He lined the sights on the gap in the body armor where the arms usually hung. Van Sciver's tumble had twisted the vest around his torso, the vulnerable strip pulled toward his belly.

Evan fired his last round.

The fabric frayed as the bullet entered Van Sciver's abdomen.

A clod of air left him.

Blood poured from the hole.

Evan kept the pistol raised, images spinning through his mind.

Jack leaning back in his armchair and closing his eyes, letting the opera music move right through him. Young Evan at his feet, soaking it in by osmosis, these strange and beautiful sounds from another life that was now somehow his as well.

Van Sciver fought himself up to a sitting position against the Tahoe.

Evan cast his empty gun aside and advanced on him. The fallen rifle lay between them. He could pick it up, stave in Van Sciver's skull with the butt.

Firelight playing across Jack's face in the study as he read Greek mythology out loud to Evan, his excitement contagious, the stories coming to life, winged horses and impossible labors, Gorgons and demigods, underworlds and Elysian fields.

Van Sciver pressed his hands to his stomach. He'd been gut-shot, the bullet entering the mid-abdominal area north of the belly button and beneath the zyphoid, where the ribs came together. Judging from the rush of bright red seeping through Van Sciver's hands, the bullet had severed the superior mesenteric artery. He was held together by the Kevlar vest and little else. The vest just might prove sufficient to hold him together long enough to get to a surgical suite.

The Black Hereafter

Which was why Evan would beat him to death with his bare hands.

Jack stepping off into the black hereafter, not a trace of fear in his eyes. What could have filled him with such peace as he'd spun to his impact?

Van Sciver's permanently dilated pupil stared out, glossy with hidden depths, a bull's-eye waiting for a round. Evan pictured his thumb sinking through it, scrambling the frontal lobe.

Evan closed to within ten yards of him when something stopped him in his tracks.

Van Sciver was smiling.

With some effort he raised his arm and pointed behind Evan.

As Evan turned, Joey stumbled off the lowered platform lift onto the dirt, both hands locked around her thigh just above the knee.

She wobbled on her feet.

Bleeding out.

74

Brightness Off Her Skin

Evan froze between Van Sciver and Joey, his body tugged in opposite directions. A few strides ahead was the man who had killed Jack. And fifteen yards behind, Joey stood doubled over, the life draining from her body.

A feeling overtook Evan, that of free-falling through the night sky just as Jack had. There were no bearings, just a spin of sensation and the pinpoint light of distant stars.

He stared at the butt of the fallen rifle ahead, the dilated pupil beckoning his thumb.

Van Sciver was breathing hard. "Looks like I clipped her superficial femoral artery."

Evan glanced back at Joey. She gasped, her legs nearly buckling.

Evan tore his gaze away, took another step for Van Sciver.

"She's gonna die," Van Sciver said. "You wanna be with her when she does."

Evan halted again, teeth locked in a grimace.

He thought about Jack plummeting through a void, his willingness to step off a helicopter to protect Evan.

The best part of me.

Evan took an uneven step backward. And then another. Then he spun and ran to Joey.

Behind him he heard Van Sciver's laugh, the rasp of sandpaper. "That's the difference between me and you."

Evan reached Joey as her legs gave out, catching her as she collapsed.

He flicked out his Strider knife and sheared her jeans to the thigh, exposing the bullet hole. There was blood, so much blood.

The femoral artery, just as Van Sciver had said.

Evan initiated the bone phone. "Tommy, get here. Now. Get here now."

He did not recognize his own voice.

He clamped his hand over Joey's thigh.

"Copy that," Tommy said. "En route."

"*Now.* We have to get her to medical."

Across the stretch of dirt, Evan watched Van Sciver wriggle his shoulders up the side of the Tahoe, shoving himself to a standing position. He fell into the driver's seat.

The SUV drove off, its momentum kicking the door shut.

"You let Van Sciver . . . go," Joey said weakly.

Evan pictured again the serene expression on Jack's face as he'd stepped from the Black Hawk, and he understood at last what had filled him with such peace.

Joey blinked languidly. "Why'd . . . come back for me?"

Evan drew in a breath that felt like broken glass. He said, "That's what my father taught me."

He bent over Joey, his hand still sealed on her leg. The sound of the Tahoe faded, leaving the valley desolate, overtaken by late-twilight gloom. They were a stone's throw from the busiest freeway intersection in the world and yet not another human was in sight.

She looked up at him, her emerald eyes glazed.

"You were supposed to jump," he said. "Across the freeway.

Away from all this." His eyes were wet. "Goddamn it. What did I teach you?"

She said, "Everything."

Her dark hair was thrown back, exposing the bristle of that shaved strip, the faraway city lights turning a few strands golden, and he realized that at some point over their days and nights he'd come to know the scent of her, a citrus brightness off her skin.

"You're okay," he said.

"You're gonna be fine," he said.

"You're worth it," he said.

Her lips pressed together. A weak smile.

He tightened his clamp on her leg.

Headlights swept the valley, a vehicle approaching. It parked, the glare making him squint.

The door slammed shut. A figure stepped forward, cut from the brilliance of the headlights.

Not Tommy.

Candy.

Evan's last ray of hope left him.

Candy approached, appraising them.

"Find what they love," she said. "And make them pay for it."

Evan would have to let go of Joey's leg to reach for his knife on the ground.

He did not.

He stayed where he was, his palm covering her wound.

He closed his eyes, saw his tiny feet filling Jack's footsteps in the woods. This was the path he was born to follow. A path into life, no matter the cost.

When he opened his eyes, Candy was standing right over him, the barrel of her pistol inches from his forehead. In his arms he could feel Joey's breaths, each more fragile than the last.

Evan stared up the barrel at Candy. "After you kill me, clamp this artery."

Candy said nothing.

He said, "Please."

The end of Candy's pistol trembled ever so slightly. Her face contorted.

Brightness Off Her Skin

Evan looked back down at Joey. After a moment he sensed the pistol lower. Candy eased back from view. He barely registered the sound of the SUV driving away.

Joey jerked in a few shallow breaths. She raised a hand to his cheek, left a smudge of blood under his eye. He sensed it there, a weighted shadow.

"I see you," she said. "You're still real."

As he heard Tommy's truck shudder to a stop behind him, her eyes rolled up and closed, and her head nodded back in his arms.

75

The Blackness to Come

Evan's hands rested in his lap, covered with blood.

Crimson gloves.

Tommy drove through darkest night. Los Angeles was well behind them, Las Vegas well ahead.

They had handled what they'd needed to handle.

"I know you're emotional," Tommy said, "but we gotta think straight."

Evan said, "I'm not emotional." His voice shook.

"This is next-level shit," Tommy said. "We gotta go to ground. A few weeks, minimum. See what shakes out. I got a ranch in Victorville, completely off the grid."

Evan stared out the window. The blackness sweeping by looked like the blackness before and the blackness to come.

Tommy kept talking, but Evan didn't hear him.

———

The Blackness to Come

Candy McClure sat on the carpet of her empty safe house, knees drawn to her chest. Past the tips of her bare feet, her phone rested on the floor. It was after midnight, and yet she'd felt no need to turn on the lights.

She had no idea how long she'd been sitting like this. Her hamstrings and calves ached. Even her Achilles tendons throbbed.

She was having what more poetic types might call a crisis of conscience.

The Samsung might ring.

Or it might never ring again.

If it did, she had no idea what she'd do.

It was one of those wait-and-see things, and she wasn't really a wait-and-see girl. Or at least she didn't used to be.

What was she now?

The phone vibrated against the carpet, uplighting her face with a bluish glow. The Signal application, presenting her with a two-word code.

It was Van Sciver.

Somehow alive.

She found herself not answering.

An unanswered phone seems to ring forever.

At last it stopped rattling against the floorboards.

She picked it up.

She keyed in a different phone number.

1-855-2-NOWHERE.

She stared at the phone, the empty house seeming to curl around her like the rib cage of some long-dead beast.

She hung up before the call could ring through.

She pressed the Samsung to her lips and thought for a time. Then she set it on the floor, rose, and walked out.

She took nothing. She didn't bother to lock the door behind her.

She wouldn't be coming back.

76

Something Flat and Unchanging

Van Sciver reclined on his bed in the ICU, his face washed of color. A gray sweat layered his flesh as he dozed, his eyelids flickering. A urinary catheter threaded between his legs. A monitor read his heart rate, oxygen saturation, respiratory rate, blood pressure, and half a dozen other vitals. A central line on the left side of his chest fed in nutrition and vitamins from a bright yellow bag of TPN.

It was a private room, the curtains pulled around to shield his bed from the glass walls and door.

In one hand he clutched his Samsung.

It chimed, awakening him.

The Signal application. Was it Candy, finally back in contact?

Weakly, he raised the phone to his unshaven cheek. "Code," he said.

Orphan X's voice said, "Behind you."

The words came at Van Sciver in stereo. Through the phone, yes. But also from inside the room.

Evan stepped into view, let the Samsung slide from his hand

onto the sheets. Van Sciver stared at him, mouth open, jaw slightly askew.

Evan lifted Van Sciver's personal Samsung from his frail clutch.

Finding him hadn't been easy. But it hadn't been hard either.

Without immediate surgical intervention and repair, an injury to the superior mesenteric artery compromised blood flow, which in turn meant that the patient usually lost most of the small bowel to necrosis.

Small-bowel transplants were rare and donors rarer yet, but given Van Sciver's resources, he'd know how to get himself to the top of the list. Due to the severity of the injury, he would not have been able to travel far. The UCLA Medical Center was the only adult small-bowel transplant center in the Greater Los Angeles Area.

Without Joey around to help, it had taken some doing for Evan to hack into UCLA's Epic medical-records system, but when he had, he'd found an anonymous patient admitted on December 4, two weeks back, who showed no health-care history.

Evan eased forward so Van Sciver could see him without straining.

"I did go back for Joey," Evan said. "And that does make us different. You know what else makes us different? You're in that bed now. And I'm standing." He held up an empty syringe. "With this."

Van Sciver peered up helplessly. His hand fished in the rumpled sheets and emerged with the call button. His thumb clicked it a few times.

"I disconnected it," Evan told him. "Then I watched you sleep for a while."

Through gaps in the curtain, they could see doctors and nurses passing by, their faces lowered to charts. Evan knew that Van Sciver wouldn't cry out for help. Help would come too late, and he had too much pride for that anyway.

Van Sciver's features grew lax, defeated. A milky starburst showed in that blown pupil, floating like a distant galaxy.

Evan reached over and crimped the tube feeding the central line, stopping the flow of fluorescent yellow nutrition into Van Sciver's chest.

"You killed Jack to get to me," Evan said. "Congratulations. You got your wish."

He slid the needle into the tube above the crimp, closer to Van Sciver's body.

Together they watched the air bubble creep along the line, nearing Van Sciver's chest. It would ride his central vein into his heart, causing an embolism. The dot of air inched along, ever closer.

Van Sciver's face settled with resignation. He said, "It is what it is and that's all that it is."

"No," Evan said, "it's more than that."

The air bubble slipped through the line into Van Sciver's chest.

A moment later he shuddered.

His left eye dilated, at last matching the right.

The symphony of beeps and hums from the monitor changed their melody into something flat and unchanging.

When doctors and nurses crashed into the room, they found the motionless body and no one else.

77

Original S.W.A.T.

She remembered two rough men minding her in the darkness, one scented of soap and sweat, the other moving through a haze of cigarette smoke and wintergreen tobacco. And there was a hospital room that was not in a hospital and a doctor or two drifting through the miasma of her drugged thoughts.

Now she looked out her dorm window onto the stunning view beyond—Lake Lugano and the snowcapped Alps. It was an English-speaking school filled with affluent kids, a demographic to which she supposed she now belonged. Seven hundred ninety-three students from sixty-two countries speaking forty different languages.

A good pot to melt into and disappear.

Her passport and papers had her at eighteen years old, a legal adult, so she could oversee her own affairs. Her cover was thorough and backstopped. She'd been recently orphaned, set up with a trust fund that released like a widening faucet, a little more money every year. She was repeating coursework here after some understandable emotional difficulties given the fresh loss of her parents. She'd pick up courses at the second semester, which began in a few weeks.

The campus was spectacular, the resources seemingly unlimited. There was a downhill-ski team and horseback riding and kickboxing, though she'd have to be careful if she chose to indulge in the last.

She was due to matriculate today, a simple ceremony. Her roommate, an unreasonably lovely Dutch teenager, was coming to fetch her at any minute.

She set her foot on her bed and leaned over it, stretching the scar tissue. The last thing she'd remembered before going out was looking up at Evan, his hand over her leg, holding her blood in her veins.

Holding her tight enough to keep her alive.

They could never see each other again. Given who he was, it was too risky, and he was unwilling to put her in harm's way.

But he had given her this.

He had given her the world.

She pulled open the window and breathed in the air, fresher than any she'd ever tasted.

There was a knock at her door.

She opened it, expecting Sara, but instead it was the school porter, a kindly man with chapped cheeks. He handed her a rectangular box wrapped in plain brown paper and said, in gently accented English, "This came for you, Ms. Vera."

"Thank you, Calvin."

She took it over to the bed and sat. The package bore no return address. Postage imprints indicated that it had traveled through various mail-forwarding services.

She tore back the brown wrapping and saw that it was a wide shoe box. Lettered on the lid: ORIGINAL S.W.A.T. BOOTS.

Her heart changed its movement inside her chest.

She opened the shoe box's lid.

Inside, dozens and dozens of sealed envelopes formed razor-neat rows.

With a trembling hand, she lifted the first one.

On the front, written in precise block lettering: OPEN NOW.

She ran a finger beneath the envelope flap and slid out an undecorated card. She opened it.

Inside, the same block lettering.

IT'S YOUR FIRST DAY. TRY NOT TO SCREW IT UP TOO BAD.

X

Her hand had moved to her mouth. She stared at the words and then over at the box of envelopes. The next one up said CHRISTMAS.

As she slipped the card back into the envelope, she noticed some lettering on the back.

Y.A.S.

Y.A.L.

It took a moment for the meaning to drop. These were the words she'd overheard that young father speak to his newborn in the park the day she'd wandered by, bleeding from one ear.

You are safe.

You are loved.

Another knock sounded, and she wiped at her eyes.

Sara's gentle voice carried through the door. "Are you ready?"

Joey slid the shoe box beneath her bed and rose.

"Yeah," she said. "I am."

78

Worth the Trying

As Evan crossed the lobby of Castle Heights, Lorilee looked up from her mail slot and caught his eye. She was alone. She smiled at him, and the smile held deeper meaning.

He nodded, accepting her thanks.

He neared the security desk across from the elevator. "Twenty-one, please, Joaquin."

Joaquin looked up, his security hat tilted. "Hey, Mr. Smoak. Haven't seen you in a while."

Evan grimaced. "Sales conferences."

"Livin' for the weekend."

"You got that right."

A voice floated from behind Evan. "Twelfth floor, too, Joaquin."

"Sure thing, Mrs. Hall."

Evan held the elevator doors, and Mia slipped past him, her curly hair brushing his cheek.

The doors closed, and they regarded each other.

He tried not to notice the birthmark at her temple. The line of her neck. Her bottom lip.

"Sales conferences." She smirked. "Ever wonder which identity is the real one?"

He said, "Lately."

And now that full grin broke across her face, the one he felt in his spinal cord. "How are you, Evan? Really, how are you?"

"Good. I'm good."

And he was.

At long last Charles Van Sciver was wiped off the books. All that remained of him was the Samsung in the right front pocket of Evan's cargo pants, pressing against his thigh.

Other matters had been put to rest as well.

Benito Orellana's next credit-card bill would show a balance of zero, the medical debts from his wife's illness settled in full. He would still have his primary mortgage, but the second lender who had nailed him with a predatory rate had been paid off. An unfortunate glitch in the same lender's system had led to the disappearance of a six-figure chunk from the escrow account.

This morning the McClair Children's Mental Health Center in Richmond had received an anonymous donation that happened to match the six-figure chunk that had gone missing from the escrow account. The money had been earmarked for improving living conditions, quality of care, and the security system.

It could also pay for a lot of Lego Snowspeeders.

The package of letters that Evan had sent would have arrived today, helping kick off a new life for a sixteen-year-old girl an ocean away.

Jack had always taught Evan that the hard part wasn't being a killer. The hard part was staying human. He was superb at the former. And growing proficient at the latter.

It was worth the trying.

"I'm sad it didn't work out between us like we hoped," Mia said.

"Me, too."

"Peter misses you. I miss you, too."

Evan thought about a different life in which he could have been another man for them. For himself.

"I have to look out for him," Mia said. "No matter what I might want for myself, I have to protect him at all costs."

Evan said, "I get it."

She tilted her head, seemingly moved. "Do you?"

"Yes," he said. "I do."

The doors opened at the twelfth floor, and Mia got out. She turned and faced him, as if she wanted to say something else, though there was nothing else to say.

He knew the feeling.

The doors slid shut between them.

He rode to his floor, entered the penthouse. He went immediately to the freezer and removed the walnut chest. Opening the hand-blown glass bottle, he poured himself two fingers of Stoli Elit: Himalayan Edition, at about a hundred bucks a finger.

He'd earned it.

The penthouse felt vast and empty. A ring remained on the counter from Joey's OJ glass. He'd have to scrub it in the morning. He thought about the mess of gear awaiting him in the Vault, a mirror for the exquisite complexities inside Joey's head. The equipment would take days to untangle.

He paused at the base of the spiral staircase. Her absence flowed down from the loft, a stillness in the air. He found himself listening for the clack of her speed cube. Or the bump of a kite against his bedroom window.

But now there would only be quiet.

Drifting to the floor-to-ceiling windows, he let the first sip burn its way down his throat, exquisite and cleansing. He looked out at all those apartments on vertical display. Families were beginning to light up their Christmas trees.

He heard Jack's voice in his ear: *I love you, son.*

Evan raised his glass in a toast. "Copy that," he said.

Only once he'd finished the two fingers of vodka, only once he'd washed and dried the glass and set it back in its place in the cupboard did he remove Van Sciver's Samsung from his pocket.

He read the last texted exchange from December 4 yet again.

Worth the Trying

VS: AFTER I GET X, CAN THE GIRL LIVE?

And the reply: NO ONE LIVES.

The sender of the response was coded as *DR*.

Dark Road.

It was amazing that someone so high up would risk so much because of a mission Evan had carried out nineteen years ago. He didn't know where the tendrils of that job culminated, but he intended to follow them. They led, no doubt, to the farthest reaches of power. That's where the darkness was. And the gold.

He'd raised the question himself, to Joey: *How much is regime change worth? A well-placed bullet can change the direction of a nation. Tip the balance of power so a country's interests align with ours.*

He had fired a number of such bullets in his lifetime. Maybe the round he'd let fly in 1997 had been one of them.

Clearly he'd been a link in a chain, and he would devote himself now to discerning the contours of that chain, to seeing just how far up it stretched.

He stared at that text once again: NO ONE LIVES.

He had something else to devote himself to as well.

He crossed to the kitchen island where the red notebook waited. He flipped it open, that scrawl standing out in relief where Joey had shaded the page.

"*6-1414 Dark Road 32.*"

A switchboard. A code word. An extension.

He took out his RoamZone.

And he dialed.

On the Resolute desk, the middle of the three black phones rang.

President Bennett was not sitting there waiting.

He remained on the couch alone, holding a glass of Premier Cru Bordeaux in his famously steady hand.

No sweat sparkling at his graying temples. His breath slow and steady. The past few weeks would have reduced a lesser man to a stressed-out wreck, but he was Jonathan Bennett and his body obeyed his will.

He crossed the Oval Office and lifted the receiver.

He said nothing.

A voice said, "You should have left 1997 in the past."

Bennett gave his allotted two-second pause and then said, "If you look into it, I will crush you."

Orphan X saw Bennett's two seconds and raised him a few more. Then he said, "I think you misunderstand the purpose of this call, Mr. President. Looking into it's not good enough for me."

"What does that mean?" Bennett said, only now realizing he'd rushed his response.

The disembodied voice said, "You greenlit Jack Johns's death. And the girl's death. And so many others."

Bennett reseated his eyeglasses on the bridge of his nose, which felt suddenly moist. "I'm listening."

Orphan X said, "This is me greenlighting yours."

The phone clicked, the line severed.

Bennett breathed and breathed again. He placed the phone receiver back in its cradle. He circled the Resolute desk, sat down, and set his hands on the blotter.

They were shaking.

Acknowledgments

Despite his propensity for operating alone, Evan Smoak gets a lot of air support. I owe a slew of thanks to my team and to my advisers.

First and foremost, I need to thank my dear friend Billy Stojack, my inspiration for Tommy. A few months prior to publication, he passed away. You may have seen his initials in previous acknowledgments, the rest of his identity redacted at his request. Now I can finally thank him in full. Billy was a gentle soul wrapped in a warrior's battle-scarred body. I can't overstate his impact on Orphan X and the world I built around him. Not only did Billy lend me his unimprovable last name, but he got me onto every weapon Evan shoots—from combat shotguns to custom 1911s and even some what-happens-in-Vegas-stays-in-Vegas firepower that I won't mention here. His patience was matched only by his kindness. I hope he's out there somewhere smoking his Camel Wides, spitting tobacco, slurping coffee, and smiling that Tommy Lee Jones smile,

Acknowledgments

the one that textured his eyes with warmth. And I hope I do him justice in these pages and the pages of books to come.

I am privileged to have an exceptional crew at Minotaur Books. Thanks to Keith Kahla, Andrew Martin, Hannah Braaten, Hector DeJean, Jennifer Enderlin, Paul Hochman, Kelley Ragland, Sally Richardson, and Martin Quinn.

And to Rowland White and his team at Michael Joseph/Penguin Group UK, as well as my other foreign publishers who have deployed Evan around the world.

And to my representatives—Lisa Erbach Vance and Aaron Priest of the Aaron Priest Agency; Caspian Dennis of the Abner Stein Agency; Trevor Astbury, Rob Kenneally, Peter Micelli, and Michelle Weiner of Creative Artists Agency; Marc H. Glick of Glick & Weintraub; and Stephen F. Breimer of Bloom, Hergott, Diemer et al.

And to my subject-matter experts—Geoff Baehr (hacking), Philip Eisner (early-warning system), Dana Kaye (propaganda), Dr. Bret Nelson and Dr. Melissa Hurwitz (medical), Maureen Sugden (IQ), Jake Wetzel (cubing), and Rollie White (geography).

And my family. In the words of the Beach Boys, patron saints of the sun-kissed and the charmed: God only knows what I'd be without you.